To Hannah and Chris

LOSING IT

Helen is probably best known for her role as the dippy Catriona in *Absolutely Fabulous*, in which she appeared alongside Jennifer Saunders in all six series of the show, as well as for creating the 'girl at the bar' in *Naked Video*. However, to many she is known for her unique brand of wit and observational humour. A comedy writer with an extensive portfolio that includes writing and performing her own material, Helen has starred in a great number of top TV comedy and radio shows.

Helen was part of a group of early 1980s comedians, including French and Saunders, the late Rik Mayall, and Ben Elton, who made their names at London's famous Comedy Store. She was a guest on ITV's *Saturday Night Live* with her solo comedy act, as well as performing at the first Just for Laughs comedy festival in Montreal along with Lenny Henry. TV appearances span such shows as *The Young Ones*, *French and Saunders*, *Happy Families*, *One Foot in the Grave*, *Bottom*, *Love Soup*, *Miss Marple*, *Casualty* and *Hollyoaks*. She plays Miss Bowline-Hitch alongside Bernard Cribbins in the much-loved children's TV series *Old Jack's Boat*. Helen also played Rich Aunt Ruby in *Horrid Henry: The Movie*. On BBC radio, she has been a regular panellist on shows including *Just a Minute*, *Quote . . . Unquote*, *Open Book*, *A Good Read* and *Woman's Hour*, as well as writing and performing in two of her own comedy series, *All Change* and *Life with Lederer*. Her columns include *Woman & Home*, the *Independent*, the *Mail on Sunday* and the *Daily Telegraph*, and she is currently the 'agony aunt' for

Woman's Weekly. Helen's comedy books include *Coping with Helen Lederer* and *Single Minding*.

She's done a variety of theatre work, following hot on the heels of Julie Walters in *Educating Rita*, playing Doreen in Alan Bleasdale's *Having a Ball*, as well as appearing in *The Vagina Monologues*, *Calendar Girls* and *The Killing of Sister George* in London's West End, interspersed with many fringe theatre plays.

To Margaret

LOSING IT

HELEN LEDERER

lu You

Helen
Lederer
x

PAN BOOKS

First published 2015 by Pan Books
an imprint of Pan Macmillan, a division of Macmillan Publishers Limited
Pan Macmillan, 20 New Wharf Road, London N1 9RR
Basingstoke and Oxford
Associated companies throughout the world
www.panmacmillan.com

ISBN 978-1-4472-6764-5

This book is a work of fiction. Names, characters, places, organizations
and incidents are either products of the author's imagination or used fictitiously.
Any resemblance to actual events, places, organizations or persons,
living or dead, is entirely coincidental.

5 7 9 8 6 4

A CIP catalogue record for this book is available from the British Library.

Typeset by Ellipsis Digital Limited, Glasgow
Printed and bound by CPI Group (UK) Ltd, Croydon, CR0 4YY

Visit www.panmacmillan.com to read more about all our books
and to buy them. You will also find features, author interviews and
news of any author events, and you can sign up for e-newsletters
so that you're always first to hear about our new releases.

ACKNOWLEDGEMENTS

Thanks to:

Wayne Brookes for absolutely making everything happen. His directness, warmth and commitment are a dream come true. Jeremy Trevathan for his contagious humour, steadfast belief and total intelligence. Everyone at Pan Macmillan, who are so efficient, kind, fun and amazing, particularly Emma Bravo, Louise Buckley, Becky Lloyd and Eloise Wood, and Emma Donnan from Busy Bee PR.

My girl, Hannah Lederer, for her belief in me and reading in one sitting on the sofa.

Susan Opie, editor supreme, for such care and diligent application (and maths).

Maggie Phillips, queen of the comma, for believing in me always.

The totally wonderful Caroline Michel and all at PFD.

Anne Reckless, who began the reading and correcting journey and kept cheering in spite of all.

Lawrence Pumfrey, for brave early editing, wit, supreme cleverness and skill.

Anna Pitt, whose unfailing help on all matters technical and artistic is so very valued.

Sara Starbuck, for giving so generously her passion, humour and commitment.

Laurie Peters, for complete comprehension of the thing.

Helena Appio, Paul Burston, Jane Compton, DJ Connel, Elinor Day, Christine Folker, Dawn French, Vanessa Gray, Jonathan Harvey, John Hegley, Julia Hobsbawm, Fiona Maddocks, Chris Manby, Mahvash Tavassoli.

Janet, Lucy and Netty.

Marco Polo Travel.

Miguel Vieira, for assistance with Papua New Guinea.

Dr Chris Browne, for assistance with maths, medical areas, supreme patience and beyond.

To Ruby Wax, for kindly allowing me the title.

Note: *Losing It* is fiction. The relationships and organizations are totally invented.

LOSING IT

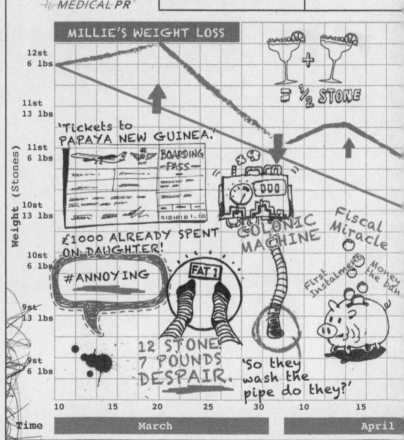

Start weight: 12 st 6 lbs > Goal weight: 9 st 6 lbs

IENT AGREES   TO LOSE 3 STONE IN 3 MONTHS FOR A FEE OF £20,000.

'o be paid monthly) Failure for client to reach
arget necessitates repayment of ALL monies

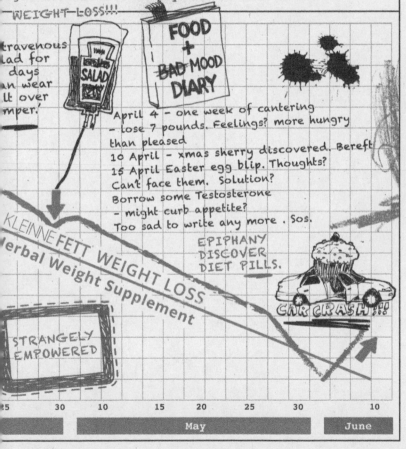

~~WEIGHT LOSS!!!~~

travenous
lad for
 days
an wear
lt over
mper.'

FOOD
+
~~BAD MOOD~~
DIARY

SALAD

April 4 - one week of cantering
- lose 7 pounds. Feelings? more hungry
than pleased
10 April - xmas sherry discovered. Bereft
15 April Easter egg blip. Thoughts?
Can't face them. Solution?
Borrow some Testosterone
- might curb appetite?
Too sad to write any more . Sos.

EPIPHANY
DISCOVER
DIET PILLS.

KLEINNE FETT WEIGHT LOSS
erbal Weight Supplement

STRANGELY
EMPOWERED

CAR CRASH!!!

|25| 30 | 10 | 15 | 20 | 25 | 30 | | 10 |

May

June

ONE

AFFIRMATION 1:
'I radiate generosity. Unless it is my round'

MONDAY 3 MARCH

Millie Tucker allowed herself a brisk check for glitches as she paused in front of the small hall mirror. Escaped nasal hair would, after all, be an avoidable own goal. The eyebrows could do with a tint, which was depressing. She smiled. This was a new habit. And would need practice. She experimented with what might be considered a warm expression and enunciated carefully from *The Pocket Book of Life Affirmations: an Inspirational Handbook for Busy People*, 'I love myself and behave in a loving way to all people, including people I'm not that close to or don't even like that much.' The book encouraged the busy reader to adapt the suggested affirmation according to their own needs. Millie had many of these.

Florence was Millie's second-best friend. No one has first-best friends after fifty, reflected Millie. They were either dead or too successful. She allowed her black jacket to flap open, to give an illusion of tailoring without the strain. How women had the audacity to wear belts over jumpers was beyond her.

Also, Florence wasn't married, which helped significantly. There had to be at least some parity if one was to invest in a night out of single-sex drinking. After all, what would one talk about otherwise?

By the time Millie got there, Florence was already in position on the plastic sofa in the window at the Bolt Whole. She smiled at Millie and raised her hand in greeting, leaving it there while she continued speaking into her phone. A selection of silver bangles tinkled down her freckled arm. Millie walked past her and towards the bar, irritated. Florence continued her conversation, keeping the arm skywards in a salute as Millie swiped the cocktail menu off the counter.

She sat on the cushioned bar stool and unconsciously began caressing the furry fabric of her jumper dress over her thighs, but stopped when she felt the girl behind the bar staring. No need to advertise she lived alone.

She was aware the menu had two cocktails that began with an 'M', but as her readers were on the floor of her Ford Escort, she had to commit to one of them. She knew she liked one and not the other. She tapped her acrylics on the shiny grey bar top. If she got it wrong and ordered the short one that came in the triangular glass which took ages to assemble but hardly contained any liquid, it would inevitably colour the evening. But she needed a drink. And she wanted a cocktail. Millie ordered herself a margarita, thinking it was a mojito.

Florence was clearly oblivious to these concerns. She looked up from her plastic banquette in the window and called over to the bar. This seating unit was meant to be a winning feature of the Bolt Whole and had glass poppers embedded in the back to signal that it wasn't afraid of being camp.

'Just had kittens.' Florence pointed at the phone.

Millie vaguely remembered Florence did something with cats every year, but had never been the kind of friend who felt obliged to take an undue interest.

The whole point of Florence being second-best friend was that she was available, so Millie would have to overlook the weird cat obsession or it might become a problem.

'Don't worry too much about the salt!' Millie forced a light little laugh as the barmaid began to rotate a glass in a grimy saucer of speckled salt. She noticed a student ring binder open next to the list of margarita ingredients: 'Screen and Musicology, Year 3'. Surely the bar staff weren't allowed to do homework on the job? Worse, Millie now knew she had ordered herself the wrong drink. She was getting the short, annoying one. Millie caught sight of her troubled round face in the bar mirror and pouted to give her lips a chance of featuring. Her jacket was straining over her too-tight jumper dress, making her top half look decidedly bulky. She looked like a Russian doll in a chunky knit.

'Is that it, then?' Millie enquired, looking at the only drink placed on the shiny counter. It was not the one she wanted.

The girl looked confused.

'Yes? Oh. Do you want a straw with that?' she asked.

'Will that take long, do you think?' asked Millie.

'No, I don't think so. They're just here.' The girl pointed at a straw holder next to Millie's glass. She didn't seem overly concerned. But then she was probably too young and thin to be able to relate to Millie's trauma at seeing her reflection.

'I could bring it over to you if you'd like.' The girl planted a straw in the glass and looked pleased.

'I'll take it with me, thanks,' Millie said firmly. She'd finally received an alcoholic drink. With a straw. She just had to make the best of it.

Millie drank as she walked. Half the contents disappeared in two sucks. Why had she left her readers in the car? And why was Florence wearing popsocks? This was new. Where were the usual denim leggings, which Florence always called jeans?

Florence had clearly not made her usual frothy 'look at me – I'm not really sixty' effort, which was the opposite of Millie's 'trick the eye downwards' method. She was sipping peaceably enough from a tumbler of Baileys, but the beige popsocks made her legs look as if they'd been in an accident, and fought with the allure of the lace and floral tiered skirt. Or perhaps it was the way Florence was sitting – knees apart and leaning forward to take her call. She looked vulnerable – as if there'd been some kind of distraction when she had got herself dressed. And Millie wasn't quite sure, at this stage, if it was going to work for her, to be seen sitting with such a person – especially tonight.

'Millie, how *are* you?'

'Well . . . you know, still here.'

'And how's the gym going?' asked Florence.

'Didn't I tell you? I haven't been going.' It hadn't seemed worth a phone call.

· Florence was different from Millie. She had an inoffensive figure. Bosomy, short, but three classes a week of bums, tums and abs had kept her body in the normal range for an older person. She also did early morning yoga, which Millie found excessive.

'Well, it's hard, isn't it, to keep it up, what with everything.' Florence looked at her sympathetically.

To Florence, a gym was a temple; for Millie, it was a place to drive past.

'And sitting down for hours on end like you have to with your work increases your bottom circumference without you even having to do anything. It just spreads.'

Florence was only able to offer this judgement, Millie decided, because she lacked her own complexity and awareness around the whole keeping-fit imperative. Millie felt justifiably defensive.

'Mine hasn't been increased by sitting. Anyway, I get up early to do things.'

'I know you do,' agreed Florence hastily. 'Do you want to see the cats?' Florence held out her phone. 'Just quickly. They're so cute.'

'Absolutely,' Millie lied. 'Who's looking after them?'

'Jack.'

'The one you met on that dating thing?'

'Yes.'

Florence was sixty-three.

'Jack is looking after your kittens?'

'He'll be all right. It's lovely to see you.' Florence crossed her legs and yawned without raising her hand to cover her veneers. There were the popsocks again and a glimpse of white, which was unfortunate.

Florence handed over her phone. Millie peered at the screen and was immediately taken aback. Then appalled.

The hairless beings did not appear to be catlike in any immediate way at all, which was quite disconcerting. But they had been referred to as 'cats', so cats they must be. Millie was moved to make a comparison with her own cat, if only because Vernon was covered in hair – a fact that, until now, she had rather taken for granted.

These were a cross between greyhound and E.T., and carried a worried expression.

'Aren't they cute?' asked Florence.

'Very much so,' replied Millie, and quickly handed the phone back to nudge a close of topic.

Millie and Florence had met at a school open day ten years ago, when both of them wanted their child to get in, but since Florence's testosterone implant, their intimacy levels had intensified considerably and Millie was very grateful. Florence had become more open, while she had become more solitary.

She'd been hoping to hear more about Florence's Belgian truck driver, whom she'd met on holiday in Spain and snogged in a cafe, then met up with again a few weeks later in Belgium. Of particular interest was the fact that Florence had been asked to bring high heels when they'd met up again in Belgium. Florence's beige patent wedges had to be worn throughout their lovemaking, which only took place in a set order of positions. This was proof the Belgian watched porn, apparently. Millie had absolutely no idea why this should be. At least the Belgian had been 'tidy', Florence had told Millie.

'Tidy as in . . . ?' Millie was still in the dark.

'Considerate,' had been the reply. Millie had no idea what that meant either, but asked if Florence had told Jack about the Belgian and the shoes. Florence hadn't, which to Millie showed an impressive lack of morals and passion for life. These detailed exchanges about sex were life-affirming, since it was Millie's only window into how life had been once – only without the shoes.

Since Florence had been given the trial implant, she'd gone from 'sensible parent' to 'sexed-up cougar in lace cardigans' in three months. The facelift was relatively subtle, and the hair extensions helped matters hugely, particularly from behind.

'So how's Mary?' asked Florence.

'Fine. Enjoying it. Yes. What about Amelia?'

'Still with the same one, unfortunately.'

'Oh no.' Millie offered Florence a sympathetic face, as this was expected, before resuming her more diverting enquiry. 'And how often does your implant have to be topped up?'

Florence looked slightly surprised at the speed of subject change.

'I mean, does it fade?' said Millie helpfully, to rephrase the same question.

'They do it every month. I get a bit jumpy straight after, but I really notice it dwindling, so I do need it. I might be due another one, actually.' Florence looked around vaguely, in case anyone might be available to do it then and there.

Millie looked around as well. She was pleased to feel complicit in this artificially induced sexual radicalization of her friend. For Millie, as a topic, Florence's implant dosage had more scope than either of their daughters or the cats. Mary lived abroad, and she could never remember what Amelia actually did. Something with hair, or possibly event management with hair, or just hair on its own.

Florence's well-being had been very cheaply transformed by the NHS and Millie needed to hear more.

'And did you tell Jack and the Belgian about your implant?'

'No!' said Florence, laughing.

Millie was struggling to imagine how Florence, who was actually older than she was by a few significant years, could now be so fearless when it came to men. How could she be so brazen at taking the initiative, or at least be so responsive if she got a sniff of interest, which she appeared to get with great alacrity? How did she actually make the transformation from being fully clothed and upright in a room to lying down and naked in a bed and then, well, probably looking somewhat ungainly for a few short moments if memory served, and all without feeling the slightest bit awkward?

'But didn't you get inhibited when you had to get into the bed with him, or even when you first met him at the airport?' Millie had tried to imagine how she would feel meeting a man in a foreign city, at an airport, when she might be carrying hand luggage and pulling a suitcase at the same time, and looking a bit tired, a man with whom she'd only exchanged emails after one meeting. This might be worse than actually being inside the bed. Or having to get out of a bath with the door open. Or wearing a swimming costume for the first time in the hotel whirlpool.

'No,' said Florence again. She seemed surprised. 'But then I hadn't eaten for about a week before, so I was feeling OK about myself.' She appeared to be looking at Millie's overly stretched jumper dress.

'You could try classes?' Florence moved her bag to the

floor so Millie could spread more comfortably across the banquette. Again, Millie took this personally. She only needed one seating unit. Her bottom hadn't spread that far since she'd been in Florence's company.

'What for?'

'At the gym.'

'I get angry in classes. I can't keep up.'

'What if you stay at the back?'

'I always stay at the back.'

Millie took stock. So far she was not enjoying her night out at all. She'd had to look at pictorial evidence of three inbred kittens and now was being made to feel she should be signing up for further unpleasantness in a gym.

'But the gym's been redone. Haven't you been?'

'The one by the roundabout on the corner with the automatic doors?'

'Yes.'

'No.'

Local people were excited that the council had singled out their postal code for a spanking new facility. Sydenham had yet to be awarded such a luxury, which made the Dulwich folk even smugger.

'You can pay as you go.'

'I'd find that quite a commitment.'

'There's a trainer there who trained Natalie, called Paulo or Paul. I can give you his number. He's hot.'

'Why would you want your trainer to be hot?' Millie felt the implant came between them at times. She wouldn't want a hot trainer. She wouldn't be able to pant in front of someone attractive.

'Well, anyway, I can get his number off Natalie if you want it.' Florence never took offence.

'Who's Natalie?' Millie wasn't sure she wanted other people being told she needed to be found a trainer by way of an SOS from Florence. Also, she thought it quite rude when people mentioned names that meant nothing. She told Mary not to do that.

'She was at that Christmas party you asked me to. At QVC 2? Natalie? Head of something or other?'

Millie remembered. Natalie was head of QVC 2 and hadn't given her a job. Millie had only invited Florence because she needed someone to walk in with and for the first half-hour who could then be relied upon to leave of their own accord. Florence was always good at this. One of her more agreeable traits. As it turned out, Millie went home at the same time as Florence because the party had fizzled out by nine.

'Anyway, you know what Amelia did for my birthday?'

'No. Oh no. When was it?' Millie knew she had to respond, as one decently had to with birthday talk, but was more concerned that her glass was empty.

'Last Thursday.'

'Last Thursday? Oh no. Sorry. What did you do?'

'On the actual day?'

'Yes.'

Millie looked at her glass again. She nodded at it as if it were a child being told it would be fed as soon as the grown-ups had finished being boring.

'Jack came over.'

'That's nice.' Millie looked at Florence's pleasantly arranged features and expertly stretched forehead and felt a flash of jealousy. Florence was lucky to have someone to come over and see her, especially someone who liked her a lot. Millie only had Harry, who while being consistently adoring, was also a next-door neighbour and therefore exempt from having any significance. Florence was much more organized. She had a proper boyfriend as well as an occasional Belgian lover who liked her in shoes. Millie's was only a neighbour projecting his own loneliness and rather pitiful need to be loved.

'Has Amelia met him?'

'No. She hasn't, actually.'

'Does she know about him?'

'I *think* so.'

'She must do.'

This was Florence's grey area. For an uncomplicated person, Millie decided Florence had a blind spot when it came to her love life and her daughter. Whereas Millie was careful to tell Mary everything. It was just a shame there was never anything to tell, and also that Mary wouldn't be interested even if there was.

'Shall I go and get us another set of drinks?'

'I'm all right, actually.' Florence twirled her tumbler absent-mindedly, which could have been on purpose, to show Millie she didn't use drink in the same way she did, as a social anaesthetic. Or it might have been because she was thinking about the kittens. Either way Millie didn't care.

'Well, I'll just get one more for me, then, shall I?'

'OK, then. You must be missing Mary, are you?'

Millie got the feeling she was being judged.

'Papua New Guinea's not the other side of the world, Florence.'

'It is, actually,' Florence corrected her.

They laughed.

'What exactly is she doing?' Florence looked puzzled. 'She's been there for ages, hasn't she?'

'She's researching periods in young girls.'

'Isn't that a bit . . . personal?'

'Not overtly. She's not a doctor.'

'No.'

'She wants to see if the girls get bitten more by mozzies when they're on their menses.'

'Do you say "menses" still?'

'You have to. For the research.'

'And does she get paid for that?'

'Yes, as far as I know. It's not voluntary work, Florence.'

'But what does she do?'

'She's trying to prove that girls get bitten more by mosquitoes during their, you know, whatsits and that makes them more likely to get malaria.'

'Why?' asked Florence.

'Because some mosquitoes carry malaria, which they inject when they bite, so she's collecting up all this data about daily bites during their cycle and then all that information . . . gets sorted out and . . .' Millie tailed off.

'Yes?'

'Could very possibly change the world, actually, in terms of global world health.'

Florence nodded in a smiley way but said nothing. Millie would have preferred a bit more reaction. A compliment about Mary's extraordinary academic record perhaps, or even a slight intake of breath. Not everyone's daughter went off to the Third World to do good for others. Especially in what she assumed to be quite cramped conditions at night-time. Mary was brave. Braver than she had ever been, and Millie was very aware of it. She was also slim with slender feet and hands, and quite graceful when she moved, but Millie tried not to think about things like that – it was too much . . . She filled the silence.

'And, um . . . how's Amelia's hair work going?'

'She just needs to get her insurance and she can go into people's homes.'

'Excellent.'

'Yeah.' Florence didn't look that thrilled.

Millie decided to order two margaritas at once, since they were so small, and pretend one was for Florence. She didn't want to swap over to a mojito now, because that would flag up her original mistake to the bar girl. And in a funny way, the sour taste was quite agreeable once you got used to it. She went up to the bar with a twenty-pound note and left her empty purse on the table for Florence to notice.

'So what did Amelia do for your birthday?' she asked, sitting back down again. The purse hadn't been moved.

'She booked me a feng shui session,' Florence announced proudly.

'That's nice.' Millie would honour the new mood and embrace this change in subject even if it didn't appear to be entirely enthralling.

'And I got sent a wonderful lady called Dr Joan Le Measurer. We've become friends now.'

'What does Joan do?'

For the first time Florence looked just ever so slightly impatient.

'Feng shui.'

'Oh yes.'

As Florence began a detailed description of Dr Joan's clothing style – which she described as being mostly 'understated Peter Jones', which Millie thought to be a contradiction – Millie caught sight of the second round of margaritas being placed on the counter. She found herself saying, 'Yay!' which was not usual.

Florence sipped her first Baileys and Millie her second and third margaritas. She was glad she'd ordered two. It showed foresight.

'And what does a feng-shuier do when they actually feng-shui?'

'Well, I can only speak about Joan.'

'Of course.'

'So she uses a compass and a diviner and helps you place things in the house to usher in good spirits and good fortune.'

Millie thought about this as she slumped back on the banquette. There was a bit of ice left in her glass. Maybe Florence would get the next round.

'What about the kittens?' Millie crunched.

'They were fine about it.'

'I meant, did they have to be moved at all?'

'No.'

'So did you have to move bits of furniture?'

'Not much. Well, apart from in the kitchen. I'd got the microwave opposite the sink.' Florence raised her eyebrows knowingly.

'Is Joan against ready meals?' asked Millie. She wouldn't be surprised. There was a growing purism spreading through Dulwich. The skips were full of microwaves and rice cookers.

'It's like putting fire opposite water, Millie.'

'Is it?'

'It's the worst thing. I binned the microwave while she was still there.'

Millie had become agitated. No more ice cubes and now an empty third glass.

'I'd have had it. For when I rent out Mary's room . . . If I do.'

'You're never going to rent it? You couldn't live with another person. Could you?'

'Might have to.'

Millie was now tearing a bar mat into fragments and feeding tiny pieces of cardboard into her mouth.

'Millie?' Florence looked at the disappearing fragments.

Millie became conscious of what she was doing. This had to be a new low. She was now eating cardboard. She emptied the contents into a tissue and cupped it in her hand. There didn't seem to be anywhere to put it.

'I'm a bit stressed.'

'Shall I get us both some olives?' Florence said this very gently. 'Or are you past olives?'

'To be honest with you . . .' began Millie.

'What?' She waited.

'Crisps would be better.'

'I know, but they don't do them, which is why I said olives.'

Florence took the tissue containing damp beer mat from Millie's hand and placed it into her bag before wiping her hand on the floral skirt. Millie knew this was a kind act of friendship. She certainly wouldn't have done it. Not even for Mary.

'What's happened, Millie?'

She sighed. She hadn't planned on sharing the problem when she'd invited Florence for a drink, but now Florence had done that, and with such a genuinely sympathetic face . . .

'I'm involved with this loan shark.'

'For . . . ?'

'For money. They help you if all other avenues have failed.'

'Oh. Like Go Compare?'

'Almost. But no, not really. They're called QwickCash. So I asked them for two grand, quickly, because I'd be homeless if I didn't pay the mortgage.'

'Why couldn't you pay the mortgage?'

'Because I didn't have the money, Florence.'

'Oh. And these people just gave you two grand?'

'Yeah, except now I have to give them a hundred pounds every week in interest until I give the two grand back.'

'Hang on – they get more than what they gave you in the first place then.'

'And every time I'm late paying the hundred pounds, they put on an extra fifty quid.'

'What if you can't pay?'

'Bailiffs.'

Florence looked shocked. 'Bailiffs don't come after middle-class people.'

Millie nodded.

'Do they?' Florence was now unsure.

'My ones do. They're very good apparently.'

Florence's face was really concerned. Her cat birthing was now forgotten. She peeled herself off the plastic seating, and waved at the girl behind the bar. Then she shouted that they needed to have whatever they'd had before 'drinks-wise'. The request would have been more authoritative had Florence's skirt not got caught in the crease of her bottom, but Millie successfully tugged it out before she sat down again.

'Thank you,' said Florence, unsmiling but apparently grateful. Millie would have been mortified.

'No, thank you,' said Millie.

'So, I mean, how did you get into such debt?'

'My mother moved to Hythe.'

'Why?' asked Florence.

'Good question.'

Florence looked pleased.

'She sold her house and bought a smaller one in Hythe.'

'Why?'

'She wants to live out her twilight years in a gated community.'

'Why?' asked Florence.

'She doesn't want to end up having blanket baths from itinerant Polish people, she says.'

'Is she near death then?' asked Florence in a sombre voice.

'No, she just wants an on-site hairdresser and Chubb locks everywhere. So now the trustees own her house, and she can't bail me out when I can't pay the mortgage.'

'Did she do . . . a lot of that? Nothing wrong with that, of course, but did she?' Florence looked a bit uncertain about asking this. Millie didn't answer. Florence nodded.

'Which is why I . . .' She sighed again. 'Why I got a loan from QwickCash.' She winced.

'But they're loan sharks.'

'I know that, Florence. You go to them when there's nowhere else to go.'

'You must have been desperate,' said Florence, which

Millie felt was unnecessary. Her surgically altered face was managing to look almost creased with concern.

'It was that or the bank repossessed my house.'

Millie swallowed. She hated weakness. Especially her own. She also hated Florence for listening with such gravity and judgement. A light remark could have taken the sting out of things. Instead, Florence shook her head sadly.

'I had no idea.'

The bar girl, quickly this time, came to the table with Florence's emergency order. She carried a tray bearing two margaritas and one Baileys. These were Millie's fourth and fifth. There was also a bowl of nuts. Millie's first.

'I thought you might need these.' The girl looked at the nuts and smiled at Millie.

Had Millie missed something? Were they friends now?

'Thanks.' Millie put a handful into her mouth. She wondered if they were being rather loud. On the other hand, it wouldn't be difficult to sound a bit rowdy. They were the only customers.

'Let me pay,' said Florence, scrabbling in her bag. She took out the tissue of damp beer mat and put it on the table as she searched for her purse.

'I can pay,' said Millie.

'No, she can't,' said Florence to the girl, adding darkly, 'Don't let her pay, will you.'

The girl looked at Florence and said, 'I'll come back later.' She raised her eyebrow very slightly at the tissue on the table. Florence missed this, but Millie busily placed the tissue back in Florence's bag as if it contained a home-made snack. The girl nodded and went back to the bar.

'But can't your mother lend you something, if it's an emergency?'

Florence was beginning to annoy Millie now.

'No, she can't. It's all tied up in the new home, so there's nothing until she dies.' Millie didn't want to think about this. She was readying herself for the fourth and fifth margaritas.

But Florence wouldn't let it go. She seemed to be intrigued, which could get tiresome. 'But you wouldn't wish an early death on her, would you?'

Millie sighed. 'No, but she's got this girl Friday called Julie who always phones me up to say, "Hi, Millie. Just to let you know Mrs Tucker would like to place a call with you today," and I have to remain all polite and enabling and say, "Thank you so much, Julie, and do you think you could get my mother to phone me herself next time, because she might be getting deskilled, don't you think?" But they're very close, so what can you do?'

Florence bent down to collect the glass she'd just dropped. Millie wondered if she might be a bit drunk. There was a rash across the orange freckled chest and a glow about the delicately tightened-up face.

'You know what, Millie? This is the time to use your savings.'

She knew Florence was only trying to help, but really, who had savings in this day and age?

She would need the sixth and seventh ordered in good time, since the fourth was now done with. She started on her fifth but decided to sip this one, without the straw, to slow down.

'Do you have savings, Florence?' Millie asked as pleasantly as she could, given she had none.

'I don't need any.'

Millie braced herself to hear why.

'My dad bought me my first flat when I was twenty-one. It had nearly tripled in value when I sold it in the 1980s so then I bought two smaller flats, and I still live off the rent of one.' Florence smiled at this luck.

'Mm.' Millie's jaw tightened. She flexed her cheeks into a half smile of acknowledgement but no more. People who made money out of selling flats slightly annoyed her. It didn't seem like a job. As it was, Millie was having to be bought drinks out of the profits of other people's rent. In fact, Millie's margaritas were indirectly tainted. Luckily this didn't affect the taste.

'So no savings then, from your . . . earnings?'

'No, Florence, no savings.'

Florence shook her head happily, evidently pleased at the fiscal foresight of her dad.

Millie felt tempted to say something quite mean about the popsocks, but then she stopped herself. She was supposed to be practising being loving to people.

'So was it easy to get the loan?' Florence sensed she'd said the wrong thing, and put her knees together to focus better.

'It's all done on the internet. They made me get Harry to send a reference, which involved acts of depravity, of course.' Millie shuddered.

'Sex?'

'As good as. I had to watch *Countdown* with him. That's a whole afternoon.'

'Is Harry the naturist?'

'Only in the summer, but yes that's him.'

Florence nodded. She remembered about Harry.

Millie closed her eyes dramatically.

'I'm living a nightmare.'

'Do you fancy any more nuts of some kind, Millie?'

'I will if you are. So now I owe two grand, need a thousand for the mortgage and can't pay off the extra hundred, which goes up by fifty quid every time I'm late. They're earning interest off me even now as we sit and finish our . . . fifth cocktail.' Millie was pleased with her maths, which had been forced to improve recently.

'Well, at least you've got your job. You're always doing something interesting.'

'I just make it sound interesting.'

'I always read your columns. At the hairdresser's.'

'Which one?'

'Which column?'

'Hairdresser's.'

'Covent Garden.'

'I thought you went to one in the Lane?'

Florence looked affronted.

'Not for ages. I go to Covent Garden, Millie. You get wine if it's a Friday, when the extensions lady comes.'

'Nice.' Millie looked at her glass. Maybe she'd go there as well. If it was a Friday.

'It was the one you did about mugs and rugs that go together in a complementary way. You should do more like that.'

Millie wanted to do more, but the editor's middle-aged son had suddenly materialized from nowhere and expected to be given work, which was all very annoying.

'The son of my editor's after that side of things.'

'That's a compliment to you. It means the *Good Woman* magazine appeals to men as well.'

'Not really, Florence. He likes cars.'

'But they pay you there, don't they?'

'Only a retainer of three hundred pounds.'

'A year?' asked Florence.

'A month,' replied Millie. 'That's why I was thinking of getting a lodger.'

'But then you'd have to share the landing, and see their pants on the line. I wouldn't do it.' Florence smiled gently as if to soften the blow.

Millie was defeated. She knew this was true. She needed her space.

'Trevor had to sleep downstairs even when we were married.'

The couple counsellors had decided that Millie had been 'angry' and Trevor had been 'disengaged', and when Millie suggested she might be angry because Trevor was disengaged, they didn't reply. This was why Millie and Trevor stopped going to therapy. Why pay to be silent when they could do that for free at home?

'I thought you said he was an insomniac. That might not have been down to you.'

'Did I? God, can't remember now. How awful.'

'How do you sleep when Mary's there?'

'No trouble. Anyway, she doesn't count. She's a relative.'

Millie felt the divide between them. Florence wouldn't understand about work and how important it was for Millie. Being a property person, all she had to do was make sure things like taps worked when they were supposed to. Florence had finished her second Baileys. Millie pounced on this progress.

'Do you fancy . . . ?'

'I do actually, Millie. And some nuts.'

'You go this time – the girl likes you. Two more margaritas and whatever you're having. Here, take some of mine.' Millie opened her purse knowing there wouldn't be much left from the twenty-pound note. There wasn't. But at least she found some raisins.

'I'll use my card. No worries,' said Florence, heaving herself off the banquette again.

While Florence was up at the bar, for hopefully margaritas six and seven, Millie took the opportunity to put on some lip liner without a mirror. A man had just come in and was standing by the bar assessing the ceiling. Florence came back with a tray of drinks. She'd cottoned on to Millie's 'buy one and get another one while you're up there' ordering system, as well as ordering one more Baileys for herself. She failed on the nuts, which was a disappointment for Millie.

'Bloke. Six o'clock. Watching.' Florence was looking at her with some expectation, so Millie crossed her legs in what she thought might be an eye-catching way and shook her hair from side to side – as far as it could be shaken in a huge hair clip. There was no response from the man at six o'clock, who still appeared to be interested in the ceiling. Millie noticed Florence frown at the hair shake, so Millie gave up trying to be like Florence and resumed the questioning about feng shui.

'What if the microwave's *adjacent* to the tap?'

'It isn't.'

'Mine is.'

'You'll have to book a session, Millie. Honestly, Joan's brilliant.'

'How much?'

'Well, that's the thing. She's half-price if I introduce her to you – Dr Joan Le Measurer.'

'Got that. And how much would that be?'

'A hundred and twenty-five.'

'That's quite a lot.'

'She's half-price for your next follow-up if you introduce her to someone.'

'So I'm full price?'

'Yes.'

'And how have you experienced stuff to be different since she's been?'

'I had the kittens.'

'You were going to have the kittens in any case. You couldn't have stopped them coming.'

'I could have had dead ones.'

Florence could not be faulted on this. From a seated position Millie managed to catch the eye of the girl at the bar, who was now draped over the counter sucking a pencil in a thoughtful way. Millie felt drunk. Nearly seven margaritas was quite a lot in one sitting – even for her – and she'd need water quite soon to avoid falling over. This would be particularly important as men were now present.

'Could we have some tap, please?' Millie called loudly from her tightly crossed leg position. She had added a pointed foot. 'That's water, from the tap.'

How come Florence was so happy and supportive tonight? Was it because the feng shui person had told her that all would be well once the microwave had been safely removed from danger, or was it because she had Jack, who enjoyed giving her pleasure?

'Water?' Florence was brandishing a jug. She'd refreshed her lip gloss with a blob in the centre of her lower lip. It looked almost like saliva. Millie felt it was sensible to stick to liner – being the owner of dwindling lips, she thought definition was more needed than shine.

'Do you need a mirror, Millie?' asked Florence.

'Not really. Unless you think I do?' She was defensive. It seemed so unfair to have lips that disappeared over time, like cliffs.

Florence looked as if she was going to say something, but decided against it. Millie looked across at the bar area.

'You know what, Florence? I might just make do with a bottle of house white next time, don't you think? For when you go back up.'

Florence nodded.

'It's much cheaper. Well done,' she added encouragingly.

Millie hoped Florence's card would stretch to cover their total bill. The night out was proving to be quite promising. She noticed that the man assessing the ceiling had very pink skin, which, whilst unusual, was not unattractive. There was a lot of it on display due to the shorts and trainers without socks, which Millie felt was quite plucky for early March. He looked rather ethereal, sitting up at the end of the counter, but this may have been because all his clothing was beige and it had caught the light.

'When's the boss in? Do you know?' Millie could hear him ask the musicologist.

'It could be later on,' said the girl vaguely. She was listening to some music in her headphones but had taken one ear out to show willing.

'I'll wait if I may.'

'You're very welcome.'

The man pulled out an evening paper from his back pocket and shook it out to read.

Millie thought she could see him glance across at her on the window banquette. She checked. There was still no one else in her section of the Bolt Whole at this moment. It had to be her. Florence was using the waiting time to call Jack. She was parenting several cats at once, after all.

Millie breathed in and flexed her foot again. The man looked up from his paper and smiled. Was it at her? It wasn't. Was it? She smiled back very slightly. Remembering to push her lips forward, rather than to either side. This was more flattering, she felt. Another man wearing a safari jacket and carrying a canvas tool bag stamped his feet at the door before noisily greeting his mate. The smile had been for him. Millie swiftly redirected her pointy smile at Florence, who obligingly smiled back. At that moment everyone inside the Bolt Whole was smiling. Except for the musicologist.

The men talked in energized, upbeat voices. The man in the safari jacket was bald, and the man in shorts had shaved his head, which Millie felt ever so slightly gave him the edge out of the two.

Florence came back to Millie with a bucket of ice on a tray, a bottle of wine and one wine glass. She added these to their collection of glasses – some on the floor and some not.

'Did you see?' said Florence.

'I did,' said Millie.

'The bald one looks nice. Well, OK, bit fat.'

'So am I.'

'Not that fat.'

Florence saw the expression on Millie's face and mis-read it.

'Really, you're not. That fat.'

Millie wished she hadn't added the last bit.

'And how old is Jack again?'

'Oh, don't,' Florence laughed.

'No, really.' Millie needed to punish Florence.

'Thirty-two.'

'Blimey.'

'But I'm not like you, Millie.'

Florence seemed suddenly uneasy. Which made Millie feel guilty. And she certainly couldn't cope if Florence was going to be vulnerable. She didn't want any emotion. It was all quite simple. Millie wanted to get drunk, hope-fully talk about sex with Florence for a bit of recreation, go home. As far as Millie was aware, Florence didn't have deep feelings. She didn't need them. She had her implant.

'I don't have a good relationship with Amelia's dad. I've got no one else who's as interested in her as I am.'

'Well, you wouldn't, would you? Nor have I. Not any-more.'

'Well . . .' Florence's face had become anxious. She couldn't hold her drink as well as Millie. Millie hoped she wouldn't have to offer advice about the daughter. She knew nothing about hair, except that it cost the same as her mortgage when you totted it up.

'At least Mary's got a degree.'

This was true. Mary liked studying, So much so she had to go as far as Papua New Guinea to live the dream of doing even more study as a fieldwork research anthropolo-gist. If it kept her happy, Millie was thankful. She was in a hut-share with a girl from Bournemouth, but at least they had Skype. And more recently a relationship had blossomed with a son of a tribe leader, which, apart from being unusual, did prove she wasn't a lesbian, which would be fine as well, of course . . . but in a different way. Mary was an enthusiast and had horizons way beyond Millie and her struggles. She was pretty, and unbelievably nosy about how people lived their lives, unless it was about her mother. Then she could switch off quite effortlessly.

'Well, they're very different . . . characters, aren't they.'

'I wish I'd paid for extra tuition.' Florence now looked very sad indeed.

Millie couldn't remember anything about Amelia. And she couldn't help feeling a bit smug about Mary's achievements in comparison, but didn't want to allow herself to feel complacent, in case something went wrong the next time the two of them spoke. She loved Mary much more easily from afar. Longed for her at times, which was all rather troubling.

'No point having regrets, Florence. Amelia's got great . . . energy, hasn't she?' This seemed a reasonable sort of thing to say, given the lack of detail available. 'She probably gets that from you.'

'She does, actually.' Florence perked up.

'Well, I wish I had half of her energy, Florence. Honestly. I need it right now.'

'Didn't you get the new column at the magazine? The "Lovely Things" one?' Millie had the decency to feel a bit guilty that Florence had remembered this information and was touched.

'Sort of. But I'm only allowed to do it every other month.'

'Why?'

'Esther's way of controlling me. She said I can job-share it with Nathan.'

'Who's Nathan?'

'The son who's having a crisis at my expense. So when I suggested doing a poetry page while he was doing my column, she said no, my poems weren't suitable. She can't have read any of them properly. I gave her five.'

Millie poured herself a refill of white. The readers of the *Good Woman* deserved more.

'Oh, hello,' said Florence.

'What?'

'He's looking,' Florence whispered.

'He's not. Which one?'

'The fatter one.'

'They're both fat.'

'The one with the shaved head.'

'Bald?'

'Shaved. In the shorts. Pink legs. No socks.'

'I can't look. It's too obvious.'

'Oh, hello again,' Florence said with more interest.

'What?'

'The leggings.'

'What?'

'They're looking at her.'

Millie gave up. She had to see. The musicologist had come out from her hidey-hole behind the bar and was now perched on a bar stool strumming a guitar. The one in the shorts, and no socks, had been waving an empty beer glass around, but when the girl broke into song, Millie noticed he quietly slid it back on the counter. The two men were clearly disappointed that the bar service appeared to be on hold while the waitress had a musical moment, and looked over towards their banquette. They exchanged a slight nod before the one with the empty beer glass hitched up his shorts. It looked like they had decided on a plan. The other smoothed his hand over his bald head before they sauntered over, quite slowly, which gave Millie and Florence time to prepare themselves. Florence thrust her bust area upwards and smiled. Millie wasn't quite sure what action might complement this, settled on quite a ferocious pout, only stopping when the men reached the table.

'May we join you two ladies?' said the shorts man. They both looked hopefully at the bottle of white on the tray. There was a bit left, but not much.

'Feel free,' smiled Florence. 'Millie and I don't start singing till later on, do we, Millie?'

'No, we don't,' repeated Millie obediently, although she sensed a joke had been made.

Both men laughed. It was generous of Florence to name-check her twice.

Florence had this knack for making make men feel as if they were really interesting. Millie had trouble with this.

'I'm Al,' said the shorts man in an easy way, 'and this is my partner.'

'And do you have a name as well?' asked Millie in a high-pitched, completely different voice to the one she'd used all evening.

'I do. Stan. Our card. We're doing the Bolt Whole's electrics. Complete makeover. Floor lights, side lights, over lights, the lot.'

'Ah, the twenty-first century . . .' said Millie.

Florence gave her a sharp look. Which was out of character.

When Millie began to see double, she knew for certain she was drunk. It was quite a nice feeling, but better when one had the luxury of lying down. Efforts would have to be made to get home with dignity. Florence had called Jack on her mobile to collect her. She said she didn't want to be away from the kittens for too long, in case the mother started eating them, which was certainly one way of getting Jack to collect her.

Eventually the doors of the Bolt Whole were closed behind them and Stan remembered he had to get back to his wife, who might still be up. This left just Al, Millie and Florence gathering on the pavement to agree what a good night it had been in spite of the singing. Eventually Jack drew up beside them all in a rather small car. He leaped out to shake everyone's hand, which made Millie think he might work in hospitality, and guided Florence, who was now very unsteady on her feet, into the front seat. He was even mildly good-looking. How did Florence do it?

Millie set off to find her Ford Escort and wondered why she hadn't visited the ladies' before she left.

'Promise me you're not going to drive,' said Al, who had hurried up behind her, zipping up a large parka at the same time.

'I'm fine. I'm very adept.'

They had reached the car. Millie leaned on it to stop spinning before grabbing the door handle.

'I'll walk you home.'

'No point – it's really close.'

'Come on.'

He took her arm and for one second she thought he was going to kiss her. He leaned forward and with one rough jerk managed to prise the door handle out of her grip. She was left feeling excited and also full of dread. She was not the kind of woman to connect with an electrician on a female-only outing. But he didn't make her feel as nauseous as Harry had when he'd reached across with his biscuit breath to claim the remote. Was this attraction?

They walked to her house and Al fished the door keys from her duffel bag.

She managed to teeter into the kitchen and made it onto the sofa – any thoughts of going to the loo would have to wait. Hopefully.

Normally when she was this drunk, Millie would head to the fridge and pounce on the stash of chocolate she'd secreted there for a *freddo* feast. Topics and Milky Bars, but usually Kit Kats would transform her into a happy person for the amount of time it took to rip the wrapper off and bite down.

Tonight any thoughts of chocolate had to be put on hold. In any case, there was only cheese. And eating slabs of cheese in front of a man was unthinkable.

Al seemed to be very at home in her kitchen. He gave the cat a male sort of cuff with his big hand and allowed Vernon to lick his knuckle by way of a matey reply. Al shook a few tins, laid out some mugs and switched on the kettle before looking at her. She suddenly felt so shy she could hardly bear to meet his eyes. Al took off his big parka and sat next to her. They waited for the kettle to stop boiling.

They waited some more before it got quite noisy and it became obvious the kettle had got stuck. There was just enough time for Al to mention that he was separated from his wife and ate a fair amount of Indian food. Millie couldn't quite believe that a man was now sitting in her house, with a boiling kettle. She'd forgotten what she should look like in such circumstances. Apart from a pressing bladder, she was very hot. She didn't want to take her jacket off, so they both sat there, paralysed. Vernon watched their stillness proprietorially from the sink unit where he'd been drinking out of the tap. She must remember to put out a bowl.

Eventually, Al got up and switched off the kettle.

As he sat down again, he licked his lips and turned to her.

Millie waited. Was this a precursor to a kiss, or was he going to tell her something dramatic?

'I missed my tea today,' said Al.

'Did you?'

Neither of those, then, thought Millie, only half disappointed.

'It's in one of these.'

Al suddenly thrust his pelvis upwards. Millie felt a sudden dip in her stomach. What was required? Cook him an omelette or straddle him, tabletop-style? Neither seemed right, but either was perfectly possible, in principle, which was pressurizing.

He said, 'Feel this,' and took her hand and gently guided it into one of the many pockets in his shorts.

Al was very comfortable with himself.

'Found it, I think.'

'That's good.'

Al took out a brown bag. In it was a chapatti wrap.

'Can I heat it up perhaps?'

'By all means, yes. The microwave is over there opposite the sink.' Oh God.

Then she stood up. She was going to be sick . . .

TWO

TUESDAY 4 MARCH TO THURSDAY 6 MARCH

Al had elected to sleep on the sofa, which was a relief. However, it brought with it some concerns. It had been a long time since another person had actually spent the whole night in her house. As soon as Millie woke up, still in her tights and jumper dress, but without the jacket, her first thought was, There's no hand towel in the downstairs loo. How could she sneak one in there without Al knowing that she'd just put it there?

And then there was the problem of conversation. She squinted at the alarm clock. Eleven thirty. She wasn't used to speaking before lunch.

She pulled on a dressing gown over her clothes in case Al was still there. There was a definite smell coming from downstairs. Could this be the legacy of Al's chapatti wrap?

There was a note on the bottom stair. Al had printed something in large capitals on the back of her payslip from the *Good Woman* magazine: 'Fuse box needs a refit. Very best, Al.'

At least there was a smiley face. On closer inspection, it was a smudge, but Millie was upbeat. She had a choice. She could either remain in debt and bitter *or* she could remain in debt and use this new brush with a sockless man to serve as the catalyst for change. It was a sign.

She had to listen to Dr Joan's long answering-machine message before being invited to speak. A very soft-spoken voice suggested the caller leave a reason why they were seeking spiritual clearance, adding they should give their own number and enunciate any difficult digits clearly.

Millie didn't want to go into too much detail at this early stage in case her message might later be used for training purposes, so she kept things casual by stating that nothing was working in her life and asking, 'Could it simply be due to the vibes in my house, or could there be other failings of a psychological nature that might need feng shuic help?' and concluding, 'It would be good to know which way to go.'

She added that her friend Florence McGee had suggested she call on the feng shui voucher-system thing, which as far as she understood 'would enable Florence to receive a follow-up visit for half the price or something in that vein'.

Ten minutes later Dr Joan called back to suggest a time to drop over for an 'assessment visit' and to go through the money side. She cautioned that she would be bringing a mature student who was shadowing her as part of his distance-learning MBA in digital marketing. Luckily, Jon was the kind of student who knew when to step back while Joan was channelling, so Millie would have nothing to fear from being observed by a trainee.

'That's fine, then,' said Millie, annoyed about the imposition of a third party, and immediately went to the fridge to hack off a chunk of Cheddar.

In fact, Dr Joan and her mature student were able to assess Millie's potential vibe damage later that same afternoon. There had been a cancellation, which Millie decided to believe was true, since it was costing her £125 of her emergency Crème de la Mer fund and she couldn't afford to harbour any doubt. Dr Joan was blonde and petite, and wore white linen slacks under a silk mandarin-collared top which strategically covered her non-existent behind. There was also a discreet velvet Alice band, which made Millie see what Florence meant about Joan's allegiance to Peter Jones – they were probably one of the last shops to stock them. Jon looked about sixty, had thinning chestnut-brown hair and was wearing a short-sleeved spotted shirt, which was quite clown-like, and pink cords, which gave away his roots as an estate agent. To the untrained eye, they could have been a couple of friends popping over for a book club, if Millie did that sort of thing. Harry from next door would be intrigued.

They both took off their moccasins at the same time and left them side by side at the front door. Then they sat either side of Millie on her sofa to take in the vibe damage.

No one spoke at all for some time – until the pressure got the better of Millie and she offered the mature student one of her Bourbons. They were on a plate on the coffee table right by his hand, so all she had to do was indicate where the plate was and he could help himself. Only the purring from Vernon broke through this wall of silence, to be later joined by subdued crunching from Millie. She had high hopes for the spiritual intervention, but then again, the pair were very, very quiet, which gave cause for her own disquiet. She had to say something.

'So what do you think, then? Can you pick anything up?'

'All houses have energies,' came the barely audible reply.

'Pardon?' said Millie.

'All houses have energies,' Dr Joan said again.

Millie nodded. Vernon's purring had gone to his diaphragm. He had clearly been transported by the spiritual vibe of the two specialist visitors. Millie should take this as proof of authenticity.

While Millie's advisers padded about upstairs, Millie was told to stay put on the sofa with her water. She hoped her linen basket was acceptably empty, as if it were a mere wicker ornament from the Orient, as opposed to a container of soiled materials.

Dr Joan and the mature student came back after ten minutes and suggested they send Millie an action plan of the pending cleansing.

Millie was disappointed. She thought it would all happen on the same day.

She would have to pay twice. Once for this assessment and then for the actual visit if she intended to go ahead. Florence hadn't told her about this.

'That's fine,' said Millie. 'Look forward to it.'

Dr Joan advised Millie to invest urgently in some crystals as a precaution and gave her the address of a shop in Crystal Palace who she knew stocked them, and not just because of its location.

Two days later a beautifully presented feng shui cleansing plan plopped onto the mat, including a suggestion that she assemble the recently purchased crystals in readiness for the session that was to take place at some point in the day. Naturally, Joan knew exactly how many crystals had been bought and requested that all three were to be washed with salt and left to dry in the sun to await their arrival.

This was tiresome, as it was early March without much sun, but she was on a mission. Joan was going to cleanse her corners.

There was a very watery sun, so Millie dashed out in her nightie and put the large crystal and the two small crystals on her tiny square of decking to catch any rays going. If Harry wanted to make anything of it, he could. This was required behaviour if you wanted to get cleansed.

Millie hoped the visit wouldn't take too long, as she needed to finish her agony page. This month she had the additional excitement of writing in a highlighted box about grandparents who couldn't let go of their children, which would take up a bit more time. Pity it didn't pay more.

Joan and the mature student arrived halfway through Millie's elevenses, which so far had consisted of five Bourbons and would have been fortified by a bowl of granola had she been afforded the time. She had just poured on the apple juice and was about to make a start when the text came through that they were outside. Millie noted that Joan's serenity had not inhibited her willingness to self-publicize. Anyone looking out of their windows at the purple Smart car would immediately know how to get in touch with Joan. It was plastered with a phone number, her website and even a short testimonial from a satisfied client across the bonnet.

Millie opened the door, to save them pressing the bell and to be extra welcoming. Jon was wearing a drum attached to a furry strap. Millie tried not to judge. He'd probably been told to wear it like that – like a baby sling, only without a baby inside. Joan was brandishing her divining shears importantly, the handles of which, Millie noticed, had been covered in the same floral fabric as Joan's travel bag. She looked as if she meant business with the spirits. Millie unplugged all the electrical items except her landline, in case she needed the police for any reason.

The three adults and Vernon stepped lightly through the house in candlelight with a broom, Jon's drum and some oil, all equally intent on their mutual goal – to release trapped energy. Millie was curious where the oil was going but didn't like to ask. Jon put it on the windows. Millie wondered how long the oil would have to stay there before it could be wiped off. Joan suggested that Millie's desk should face the garden rather than the wall. Millie felt foolish to have been facing a partitioned wall for all these years without realizing the damage. She was then asked to collect the crystals so they could be solemnly arranged in the sitting room. They were damp from a sprinkling of rain, but Joan assured her they would still offer a protective aura in their own way.

At the herbal tea break Joan asked Millie to check out someone called Brigid.

'Brigid?' Millie asked. Was she a friend? No. Brigid was a Celtic figure of poetry and smithery who could help with Millie's problem page and column work and possibly varied styles of traditional poetry. 'Will do,' said Millie. 'Brigid. And is she a fan of the sonnet?'

Joan nodded without saying anything, which was a bit frustrating for Millie. She'd always wanted to be a poet but stopped reading out her work in clubs because of the folk music. And the quiet people who came to listen in silence. But now she was at the magazine, she wanted to progress her poetry to reach a wider audience. Poetry eased the burden of whatever it was inside her that felt like a burden. Birthdays were particularly welcome opportunities for release, although her mother's reaction to the last significant-birthday poem had been disappointing. 'It must have taken you ages, did it?' she had asked in a slightly puzzled way.

And then it all went rather odd. Jon grabbed the back of Joan's mandarin silk top, and as his hand slipped off the shiny fabric, he toppled onto Millie, knocking her down the stairs. Jon's clipboard tumbled on top of her.

'Oh,' Millie said quite loudly.

'Shh,' admonished Joan as she narrowed her eyes at the ceiling. Jon did the same. 'Can you feel it?' asked Joan.

'I can, thanks,' said Millie. 'On my coccyx.'

Jon glanced down at Millie, who was now wound round the banister trying to heave herself up. He closed his eyes quickly without helping her up.

'Yes. Yes, I can. I can feel it,' he said.

Millie felt Jon was just copying Joan, which lost him respect. On the other hand, Joan was being very convincing and Millie didn't want to make assumptions so early on in her spiritual journey. They had a long way to go. Millie murmured an approving 'Mm.' Joan let out a very long, loud sigh. Jon held his breath and went red. The sigh somehow made Millie want to stand to attention. They all waited.

'Is there a problem?'

'Hold hands,' commanded Joan.

Jon reached out and Millie allowed her hands to be held by these two strangers. She wondered why Florence hadn't mentioned this element of the visit. Maybe Florence thought it was normal.

The clearing of Millie's banister area had never felt quite so important to her future happiness. She loved her home, and she wanted it to feel right again. It might be a bit scruffy around the skirting boards and have a slight smell of mushroom, but keeping it gave her a purpose. She could still locate the very spot on the carpet in the sitting room where Mary had been conceived out of politeness. A coffee table stood there now with a bowl of marble eggs on top, which was somehow commemorative. The new damp crystals looked a bit scruffy in comparison.

The three of them stood on different steps and held hands.

After what Millie considered to be a reasonable period of reflection, she ventured, 'So . . . shall we . . . go up or down . . . the stairs?'

'Shh,' said Joan sharply. 'You can go! Go on, now! Go now . . . Leave . . . Come on, now!' Her face had gone quite pale. Or maybe Millie imagined it had.

Joan suddenly let go of her hand to click her fingers. Millie immediately stood up very straight. Jon did the same.

Millie wondered if she was supposed to leave as well. Where would she go?

'It's all right now.' Joan said this as if she were talking to a child. 'You can go . . . Go on, now. Go over.' Joan took a packet of mini wet wipes out of her pocket and wiped her face, removing a large amount of beige foundation at the same time.

Jon was there to take them from her. He used the same wet wipe on himself. They must know each other quite well, thought Millie.

'Yes, it's all right,' said Jon. 'Now. Go . . . It's fine. Really. Just go.'

Millie looked at the two of them with growing terror.

'It was a lady,' Joan explained in a kindly voice to Millie, as if this would make everything all right for her.

Jon nodded.

'Yeah, she was. A woman.'

'With a child. A dead child. She was stuck.'

'Dead?'

'Very,' said Joan in a firm voice.

Joan dropped Millie's hand and quickly wiped hers clean on the new wet wipe that Jon was proffering.

'We needed to let her pass over.'

'Is she . . . is she over now? Has she passed?' Millie tried to keep an open mind but didn't want to know where she'd passed to. She couldn't vex herself about the afterlife. But she didn't want to risk annoying Joan. It was enough that she'd been sharing her house with a dead woman and a child. The main thing was that, according to Joan Le Measurer, she wasn't going to be doing that anymore.

For twenty-two years it had been herself and her daughter – if you didn't count a three-year relationship with a man in Scotland who'd had a vasectomy for no other reason than because his first wife asked him to. Millie hadn't been ready to share a readymade family with him and had to end it, which was hard at the time but necessary, especially when Mary bit his thigh. Theirs wasn't a natural fit really. And apart from a few minor skirmishes that involved rejection on one side or the other – mostly theirs – Millie had been alone. Trevor and she had been married for exactly one year after Mary was born, but various factors conspired to put an end to that. Friends, family and Trevor's abiding interest in seeing past girlfriends being just a few. Also, he wanted to leave.

Now it turned out she'd been living with a spirit and her dead baby.

'Yes. She's gone.' Joan appeared to be very pleased with her work and handed the floral travel bag to Jon, who took it and gave it a little shake of satisfaction, which Millie thought overplayed his role in the clearing. 'I'm pretty sure of it.'

'How will I know she's . . . ? I mean, if they've gone?'

'If it feels suddenly cold or the lights start flickering . . .'

'Yes?'

'She might be back.'

Suddenly, they could hear an insistent flapping from the letter box.

'Is that her? It can't be. You said she's gone!' Millie almost shrieked.

'Hello! Anyone at home?'

'Oh. It's just Harry from next door. Ignore him. He's probably after a biscuit,' said Millie.

Harry flapped the letter box again.

'Hello there! I heard drumming. Are you in there, Millie?'

'I'm fine,' she yelled at the door. 'Just getting rid of a ghost, Harry. Go home.'

If only Millie hadn't gone for that drink with Florence. She'd only arranged it because she hadn't spoken to anyone in her own age group for a few weeks. And she'd needed to act out her affirmations for busy people.

Everything felt spoilt by their visit. The familiarity of her fridge was now sullied. How would she ever feel really free to ransack the freezer with her usual abandonment if the dead woman and infant might be gloating at her somewhere from the pelmet? Could she be sure she was safe?

But it was too late. She'd used up the Crème de la Mer fund for two sessions of feng shui cleansing. Hopefully this would be the end of it.

Joan took Millie down the side of her house for a final check of potential dangers associated with uncovered drains. Harry was reading the advert across Joan's bonnet. He spoke the words out loud – 'Dr Joan Le Measurer, feng shui specialist' – and then he put a question mark at the end as he said it. She hated Harry.

He was spry, wrinkled, with dyed chestnut hair and wore heavy-framed glasses, which Millie considered an affectation and too busy for such a boring face. Anyone who spent as many hours in Homebase as Harry without buying anything could never be considered an interesting person. Merely sad, with a tendency to obsess over DIY to give himself purpose. He was 'no tool and no trouser', as Millie had told Florence once, when she enquired if Harry might be romantic material.

She stared at Joan's checklist of items to buy to activate further cleansing for the long term: one mirror, five coins and a red candle with a trimmed wick and no wider than five centimetres. Joan Le Measurer certainly measured up to her name.

FRIDAY 7 MARCH

Harry had moved next door to Millie five years ago. On Millie's other side was a residential home for the blind. A visiting friend of Millie's had once parked across the entrance in error and one of the residents had left a note on the windscreen: 'Selfish bitch.'

Harry had erected two Grecian pillars either side of his front door, which had remained in plastic sheeting for at least a year. No one knew why they were there, or why he had taken the sheeting off recently. Millie didn't want to waste her time talking to Harry, so never asked. Whenever he could catch her – usually between her front door and her car – he offered as much information as he possibly could on a variety of subjects. This was how she knew he'd had a CCTV camera installed over his front door to protect his lights at Christmas. Millie suggested this seemed quite a lot of effort for a small suburban door with a frosted-glass porch when the lights were only at risk once a year, but Harry didn't take offence. He just liked her company. Sometimes Harry lined up her dustbins for her if they had been carelessly left askew on the pavement by the bin men. Sometimes he just moved them out onto the street himself so he could move them back and tell her he'd done it.

'Been shopping, Millie?' asked Harry, straightening up from his trowel work. It was early. But clearly not too early to catch a glimpse of his darling, which was all very irksome for Millie.

'Not really.' She looked down at the flimsy bag and shook it for effect. Then she smiled the special non-committal smile she reserved for Harry.

'Can I carry anything?' he said eagerly.

Millie shook her head and walked into her once-haunted house. Harry had seen two Chunky Kit Kats through the translucent bag. She knew that he knew what she was now going to do with them. Millie especially hated Harry at times like these.

The first chunk of the first Chunky Kit Kat was going down nicely when the phone rang. It was Esther from the *Good Woman* magazine. This was annoying, but Millie had to take it. Esther might be asking her to write something or other. It was a pity Esther wasn't more agreeable, but theirs was a work relationship and had to be managed. Millie offered Esther sycophancy, while Esther offered Millie columns. There was a sense of urgency whenever Esther spoke to Millie or indeed anyone – as if life might pass her by if she didn't get her point across immediately. She'd been married twice, and commanded respect at the magazine, although no one that Millie knew there liked her particularly. But she was always very groomed, if big-boned, with a keen interest in wrap-over jersey dresses.

Millie and she had recently gone to a private viewing of paintings about sisters at a London gallery, which was so unattended they were forced to talk to each other. This was where Esther revealed that her grown-up son, Nathan, had moved back into his old bedroom at the top of the house while he sorted out his divorce. She explained that although Nathan's first love had always been cars, he would now be sharing Millie's column work, as well as the odd restaurant review. Restaurant reviews paid £75. Millie knew she wouldn't like Nathan if she met him and, when she did, wasn't surprised to observe he wore baggy denims with frayed bottoms, and slip-on shoes.

'Ao?' said Millie, which was Chocolate for 'hello'.

'It's Esther.'

'Hi, Esther.'

Millie was peeling down the wrapper and going for the next bite. There were normally three bites in one Chunky, unless she took an unusually large bite, making it one and a half.

'Are you eating?' asked Esther.

'No.'

'Oh. Well, never mind. So how are you?' asked Esther briskly.

Millie sensed she needed to get the pleasantries dispensed with as quickly as she was able, but didn't see why Esther should be let off the hook quite so easily since Millie was in the mood to chat, and a conversation with another human might take her mind off the chocolate.

'Fine. Well, not totally fine . . .'

Millie had taken a breath to swallow and Esther jumped in to get through her checklist.

'And Mary and Eugene, is it? That's her Papua New Guinean herdsman, is it? All well there?'

'Tribesman, actually, Esther, thank you for asking. Not completely well, actually, because Mary got an infection last week. Probably the water, but could have been from

Eugene in some shape or form. I'd rather not think about it. I want to tell Mary to keep a bit of herself back, but Skype's not the best medium to offer advice and to tell your daughter she might be wasting her life on a Papua New Guinean tribesman, even if he has studied something or other in Richmond upon Thames. And they might just be friends who are still at the talking phase. Who knows?'

'So anyway, I've got a proposal.'

Millie inserted the final chunk of the first Chunky Kit Kat and crunched as soundlessly as she could while she fingered the next bar. As her mouth emptied, she began to very, very quietly unwrap it.

'I was at my monthly Power meeting this morning.'

'Where?'

'Claridge's. I've got a proposition for you. I've suddenly had this . . . epiphany and I think you'd be perfect.'

Millie wondered why she was being propositioned. They both knew Esther only troubled herself with celebrities. Esther must be feeling the effects of the Buck's Fizz. There'd been a small burp, which Esther had tried to pass off as a chair moving, but Millie knew wasn't.

'I thought you only worked with celebrities for the campaign stuff?'

'I do, I do. But in this case your . . . Hope you don't mind me saying this, but your ordinariness, middle-class poverty and, er, sweet tooth – shall we say? – promise to be quite expedient . . . for us both. It really chimes with Middle England right now. People will identify with you.'

Esther sounded very pleased with her epiphany. Millie was doubtful.

'You mean I'm part of the new Middle England's "old, fat and poor"?'

'Did you know Tessa Keltz lives near you?' Esther clearly needed to crack on and make a point.

'I didn't.'

'We did a piece on her house.'

'With the entirely paved-over garden?'

'And we got on really well.'

'You get on with everyone, Esther.'

This wasn't true.

'Well, she's been asked by Kleinne Fett to front their campaign.'

'Kleinne Fett.'

'Yes. They're German.'

'Hosiery?'

'Close. Herbal diet pills.'

'Oh yes, I know.' Millie had not heard of Kleinne Fett.

'So Tessa was asked to front it. But she's off to Hong Kong.'

'Did she do *This Morning*?'

'No. Look, she's got to go to Hong Kong, but Kleinne Fett needs the control candidate to start the campaign. To take the drug and be seen to share a healthy food journey with everyone's favourite celebrity. If we can't get Tessa, I know Lindy Farton's a yo-yo dieter . . . but we can't use the word "diet". Ever. Except between ourselves, of course.'

'Is it a diet drug?'

'No. It's an entirely herbal supplement.'

Millie felt momentary disappointment.

'Why me?'

'Well, you're not famous, and you're also fat, aren't you, which is lucky. No offence.'

'Only some taken, then,' Millie said as sharply as she dared.

'Very Medical are doing the PR.'

'And they are . . . ?'

'A medical PR company. Two girls, very bright. Well, not *very* bright, but bright enough to be guests at the Magic Power breakfast this morning.'

'I thought you had to pay to go there.'

'They have guests as a one-off. If they're bright enough. And they've got the campaign and I'm acting as the go-between as per this morning. Shall I carry on?'

Esther was sounding quite sharp.

'OK. By all means.'

Esther could be very bullish at times. And hurtful.

'So the Very Medical girls asked me to find one non-celebrity to act as the control group for the German herbal diet pill. It's a trial, you see. That'll get masses of publicity when the real celebrity comes in at the end. Or before, if we get lucky. The two of you can share notes on your diet journey, which will appeal to a wider demographic without saying the word "diet", unless the brief changes by then.'

'Still not quite sure about something, Esther. Why are you asking me?'

Esther paused.

'I've just explained.'

'I must have missed it.'

'Because while you're not a Keltz, you're a Keltz neighbour, and apart from saving on their transport costs for the odd photo shoot, assuming Tessa might be prepared to share a cab with you, or even *do* it, which we don't know yet, I told them you were interested.'

'And will the famous person have to lose weight?'

'Obviously.'

'What if they don't?'

Esther tried again, but she was annoyed now.

'If they don't, we can PhotoShop it or something.'

'Oh.'

'And why now?' Millie had finished the second Kit Kat and was feeling around in her handbag. She found the Bounty in the side pocket. She lined it up on the table and patted it.

'Because it needs to dovetail with the American campaign, which is ready to go. They've pencilled in an Osmond and booked a nurse from Ohio.'

'Is there a fat Osmond currently needing to diet?'

Esther coughed. The neutral, nothing kind of cough she used at work to move things along if they were lagging. It was strangely authoritative.

'So obviously I get a commission from your fee.'

'How much?'

'My commission, or the fee?'

'Er, fee first.'

'Are you sitting down?'

'I am,' said Millie.

'Twenty thousand.' Esther said this as if she were delivering a great prize.

'What?'

'And I'd take 20 per cent.'

'Of £20,000?' Millie was incredulous. She did some sums.

'OK. I'll go to 17.5 per cent.' Esther was miffed. She'd put a lot of work into this.

'You're kidding.' Millie couldn't believe that amount.

'Fifteen. That's it. Otherwise I lose out.'

Esther muttered something Millie couldn't quite hear.

'OK. OK, yes.'

'Great! So the *Good Woman* will have two semi-neighbours fronting the campaign, which could work quite well, as a brand by-product. If Tessa comes on board, you're both already connected, indirectly, to the same post-code – one famous and talented, and one who's . . .'

'Me.'

'Yes.'

'It's perfect. We could even say you were local friends if Tessa doesn't mind. I'll check when she gets back.'

'OK.'

'Perhaps you could meet, but actually . . . maybe that's not necessary.'

'OK.'

'You just have to lose the weight.'

'OK.' Half of the bar went into her mouth.

There was a silence.

'How long have I got?' Her mouth sounded full, but she didn't care. She was rich now.

'Three months.'

'How much do I have to lose?'

'Three stone.'

Millie nodded and quietly rid her mouth of the Bounty into its wrapping.

'OK. That's doable.'

There was a short pause while Millie digested what had been said. Then it sank in. She allowed herself to feel one moment of pure, unreserved joy. Maybe, just maybe with £20,000 she would be able to pay off the loan shark and secure her house without worry. Things had been esca-lating. She had been too proud to tell anyone – except

Florence, which had led her to Joan, and one visit from Joan had changed everything. The freed-up chi from the dead woman had gifted her £20,000. Not only that, it had taken one day.

Millie was a believer. Now, thanks to Dr Joan Le Measurer, she would be free. She called Florence immediately. She loved Florence.

THREE

AFFIRMATION 3:
*'I only eat what I feel I need, which may look like
an excessive amount to other people'*

'Hi. It's me . . . Oh, hang on.' Millie became distracted by
something under her mug of coffee. It was the remains of
the Bounty, which explained why the mug was tilting.

She would not be eating that.

'Hi, Millie.' Florence sounded a touch underwhelmed
to hear from Millie. There were faint police sirens in the
background. 'Can you hang on a sec?' She seemed flustered.

'Sure.' Millie stared at the Bounty. She moved it slightly
to the left of the mug, caressing its bumps softly as she
did so.

Millie sat and waited. This was slightly rude of Florence. Florence didn't have anywhere important to go, as
far as she knew. She was a stay-at-home cat-carer.

'Florence?' Millie called into the phone rather point-
lessly. 'Hello. Hello?' Millie said into the silence again.

She turned the sound up on the Food Network. Nigella
was sitting in front of a beach hut, surrounded by various

adults and children eating from a camping table. This was the end bit of the show where a group of close friends all had to join together and eat up, and generally look pleased.

She threw the Bounty towards the waste-paper bin. It missed and landed on the rug. She would make herself ignore it, as a test.

She'd have to tell Mary about this windfall as soon as she could get her on Skype. Millie had a duty of care to impart family information. And anyway, she had to tell someone, since Florence was annoyingly absent. She was going to be in the black; she was going to be a thin person, without debts, who wore stretch jeans and very possibly a thong that showed above the waistband – or at least the kind of person who could ditch the black jacket and wear – God forbid – a blouse on its own.

Nigella and some adults with other people's children were switched off. She ended her call to Florence and picked up the Bounty before placing it in the bin. Then she sprinkled a bit of Vernon's dried food on top as a precaution and moved away from danger to her desk.

Would Mary be available? Normally one had to book a Skype call with her, but if Mary was nine hours ahead, she might just catch her in the early evening. Recovering perhaps from bouts of reading Henry James to the village teens or collating some data in a research hut or even having sex with Eugene, if they'd got that far. It was hard to know how far this relationship had been taken, but Mary was twenty-three and free to confide or conceal as she saw fit. Millie certainly didn't relish getting her head bitten off for asking about intimate things like that. She would feel her way, avoiding questions like, 'And are you having sex now? If so, shall we chat it through?' As this would not be helpful. Or welcome.

She was in luck. Mary had taken some time out of her evening for essential grooming. The hut-mate had tactfully vacated. She would now have precious time alone with her child who had chosen to station herself overseas. Papua New Guinea was nearly nine thousand miles from London, which felt very far away, even if it did have Fox News.

Millie had forgotten how exciting it was to see the tiny grey half-face of her child squinting back at her. Mary's absence for nearly a year had made it almost possible to forget she had a child. But not quite. There was no mistaking the unique fluttering of recognition around the general heart area. Mary had a delicate face and beautifully even teeth, which were a result of upper and lower braces worn at exactly the right time during puberty. This had given a perfect profile. In fact, there were no ugly children to be found in Dulwich, due to the one dentist, who wired them all up in the same way. Millie noticed that her brown hair had been streaked by the sun and she looked quite fragile, but well, from what could be deduced in the blur. She was possibly a bit shorter, but then that could have been because she was only visible at the bottom of the screen.

'Hey, Mummy! You caught me!' Mary waved a razor high in the air to make sure this, at least, was captured.

For a short second Millie thought she'd intercepted her own daughter's suicide.

'Richenda's gone for the plasters, so we're all alone. Eugene hates any vestige of a follicle. He's got no chest hair whatsoever, which is a first for me. I hope he appreciates all this effort. How are you, Mummy? I'm not great.'

The sound of Mary's voice triggered a surprise lump in

her throat. As she swallowed to beat it down, her mobile rang.

'Hello?'

'Hello?' said Mary from nearly nine thousand miles away.

Millie was reminded that these cross-continent exchanges weren't always entirely straightforward. Last time, they'd had a row because Mary was tired. They'd both decided to agree that was the reason. In reality, it was because Mary was spoilt. It was Millie's fault. She'd overcompensated because she had no idea about childrearing and thought being nice was often the best course in the face of conflict.

'Hello?' Florence was now available to speak to her friend. 'Sorry about before, Millie,' she said. 'One of the kittens had a seizure.'

'Can I call you back?' said Millie. 'Sorry – I thought we'd got cut off.'

'Oh.' Florence sounded hurt.

'Mum?' Mary sounded mildly indignant. 'Erm, you just called me and I was actually in the middle of something important. Are you on the phone?'

Millie could see Mary sneak a quick look behind her and then lean into the screen to make extra sure she had Millie's attention. Even as a child Mary knew how to get Millie to drop what she was doing and drive to the school with some forgotten homework, or rush over some nicer pens for an art lesson on one occasion.

'Richenda's coming back any minute. And it's also quite hurtful if you're speaking to someone else at the same time as me.'

Mary's slightly stressed tone reminded Millie of waving her off at Heathrow, just before she disappeared through passport control. Mary had chosen this moment to suggest Millie might want to get herself tested on the ADHD spectrum. Millie pretended she hadn't heard. No one could have predicted the car keys would be concealed by a newspaper and remain undiscovered for quite so long. And anyway, anyone could be late for a plane without having to be linked to a behavioural spectrum.

'I'm not on the phone, darling.'

Millie moved the mobile onto her lap and kept her hand over it. There was a muffled 'But it's fine now. I can talk. They've gone.' Florence's voice rang out with excitement. 'The fire brigade were fabulous.' She was cracking on. 'They offered to do mouth-to-mouth through a plastic bag, but I said, "No need – go for it with the lips."'

This was when Millie cut her off. She had to concentrate on her child. The same child she had blocked out ever since she'd moved to Papua New Guinea by eating herself plump with grief. The same child who had caused her such gyp for twenty-three years. And love.

'Mum, so much has happened!'

'Same.'

'Me more, though, I expect.'

This was a good sign. At least they were still competitive.

'You go first, then. Actually, can I just tell you that I got a call from Esther?' Millie had to speak fast. That lumpy hut-mate would be back, knowing her luck.

'Who's Esther?' Mary tapped her leg up and down on the hut floor to make her mother speak more quickly.

'You know who Esther is.'

'I don't.'

'The editor of the *Good Woman*. The magazine I write for. You might remember.'

'Oh yes.'

Millie knew she was lying. She'd forgotten how genuinely uninterested young people are in their elders. Maybe Millie should have let Mary speak first. But the hut-mate would come back with the plasters and they'd have to share pleasantries about her research methods, which seemed to be all they talked about. Or even Eugene himself. Although this was unlikely. As far as she knew, Mary was conducting her courtship with Eugene in private. She hoped he wasn't fat or spoilt. Maybe he already had other wives. She didn't want Mary throwing herself at an unsuitable man whose ego couldn't cope with having a brainy girlfriend. In any case, the research funders might not be too keen on one of their beneficiaries cavorting with a key member of the male tribal infrastructure. She might have to say something. She would have to tell Mary to keep her distance but still have fun, of course.

When Millie revealed the actual amount, Mary interrupted, 'You can come here, then?'

'Er, when?'

'With that money. You can come here for a visit. And bring some of my stuff.'

'I can?'

'Yes . . . I'm lonely. And I've got issues.'

'Oh.'

'I need you.'

'Oh.'

This was sudden. And a shock. Millie couldn't bear to see her child vulnerable and far away. There was an actual ache at facing her daughter's struggle. Millie didn't know quite what to do, so she made a rather inappropriate childish face.

'Eek.'

Mary said, 'What?' as she squinted back up into where she thought the camera might be. She suddenly looked slightly lost and forlorn.

Millie felt a terrible surge of something with a name that she didn't know. Whatever it was, it shot through her.

'And I miss you,' said Mary.

'I miss you too.' Millie didn't have time to edit her words and the lump in her throat made her speech sound oddly masculine, which surprised them both.

'I keep thinking how awful I must have been to you.' Mary screwed up her face to make it look worried.

There was a time not very long ago when Millie would have paid to hear that sentence. Several times over. Nevertheless, Millie sensed her words weren't strictly true. She might give some passing thought to her mother when she was bored, or had gripe from the flatbread, but she had her Settlers for that. Millie remembered packing them.

'You weren't. Not that awful,' she offered kindly.

'I was.'

'That wasn't you. It was more Sheila who made you do the actual stealing.'

'I know, but I could have walked away.'

'I'm sure it was normal. For some of you. There's always going to be pressure in the lower sixth. To shoplift.'

'You must have been so worried. I often think about what I put you through when I talk to the mothers here.'

'Do you?' This was nice. And a bit unsettling. What did she tell them?

'I don't know why I did it. I didn't even want half the stuff we took.'

'I think it was the lying to me that must have been hard to bear.'

'Not really.'

'Oh.'

'It was just the adrenalin rush and Sheila egging me on and then us laughing about it afterwards.'

'But you wouldn't have done it if it wasn't for her.'

'I'd have done something bad.'

'You could have ended up with a tag.'

'I know. You were amazing.' Mary had become brisk. Millie realized there was only so long a young person could hold the same note of remorse before having to move on.

'I blame Sheila's mother.' Millie felt encouraged enough to have another go.

'If that helps process it, Mum.'

'Well, she's never out of a tennis skirt, is she? I saw her in the overpriced bakery in the village the other day.'

'What was she buying?'

Mary had always been curious about minutiae. This is why she did research.

'Didn't see.'

'What did she say?'

'She was in a rush. I can't remember. It was a bit awkward.'

'What were you buying?'

'Why?'

'I just want to hear about normal things.'

'Some soup.'

Millie didn't mention the cheese straws, the avocado baguette and spinach muffin to go in the same bag.

'So can you come over, now you've got the money?'

'I haven't got it yet.'

Mary was making Papua New Guinea sound positively local.

'It would be great, Mummy.'

'I mean, I could. Yes, I could. I could find a package to, to, um . . . the jungle. They must fly there because you did, didn't you? God, was it three planes, Mary? That's a lot of flying for one person.'

Millie was now experiencing reactive anxiety. It was miles away and she had a lot on at home. Why did children do this?

'What's the nearest airport again?'

'Jackson's.'

'Jackson's what?'

'Jackson's International Airport.'

'Where's that?' asked Millie.

'In Port Moresby,' answered Mary patiently.

'Which is where exactly?'

'It's the capital city, Mum.'

This sounded more promising. If the airport was in a capital city then it would have to be more than an airstrip with just a few shops and what have you.

'You have to change twice, or sometimes four times, and then we get a small plane to Goroka. I'll meet you.'

'Goroka? Where the hell is that?'

'It's by the swamp. Three hundred miles further south. It's where I live, Mum. No swamp, no mosquitoes, no research.'

'I know.'

'We can have girl chats. Richenda's OK, but she farts on purpose and I'm so over it now. I need the GHD tongs. They're in the bottom of my wardrobe.'

Millie couldn't remember ever having any girl chats with Mary. In fact, she would have given anything to have girl chats before Mary moved out. But it was a big ask to travel to a mud hut in the middle of a swamp. And there'd be no Liberty's as a backup plan.

Mary leaned her face into the screen for the benefit of her mother.

'I miss you.'

'No, I'll come. I'll come. I'll get an advance of some sort off Esther. Once I've signed up with Very Medical.'

Fabulous, thought Millie. She would be flying for several days to get to a swamp she didn't particularly need to see, while Mary might be getting betrothed to the Papua New Guinean heir to a tribe and bunking up with a windy hut-mate from Bournemouth. And if that wasn't taxing enough, Millie would be losing three stone in three months to keep her house, while Mary carried on with her PhD connecting malaria to menstruating young females. They both had a lot on.

But at least Mary seemed pleased at her mother's response. Which was nice.

'Do you have to do anything else to get the money?'

Why are the young so stupid? Or was it just Mary? Who knew?

'Yes. I have to lose three stone as well. In quite a short time frame, actually.'

MONDAY 10 MARCH

The offices of Very Medical PR had been colour-coded. The sofa, cushions, pens and notebooks in the conference room had all been chosen for being purple to some degree. There was a mission statement on the signature lavender wall in reception. It read, 'Very Medical is very credible.'

Today, for the meeting, Lucy was wearing a thin black gabardine jacket with a tie belt that looked a bit like a sawn-off dressing gown, and black trousers that stopped short of her ankles. This was a pity, Millie decided. The wearer of too-short trousers was usually out of touch with themselves and how they came across to other people. This view was borne out when Lucy topped up a beaker from a mauve pitcher of water and drank from it herself before waving the jug invitingly at Esther.

'I'm fine, thanks, Lucy,' Esther said from across the table.

Esther had already briefed Millie on the qualities of the sisters on the drive to Chiswick, but Millie hadn't really engaged, apart from learning Esther felt it was 'serendipitous' that she was there to bring everyone together onto the same page. This was Esther-speak for getting a good cut without anyone being bold enough to stop her. All Millie wanted was an up-front aeroplane ticket; after that she would deal with the rest of the challenges as they came up. Very Medical PR certainly had a lot of 'self-belief as a new company', as Esther put it, if the confidence in purple was anything to go by.

Millie tried to see the resemblance, since Lucy and Terri were sisters in their late twenties. Apart from mousy hair, Lucy was thin and pointed-looking, while Terri was thin and ill-looking. A subtle difference. Terri also tended towards bland jeans with heels and a blazer, leaving Lucy to enjoy the gabardine ankle-swingers and flats that a traffic warden might wear for a touch of fashion but with comfort.

'Molly? Water?' asked Lucy.

'I'm good, thanks,' said Millie, jiggling her beaker back at Lucy. This was slightly awkward. Who was going to break it to the girls that their non-celebrity client was not called Molly?

'I'll have some, Lucy, thanks,' said Terri. Terri was so thin water was probably the only thing that was allowed past her lips. She might manage solids at weekends to stay alive, but that would be it.

The business of pouring and passing was made much of and there was a real danger of the beaker activity taking over until Esther took the lead.

'So! It's very exciting. Oh, by the way, I bumped into Lindy Farton, who thinks the whole idea sounds really interesting.'

Millie was familiar with Esther's trick of undermining and pulling rank at the outset of a meeting. She did it at the magazine when she was being enthusiastic at the same time so no one noticed.

Terri and Lucy looked at each other with alarm. They seemed easily unnerved. The Farton sister was famous. She had been on *Loose Women*. Possibly as a regular pundit. Millie felt a bit sorry for them.

Esther continued, 'So . . . Lucy, do you have your contracts?'

'Ah yes. We've got one for both of you – Molly as well!' Lucy leafed through a pile of papers and tapped a plastic folder importantly.

'Will you need to measure her today?' asked Esther,

cocking her face in Millie's direction but without taking her eyes off Lucy.

Such a missed opportunity: Esther could have injected her name quite easily. She could have said, 'Will you need to measure *Millie* today?'

'Yes. We've got a tape measure and scales, so if you want to just step on here . . .' Lucy stood up and placed a slim pair of scales at Millie's feet. 'You'll need bare feet for it. Sorry – we should have said.' Lucy didn't sound sorry at all as she sat back down.

'We'll need a printout of your visceral fat,' explained Terri importantly. She had just checked her notes and this was what it was called. 'I'll be in charge of all measurements.'

'And her BMI, of course,' added Esther, getting into the groove.

'Fine. Whatever you need. Saliva?' asked Millie, keen to be ironic at the start of this new professional relationship.

'No, we won't need that, actually, Molly,' said Terri, who was wrenching a portable fat-measuring device out of its tight-fitting polystyrene encasement. This made a lot of noise and conversation had to cease until it had been fully unwrapped. Millie used the interlude to work out how she could get Esther to say her name.

She looked around for somewhere to change, but it was clear they all expected her to disrobe then and there. She was going to have to take off her jeans and her support tights and pull her jumper down without looking as if she was pulling it down, and then she would have to take it off altogether. She wasn't going to remove her Spanx, though. They would stay on. She could do this. She needed the money.

Terri seemed to take a very long time locating her tape measure from a faux doctor's bag in patent leather. She might be doing this on purpose. Millie was beginning to doubt their humanity.

'Quick as you like, Terri!' said Millie, breathing in and trying to look impassive. Out of the corner of her eye she could see a delivery man in the courtyard, who was dangerously close to the window. He appeared to be delivering more water.

'Any blinds? Never mind – too late.' The delivery man's co-driver had now been summoned for a look.

Terri leaned in to record the width of Millie's neck. The slight smell of stale vomit forced Millie to look towards the window again. The two water cooler delivery men looked back at her with naked curiosity. They couldn't quite believe what they were seeing. Millie smiled back at them, hoping to shame them into averting their gaze. Unfortunately, they took this as an invitation to smile back. One gave her a thumbs-up. Terri continued with her measuring.

'All done now?' said Millie through gritted teeth. She had been holding her breath for as long as was safe without dying.

'*Think* so,' said Terri, oblivious to the trauma and humiliation caused, standing back to assess the body she'd just manhandled.

Terri did a few crisp taps on her calculator and seemed pleased to announce that Millie was very unhealthy indeed.

'On Monday 10 March I can announce that Molly's official start weight is twelve stone six pounds.'

'Gosh,' said Esther, sucking in her cheeks, 'that's high.'

Terri tapped her calculator again. 'So, going forward to the first official weigh-in, which will be just over two weeks away, on Thursday 27 March, you should have lost . . .' Terri stuck her tongue out to concentrate, which forced Millie to look away again. 'Seven pounds! That's . . . how many pounds a week, Lucy?'

Millie looked vacantly out of the window. Terri wasn't the kind of person to command respect and Millie wanted to demonstrate this wherever possible. This seemed like a good time.

'You're the one with the calculator, Terri.'

The sisters exchanged a sisterly look and Lucy added, 'In charge of measuring.'

'Ah. I know this! She'll have to lose just under three pounds per week before the first weigh-in,' said Esther, intervening smugly. 'If we're talking almost two and a half weeks away. Which I think we all are, if our diaries tally.'

Lucy consulted her lilac clipboard.

'Yes. After that, for the next two weigh-ins, she'll have to lose three and a half pounds a week. She'll be being weighed three times in the three months between now and 10 June.'

'So that's three months and three weigh-ins after today.' Esther was quick off the mark.

Lucy said, 'That's what I said, Esther. But the first weigh-in is after two and a half weeks to prove to us that Molly can actually lose the weight.'

'Oh, she can, dear,' said Esther smoothly.

'And then the second weigh-in will be six weeks later – to maybe give you a nice run in.' Lucy tried to make this clause sound attractive, and made a mark on her clipboard with a purple biro.

'Another lovely touch,' murmured Esther.

'And then the final one will be just under five weeks later. Can we all go with that?' Lucy looked around briefly before continuing, 'Receiving three instalments of the total fee . . .'

'Which is the block of £20,000, I believe.' Millie tried to sound casual, but she needed to get dressed. Surely they could see she was embarrassed.

'Yes, that's the total fee, Molly, but in three instalments it's £6,666 per month.'

'Oh no,' Millie interrupted. 'Hang on.'

'What?' Esther looked worried.

They all looked at Millie.

'The sign of the Devil is "666", isn't it?'

'Funny. So anyway . . .' said Esther quickly, and launched into her own plan of action, stating the same thing but in her own way.

Millie would follow the Kleinne Fett Diet, culminating in a huge press call at the end, when the famous popular but unthreatening household name would turn up to compare diet journeys. Esther would also ramp up her own individual press campaign towards the end of Millie's 'weight journey', but would not involve swimwear shoots for obvious reasons, given Millie's cellulite issue and thighs. But she had received interest from one editor who liked the idea of Millie popping out of the shower looking wet and mischievous, as a way forward. Towels could be strategically placed, and Esther urged everyone to seriously consider a wet-room approach on camera to best showcase Millie's loss. She would also have to insist on an advance of £2,000 for Millie to fly to Papua New Guinea in three days' time on humanitarian grounds. The flight ticket was already on hold, and the pills would go with her, of course, explained Esther to the girls, adding, 'In her hand luggage, depending on how many have to be taken per day.' Both Lucy and Terri looked impressed that Millie would put this money to a humanitarian charitable cause so early on. When Millie explained she had a daughter out there who was studying periods and needed her GHD hair tongs brought over, they were less impressed, but agreed the money should be released forthwith.

Esther then handed out copies of her own contract, which, she informed everyone, she'd had drawn up by her family solicitor stating her bespoke commission. 'Just for safety.'

'I'll put yours in your bag,' said Esther briskly, and stuffed it into Millie's large, chaotic holdall. 'Should she get dressed, ladies?'

'Oh yes, do!' said Lucy, as if getting dressed might be as exciting as having a second glass of water. 'Feel free, Molly!'

'What kind of diet am I following?' Millie had never put clothes on as quickly as this in her life. She might need her Ventolin, but didn't want to admit to any more weakness in front of the pointed sisters. Having her breast lifted up by smelly Terri to get to her non-existent ribcage and being stared at by the water cooler men was exposing enough for one day.

'Ah yes.' Lucy handed her a small piece of paper. 'It's quite straightforward.'

Millie looked at the handwritten list. It read, 'No fattening food for three months, a lot of water (more than normal) and some exercises including running.'

'What diet is that?'

'We adapted it for you,' said Terri. 'The one from Kleinne Fett was in German and suited to German shopping habits. We thought this should work if you stick to it. We can give you support over the phone as well.'

'In what way?'

'Well, if you want to chat . . . one of us can come to the phone and listen and suggest things to monitor where you're at and whatnot,' said Lucy, adding a supportive smile after she had finished speaking.

Even Esther looked unimpressed.

Terri had lost interest now. She seemed utterly exhausted and distracted after her measuring. Millie was tempted to offer her some water to pep her up, but decided she didn't like her enough. Lucy appeared quite comfortable with the pastoral-care package they'd made available to Millie and was busily unstapling forms and handing them out with authority. Millie thought an envelope would have helped, but maybe they didn't do them in purple.

'That's a loss of just a stone a month,' said Lucy. 'Excited?'

'Very,' Millie lied.

'So shall we sign, then, ladies?' Esther stopped short of rubbing her hands but had placed them palm down on the table.

Lucy handed out copies of the contract. Esther put her version on top. Everyone solemnly signed.

'You can sign my one when you get home,' said Esther to Millie. 'Gosh, this is a historic day for us all!'

Esther grabbed a beaker and raised it. The sisters did the same. Millie declined the water jug that Terri was jigging up and down in her direction as if they were now close friends. Terri had touched where her ribcage might be, which would make further intimacy unthinkable.

It was just cruel that she had to blow her advance on a ticket to Papua New Guinea when she should be paying off QwickCash so they would stop ruining her life.

'I think you came across very well, Millie,' said Esther as they crawled down Chiswick High Road in Esther's open-top sports car. Millie wished she'd been told to bring a headscarf. Esther was more than prepared, with what looked like a beekeeper's hat and veil, which might be why people were staring.

'So did you. They were impressed you bumped into a Farton.'

'Well, you know, it's always worth a mention.'

'And did you?'

'Did I what?' Esther looked at Millie sharply.

'No, that's good. That you bumped into her,' Millie said quickly.

'Anyway, if I can't get a Farton, I might pull in a Dimbleby.'

'And will a normal-sized male mesh with the female target demographic, do you think?' Millie asked pleasantly.

Esther checked her rearview mirror and said nothing.

'Anyway, they seemed impressed with your contacts,' Millie soothed. Esther had her own way of doing things. It was pointless getting overly involved.

'Well, you know, sometimes experience shows. They've only been in the game for a year. But they're good, though.' She glanced at Millie, unsure. 'They're very good.'

'Oh yes. I could tell,' Millie lied. 'Thank you for getting me the advance for the flight money.'

'No problem.'

'Well, let's hope Mary appreciates me. And the effort.'

'You might need to get immunized, Millie. Don't you get dysentery over there?'

'I'll be fine, Esther. I've got a strong constitution.'

But this thought had given Millie an idea. Perhaps she might catch dysentery while she was out there. Only a mild form – she didn't want to get hospitalized, but a nudge towards involuntary food release would surely be a gift. It shouldn't be too painful. This idea was not only genius, it demonstrated the far-reaching power of Joan Le Measurer. Ever since Joan had released the chi in her home Millie was being shown how the universe was making connections on her behalf.

Bless Florence for leading her to Joan, who had so successfully repatriated the dead woman and baby. She'd take Florence out immediately and ask about the cat seizure as a special kindness.

There were roadworks on Chiswick High Road and the slow progress made conversation quite strained. After a round-up of all the people at the magazine who they didn't like but respected, of course, the only sensible thing to do was sit back and listen to Melody Radio. Mungo Jerry and the Electric Light Orchestra could take up the slack. Three hours later they arrived at Millie's house.

Predictably, Harry rushed out onto the front lawn when he saw the car and began his silver-service yoga routine in earnest, for their benefit.

Through clenched teeth Millie said, 'Don't encourage him.'

'He's just being friendly.'

'You don't know him like I do,' said Millie.

Esther ignored her and waved at him from the car, which encouraged Harry into a proud leg split. This forced them both to look away at the same time.

Esther wrote out a cheque for £2,000 and tore it off, saying vaguely, 'So, Millie, that's ten per cent of twenty thousand.'

She leaned across and touched Millie's hand, which was unusual for Esther, but money often excited her and she was giving in to it.

'I won't take my commission,' Esther smiled.

'Thank you,' said Millie, surprised.

'On the first instalment.'

Millie didn't look at the cheque as she stuffed it into her bag. She found money embarrassing. Whether you had it or you didn't, it always caused arguments.

'Do you think you could tell the girls my proper name?'

'They know your name.'

'Why did they call me Molly, then?'

'Did they?'

'Several times. Will you tell them?'

'Of course. If it's important to you.' Esther paused and tapped her hands on the wheel. 'Do you think you can do it?'

'Of course.'

It was becoming impossible to ignore Harry, who was now peering into the car on his way up from a lunge.

'Do you want to come in for a drink?' asked Millie as she got out of the car and stepped round Harry, who was now showing off his child pose, which didn't look too taxing. He just looked very draped, like a section of curtain supplicated over his crazy paving. She might use Esther as a human shield while she walked to her front door.

'A drink?'

Millie remembered.

'Of water. I've got to drink more than usual.'

'Tempting, but I'll say no.'

Millie walked alone up the footpath searching for her keys. Harry had jumped over his footpath to land on hers.

'Want to join me in a mild stretch?'

'Not really.'

At last Millie found her keys.

'Why not?'

'I need my body taut and alert – stretching is for old people.'

Harry looked brave but crushed.

'Only thinking of you,' said Millie almost kindly.

With that she let herself in and shut the door.

FOUR

~

AFFIRMATION 4:
*'Today I am filled with courage.
I no longer look left and right before I cross my legs'*

THURSDAY 13 MARCH TO FRIDAY 14 MARCH

Florence offered to drive Millie to Heathrow as long as she didn't mind sharing the car with her still-unfortunate-looking kittens. She was convinced the mother might eat them if left unattended and Jack had absented himself from early evening cat care. This was very generous of Florence. Millie wouldn't have offered to do it if the tables were turned. But then they both accepted she wasn't as nice in that way as Florence. Millie squared this by thinking Florence's niceness was a displacement for needing affirmation, whereas she was more self-sufficient.

As she hugged her friend goodbye, Florence said, 'I'll check in on Harry, shall I?'

'Why would you put yourself through that?'

'Because he's got your spare key. To feed Vernon.'

'Oh yes.' Millie was not happy about this.

'Just so I know, is upstairs out of bounds?' Florence sounded brisk. The car was on a yellow.

77

'Yes, and tell him not to snoop.'

Millie chose to fly overnight with Emirates, believing this would offer a better choice of food and fewer flight changes – although two stop-offs, at Dubai and Singapore, still seemed excessive. All she wanted to do was get there, say hello, be nice and then leave. She wasn't going to vex about her diet while airborne. The joy of an in-flight mini pretzel packet and a vodka and tonic was often the best part of a holiday. Millie wasn't sure about the standard of the local plane that awaited her at Papua New Guinea. Mary hadn't told her much about the airport except to say there were no finished roads in Papua and everyone had to fly if they wanted to travel anywhere at all. Millie didn't believe this. But looking at her itinerary, it did seem she'd be spending most of the time away up in the air.

Millie had requested a window seat, which was foolish, given her recent uptake of water. She felt the now familiar urge to urinate as she half wheeled, half lifted her bag through economy seating. Row 17 was empty. She quickly plonked her magazine and biscuits on the middle seat. She stopped short of putting any objects on the aisle seat just in case she got told off before take-off when it was quiet and everyone would hear. Once seated and belted, she took out the crumpled sheet of paper from her handbag that detailed her travel itinerary. This had been taken out and put back several times. Millie had asked Mary to email a list of 'at a glance' travel requisites.

Millie checked her itinerary again. 'After arrival at Jackson's International in Port Moresby, look very carefully to take correct exit to domestic departures or you'll end up where you started from. Some people get lost and miss their connecting flight.'

Mary had then put, 'We can bond here,' in bold type-face. This was nice, and almost made up for the terror ahead about missing this connection.

As she rummaged in her handbag to locate her giant-sized headphones among copious packets of the Kleinne Fett pills stuffed in all the pockets, which had to be taken out before being put back, she became aware of a presence. A man was standing in the aisle. She could feel him assess the pill display, which was now scattered across both empty seats and included a sponge bag. He removed his Barbour and folded it into a small rectangle with a series of neat little movements. He was posh, judging by the gingham shirt and knitted tie. A posh person would be likely to be as insular as she was, so she should be safe. Before he slipped into the aisle seat, he took out a Kindle from his blazer pocket.

The first leg of her journey, to Dubai, appeared to be quite full, but the empty middle seat was still cause for cautious optimism. While Millie stared out of her window and the posh man continued to read on his Kindle, she felt a connection of mutual hostility flow between them. As long as he let her through to the WC with good grace, she would settle. The most promising element was that he'd territorially placed the *Financial Times* on his side of the divide. They were almost a team.

And then Millie's optimism came to an abrupt end. From down the aisle she could hear a woman's voice, breathy from running: 'Which side are the "H"es, Gerard? Have you got my glasses?'

'No,' a male voice replied, 'and I'm not going back for them. The "H"es are left, Maureen. Just keep moving.'

Millie reassured herself. At least they would sit once

they'd found their seats and be out of sight. She would not be affected by their existence.

'Who's got Jacob's monkey?'

'Jacob's got it. Jacob? Keep going.'

Trailing behind Gerard was a small boy holding a sandwich box, headphones and a bag shaped like a monkey. He looked to be about eight, wore glasses and had spiked hair, a fashion his mother must have deemed suitable for a child. Clearly a family of Harry Potter devotees.

'Quickly now.'

Gerard stopped at 17H. As Millie knew he would.

'Room for a little one?'

The man with the Kindle, without raising his face, levered his legs to the side to allow the child access before returning to his Kindle in one move. Millie stared hard at the window. She wanted to cry. A child. A boy child.

'Sorry.' Millie removed her sponge bag from the middle seat, which she'd put back after the Kindle man had settled. She now stuffed it into a groaning front pouch – full, along with the rest of her travel armoury.

'That's OK, love. Jacob, this lady will see you all right!'

If Millie remained very still, they might go away now.

'Won't you?'

'Sure,' Millie said in a tight little voice.

Jacob squeezed past the man with the Kindle and unloaded his items into the seat pocket in front. He was small and serious. Millie assessed the damage. Sandwiches, crayons, two books, a puzzle book and jelly babies.

Millie looked out of the window feeling very low indeed.

Gerard was back. 'Here, son. Your pills.' He thrust a bottle into Jacob's hand. 'His pills,' he explained to Kindle Man and Millie.

'His mum and me are down there, OK? It was a late booking.' Gerard shrugged his shoulders a little too eagerly. It occurred to Millie that both parents seemed a little too keen to rid themselves of their child. Why hadn't one of them offered to swap seats with her so at least one parent could sit with the boy? It was too late. She succumbed to the familiar feeling of somehow being responsible for her own downfall. Millie had now been made responsible for a child who needed pills. And out of the two potential carers she'd been singled out as the main one.

'It's all right, Mo. There's a nice lady next to him . . .' He looked back and gave Millie a joyous little wave.

Why her?

Soon after take-off Jacob turned to Millie and asked, 'Do you think creationism in schools should be taught or banned?'

Millie pretended not to hear.

Jacob tapped her arm.

''Scuse me . . .'

'I don't have a position, Jacob, thank you.' Millie turned back to her clouds.

As the flight wore on, Millie felt an increasing desire to put things in her mouth. She couldn't control it. Perhaps it was the anxiety caused by Mary's cautionary travel itinerary and the fear that had been put in her mind about missing her connecting flight to Goroka. Or that she might not be able to find the visa desk or work the ATM machine. There was a lot to go wrong. Overcome by anxiety, she decided she had to eat everything, including Jacob's bread roll and chicken chasseur, and his jam sandwiches. She would eat now and worry later. At least she had a tentative backup plan: if she managed to catch a *mild* form of tummy bug – without doing too much harm to any important body part – she could allow herself just one more After Eight mint and then perhaps check if Jacob wanted his.

Jacob was happy to part with his After Eight if Millie didn't mind him eating all his own jelly babies without sharing. He also wondered aloud why Millie was *quite* so hungry. He observed that other passengers didn't seem to be eating up other people's extras. Millie explained it was a mild travel disorder that plagued her on long flights. Jacob was sympathetic and offered to play hangman to take her mind off it. Millie said she might later. It would be something to look forward to. They settled into an easy companionship and touched on the subject of 'what is goodness?' Millie decided it was 'where you sacrificed yourself for others' and Jacob suggested it was a utopian society where one's parents were dead.

Jacob wanted to see her itinerary and studied it carefully.

'How do you know your girl will be waiting for you?'

'Because it says so.'

He considered this.

'What if she forgets?'

'She won't. She asked me to come.'

'But she might have something else to do this morning.'

'She knows I'm coming.' There was now a seed of doubt in Millie's mind.

'Does she want you to come?'

'She asked me, didn't she?'

'I ask my mother to do things for me, but sometimes I trick her into doing them just to see if she will.'

'Well, that's not very nice.'

'Mary might not be very nice,' suggested Jacob.

'She isn't. All the time.'

'Have you got a contingency plan?'

Millie wished she had packed wet wipes. She was sweating. She'd drunk too much vodka.

'I won't need one.'

As they said their final farewells at Dubai, Jacob gave Millie half his pain au chocolat to help with her travel disorder. It was wrapped in a sick bag for safe keeping. He had saved it for her, he said, since he assumed she might want to be alone in both the Dubai and Singapore transit lounges and because they had been allocated separate seating for these later flights. Millie replied that this was very emotionally intelligent for a person of eight years old and thanked him for his sensitivity.

They shook hands and Jacob solemnly announced, 'I really, really hope you get dysentery.'

Gerard swung round at him.

'Jacob! That's an evil thing to say! Apologize!'

'She wants to get it!' protested Jacob.

'Anyway, enjoy your trip!' said Millie, backing away in a fog of vodka and excess.

Millie was sorry to see the back of Jacob, which was a bit disconcerting. He'd donated all his cream cheese and butter.

When Millie finally arrived at Jackson's International in the early hours of the following day, the terminal building was already bustling and hot. Crates of livestock and smiley relatives gathered noisily as they waited to greet loved ones. Where was her loved one? The sight of welcoming strangers made her feel lonely and triggered a surprise longing for Florence and the ugly kittens. And there were queues everywhere she looked, which made her want to stand still and make it all stop. But she couldn't. With Mary's itinerary in her hand, she tried to block out the rising panic and believe that people weren't staring at her. She felt she had a label on her head: 'Woman travelling alone. Could be needy or stupid. Either way, avoid.'

She must focus on objectives. These were: withdraw money, get visa and meet Mary. She found an ATM and tried to see what the person in front was doing. This proved fruitless, as the person was shielding any action with his hand, so when it was her turn she was none the wiser. Millie froze. She couldn't remember the number of kina to the pound. With a shaking finger she punched in '1,200', thinking this would give her a sensible amount of £300 for the week. Not too much and not too stingy. The decimal point must have gone awry, as the machine spat out 12,000. This seemed an awful lot, but she tried to look nonchalant as she shoved the massive wad of banknotes into her purse.

There were only two officials in the whole airport arrivals bay, both of whom may well have shared the same tranquillizer. The two men spent a very long time issuing her with a visa. They had a system by which one of them thumbed through a list of names while the other one watched. Then the one who had been watching spoke to someone on a mobile phone while the other one waited. Finally, a stamped piece of paper was sleepily handed over. Millie would have thanked them but discovered she was unable to speak at this point. Instead, she pointed at the word 'Goroka' on her itinerary and nodded at it hopefully. One of the men roused himself to show her a very small sign that said, 'Domestic flights'. This was promising. Millie headed towards it but got distracted by a sweet dispenser and found herself assessing the Papua New Guinean crisp situation. This is what anxiety did to her. It went straight to whatever gland it was that stimulated her hormones and told her to store fat for emergencies.

There were a few smiley locals, one Australian tour guide with the inevitable clipboard at arrivals, but no sign of Mary. Anger now replaced the anxiety. She'd put her diet on hold to make this trip. She'd been played. She might as well leave the GHD tongs in lost property and book the next flight back. Suddenly, from behind her Millie heard a familiar voice. 'There you are! What are you doing, Mum?'

Millie hadn't heard anyone say 'Mum' for a long time. It immediately made her want to cry. She arranged her mouth into a surprised smile.

'Nothing.'

They hugged awkwardly, which was to be expected, since hugging had always been awkward.

'You look tired, darling.'

'So do you.'

'It's a long flight, isn't it? Once you've chopped and changed . . .' It was impossible to state this fact without any tinge of resentment, and needless to say Mary picked up on it.

'And we've got another one in twenty minutes, so best brace yourself.'

They both looked away from each other. Millie was not at her best. Not in this chaotic airport, with only two sedated officials and nine hours ahead of her normal time. But nor was Mary.

Mary was looking skinny and pale with longer hair than before and she was wearing a pair of huge hooped earrings that looked extremely painful. She strode ahead of her mother talking quickly and purposefully.

'We're catching a really sweet little flight, Mum. It's only for two hours. And the main thing about twin engines is that they're really safe apparently.'

'That should be more than the main thing.'

'They only fly if they can see where they're going, because we're so close to the mountains.'

This offered scant comfort to Millie, who had a fear of small spaces and who now had to run to keep up with her child. Mary was leading the way along a fenced-off connecting walkway, and going very fast. The walkway was an open fenced path covered by tarpaulin, which created even more heat on an already hot afternoon.

'Can you slow down, darling?'

But Mary said they were late and now had ten minutes to catch their PNG plane. Millie felt guilty about dallying over the crisps but felt this half walk, half run was more of an assertion of power for Mary. Millie was not in the mood to be disrespected. She'd just traversed several time zones and now here she was, almost running to keep up with her child, to catch yet another aeroplane, with two miniature engines, to Lord knew where. The land was very flat and there were no taxis, but Millie could see a series of lush green hills in the distance beyond the dilapidated weatherboard buildings and beaten-up trucks outside. Perhaps she could run to the hills and stay there . . . and lose weight quietly on her own. All she could do was focus on the khaki shorts wrapped around her daughter's pert buttocks and follow on doggedly.

Suddenly, Mary stopped, which gave Millie a chance to take a swift suck of her inhaler. Her rucksack was heavy and as yet Mary had not offered to carry it. Both were sulking, without quite knowing why. It was part of a ritual they performed with each other after spells apart.

'Have you got any cash, Mum?' asked Mary.

'I may have. A bit.' Millie didn't want to make things too easy for her recalcitrant child.

'There might be stuff you can buy on the plane.'

This felt friendlier. Millie was encouraged.

'Could you bear to take this, darling?' Millie handed over the rucksack.

In spite of their instant mutual irritation with each other, Millie was in fact relieved to be anywhere with her daughter. Mary seemed in charge and more mature, even if she did look a bit unkempt. Millie would follow her daughter's instructions and simply stand or sit when required.

Millie was relieved they were the only two passengers in this very old and light aircraft to Goroka. Some of the more uncertain moments – particularly the ones when she thought the engine had cut out, and when she heard the pilot swear in a Papuan dialect, or when she saw a large crack on the plane's left wing that seemed to get bigger with altitude – were best experienced in relative privacy. Clutching the hand of one's adult daughter and sobbing into her armpit could never be dignified. Looking out of the window to distract herself made things worse. Dense green forest, glimpsed through a nasty grey mist and plumes of smoke from forest fires, seemed rather ominous and full of danger. And there didn't seem to be any buildings of any description, which was another worry. No sparkly stamp of a swimming pool or tennis court for the traveller in need of downtime. The less she looked at the inner, probably treacherous, hinterland, the better it would be. Instead she focused on Mary's face and tried to memorize it, which would be useful if her face was to be the last thing she ever saw.

Unfortunately, Mary thought this was funny, which was disappointing.

'Mum, relax. They only use pilots who know the Eastern Highlands intimately and if they can see. Visibility's a fairly high priority here. More so after the crash.'

'What?' It was getting late. Millie hoped there would be lights on the plane.

'Nothing. It was ages ago – 2011.'

'Any fatalities?' asked Millie.

'About twenty-eight. Maybe less.' Mary shrugged and hugged her mother's arm. Millie resolved she wouldn't be taking the flight back. She'd use those kina for a taxi and go without snacks.

'Here we are, then!' Mary proudly opened the door of a bashed-up Toyota. She tossed Millie's rucksack casually into the back.

Millie looked around for someone from the settlement to drive them to the hotel. Someone in authority would be reassuring. What would they do if a snake suddenly attached itself to the windscreen?

'You're going to drive us?'

'Yes?' Mary said defensively.

'Great!'

Millie held on to the truck door tightly and remained silent for the next leg of the journey.

The hotel looked like a Premier Inn that had been given a tropical makeover. It appeared to be modern, well equipped and clean. Millie's hope of catching any bugs dwindled in an instant. Even the male receptionist looked very scrubbed and shiny. There was a well-stocked kiosk selling flowery flip-flops and all manner of toiletries for the intrepid traveller who had forgotten their travel wash.

On the other hand, Millie felt immediately calmed by these symbols of civilization and resolved to put the trauma of the journey behind her. So what that there had been a few bloodied dead chickens strewn across the road? She should be proud of Mary's driving skills – much improved since she had driven her mother at three miles an hour round Hyde Park Corner when she was learning. She must make the most of every second. Soon the trip would come to an end. Hopefully. She hated feeling so out of control.

As they waited behind a group of scuba-divers, Millie decided to use the time to get to know Mary's world.

'So, do your girls mind you asking about their periods, or do they get a bit embarrassed?'

'Why would they do that?'

'No reason.' Millie wished she hadn't said anything.

'No, they don't actually.'

'Well done you, then.' Millie noticed a cleaner with a disinfectant spray heading straight for them. She ducked instinctively.

'Seriously, Mum. My methods have got all sorts of attention from the settlement, and the university's really promoting it now, because of the implications.'

'Of course they are.'

Now there was another cleaner, wiping the marble floor with a mop. The hotel was so clean even the good bacteria were being heartily zapped at source.

'And what are the full implications again, darling?'

Mary looked at her mother, but with patience this time.

'That if we can eradicate mosquito larvae in standing water, we can reduce the risk of malaria in the girls. I'm using the stuff I did at Durham as well. God, I'm so happy I did that before I got here.'

'Absolutely,' Millie agreed. 'And it's amazing to think . . . Well, it's a bit of leap, isn't it, to think you get bitten more when you're . . . you know . . . having a . . . ?'

'Period,' said Mary.

Millie smiled extra brightly at a couple more divers who were now behind them in the queue.

'Well, it would to you, wouldn't it,' Mary said sharply.

It felt like old times. This push me, pull you of irritation followed by acquiescence, followed by love.

'Are you ready to check in now, madam?' The hotel clerk's smile had dropped a little.

'She is, yes,' said Mary, before turning back to Millie. 'Basically, Mum, if I work out how women synchronize their periods in certain climates, I can adjust the environment to eradicate disease.'

Millie could see Mary really wanted her mother to get this. And while Millie thought Mary's vision to be somewhat far-fetched, so was her plan to get a mild dose of diarrhoea on purpose.

'If you could sign here, madam . . .' The clerk had unclicked his biro and was smiling again. ·

'Sure I can't come and double up with you in your hut?' asked Millie out of sudden panic. She didn't want to be alone in a clean, Hawaiian-themed room. She wanted to be in a dirty hut with Mary.

'Where would Richenda sleep? You'll be safe here.'

Mary looked at the hotel receptionist apologetically.

'She hasn't seen me for a while.'

'I'm her mother,' added Millie.

The receptionist nodded and called for backup on the front desk.

'How do you know Richenda doesn't want my hotel room? She might like it.'

'She's studying the anopheles mosquito, Mum. She can't stay in a three-star hotel. She's got to rough it. Like me.'

'Of course she has. Sorry. So when shall you and I bond, then, do you think? It's on the itinerary.'

A porter had materialized and was tugging at Millie's rucksack.

'Let him have the rucksack, Mum.'

'OK.' This would be a worry. Millie didn't know how many notes to give as a tip.

'I'll come round and have drinks with you at seven. When you've had time to change.'

'Should I change, then?'

'Oh. OK, then, fine.'

'What?'

'No, fine.'

'What?'

'It's just . . . I told Eugene you were quite glamorous.'

Mary went back to the settlement, and Millie lay on her hotel bed working out how she was going to lose weight when there was a minibar in her room stashed with a giant Cadbury Fruit & Nut and Pringles. Mary had told her there was a hospitality allowance for a close relative.

She would eat today and diet tomorrow. Perhaps if there were any peanuts in the bar, she could give them a good fingering and possibly pick up a mild strain of man virus. Job done.

She unpacked a pashmina that had been given as a Christmas present and never worn. It was probably recycled. No one ever bought pashminas new. She draped it over her large, baggy black T-shirt before cleaning her teeth. This was as glamorous as it could get. Eugene wouldn't know what had hit him. Draped with a shawl and spritzed with a whisper of spearmint.

Millie waited in the hotel bar, the Mango Fountain, for Mary and the mystery boyfriend. She didn't know what to expect but was determined not to be judgemental whoever walked in with Mary. The bar stool was very high indeed. She perched, lopsided, and tried to zone out from a group of young men from Manchester who were reading from a shiny folder labelled 'Eco Tourism and Trekking'.

Millie ordered a gin and tonic from a Papua New Guinean waiter in a bow tie. He was also wearing tight plastic gloves. Perhaps the hotel was on a hygiene alert – which would be bad luck.

Millie had forgotten to bring the in-flight magazine downstairs to flick through in a casual way while she waited. She gazed at the bottles behind the bar in what she hoped was a self-contained manner and reflected on what was to be achieved in the days ahead. Apart from bonding with Mary, and hopefully acquiring a minor stomach bug to fast-track the weight loss, what else was there for her to achieve here? Mary hadn't seemed particularly upset about any 'issues' at the airport. Most unlike the pathetic creature that had tugged at her heart on the Skype call. But that was young people all over. Changeable. Manipulative and innately selfish. The clever thing to do here was not to expect any thanks.

As the eco tourists wandered out of the bar, in search of the kind of meal Millie would have liked, a chubby man in his late twenties with a centre parting and a neatly cut shoulder-length bob walked in. He was wearing a clay half-moon round his neck and some sacking round his girth.

Mary rushed in and said, 'There you are, Eugene!'

So this was Eugene. The surprise was tempered by a sense of inevitability. Why had she assumed Mary would fall for someone normal? There was another more diverting element: Eugene's height, or lack of it. Her daughter's boyfriend was extremely short.

'Wow. Eugene, I presume!' Millie managed a warm smile.

'Yes, Momma. I am that man.'

'"*Momma*" is Papuan for "older woman", Mum,' explained Mary.

'Lovely.' Millie's smile hadn't slipped.

'Or I suppose that would be "crone" in the traditional sense, wouldn't it?' said Mary.

Millie's smile slipped a little. Mary had at least prepared her for one thing: Eugene had no chest hair whatsoever, even though it didn't feel appropriate to be looking at his bouncy man boobs quite so early on in the proceedings.

His look was direct and curious, and seemed to be taking in all of her body from top to toe. After a few seconds of general assessment, which felt less than entirely comfortable, he spoke again.

'You are round.'

'I'll take that as a compliment. Thank you.'

Eugene nodded.

'You're welcome, Momma.' Then he smiled, which revealed lots of shiny white teeth. If one was to find a winning feature, it would have to be the teeth.

He took Millie's hand and raised it to his lips, where his mouth hovered. Millie could feel his warm breath on her knuckles. She co-opted one of Esther's diverting coughs before reclaiming her hand and letting it fall. This was all rather unexpected.

'So! Shall we eat, ladies?' said Eugene brightly.

'Well, that's the thing. I'm not really—'

'My mother's dieting in the UK, Eugene,' said Mary pointedly, as if this was Millie's full-time career.

'I have studied in Richmond upon Thames, Momma. In the UK.'

'How lovely. Near the river?'

'No.'

'That's a shame. It's lovely there on the weekends, if you've got the weather for it.'

'We had weather, Mommy.'

'Ah well. There you are, you see. Even better.'

They looked at each other significantly without quite knowing why. Millie thought he was looking at her chest for longer than might be considered usual, but maybe he just liked the pashmina. No, Eugene was not what she had expected at all.

'So . . . We thought we'd go over to the settlement as it's your first night,' said Mary.

'Lovely!'

'You are a big mother. You must eat. We celebrate you,' said Eugene. 'And my Mary!' he added.

'Did you know that "Mary" is Papuan for "younger woman" in this dialect, Mum? Isn't that amazing, don't you think?'

'I do, Mary. How prophetic! It's as if Eugene knew we were both coming!'

Millie had a lot to take in, but she was going to be positive. Even if her daughter's boyfriend was a little overfamiliar. And tubby. How dare he call her round?

The Swamp Study settlement was a short walk from the hotel across a couple of roads. It was easy to spot because of the bright bunting plastered with sponsors' names draped over the entrance. An impressive range of pharmaceutical companies and government agencies had stated they were proud to lend their name to the settlement: Water Gift, Pharma de Veer, Mary's anthropology department from Durham and, more randomly, Michelin Tyres.

The Checkpoint Charlie entrance was operated by two Papuan girls, who saluted the three of them as they walked through. Millie decided to ignore their smirking, although she was tempted to turn and wave two fingers at the hussies. It wouldn't help her cause. She accepted that the three of them might make for a humorous tableau, but Eugene had insisted on linking arms, and since he was so much shorter than either of them, walking in a straight line was unpredictable.

The actual settlement appeared to be made up of temporary prefab huts surrounding a courtyard, which was well equipped with yurt wood burners, campfire tripods and Baby Bellings. Harry would be in heaven, although he wouldn't like the flies. Millie smiled, as much as she dared, in case any of the women might think she was mocking, or inappropriately embarrassed by their naked breasts. There was an element of Glastonbury mixed with redbrick university campus. Millie felt slightly intimidated by this mix of study and community spirit. A few academic-looking gentlemen in safari jackets wandered cheerfully among their Papuan subjects before retreating into huts with names like 'Graham's Faraday Suite' and 'Methods of Social Investigation Centre'. At least there was a medical hut . . . Useful to know.

Mary sat down on a wooden bench in front of the cooking units and patted the space next to her, indicating her mother should sit down as well. This at least felt cosy and welcoming. And quite timely, since they'd just skirted round a cauldron containing what looked like reptilian body parts.

'I'll show you my hut later, Mum.' Mary waved at a couple of teenagers who were kneading lumps of dough into little pancakes before tossing them into a massive pan. Millie wasn't sure if one of these dainties would be coming her way, but if it did, a mild form of tummy upset from foreign flour would be welcome. The stew in the cauldron, on the other hand, was another matter. She wasn't sure if she could manage the fish gills and the strange hands and feet that seemed to be bobbing about on the surface in glutinous grease. Maybe they had belonged to frogs from the swamp.

'And where do the lecturers live?' Mary had just waved at a bespectacled man retreating into the Faraday Suite with a file.

'That's Graham. They're not lecturers, Mum. They're research fellows.'

'Fellows, then. Where do the fellows sleep?'

'They've got their own unit, behind the offices. Richenda and I are near the girls. They take turns in staying over.'

'And what about the parents?'

'They get bussed in from the village.'

It all felt very weird and manufactured.

Mary was looking around expectantly. Clearly something was about to happen. Eugene was nowhere to be seen.

'Is this normal?' Millie whispered. She nodded at a couple of young men, whom she assumed were fellow anthropologists, and smiling Papuan girls in sarongs who had joined their bench.

'What do you mean, "normal"?' Mary whispered sharply. 'What's normal?'

Millie wanted to suggest, 'Possibly not this,' but refrained. 'Normal' wasn't a word recognized by anthropologists.

'Shh. It's starting,' Mary said.

A short, squat man ran into the centre of the courtyard and took up his place behind a drum. He started to beat out a slow but persistent rhythm.

Mary relented by allowing some information. 'It's a welcome. For you.' She stole a look at her mother, who returned it with a nervous smile.

A line of younger men, wearing plumage on their heads and clanking silverware round their necks, then stomped into the centre, joined the drumming elder and crooned a soft chant. Millie felt overcome with the enormity of the occasion. She worried she was not deserving enough. She tried to look grateful and avert her gaze from any male body parts she'd not seen for a long time. The elder had covered his modesty with a beach towel, which she was thankful for, as he was sat astride a kettledrum in front of Millie, but some of the other men were more relaxed about their pouches being more mobile.

'That's Eugene's dad,' said Mary, nodding at the man behind the drum.

Somehow Millie was not surprised. She felt herself respond to the insistent build of beats . . . and began to do some nodding. This would not do. She might fall off her bench. She reached into her shoulder bag to wake herself up with a surreptitious spray of mosquito repellent, while Mary swayed and chatted to some girls sitting on the other side of her.

Several women now joined the men and gathered in a circle of stomping and clapping. Millie became overwhelmed by the rhythm and joy of group singing. She had been affected the same way at Disneyland Paris, but Mary had been too little then to know what to do. It must have been hard being in a boat with a crying mother moved to loud sobs by Eskimo children singing 'It's a Small World'. Now Mary kept a watchful eye in case the rhythm and singing took hold and she went weird again. But the drumming was persistent and compelling. She could feel herself falling into a trance when suddenly . . . there was Eugene, singing lustily in front of her. 'Oh, tatigo . . . oh

de oooo.' This brought Millie to her senses. The towel
only covered his front lower half and she felt obliged to
avert her gaze again, in case he turned round or, worse,
had to pick something up. She felt her daughter's boyfriend's buttocks were not to be viewed at a first meeting.
There had to be some boundaries.

Mary leaned in to Millie's ear to reveal, 'They've just
come back from the Prague International Folk Festival.
They came fourth.'

'I'm not surprised!' said Millie enthusiastically.

Again this was wrong.

'They should have come first, don't you think?' Mary
shook her head.

Millie wondered if this was to be the argument they
needed to have before they could settle down and be nice
to each other. It was their ritual after all.

Suddenly, one of the girls stood in front of Millie, smiling while she shook a bowl of stew at her. She did this in
time to the drumming and she seemed to be offering it to
her. Millie shook her head as if to refuse the bowl but in
a smiley way. She'd seen what was in it and would have
said a firm 'Not for me – just eaten on the plane' had it
not been so public, and she didn't want to offend. The girl
wouldn't go away. She nodded back, swayed some more
and shook the bowl again. Eventually, and to show Mary
how committed she was to her daughter's community,
Millie took the bowl and drank from it quickly. If she did
it fast, it would be bearable. The girl looked at the empty
bowl in shock, as did everyone else on the benches. The
girl backed away from Millie, who suddenly realized she
was supposed to have bowed at the stew, as everyone else
was now doing.

'So . . . that stew wasn't to be eaten?'

Mary was open-mouthed. Millie could see that she was appalled. And who wouldn't be? Her mother had just made light work of some fish gills. And she was even dribbling.

'No,' Mary replied eventually.

Millie could understand this. It had tasted horrific.

'You could have told me before,' she hissed.

'I was about to tell you.' Mary still looked a bit disgusted.

Apparently, the bowing to the stew was to thank the spirit world for bringing a visitor into the settlement.

After the shock had died down, Millie offered her profuse apologies to the Papuan cooks, who forgave her. Eugene's father also waved away her apology, before wiping himself down with his towel to recover from his drumming. Millie was relieved when Mary suggested Millie go with her to see her hut. Eugene had changed out of his skirt and into a tracksuit. He would be busy with his iPad, he told them. Apparently Richenda was keen to meet Millie but was giving the drumming a miss tonight and was in the hut. She hoped they'd forgive her, but she was behind with her data-collating.

The two women were sharing until a bigger hut could be allocated, but no one knew when that would be, even though Eugene was apparently pulling strings with his dad, who had something to do with one of the sponsors – the tyre people.

The hut was in fact made out of wood and very hot, with two tiny futons, one on either side, separated by a huge electric power adapter point for all their various items. No wonder Mary sought solace in her boyfriend, and who could blame her? Perhaps that was what kept them together – the promise of superior bedding? It was too early to tell.

Richenda was tall with the kind of hair that could never grow long and an athletic build that was more lumpy than bony. Millie couldn't help feeling smug her daughter hadn't turned out as plain as Richenda, even though they were both academics and had to dress in a similar way. Some people looked pert and cute in shorts, and some people looked more like builders. Mary's hut-mate was one of these.

Richenda wondered if Millie might like to try out some swinging on the hammock. She might enjoy hitting each side of the hut with her foot, if she was given a really big push. Millie allowed herself to be helped into a hammock to duly try out the suggestion, but regretted it immediately. It was not easy to cling on to the sides of a hammock and look as if being pushed from side to side in a small hut was in any way pleasurable.

While Millie was contained in the hammock, Richenda over-shared about her girlfriend, who was at the Bournemouth University, like her.

'Look – she sends me photos.'

Richenda pointed to a corkboard covered with post-cards of Bournemouth, including the town hall, the shopping centre, a church . . . Millie was reminded again that academics were indeed a strange species.

'How thoughtful,' was all she could think of to say.

Eventually, after a few dark looks from Mary, Richenda took the hint and loped off to take her musings elsewhere.

'Do you regret coming here, darling? Tell me honestly,' said Millie. It was exciting to have Mary all to herself at last, without the added pressure of being airborne and hysterical. But she was getting a slight sweating feeling, as if she'd had too much rice pudding.

'No. I needed to get away from home.'

This was hurtful.

'And the research is really full on, Mum. If I can get to grips with the patterns of period overlap, then I think I can crack malaria. Don't tell anyone in London yet, or Richenda, but it's coming together.'

'That's such an achievement.'

'I know. The university are in touch all the time. I couldn't do it on my own.'

'I'm sure you could,' said Millie loyally. 'And what about Eugene?'

'You've just met him. He's the son of the tribe leader. Make up your own mind.' There she was, being prickly again.

'I know, but is he nice?'

There was a pause.

'He makes me go off in a sort of trance when I'm with him.'

'How does he do that?'

'He makes a kind of whistling sound.'

'Really? That's odd.'

'I know, but then it all goes very relaxing afterwards, as if I'm sinking.'

'Is it a sort of reiki thing, do you think?'

'No.'

'How do you know?'

'I asked him.'

'Maybe it's another kind of technique.'

'And when I wake up, I feel weird. And more tired.'

'What kind of weird and tired?'

'I don't know.'

'You're not pregnant?' Millie felt immediately depressed. Her own mother would have to be told, of course, which would be unpleasant.

'No!'

'I had to ask.'

'Why?'

'Granny will want to know.'

'But I'm not. I've just said I'm not.'

They were silent. Millie lay very still in the hammock. She knew she had disappointed Mary by asking, but she had to be sure.

'How do you know you're not?'

'What are you like, Mum? I'm studying periods. I think I'd know.'

'I meant, um, have you, you know . . . ?'

'What?'

'Been intimate?'

'Of course we've been intimate.'

'Oh.'

'We talk about everything. He's really involved in what I'm doing and how my work affects the environment from his point of view, which is at odds with mine, but we talk it through all the time – we're very open, Mum. We always make up after a row about me killing his people's trees. And he loves the fact that I teach the girls English as well as carry out research. He says it makes him broody.'

This was not good news.

'But you're not . . . are you?'

Mary looked wounded and raised her voice. 'Nooo. Goddd.'

Millie immediately felt that she had been intrusive, but she was in too deep to stop now.

'And physically?'

There was a slight blush from her child, which was disarming.

'Yes. I mean, yes, of course.'

'That's nice, then.'

Millie was none the wiser. She still didn't know if Mary had actually done the deed with Eugene or anyone else for that matter. She knew she'd liked a lecturer at Durham, but that would have been against the law at the time probably.

'It's just he's weird. And asks lots of questions about if we use pesticides in our research, and because he's so into nature, I don't want to upset him, so I kind of lie.'

'Well, why can't you loosen the relationship a bit and talk about trivial things?'

'How do you mean, Mum?'

Millie forgot Mary was a young twenty-three, which may somehow be her fault, of course.

'He's not a . . . Oh God. Mary, he's not a . . . ?'

At that moment Millie had the horrible thought that Eugene might be teaching Mary cannibalism. She had to stop her from being infected by human remains – it might be passed on as defective genes to her potential grandchildren. At this last thought, Millie's insides started to erupt. She suddenly felt woozy. Her stomach rumbled loudly and she hurled herself out of the hammock onto all fours as she'd seen mothers do on television when about to give birth. The least she could do was aim high.

'Errgh.' Mary looked shocked. 'What are you doing? That's Richenda's futon! She'll go mad. Stop that, Mother. Just stop it!'

Sadly, Millie was not in a position to call a halt.

FIVE

AFFIRMATION 5:
'As a woman of weight, I am grateful I can still reach my "silver bowl" area. All is well with my bowl'

SATURDAY 15 MARCH

Millie opened the eye that was able to respond and wondered if she'd been kidnapped. Her guard appeared to be doing the crossword. She assumed she'd also been drugged and possibly strapped down, since her arms seemed to be inside a sheet. Perhaps she'd put up a fight and been sedated. She hoped she hadn't dribbled.

Opposite her, with his legs astride a chair, sat Eugene. He was wearing a toga arrangement today with reams of calico bunched round his middle. The bunching revealed a lot of leg. And thigh. He was cradling a battered transistor radio and not doing a crossword at all. She ought to say something.

The first step would be to wrench her tongue back from its resting place so she could prepare for speech. The move made a rather dry, clicky noise, which was unfortunate.

She was lying down in a hotel room that smelt of rice pudding in the presence of her daughter's boyfriend.

'He had the look of one who had drunk the cup of life and found a dead beetle at the bottom,' said Eugene sagely and with feeling.

Millie would have said, 'Pardon?' but this involved a plosive. As things were, she managed an 'Mm?'

'P. G. Wodehouse,' offered Eugene, tapping the small radio in a knowing way.

Millie really wanted a glass of water, but didn't want Eugene to come over to the bed in case he saw her asthma inhaler and dental floss. She'd rather keep some distance between them until she worked out why she was in her nightie. And who had put her in it.

She looked down. Yup. Eugene clearly had full view of a nipple. This was the absolute worst thing that could have happened to her. Ever. He must have seen it. If she could see it, he must have. She needed to flip the breast back into its holder. Then she made another discovery. Not only was she wearing a bra, but it was the one she had packed. Someone must have got it out of her ruck-sack . . . But this was not the kind of mystery she felt she could solve at this moment of mortification. She scooped the breast back into its cup with one hand and tugged the fabric over it with the other. Unfortunately, this wasn't an action that lent itself to a casual flick. Millie's breast was too noticeable an item to squirrel away with sleight of hand.

'Radio paints pictures, don't you think?' Eugene was staring intently at her again. 'I always listen to the play after the news,' he added, and gave the radio a little comfy caress for emphasis before darting a glance back at her.

Millie noticed his very long eyelashes and very round

cheeks. And an unusually small, but chunky, body. Not unlike a Papuan Father Christmas elf.

Millie returned his gaze as best she could and placed her arms protectively across her chest. Her tongue at last broke through the moss and she found she could speak.

'Eugene, can I just ask—'

'The World Service is a lifeline for Papua New Guinean rebels.'

Millie's listening was confined to *Woman's Hour* and, more recently, Melody Radio. She would have no idea how to find the World Service. The last she heard, it had been moved to make way for a car park.

'The World Service is the only voice to expose our corrupt elections. The bribes they receive are from the West, but no one hears that.'

Eugene looked at her significantly. Millie wondered if she should feel responsible.

'Have you tried the internet? Or Twitter, as an alternative?'

Eugene shook his head slowly.

'We don't trust. We have to fight corruption, Momma.'

'We do, Eugene. Um, can I just . . . ? What happened? How did . . . ?'

'You did a toilet, Momma.' Eugene was now by the bed. He took the transistor off his wrist and put it on the bedside table.

'Ah.' Millie was shocked.

'Yes. And I'm afraid, my lady . . .'

'Yes?'

Eugene sat on the bed and looked at her in a kind way. 'It was a very big one.'

'Gosh. I see.'

'The stew was a symbolic sacrifice, Momma.'

'Yes, I realize that now, thank you. Any idea what might have been included in it?'

'Yes.'

'And would you tell me, please?'

'Fox. It is a symbol of running fast.'

'And . . . Any other symbols in there?'

'Flying fish, Momma.'

He smiled.

'No humans.'

'Well, no, of course not.' The flying fish was a worry.

'It was an accident, Momma. No one blames you.'

His kindness was unnerving her. He was forcing her to feel grateful, which did not sit well with her mortification over the nipple.

'So . . . how long have I and, indeed, how long have you been here, Eugene?'

'Some of the night and some of the morning.'

'And where is Mary?'

She should have asked about Mary first. Where had she spent her night and her morning having been humiliated by her mother within hours of arrival?

'At the hut.'

'Is she there now?'

'Mary is always busy with her tutor. She Skypes him when she could be playing with me. I feel pain.'

'She gets busy with her research, I imagine.'

'And you were sleeping like a noisy little baby.' He smiled again. Eugene would be a perfect candidate for a tooth-whitening campaign.

'Yes, thank you.'

The last thing she could remember was feeling she was

about to give birth on the floor of Mary's hut. Poor Mary. And what would Richenda say about her futon?

The only positive – if lying down in a hotel room in one's nightie in the presence of one's daughter's boyfriend who may or may not have been looking at one's nipple could be seen as a positive – was that weight had been lost. She felt flatter. She would weigh herself in the hotel spa as soon as she was mobile, but she was sure she'd lost at least three pounds, if not four. And each pound equalled £476.19 in the bank. She knew this because Esther had got someone at the magazine to do the maths. Not a bad trade-off for the zoo-casserole disaster, as far as sacrifices went.

'Would you like to know something naughty, Momma?'

Eugene looked at her gently. She wouldn't have minded, if he hadn't been adjusting his calico toga at the same time. Millie looked away discreetly.

'Go on, then.'

'The rebels of Papua are not being heard because of the distorted news coverage.'

'That must be quite a worry. Particularly if you happen to be a rebel.'

'It is.' Eugene looked troubled.

'And did I . . . ? How did I make my way from the hut to . . . here?'

'Mary and the big lady took you to the medical centre.'

Millie braced herself.

'And then?'

Two large brown tiger eyes stared down into her less exotic pair. She thought she caught a whiff of Imperial Leather.

'I arrived and I carried you to your resting place.'

He stretched out a chubby arm. Millie blinked hard. A

bit of fish stew had found its way into her left eye. She focused on blinking to shift it.

Eugene's hand hovered over Millie's face and chest as if conducting some sort of cosmetic surgery appraisal. There was a strange sucking noise coming from his mouth. This could have been the whistle effect Mary had experienced. And now he was breathing out, making sounds of the sea from his throat. Images of Camber Sands and a lighthouse . . . Oh dear, what would Mary think if she knew about the nipple?

An unmistakable sensation of heat came off Eugene's hand. As Eugene fixed his eyes on hers, he lowered his hand to hover above the now-secured breast. Millie maintained a neutral smile but panicked inside. Then she closed her eyes. She couldn't think why she hadn't done this before. At least it was dark now. Well, pinkish, but darker than before. Could she phone reception? She didn't know what number it was on the phone. Even harder with her eyes shut. And it would be unlikely that a person with their eyes shut would hit the exact button they wanted . . . It was probably nought, but that might get her room service. And what would she order? The worst thing, apart from the fear and panic, was that she couldn't seem to stop the turmoil in her lower body. The heat from his hand was palpable. Was he actually on her breast now or still hovering? The tiny whisper of tingling could mean his fingers were now toying with her very, very suggestively . . . Had he, or hadn't he? The heat came on and came off, and then it came on again. Was he or wasn't he teasing her? Was he actually touching her? Was there a finger on her? It was unbearable, but she wouldn't open her eyes.

The last time she'd felt this kind of stirring was when she was twenty-three and a half. The same age as Mary. What could be happening to her? Had her brain been rewired by Eugene in a secret, one-on-one Papuan ceremony overnight in this hotel room, a dark, ritualistic exchange that even her daughter didn't know about? With a growing horror and shame Millie found herself alert to feelings that had been dormant for years. Except in a muted version in the cinema. This could not be happening. She was a middle-aged and involuntarily celibate woman. Even the vasectomy lover had a tendency to turn over and just go to sleep – giving the meaning 'good in bed' a sad twist.

These kinds of feelings were off limits for someone like her. She hadn't asked to be ignited. Nor was she looking to be ignited. Florence had her implant, and Millie had . . . her life. But now part of her was willing Eugene's hand to land on her breast just as fervently as she was willing it to be removed. This was now an official nightmare. Her daughter's boyfriend was making her very, very confused, and what's more, he didn't seem to have any idea about the turmoil he was causing. No, this was all in her mind. And would just have to be channelled. She said nothing, but accepted she couldn't lie there with her eyes shut for much longer. It was daytime. It might look as if she were lazy. Blinking would be good. It was the most neutralizing thing she could think of. And at least she'd shift the fish.

They stayed like that for about a minute and a half, Eugene with his hand held high and Millie furiously blinking skywards. She could feel the heat, but wasn't sure if that was her own hot flush or his energy flow. Her 'silver bowl' area, as Florence's yoga teacher described it, was being given an involuntary stirring and the effect was most disconcerting.

'I liked it, Mommy,' he whispered.

So this wasn't her imagination. He had seen the escaped body part. Or had he? What was it that Eugene liked?

'What did you like?' She thought she'd risk it even though she couldn't bear to know the answer either way. She was feeling a mix of shame, arousal and repulsion. Only Joan might know what was going on inside her head right now. Millie must nip this in the bud before she got herself a reputation, even if it was only in the spirit world she would be judged to be craven and immoral. This was wrong.

Eugene looked surprised but removed his hand while continuing to stare.

'The play, before the news.'

'I must give the World Service a go when I get back to England. It's one of those things you always intend to do but never quite get round to.' Millie made her voice sound conversational, as if she were idly planning a car boot sale in her back garden.

She raised herself up on the pillows, all notion of desire forgotten, but to her dismay was not fast enough to prevent passing wind very slightly. This took them both by surprise.

'Yes, my dressing gown, if you would. It's on top of the rucksack, Eugene.'

Eugene nodded as he located the dressing gown. He hiked up his toga and brought a chair to stand on so he could reach it. He glanced back at her.

'The UK doesn't care about their countries.'

'We do a lot of work with the Channel Islands. You just don't hear about it as much.'

'Our country was your protectorate, Momma. We let you boss us.'

Eugene made himself stand tall, which brought him more or less on a level with the trouser press by the wardrobe, and strode over to the bed. From behind he looked quite muscular, until he turned round and the man boobs rather dominated.

'And our mess is your legacy.' He held out the dressing gown.

'I can only apologize on behalf of the British consulate, then,' said Millie, grabbing it and putting her arms in as quickly as she could. 'I have to admit I'm not happy with a lot of what we've done around the world, Eugene. I mean, look at what we didn't do for the Irish Potato Famine. Shameful! And we were the first to invent guns in a big way, weren't we, in the First World War? And look how we monetize religion on our own doorstep. It costs ten pounds to get permission to do a brass rubbing, and for why? It's outrageous. Anyway, I thought you belonged to Australia now. Not that I'm shifting blame in any way.'

It felt odd to be having this kind of potted geographical exchange when her body had revealed rather more than it should.

'Papua is not a puppet.'

Millie wondered if she would be able to say this after seven margaritas. Probably not.

'We need the right friends to help us.' Eugene almost spat this last sentence. It made him appear quite masterful, even though he was in flip-flops.

She wondered what Mary said to placate him at times like this. Mary had always been apolitical. Except about tuna.

'Will you be seeing her later, Eugene?'

'Who?'

Eugene's pupils were suddenly huge. Millie wondered if he'd taken any betel nut while she'd been in recovery.

'Mary.' Millie felt a bit more on the ball now she had her dressing gown. She would get Mary to solve the mystery about the change of bra. The one she was wearing was her T-shirt bra and offered far less support.

'Yes.' The mention of his girl's name seemed to have brought him back into the present day and the musky hotel room.

'That's nice.'

There was a pause. She was obviously supposed to say something else. He had put her to bed after all, and it can't have been pretty.

'And are you a terrorist, Eugene?' Millie asked.

'Are you, Mommy?'

'No.'

'But you don't want your country to be served by dictatorship?'

'Who does?'

'So what is a terrorist, Mommy?' Eugene folded his arms across his chest.

'Do you know, Eugene, I've never met one. I don't know where you'd tend to meet any. Apart from maybe along the Edgware Road.'

There was a pause.

'I am a member of the VPL, Mommy.'

Millie wasn't quite sure what to say. She didn't want to appear rude or disrespectful.

'Which stands for . . . ?' she had to ask.

'Virtual Papuan Liberators.'

'Ah yes.'

'Yes, Mommy.' He looked at her intently. 'So you are better now, my lady? After your mishap.'

'Yes. Absolutely. Thank you so much for your help.'

But Millie owed Eugene. Especially as he'd been the one to haul her out of the hut, over the road, into the lift, out of her clothes and, very possibly, into her spare bra.

'Will I take the radio away, then?'

'Yes, do, please. By all means.'

'I like Mary, Mommy.'

'So do I.'

'She has good ideas to stop malaria.'

'Yes.'

'But she must watch who is paying for them.'

'I think it's the university.'

'But who is paying the university? I tell you who pays them, Mommy: the pharmaceutical companies who bribe our government to buy unlicensed drugs and let them loose on our people. They pay, Momma. Their bribes let the government build casinos and hotels on protected land, and *that* is why they want the settlement to exist! They don't care about curing Mary's malaria. The more malaria we have here, the more they like it – the more investment money, the more corruption. I need to protect our land from our own government and tell the world what is going on.' Eugene paused for breath. He was sweating a little.

Millie sensed there was more. He had a checklist of injustices. The VPL must be kept very busy.

'I have a responsibility to stop the logging and robbing of our trees. Without trees, we get manmade swamps, and we don't need artificial swamps on this settlement. And yes, I see that without the swamp, Mary can't study the mosquito, but hey, lady, let us be clear whose side Mary is on – saving the planet or killing it? Let's face the facts, Mommy.'

'I'm very much one for facts, Eugene.'

'The logging is wrong, Momma. We need to stop the robbing of our trees. They absorb the rain, and if there are no trees, the rain forms puddles, which form swamps and malaria comes calling.'

'Ah yes, Mary's malaria.'

'Yes, Momma. You see, Mary wants swamps to study the malaria, but . . .' Eugene suddenly trailed off.

Millie wondered if he might be confused. She certainly was.

She thought this a good moment for her to get some clarity.

'Indeed . . . So nothing happened, Eugene, just then?'

'We will not speak of it.'

'No, that's best.'

But what were they not speaking about?

Eugene bowed and closed the door very gently.

Millie felt uneasy. What had happened? Had anything happened? Had she made something happen? Was she responsible for feeling attracted to Eugene even though she knew she couldn't be attracted in any way to this small, fat man? Perhaps it was the stew. An hallucinogenic reaction? It would help her turmoil if this was the case, but somehow she doubted it was.

She staggered into the bathroom and began the long task of making herself presentable for Mary.

Millie decided to pop into the hotel spa to weigh herself before meeting Mary in the bar for lunch as it was her day off. She also bought herself a floral hair slide at the hotel shop. This was out of character, but she decided not to give herself a hard time over a plastic poppy that could possibly lift her mood.

She asked the spa receptionist if she could take the scales into a shower cubicle to use them in private. The receptionist agreed, but followed her into the changing rooms, explaining they'd been told to look out for thefts. Apparently hairdryers were popular with Westerners. And for every dryer stolen, the staff had to contribute half their weekly wages. Millie could hear the receptionist humming directly outside the cubicle while Millie disrobed. She stood on the scales. She now weighed twelve stone three. She let out a loud and triumphant 'Yes! Twelve stone three!' She'd lost three pounds. Thanks be to the fox.

When she'd put all her clothes back on, which took some time, Millie emerged from the cubicle feeling quite jubilant. It would have been nice for the receptionist to agree that twelve stone three might be quite a light bodyweight taken as a whole, but she just took the scales off her and hurried back to the reception.

Esther had emailed her three 'motivational mind maps' that she thought Millie might find entertaining. She was very pleased with them. Apparently Nathan had thought them up one night on his computer and had called them 'Millie's Life-Changing Health and Wealth Challenge'. One was a 'concept map' using bubbles that linked to a face that she assumed was supposed to be her. Nathan had made her face look rather fat. The writing in the bubbles stated that for every stone lost, Millie would earn £6,666. The same information was repeated in different languages, which Millie thought could be a mistake with Nathan's computer.

A similar map showed that for every four pounds lost, Millie would earn £1,904.76. For this one, Nathan had replaced Millie's face with an image of a fat woman wearing a leotard that was worryingly detailed.

The spider diagram was the most irritating, though. A messy drawing showed Millie would only get her money after each month and only if she was on target. She would also get eaten by a spider if she didn't. This was subtitled 'Meaningful Information', which Millie found meaningless and extraneous.

Finally, there was a stern warning in blue that she had already received £2,000 up front, so the first instalment would reflect that and be *less*. By now Millie felt dizzy. It was none of Nathan's beeswax anyway. She would have to tell Esther to forbid her son from doing any more mind maps. They were not helping.

Mary appeared to be in the mood to talk, which was good news for Millie. The more distance she could put between herself and Eugene's hovering-hand moment, the better. Apparently Mary had other problems with Richenda apart from having her futon sullied, and Millie was all ears.

She ordered Mary an iced water and suggested they retire to a pair of highly sanded-down tree-trunk stumps to drink it calmly. Millie had been perched at the bar waiting for Mary and coveting the menu options. If she couldn't eat food, she could read about it. Millie was wearing a blouse tucked into her jeans and the flower hair slide to celebrate the fact that she could tuck the blouse into her jeans.

'So what is it about Richenda that you don't like? Apart from her looks.'

'I didn't say anything about her looks.'

'Didn't you? Oh, sorry.'

'She's just not . . .' Mary struggled for the right word.

'Nice in any tangible way?' suggested Millie.

'Like us?' Mary asked.

Millie nodded.

'It's not that I don't like her – it's just she's kind of sabotaging my work.'

'That might be something to challenge?'

'I don't want to alienate her.'

'But if she's sabotaging your work, I wouldn't worry about alienation. This isn't a relationship you need to protect.'

'Yeah, but you've got no experience of relationships, Mum.'

This was true, but it seemed a bit blunt the way Mary had said it.

'I've got my local friends. Friend.' Millie was defensive.

'That doesn't count. I'm talking about where you have to work at a relationship, where you're sharing the same roof.'

Millie looked away to hide some quick tears. This was all too much. She caught the eye of a waiter laying out a series of tempting-looking coconut shells of small, crunchy balls. She nodded at him sneakily while reaching across to the water jug and hoped Mary wouldn't notice. A quick nibble on some salty protein would be a way to solve any untidy welling-up of emotions.

Mary was in full flow.

'She always seems to take her saliva swabs from the girls just before I start a class.'

'How mean.'

'How do you mean, mean?'

'That it's mean to interrupt you before your classes.'

'Mum, do you have any idea what I'm talking about?'

'No.' Millie kept smiling.

At least they were having girlie chats. This was what Mary had asked for.

Maybe she could sneak to the loo and snitch a crunchy thing from the bar top on the way. But she had a feeling that the account of Richenda's sabotage was only just beginning and she didn't want to appear uninterested.

'If she swabs the girls when I start teaching, then I don't have a full class. Then the other girls get distracted by the ones that are missing, then they leave, and then I'm left with hardly any girls, which looks bad and then the team leader thinks I can't maintain a full class.'

'Why don't you ask her not to swab when you're about to start teaching?'

Mary looked at her mother with exasperation.

'It doesn't work like that.'

'No,' nodded Millie. She wanted to support Mary, she really did, but she was also dealing with a renewed compulsion to forage for processed food. It didn't help that Mary was making her feel one step behind all the time, and this lack of control made her want to eat all the more.

'Do you think we could have a little snack just to line my stomach?'

'And if I do a treasure hunt,' continued Mary, 'or another creative activity, Richenda always seems to want to tag along, and then it looks as if we've both set it up – and my findings go on her research data.'

Millie would obviously need to solve this outrage before any snacking.

'Why don't you talk to your team leader and say you've got issues with Richenda sabotaging you and claiming your data as her own?'

'I can't.'

'Why?'

'He likes her.'

'In what way?'

'Oh, never mind,' Mary sighed. 'What about you?'

'I'm fine! Except for the cash flow and the diet.'

She caught the attention of the waiter and ordered another jug of water and somthing called 'kau kau' which sounded jolly and a bit potato-based.

'Richenda's got the team leader eating out of her hand.'

'How do you mean?' Millie asked.

'The team leader's being given funding by Eugene's dad, Mum. He likes Richenda and he doesn't like me because he doesn't want his son to go off with a Western girl.'

'And is Eugene's dad influential? Apart from being a tribe leader with great drumming skills – which I imagine carries some weight, does it?'

'He supports Manchester United.' Mary was defensive. Millie nodded.

'He's quite modern.'

'Must be – to send Eugene to England. Shows fore-sight.' Millie wanted to demonstrate that she'd been following events in great detail. 'And did Eugene study politics, by any chance?'

'Accountancy.'

The waiter was coming over to their tree trunk. He

placed the jug of water on the table, which Millie eagerly moved to one side in readiness for him to position a small bowl of things that looked like cheesy puffs but probably weren't.

'And if people don't believe I've done my own research, my tutor at Durham might have to drop me.' Mary looked quite stricken at this as a possibility. 'I need credibility.'

'You've got tons of credibility. Look at you. You're tired, scruffy and totally dedicated to your cause.'

'You're just saying that because you're my mother.' But Mary looked pleased.

'Couldn't you transfer to London? I'm sure you'd still get postgraduate funding if you explained the problems you're having here.'

'How can I collate women's menstrual patterns in London and link it to the anopheles mosquito when every female over twelve is on the Pill?'

'Well, couldn't you find someone else to do it here and then get them to post them to you?'

The exchange meandered on, with Millie trying to be helpful and Mary finding fault with everything. Occasionally Mary appeared happy and animated, but not often. The waiter arrived to replace the empty bowl of crispy balls with another one as well as a plate of what could be battered ants. Mary was about to wave it away when Millie said sharply, 'Just put them there, thank you . . . Lovely.' She couldn't stop herself.

Millie smiled protectively back at her pinched-looking child and then felt immediately guilty. Did her daughter know that she had just made polite conversation with her boyfriend while he hovered over her breast, causing a mix of Oedipal desire and repulsion?

'Mum?' The tone went up and then down.

'Yes?' Millie was neutral yet pleasant.

'You know last night?'

'I do, yes.'

'Why did you have to eat the sacrificial stew?'

'I thought it was the done thing.'

'No one else was doing it.'

'I realize that now.'

'No one *ever* eats fox and fish gills.'

'I'm sorry. I didn't know that.'

'Fish gills are like gristle over here.' Mary was keen to underline the error.

'I said I'm sorry. I was being overreactive. And too keen to please.'

Mary looked perplexed. Perhaps she'd forgotten she could have prevented her mother's faux pas with a quick heads-up, such as 'Whatever happens, don't eat the welcome stew – it's symbolic and could kill you.'

Millie wondered if this was a good time to share the findings of her ridiculous 'Wealth and Health' mind map and decided it wasn't.

'Well, anyway . . . I'm fine now,' she said cheerfully, and popped an ant into her mouth. It tasted of batter. But not much ant.

'So tell me about you. What's going on with Eugene?'

'Well . . .'

Mary sighed. She clasped her hands together and closed her eyes.

'And . . . are you happy? Doing all that rambling about in the forest as well as the research?'

'I was. Actually, the findings are amazing, Mum.' Mary smiled for the first time. 'All the girls seem to group their cycles in a similar way, and it's not just down to the moon, because the similarities are triggered by social tension caused by the hierarchy in the tribe . . .'

As Millie listened, she ate her way through the rest of the ants, which turned out to be so salty she had to finish the jug of water.

'My tutor from Durham was going to come out and start publishing.'

'The bald one with no neck?'

'The one with glasses.'

'With the limp?'

'No one's got a limp at Durham.'

'Sorry. So is he coming out, then?'

'He wanted to. Loads. I told him not to at the moment, but I think he's still coming. I didn't want him to get . . . you know . . . upset when Eugene started hitting on me.'

'Hitting?'

Mary looked at her mother with irritation.

'He's started to like me. A lot.'

'Well, who wouldn't! You're very beautiful,' said Millie loyally. 'And in need of a manicure, but that can be fixed. They do them here, don't they? In the hotel spa. I weighed myself in the ladies' today – very swish tiles.'

'I wouldn't go here. The girls are sex slaves. I can't support trafficking or entrapment, and nor should you.'

'I'll cancel my facial immediately. So would you say it's serious with Eugene or just physical . . . if it is?'

'I had this sort of animal attraction to him at first.'

'Yes?' Millie too had found Eugene attractive, but whether it was animal or not, it was very inconvenient. The thought of his hovering hand, and her reaction to it, made her feel flushed with shame. What was wrong with her?

'But then he started saying stuff that worried me.'

'Like what?'

'Trying to find out things.'

'What things?'

'Well, we were out in his dad's utility van.'

'That's nice.'

'Not that nice. His cousins were in the back messing about.'

'He's really a family boy, though, at heart, isn't he?'

'Then he took a call. He walked away into the trees to keep it private.'

'Yes? And?'

'I think he's—' Mary broke off.

'What?'

'Well, I'm not sure.'

'You must have an idea?' Millie encouraged.

'He might be a terrorist.' Mary said the word 'terrorist' very quietly.

'I don't think so, Mary. I think he's just very confused.'

'What about?'

'Well . . . I don't know, but just because he takes a private call from a friend doesn't make him a terrorist. Maybe he didn't want the cousins to listen in.'

'But he talks about the rebels needing support.'

'Of course they do. Rebels need to have support, otherwise they wouldn't be in the minority, needing support, and they wouldn't be proper rebels. He went through all that stuff with me.'

'What stuff?'

'Well, just said that rebels needed support to make sure their voice was heard. And I can see his point, actually, can't you? I mean, I can see why he's against logging because it leaves the land swampy, but then I can see why you need it swampy because you need the mosquitoes, otherwise you won't be able to study them and cure malaria – thinking ahead, of course. So no, we don't have to think he's a terrorist, just a bit passionate, which is easily misconstrued.'

'But he belongs to a cell, Mum.'

'The VPL?'

'Oh. He told you?' Mary seemed disappointed.

'He just mentioned it. But the "Virtual Papuan Liberators" doesn't sound very active as a pressure group, does it? I expect it's all done on the internet. Virtually.'

They both fell silent. Mary looked at the empty ant bowl. Completely clean.

'Christ, Mum. You're supposed to be losing weight. That's equivalent to three battered sausages.'

'I've got a deficit of salt from last night.'

'I thought we agreed not to talk about it.'

'Did we? OK, then.'

'So, Mum, what do you think?'

'About what?'

'Do you think Eugene is . . . ?'

'Odd? Yes. Very.'

'A terrorist?' Mary was not going to let this go.

'Well, I suppose it depends on your definition, doesn't it?'

'Someone who might end up killing me in my sleep for doing something they didn't agree with?'

'Mary! Eugene isn't capable of violence!' Millie said this with such conviction it took them both by surprise. They let a beat pass for the mood to settle.

'I went on his "recent history" in the internet room just before you arrived and found out he's obsessed about

Greenpeace. If it's not drugs or corrupt governments, it's trees. He'd got all this stuff up about the UN's International Day of Forests and I'm worried he might be planning to bomb the Port Moresby parliament buildings on 21 March.'

'I think that's the day after I'm leaving.' Millie knew the date off by heart.

'Actually, he's getting the same plane as you to Jackson's International and stopping with his cousins overnight.'

'Ah, I won't be flying back to Port Moresby. My nerves can't take it. I'm going to speak to the hotel about a taxi from here.'

'You can't. The roads aren't finished. They all come to a dead end, and they don't do taxis from here.'

'I'll get a lift to a port, then.'

'It'll take you two days and you'd have to bum a ride from a local boat – assuming they'd take you.'

'Oh.' Millie was stumped.

Mary carried on oblivious that she'd delivered this crushing blow to her mother's mental stability.

'And now he's saying he wants to stay with you in Dulwich in the spring.'

'What?' Millie swapped fears of an untimely death in a clapped-out plane to illicit trysts in Dulwich with a Papuan tribesman. Both options raised her pulse to racing. 'He probably wants a base for a bit of retail therapy. I can see him in Paul Smith, can't you? Or anything shop-bought – that isn't calico.'

'Mum, did anything happen? You look funny,' Mary observed.

Millie experienced a shot of adrenalin, similar to when she started to read her bank statements. Had her daughter got inside her head?

'Did anything happen when?'

'After he carried you to your room?'

'I was a bit gone at that point. Were you there?'

'Of course I was there. I put you in your nightdress and changed your bra. It was all brown. Something must have seeped.'

'Ah! I was wondering about that . . . Thank you. That's really nice of you because I couldn't remember how I'd got into bed and into my night things.'

'I had to get back to the settlement because of the curfew, but I was worried you might swallow your tongue, so I told Eugene to stay and make sure you didn't. You didn't, did you?'

'Didn't what?' said Millie defensively.

'Swallow it. Did he have to yank it out or something gross and you're not telling?' Mary looked very angry at this possible deceit.

'No, darling. You'll be pleased to know my tongue remained in my mouth.' Millie poked her tongue out to prove it.

'Eew.' Mary pointed at the vestiges of batter on it.

Millie hurriedly withdrew her tongue.

'Anyway, thank you for doing that, Mary.'

'But you do think he's got an animal attraction, don't you?'

'Seriously, Mary! I'm a woman of fifty – where does that come from?'

'Fifty-five.'

Millie took Mary's grubby hand in hers.

'Eugene is strange, I grant you. But he's not an insurgent – he just likes his country and wants things to be better. Like you do.'

'So why does he take all these calls in private?'

'Do you want to come home?'

'No.'

Suddenly, there was a loud, 'Hi, my ladies!'

Mother and daughter looked up and there standing in front of them was Eugene, wearing a baseball cap, tracksuit bottoms and a Day-Glo rucksack. A trip to Fenwick's men's department might well be in order after all.

'Ladies! I come to take you for lunchtime *picnica*.'

He kissed Mary on the mouth and appeared as if he was about to do the same to Millie, who dodged to look in her bag for a tissue. This must be a Papuan custom. Luckily, Mary didn't seem to think his interest in her mother was odd, but for how long would that last, especially if she didn't nip it in the bud now? She had convinced herself that any rogue physical longings she may have had were due to a projected anxiety about debt, jet lag and fear about losing her house. Easy enough to get these elements confused with arousal, but not to be repeated.

'You told Mary, Momma?' asked Eugene.

'Told me what, Momma?' replied Mary accusingly.

'I told Momma I like you.'

'And I told Eugene I like you too.'

They both looked at Mary.

She looked unsettled.

SIX

AFFIRMATION 6:
'I embrace my inner child and also my real one, but not at the same time'

'Shall we move a little nearer . . . to the fire?'

'Just had a shower, Mum. Too smoky. What's wrong with here?' said Mary, showing off now that she was with her boyfriend.

'Nothing.' Millie tried to calculate how many hours left before her return flight.

She estimated around 120.

They were seated on a groundsheet in the courtyard of the settlement, which was also in the direct path of the medical centre. There was a lot of through traffic from volunteers, all of whom had heard about Millie's hut-soiling incident from Richenda. One concerned volunteer asked how she was after her 'mishap' and whether she had 'rehydrated' herself.

'Yes! Completely fine now, thank you. I'm fine, thanks.'

'A tinned picnic is safer for you.' Eugene chuckled fondly and shook three tins of luncheon meat from his rucksack onto the groundsheet. He then arranged them in a tower and looked very pleased with himself.

'No boiled sacrifices?' Millie dared ask half jokingly.

'Mum!' Mary was disapproving.

'None, my dear.' He leaned across and patted Millie's hand.

She withdrew it to fiddle with her poppy hair slide.

'For my two favourite ladies,' he beamed.

'Have you got a can opener, darling?' asked Mary.

'Ah. No. Damnation,' said Eugene with exasperation.

'What a shame!' said Millie, both relieved at the lack of tin-opening and alarmed at her daughter's sudden term of endearment. 'Darling' was new. It made her sound at least forty-five.

'Ah! Wait a minute! I've got a Toblerone in the hut.' Mary stood up and at the same time rather unceremoniously unhooked her thong from inside her shorts.

Eugene allowed himself some pleasure at the glimpse of pink lace.

'Don't fetch it on my account,' said Millie.

'OK.'

'But if it's going spare . . .' said Millie hopefully.

'You had those ants, Mum. Are you all right?'

'Fine. Just a bit tired probably.' And full of ants.

'We go to the paddock?' Eugene looked at Millie in a concerned way.

'The paddock?' asked Millie, surprised. Paddocks usually had horses in them.

'It's my fieldwork study area,' replied Mary. 'We call it "the paddock" because there's a hammock there and it's usually very private.'

'Very private,' added Eugene, and looked smug. This was annoying.

Mary raised her eyebrows knowingly at Eugene. So this may have been the scene of Mary's intimacy with him. And she was now being invited to view it as a place of significance.

'Ah,' said Millie politely. 'Lovely. Nice idea,' as if they had suggested relocating to an upstairs bar overlooking a pool, instead of risking disease in a mosquito-infested area. The paddock must also be where Mary gathered samples of stagnant water, which didn't make it entirely romantic as a deflowering location.

'Let's go, then.' Millie stood up.

She would still be polite to Eugene, but felt she could afford to be a bit short and curt with her child, as Mary was family. She hoped this would get the status quo back to how it should be, and not how it had been this morning, when Eugene's hand had hovered persistently over her breast, for whatever reason.

The three of them set off, arm in arm, on the small pilgrimage to the paddock, with Eugene and Mary helping Millie over some of the steeper terrain. They separated when a branch smacked Eugene in the face and he asked if he could go on ahead, on his own.

'Of course,' said Millie, 'go on, both of you.'

They almost looked like a normal couple from behind. This was the first boyfriend Millie had met, and if Mary favoured short and swarthy, so be it. Millie followed them past the prefab offices and huts, and down a slope towards the swamp. She struggled to keep up, as there were a few dangers underfoot that required a lot of checking – not just for snakes but also for endangered Papuan rats and mice that she'd heard about. She didn't want to be known as the Englishwoman who'd squashed a rodent. When she heard Mary's cheerful voice call, 'Over here, Mum! You look hot!' she couldn't wait to sit down.

A Hansel-and-Gretel-style cabin had been erected on stilts next to a hammock slung between two trees. If it hadn't been for a pile of logs ready to be transported away in a fleet of battered pickup trucks, she could have believed they were in Center Parcs. But the air was heady with sawn wood and general swampiness.

After Millie had been shown every inch of the hot, stuffy cabin, with its impressive display of blood samples and swabs, she couldn't stop herself from yawning. She was exhausted from her exposure to potentially endangered animals. Both Mary and Eugene looked at her hopefully. They suggested she take a nap in the swinging hammock. She would get covered with bites, but no matter – she was here to support her daughter, and if this was what Mary wanted her mother to do, then she would do it. One day it would pay off.

Over by the trucks, a few workmen were putting on their shirts and clocking off for their lunch. Eugene scowled at them as they roared off in their beaten-up open-top vehicles. This was the first time Millie had seen him frown. He looked like a little hairless bulldog.

'Ready, lady?' Eugene looked at Millie in an enquiring way that was just a little too intimate for Millie's taste.

'I believe I am, Eugene.'

She was straightened and encouraged into an upright position before being tipped into the canvas sling. This felt slightly awkward, but she allowed herself to be man-handled. Once she was stretched out, Eugene and Mary rocked her gently back and forth, which was surprisingly solicitous even if it wasn't entirely compatible with her digestive system. Then she got the idea. They wanted to be alone. She would play along. Millie pretended to be asleep and even let out a convincing little snore. She could hear them back away and disappear into the cabin to do whatever it was they wanted to do. Eugene was giggling in quite a high voice, which could be a worry if he became family.

Millie had almost dropped off when she heard raised voices from inside the cabin.

'I have to tell him what I know.'

'Why?'

'Because he's my tutor.'

'He is nosy. You should be telling me.'

'I tell you as well.'

'He is denying my people the right to trees.'

'We're giving your people the right to fight malaria.'

'You and he kill my trees.'

'We don't.'

'Do!'

'Don't!' screamed Mary.

Then in a quiet voice Millie heard Eugene say, 'The tutor like you.'

'And I like him, Eugene. OK?'

'Not OK.' Eugene was firm.

Millie was fully awake now. She heard Mary let out an exasperated 'Godddd.'

There was a slam of a door, footsteps and then silence. Millie wasn't quite sure what she should do.

She felt rather embarrassed at overhearing their tiff and didn't know whether to follow Mary out of loyalty. But the hammock was hung quite high up and she'd missed her moment for a dignified descent, as she'd need assistance to get down. She looked across to the trees. Mary was now miles away. The best bet was to stay put and settle her stomach after the rocking and the battered ants. Some of them may have been alive by the feel of things. She allowed her eyes to close again and sank back into what she considered to be a well-deserved nap.

As she drifted, she could just about hear Eugene on the phone, something about the International Day of Forests and parliament buildings, and then she felt that strange whistling on her face. She could smell a heady mix of sweat and soap. She pretended to wake up with a start.

'Ah, Eugene!'

She opened her eyes wide and checked her blouse. He was peering at her.

'Did you hear us, Mommy?'

'Not all of it.'

'I take you back to your hotel, Mommy. You want a carry?'

'I'll be fine on foot. I like looking out for the snakes and other endangered species, actually. It's quite . . . fun.'

THURSDAY 20 MARCH

Millie was packing with a bit more enthusiasm than perhaps was decent in front of Mary. She made herself slow down and fold up her new sarong, bought in the hotel boutique, with deliberation. The impulse buy was inspired by her weight loss. It would be a challenge to find an occasion to wear it at home. She wondered again how much weight she had lost altogether since she'd arrived. The hotel spa's scales had shown she'd lost three pounds after the fox expulsion, which now seemed pretty meagre given the loss came from both ends, but after a second weigh-in they'd said she'd regained a pound. Who'd have thought battered ants could be so fatty? So in fact that was a loss of two measly pounds. Her jeans were a bit loose, but that might be because they needed washing. She'd been wearing them for the whole week.

Mary was sitting on the bed watching TV and flicking channels.

'We didn't really have much time to talk after your row, did we?'

'No,' said Mary.

'Did you make up with him?'

'Mm,' said Mary. 'He came after me. Eventually.'

'Aw. That's nice.' Millie patted her rucksack fondly as if it were a well-behaved child.

She'd be fine once she could see the Hammersmith fly-over. That at least would be real. So far there were a lot of uncertainties about her time in Papua New Guinea. She had no idea if she'd been hypnotized or healed or what had taken place on her first night here, alone with Eugene. But whatever it was, she still felt very emotionally charged and raw.

Whenever she thought of Al – which she'd resolved to do twice a day as an experiment to see if she liked him – the memory of that shameful desire with Eugene popped up and she couldn't quite get rid of it. Al became smaller, and Eugene, well, he became . . . bigger. This now was the greatest worry of them all.

After a fallow period of enforced celibacy, she had

finally been gifted an electrician who would at last be someone to go to the cinema with after all these years of slipping in after the film had started. Yet here she was grappling with urges about something that could never happen, with someone who was forbidden.

Mary was now watching Oprah Winfrey on Fox News with the sound turned down. Oprah appeared to be discussing a book with some deprived-looking children, but beyond that it was unclear what was being said. Mary was looking troubled.

'The thing is, I don't really know what's going on with Eugene.' Mary looked at her mother. She wanted to talk. This was typical. Millie was all packed and psychologically bracing herself for the inordinate amount of flying time that lay ahead of her, and now she was being summoned for motherly help.

'OK. Are you serious about him?' she moved next to Mary on the bed.

'I don't know.'

'In my experience that might mean you're not sure.'

'Your experience doesn't fill me with huge confidence, Mother.'

'Just trying to help.'

'I know.' Mary's voice became kind again and Millie felt a sudden tenderness. Her changeable and perplexed daughter haunted her in the most mercurial way, and their relationship seemed to become more intense as each day passed in Papua.

'I think he has strong feelings.' Mary flicked off the TV and swivelled round on the bed to face her mother. There was no escape.

Millie removed herself to the hotel armchair to focus

on her child with a bit of distance between them. She wanted to leave their relationship in a good place.

'Do you think you and Eugene got quite close?' asked Mary.

Millie had not been expecting this.

'Not close exactly, no.'

'You must have.'

'How do you mean?'

'After your seizure.'

'My short bout of unfamiliar food reaction, you mean.'

'Did he . . . ?' Mary found a tassel on the crocheted throw and began unpicking it.

'What?' said Millie with a sense of doom. She knew she had to do some direct talking. It was her job.

'What do you mean, what?' Mary looked up and stopped fiddling.

'Of course not, Mary! He's a very *unusual* individual, I grant you, with very *unconventional* body language by Dulwich standards, but there was nothing *intimate* between us, if that's what's worrying you, along with all your other worries, my darling. I urge you to tick that one off the list. I'm a middle-aged woman.'

'I know you are.'

'Good. Thank you.'

Millie had been working hard at putting the breast incident behind her. She didn't need to be reminded about any physical urges. Except at night, when she'd been experimenting with a new fantasy that involved Al throwing her up against a wall and ordering her to undress, in a sexually bossy way. He often had his legs apart and sort of leered at her chest. In real life, she didn't think Al had it in him, but it was worth a try. If the fantasy played out well enough, it could just about block out the fear of the loan shark's interest rate and what the bailiffs might do to her in real life. When sleep eventually came, it was a huge relief.

Millie wanted to get a better picture of how Mary's relationship was being perceived by other people in her workplace. Perhaps she could get support from them after she went back.

'How is it with you and Eugene and your various colleagues? I mean, other people seem to think you're an item, do they? What do they say to you about it? What does your team leader think?'

'I don't know. I haven't asked him.' Mary looked hopeless. 'I don't want to ask, and I don't want you to ask about him either, Mum. It's too much. I'm an adult.'

'Of course you are. That's fine.' Mary was obviously muddled, but she'd just have to leave it at that.

Millie got up to collect some papers that had been put under the door. There was a fax that Esther had forwarded from Very Medical, who were concerned Millie might have run out of Kleinne Fett pills. There was also some potentially good news about Tessa Keltz, who might be interested in the campaign but was waiting to see if she'd been diagnosed with a food allergy before the agent could go ahead with any commitment. The results depended on Tessa's stool sample. The food-allergy people paid very well apparently, but stools tended to take two weeks to assess. In the meantime they couldn't align themselves to conflicting campaigns. There was also a memo from the hotel spa charging her for use of the scales. She placed these on the dressing table under her handbag. They were of no relevance to Mary.

'Because actually Eugene's quite serious, isn't he?' Mary was asking.

Millie sat down again.

'He is, yes.' She wondered if this would later be used against her or if she should remain silent.

'And I'm not sure I'm ready for . . . you know . . . commitment.'

They let the question hang between them. Millie was too scared to say anything. She didn't want to caution against Eugene in case it made Mary rebel and get engaged to him, but she didn't want to actively encourage the relationship either, because then the hand-hovering moment would never quite go away . . . completely. She felt a sharp burst of jealousy.

Also, she was going back to London that afternoon and didn't want to start anything they couldn't finish.

'I could cut your fringe if you fancied. There's time. I can call reception for some scissors.' Millie loved cutting hair.

'I'm growing it.'

'Good!' Millie enthused. 'That's good. Then you can wear it half up, half down. If you wanted.'

'No. I wouldn't do that.'

'No.' Millie nodded respectfully.

'He likes it in England, he says.'

'Does he want to go back and do more accounting?'

'Possibly. And I've always liked England.'

'You're not thinking of coming back, are you?' Millie said sharply. She thought of the £2,000 she had spent on coming here. That could have paid off twenty weeks of QwickCash interest.

'Does Eugene want to live in England, do you think?'

'He's got some friends who work for Greenpeace in Barons Court, he said, who have a sofa, and I could maybe . . .'

'Mary, you told me only the other day how much your research means to you.'

'Yes, it does – really it does – but that was before . . . he got . . . And then, you know . . .'

Millie didn't know. She had to be bold and ask, for both their sakes.

'Sorry, but I've got to ask you again, Mary – tell me about when he touches you. Did we decide it was a reiki thing that he does?'

'No, we didn't, and I told you I wasn't pregnant.'

Mary located the Tic Tacs in her mother's make-up bag and helped herself. She looked shiftily back at her.

'That's right. Well, in that case – and what do I know, Mary? – it strikes me that Eugene might, and I only mean might, be a bit of a Wicca?'

'A what?'

'I hate to tell you this, Mary, but there was an unfortunate incident.'

'Why didn't you tell me before? I kept asking.'

'Not with me,' Millie intercepted quickly. 'It was with some Wesleyan missionaries. They got sacrificed and eaten – various bits of them. They were hung up for smoked meat.'

'I don't believe you. When?' Mary was trained to doubt facts unless proven.

'A few years ago.'

Mary still looked unconvinced.

'Well, it happened here. And very possibly there may be a history in Eugene's tribe of putting people in trances for . . . for shadier ends.'

There. She had said it. It sat between them.

'OK, maybe not eat you,' said Millie. This had sounded a bit harsh.

Mary looked embarrassed. She offered her mother a Tic Tac.

'What I mean is, does he hypnotize you?' asked Millie, more for her own interest than Mary's.

'No . . .'

Millie took a Tic Tac and laid it on the bed.

'So shall we just agree that there are a few unknowns with Eugene?'

Mary nodded.

'And that he may or may not be involved in changing the world, which can take many forms.'

'Yes.'

'And that we've both got our lives ahead of us, with all their glorious twists and turns of adventure and discovery.'

Mary wasn't convinced, and Millie didn't blame her. She knew the blithe clichés were an insult to Mary's intelligence. But her hands were tied and she needed to hit on some winning formula to move them both forward.

Then she remembered Florence's enthusiasm for a book.

'You know what they say in *The Secret*?'

'I don't believe in self-help books.' Mary eyed her mother suspiciously.

'It comes as a DVD.'

'I'm a scientist. Why would I watch anything called

The Secret? How can it be based on empirical evidence if its findings are a secret?'

'Shall I tell you anyway?'

'All right. Go on, then.'

'It says that for all your wishes to manifest themselves, you have to fall in love with *you*!' Millie clapped her hands magically.

'Isn't that a bit narcissistic?'

'OK. How about doing an affirmation before I go? Can you say, "I know that I am perfect right now and in every moment"? Can you do that?'

Millie wished she had brought *The Pocket Book of Life Affirmations: an Inspirational Handbook for Busy People* with her. But something told her Mary would be quite pleased she hadn't.

Mary shook her head.

'No. I couldn't say that. It's based on a false premise.'

Mary had always been stubborn.

'That's a shame, then,' Millie said briskly. 'So shall we go shopping in my last few hours here? Can we go to the market? And can we perhaps have a light lunch back here when we finish? I'm starving.'

Millie persuaded Mary to let her buy a pair of pink denim shorts in the market. They both agreed the khaki ones had been worn quite a lot. The choice had been pink denim or a pair of boy's football shorts, and they agreed the pink denim was the better option. They were clearly in harmony during this last outing together. Millie chose a wooden crocodile-shaped ashtray for Al and told Mary this would be for her new friend.

She asked Mary if she thought the ashtray would be a fire hazard if her new friend didn't stub his cigarette out in it properly. Mary wondered what kind of idiot new friend would leave a lit cigarette in a wooden ashtray. But Millie was pleased to have at least mentioned Al's name – just in case it went anywhere. They both knew Mary was more concerned about Eugene, and the fact that her tutor from Durham might be making a visit soon, which was what she and Eugene had rowed about.

Millie was satisfied the pink shorts would herald some new energy. She asked if she could bin the old pair and Mary agreed. At least she'd been able to fix something.

SEVEN

〜

AFFIRMATION 7:
*'I am a mindful flyer. Even when people just need
a high five. In the face. With a Kindle'*

Mary was working on the afternoon of Millie's flight and
insisted her mother accept the offer of a lift from Eugene.
He was, after all, driving to the airstrip in Goroka and
taking the same internal flight to Jackson's International
Airport for his overnight trip. He had planned to stay with
some cousins and spend some time in Port Moresby to buy
some Manchester United memorabilia for his father before
coming back again the next day.

Millie reluctantly agreed to the lift. But she was worried. She remembered the phone call he'd taken when she
was in the hammock, when he'd spoken about the International Day of Forests and parliament buildings.

She didn't want to hear a loud bang and worry that her
daughter's boyfriend had been in the area when a bomb
went off.

Mary came to the hotel to wave her mother off before
hurrying away to the settlement to prepare for a class.
Millie knew she was off to have a cry. She recognized the

look. Mary had always retreated to the same spot in the garden in Dulwich by an azalea bush when she was upset, thinking that she wouldn't be found. Millie would give it a few minutes before putting on a coat and outdoor shoes to wander past the bush and say casually in a surprised voice, 'Oh, there you are! I was just thinking about popping some chicken dinosaurs on a tray. What do you reckon?'

During their shopping trip at the market that morning, Millie had finally dared slip into the conversation that Mary might want to 'keep a bit' of herself 'back from a man', adding that it was an adage her own mother had handed down to her. This wasn't true, but she'd been wanting to say this for some time. The advice made Mary snort with laughter – 'More clichés, Mum!' – which was a bit hurtful, if true. But it may have influenced Mary's gift of a yellow crocheted spectacle case for Millie to take back to Mary's grandmother: 'You can tell Granny I've got no intention of being distracted by a man.'

The drive with Eugene from the hotel to the airstrip proved to be unsettling. Mary and he had greeted each other slightly awkwardly when he came to collect Millie at the hotel. Eugene looked wistfully at the new pink shorts.

'Mary, you are princess in pink.'

'Ha, ha,' Mary said dismissively.

'She's very bad at taking compliments,' Millie felt she had to apologize. She didn't want Eugene to be hurt.

But once they were both seated up in the truck, he quickly recovered his disappointment and smiled at her.

'Ready for me, Momma?'

Was Millie imagining Eugene's desire for her? Maybe he was just being polite, but he certainly seemed to allow his eyes to linger over her cotton blouse.

'No funeral today, Momma?' he laughed.

'Pardon, Eugene?'

'You are not wearing black.'

Millie thought Eugene looked slightly taller today. It was only when he climbed out of the cabin and came level with the hubcaps, which admittedly were on unusually big wheels, that she was reminded of his lack of height.

A faded cushion had been placed on the passenger seat for her. It was a kind thought. She felt obliged to sit on it in spite of the possible livestock inside. She was after all being offered a free lift. It would be a small price to get nipped. She had no plans to reveal either of her bottoms to anyone important when she got back to the UK. Not even Al. Correction. Especially not Al.

But as they began their bumpy drive across unfinished, rocky, makeshift roads, Millie had to acknowledge to herself that she was now experiencing another surge of arousal. This could be hunger or it could be triggered by the vibrations as Eugene dodged potholes. Either way, the surge of dark contractions took her by surprise. Feelings like this had been long buried, except for the few fledgling appearances at the start of her visit.

Eugene was looking very different as well. He was out of his calico drapes, and the chunky little legs had been squeezed into a pair of brand-new chinos. She suspected they had been bought especially for this very occasion. The supposition gave Millie an awful thrill. He must care about her enough to buy new trousers. To be adored by anyone keen enough to buy trousers for her was quite humbling, but also off-putting. It was too much.

Millie knew this was all nonsense. The feelings would fade as soon as she touched down at Heathrow. It was only because it was hot and sunny and very green here. The sun always did this to people. But for an hour she would be in transit. She was no longer a concerned mother, nor was she tied in to the strictures of the diet. In fact, she had thoroughly enjoyed the packet of Milk Chews Eugene had left for her on the dashboard. Apparently these were his mother's favourites as well, which is why he thought she might like them.

It didn't help that the muddied potholes got larger as they drove the thirty kilometres to the airstrip. Millie found herself in Eugene's lap on two occasions. She apologized each time and he laughed. She didn't want him to think she'd dived there on purpose.

Millie wondered if she should ask Eugene a few important questions. What were his intentions with Mary? Did he like older women? And was he going to blow up the Houses of Parliament to commemorate the International Day of Forests when he dropped her off at Jackson's Airport, as Mary had feared? She decided she wouldn't ask him these last two, but there was something powerful and attractive about a man who wanted to improve his environment. And who was driving so masterfully round puddles at the same time. She might even join up when she got home. On the other hand, Eugene might well be a Wicca or a shaman or something else weird. This was, after all, not unknown in Papua New Guinea. Tribes had gone to war over such activities. Or were all these worries just misplaced grief for leaving her daughter behind?

At last they'd descended a mountain and avoided a few 50cc scooters and roaming livestock to reach an almost conventional twenty-four-hour garage. Millie's guilty, jumpy journey was near its end. The thought of what she was leaving and what she was returning to filled her with dread.

'What do you use, Mommy?' Eugene had asked as they turned into the garage.

'For?' Mary smiled back nervously.

'Your skin. It's a very smooth one.'

'You're very kind.'

'Like apples.'

'Thank you.'

'What make? I buy some for my aunties.'

'I just use Vaseline if I'm honest.' Millie was not going to mention the Crème de la Mer.

'I must tell my aunts,' said Eugene.

'Do.' Millie felt no guilt. Let them have Vaseline.

And Millie was now being likened to his aunts. No matter. Eugene jumped the long way down to the ground to insert the nozzle of the petrol pump into the aperture. He now looked small again. Very small.

As the petrol vibrated into the tank beneath her, Millie took out her return itinerary and tried to banish the image of Mary's worried, pinched little face waving her off.

'Cooee, Momma!'

Eugene was waving a little brown-paper bag at Millie. He bowed outside her side of the truck's passenger window, making it a tricky manoeuvre to reach down to collect it. She was sure her cleavage was on show.

Millie had to prise the bag out of his hand. She shook it with pleasure and opened it. Inside was a plastic Papua New Guinean naked lady hanging from a key ring. The figure was dressed in a feather thong and was naked from the waist up.

'I shall treasure it,' said Millie, straightening up.

'Where?' asked Eugene, staring, she thought, at her breasts.

'Where?' she echoed.

Eugene had climbed back up into the cabin.

'Allow me.'

Eugene took the key ring, with the dancing naked lady wearing the feather, out of Millie's hand and very slowly dangled it at the top of her blouse. It wasn't a low blouse, now she was sitting up again and had adjusted herself, but the feather bobbed there for quite a few seconds. Then it started to slip down the top of her blouse and in between . . . things. Eugene looked at her intently as he manipulated the doll in and out of her blouse. Millie became a seething mass of confusion and hormones and horror.

'Thank you, Eugene. That's very nice. Perhaps I'll just attach it to my handbag.' She held out her hand and took the key-ring doll from him. He looked wistfully at where the doll had been bobbing up and down.

'Your handbag?' He sounded like the characters in the afternoon play they'd listened to.

'Yes, on the strap. Like you do with a scarf.'

'Wait.' He took the key ring back and, with his eyes still boring into her, inserted the naked lady's head in his mouth and used his tongue to flick all around it.

Millie thought she might faint.

'She was a little dirty. I clean her up for you.' He kissed the naked lady and put it in her hand.

'Thank you so much. That's lovely, Eugene. Most unusual.'

Eugene started up the truck with a macho rev of the accelerator and licked his lips at the same time. He looked across at her and caught her stealing a sly look back at him. He smiled.

'Yes, that's a real . . . memento of a super . . . time all round.'

They drove the last half-kilometre in silence . . . Had he tried to arouse her with a key ring?

The short flight to Port Moresby was less of a shock than the one coming over, but she did feel the need to grip Eugene's hand quite tightly during most of the flight. He allowed this quite happily. They shook hands more formally outside Jackson's International, to go their separate ways. Eugene to very possibly bomb a building and she to a life of debt, diet and depression. As she walked inside the throbbing airport she realized that there were three revelations from her trip that had to be faced and they were all equally horrible. Firstly, she had experienced an alarming reawakening of sexual desire caused by the actions of her daughter's boyfriend. Second, she had not lost any significant weight: three pounds off and one back on was not the kind of result Esther would be looking for, unless the hotel spa scales were malfunctioning, and they weren't, because she'd asked the spa receptionist to check them. And finally, she'd been duped into coming thousands of miles as a carrier of hair tongs, only to discover her daughter might be popping back to the UK in the not-too-distant future, as well as behaving in an argumentative and needy manner for quite a lot of Millie's visit. And still she adored her.

Millie had settled into her seat and was just starting to trust in the fact that no one was going to sit next to her when a small hand tapped her on the head from the seat behind. It was Jacob. This time, she actually found she was pleased to see him and they greeted each other like old colleagues.

'I was wondering if you had any luck with the dysentery, Millie,' Jacob began conversationally.

'Quite a good result, thank you,' Millie replied, adding, 'Well, middling,' in case Jacob thought a loss of two pounds or possibly even less given the bread rolls recently consumed at the airport was not significant.

FRIDAY 21 MARCH

The last-minute purchase of a giant Toblerone, to add to gin, a triple-pack of mascara and 'Viva Glam' lipstick, had failed to alleviate Millie's growing sense of doom when she found herself in Heathrow arrivals the next day. A brave step onto the scales in the ladies' confirmed her mood. She was twelve stone seven pounds. She'd been away for eight days and had eaten food during most of them, but this gain was extreme. She'd been twelve stone four at her second weigh-in at the hotel, having gained a pound from the battered ants, and had put on three pounds since then. It must be a mistake. Either the hotel scales or the Heathrow ones were faulty, or the in-flight meals alone had gained her three pounds. She was now one pound more than her start weight. She wanted to scream but saw Florence waving her freckled, bangled arm at Millie and managed to rein in the hysteria.

She was tired, hungry and exhausted from fighting back her sexual arousal on the flight, but here was Florence, waving at her with one leg firmly on the cat basket. Surely the kittens could be left at home by now.

She swapped the duty-free bag into her other hand and called out a cheerful greeting to Florence. If she sounded cheerful, she would become cheerful. This was a proven CBT trick and had worked for her during the worry about Mary's shoplifting phase.

'Hi, Millieee,' screeched back Florence.

So here was her second-best friend waving at her with easy enthusiasm. Would Millie have got up at the crack of dawn to collect Florence from one of her weekends to Belgium and experience the stress of the short-stay car park? No.

The flight had given her time to reflect. Agonizing images of Mary's worried face would come into her mind, forcing her to switch back to thinking about Eugene, which worried her even more. But they had hugged hard in the hotel foyer before she left. A big, tight hug that was the longest either of them had allowed themselves.

Yes, there would be quite a lot to tell Florence and a few questions to ask. One would have to be, 'Does the licking of the face of a doll key ring equal foreplay?'

Instead she said, 'You look very summery. Is that Agnès B.?' before almost falling into her arms but stopping short of an embrace.

Florence looked rather surprised at this show of affection. They air-kissed to work round any confusion.

'It's Zara,' said Florence, typically ready to reveal its source. 'They didn't have a medium, but I fell in love with it.'

She was wearing what looked like a very snug petticoat as a dress over a blouse. Maybe her sheepskin was in the car. It was still March. On the other hand, Florence always said she felt heat easily.

Florence assessed her friend's face carefully.

'You look different, Millie!' she said.

'I know.' Millie waited.

'Yeah. Wow.' Florence stepped back and closed one eye to get a better look.

'Thinner?'

Florence said nothing but continued to appraise her friend.

'What, then?' Millie sighed.

'Yes, thinner,' said Florence quickly, 'but also more . . . Have you met someone? It's that or you've had a shock. Has anyone died?'

'No one's died,' said Millie. She would call her mother, though, and tell her how well Mary was doing, as instructed by Mary.

'A lot happened out there.'

She wanted to be mysterious, but first she needed to rebalance her bags. She gave Florence the gin to hold.

'Aw, thank you, Millie. How lovely.' Florence looked almost overwhelmed with quite so many gifts, which were easily visible through the duty-free bag.

Too late. She'd forgotten about the lipstick, triple mascara and Toblerone. Millie would have to fish those out when they were in the car.

'The Toblerone's for Harry,' Millie said quickly.

'That's nice of you,' exclaimed Florence. 'He's got a sweet tooth, hasn't he?' She seemed pleased for Harry. Which meant, rather annoyingly, that it looked as if he would have to be given the Toblerone.

They'd reached the short-stay car park's ticket machine. Florence fed it a twenty-pound note and waited for the change. The tinkle of a lone pound coin and a fifty-pence piece chinked back at them. Millie didn't offer to pay, but she might let Florence keep the lipstick. Not the mascaras, though.

'Harry's been amazing,' said Florence as they sped out of the car park. 'And Vernon's really come on.'

'In what way amazing?' Millie didn't really want to talk about Harry. Or Vernon coming on in her absence.

'He's fed him. He's talked to him. He . . . Well, he went in every day. He even babysat mine.'

'What about Jack?'

'Jack.' Florence's jaw clicked.

'What? Are you not . . . ?'

'We are. But the other one came over for the weekend.'

'Brussels Man?'

'Yes.' Florence looked a bit shy. But not for long. 'I got this message he was in London. Nothing for weeks and then . . .' Florence snapped her finger with her thumb. 'We stayed at the Sofitel. Back there, actually.'

She tilted her head backwards in case Millie might want a glimpse of the hotel. She didn't. Nor did she want to hear about any recent forays with the shoe man – she'd had sufficient awakenings of her own and didn't think she could stomach anyone else's just now.

The drive was depressing. Where were the sun, the rugged Eastern Highlands and lucky key ring garages? How could she retain even an iota of hope or cheerfulness right now?

'You're quiet,' said Florence. Millie saw her glance at her before she spoke. Millie pulled her jacket round to hide her stomach, which had become bloated from several airline meals, her own and Jacob's.

'Well, it's been a struggle with the food.'

'What's it like over there?'

'There was a minibar in the room.'

The women exchanged looks.

'And a few crisps. With the wine. On the flight.' No more needed to be said.

'I went to an amazing supper club last week, Millie.' Florence was always so positive about everything she did. It made her own negativity more pronounced.

'Can we not talk about food?' The reality of what Millie had eaten had hit her, and now she knew that Florence knew what she'd eaten, she couldn't pretend.

'No, this is a special supper club. Joan introduced me for half-price.'

'Feng shui Joan?'

'Yes.'

'That's nice. How is Joan?' Millie was exhausted. She didn't care about anyone except maybe Esther, who would have to be told about the weight gain.

'She's great, and it's called Tough Titty Supper Club.'

'What is it?'

'It's a club for women who want to support other women but who don't want to compete.'

'How does it get any members?'

Florence was not going to be put off. Millie was often contrary.

'There are loads of trainers and nutritionists who are members.'

'Odd they'd want to meet over supper.'

'But they'd work with you for nothing.'

'Why?'

'Because that's how a supportive, non-competitive entrepreneurial female infrastructure finances itself. I was telling Harry about it, and he said you should join and meet the members. He's found a lot of unpaid bills.'

'Well, he can pay them if he's so worried.'

'He sorted them all into piles to show their priority. He said this Kleinne Fett offer has come at the perfect moment. To avoid prison or the bailiffs.'

It was obvious Harry and Florence had spent time talking about her problems.

'I agree with him.'

'Oh good. Because Joan really thinks this is going to be the answer.'

'What is?'

'Tough Titty Supper Club. They're amazing.'

'And what do they do again?'

'It's a networking club for women who don't take any shit but who want to help each other.'

'Actually, they don't sound my sort of people, Florence. I'm too competitive.'

'You could network and find yourself a personal trainer.' Florence gave her an uncertain look in case she'd been too direct about size. But Millie knew she was trying to help.

And if Joan Le Measurer – who had already proved herself to be a soothsayer, guru and monetary miracle worker – was recommending Tough Titty, then she should probably consider it.

She probably should. What did she have to lose?

Three stone and one pound.

Florence was pleased with her soft but hard sell.

'So how much weight do you think you lost, out there in Papua?'

'Papua New Guinea. About half a stone.'

'That's good. That's what . . . ?' Florence counted on two fingers. 'That's seven pounds all in, isn't it?'

'Half a stone is seven pounds, yes.'

'That's quite significant.'

'It was. Then I put on another few pounds on the way back. Weird.'

'Horrendous.' Florence seemed angry at the injustice of the mysteriously unaccounted-for surplus.

'I know.'

'And why was that, do you think?'

'I was very ill, very ill indeed, and needed to replenish my fat stores, I assume.'

Florence looked suitably grave. The kittens were beginning to complain on the back seat.

'Or it might just have been stress-related. I blow up when I worry,' said Millie.

'Don't we all?'

Millie knew that Florence never blew up.

'Compounded by a fox and fish stew on the first night.'

'Really? They probably cook with all the entrails over there, don't they?'

'They probably do, yup.'

'And then there's the dirty water. I suppose it would have been considered rude to leave any, would it?' asked Florence.

'Quite the opposite. It was considered rude to have some, but Mary didn't tell me in time.'

Florence nodded, without understanding.

'I was hoping to get mild dysentery or diarrhoea while I was there, just to kick-start the diet. Did I say I was planning on that?'

'I don't think you did, no.'

Florence looked again at Millie's distended stomach. The jacket had fallen open.

'And . . . did it work?' Florence asked doubtfully.

'At the beginning it did and then . . .'

'What?'

'I might as well tell you. I met someone who triggered certain impulses with food – that threw me off centre.'

'Off centre?'

'Yes.'

'Gosh. Who did you meet?'

Millie was irritated.

'He's called Eugene.'

There was some reassurance in saying his name.

'Eugene? A doctor?'

But not when Florence said it.

'Mary's boyfriend.'

Florence frowned.

'The one that gave her the STD that you were worried about?'

'That was a bladder infection. I think she's still a virgin, or she might not be *now*, of course. I think they did it for the first time in the paddock.'

Florence mulled this idea over.

'Is that a custom in Papua New Guinea? That the mother has to . . . be present?'

'Oh no. I wasn't there. Well, I was, but not when they did it.'

Florence looked out of her depth. She switched on *Woman's Hour*. She switched it off again when the serial came on.

'But . . . how does Mary feel about Eugene?'

'She doesn't know her own feelings,' said Millie, and

pressed the window switch to let in some air. And to change the subject.

Florence said casually, 'Harry was wondering how much time you've got before the first weigh-in and how much weight you've already lost.'

'That's quite nosy of him. Overall, probably three, maybe two pounds.'

'Ah, because he said the contract stated – after your initial money advance for the flight – you have to lose seven pounds by the first weigh-in, which is next Thursday.'

'Shite. Next Thursday? That's . . . *six days away*.'

'To get the money. So, Millie, if you've already lost two pounds, that's only another five to go . . . to be on target . . . to get the money . . . at the first weigh-in.'

Florence had never suffered from being repetitive before. Harry must have got inside her head. This was what obsessives did . . .

'Right, but I'm not sure quite where I'm at weight-wise. What would I have to lose let's say if I'm . . . God forbid . . . twelve stone seven?'

'You'd have to lose . . . eight pounds in under a week to stay in the game.'

'Ah.'

'Harry wrote out all the options for you, after he read the contract and went through your filing cabinet and whatnot.'

'What filing cabinet?'

'The one that had all your poetry. From when you were a teenager.'

'You both read my poetry?'

'Lovely stuff, Millie.'

'What?'

'Harry brought them round. That guide camp must have been awful. Shocking and moving in a funny way.'

'That's quite intrusive.'

'I suppose it is, yes.' Florence made herself look ashamed, while Millie made herself look violated. 'Sorry.'

'I mean, why read that one?'

'We read the sonnets about saying goodbye as well and the—'

'Which?' asked Millie suspiciously.

'The girl one. About the netball captain.'

Millie shook her head in disbelief. She closed her eyes. Nothing was sacred.

'You're a really good poet. We both thought so.'

Millie nodded.

'You can read my teenage diary if you want?' offered Florence, adding, 'My mother thinks it's hilarious.'

'I'm not really into reading other people's diaries,' said Millie quietly.

She closed her eyes and tried to think about Al throwing her against the wall.

'Well, here we are! All present and correct!'

Millie opened one eye. She was home. Harry was rushing out of his house in yoga bottoms and furry slippers to open the passenger door.

'Were you asleep, Millie?' He peered at her closely.

'No . . .'

'She was in a world of her own!' said Florence fondly. 'She's knackered.'

As Millie got out, opening the boot to get her rucksack,

Florence mouthed, 'Not good,' and made a mime with her hand of a huge stomach to Harry. Millie saw this in the wing mirror.

Harry nodded.

'I'll make her a broth tonight,' he whispered.

'I'll not be having one of those, thank you, Harry.' Millie had also heard the stage whisper.

Harry looked at Millie.

'Vernon's missed you, Millie.'

'You mean you have.'

'True, I have.' Harry smiled.

Millie felt queasy.

She left some newspapers in Florence's boot for recycling. She was too jet lagged to do it herself.

'So, Florence, there's a lipstick and mascara in the duty-free bag.'

She changed her mind about the Viva Glam. She'd be needing it herself.

'Oh, thank you, Millie.'

'Can you just take the gin out and give me the rest?'

Florence looked hurt, but fished out the make-up.

'And the Toblerone's for Harry, isn't it, Millie? Shall I leave that in for him?'

Florence looked at Harry and shook the bag meaningfully. She was about to take the Toblerone out when Millie snatched the bag from her.

'Yup. Sure is. Listen, you've both been fantastic, really. That was so kind of you, Florence. Can I pay for the car park?' Millie slammed the boot shut.

'And the petrol? No, of course not.'

Harry looked suddenly melancholic.

'Do you want me to come in with you?' His role of cat

protector and nosy parker looked as if it was coming to an end.

'I don't, actually, no.'

And with that, Millie staggered into her house, fatter than when she left it.

Vernon was unmoved by the sight of his mistress. Millie felt her stomach. It had not gone down. She looked at the pile of bills. She still owed a lot of money: £2,000 to the loan shark plus interest, the usual £1,000 to the bank for her overdraft, and now there was a courtesy card from an organization called Barrington Bailiffs who wanted to introduce themselves. Apparently they had won 'Best Enforcement Team of the Year' in 1986.

Harry had opened the monthly cheque for £300 for Millie's agony page and put it in a pile labelled 'Income'. There was currently only one item in this pile. Harry had gone to a lot of trouble highlighting and underlining sections of the Very Medical PR contract in pink.

Drastic measures would now be required. She needed to lose eight pounds in under a week. Water tablets would be essential.

Esther had sent a funny card with an image by Beryl Cook of two fat ladies playing bowls. She had written, 'Welcome back. Let's get slim,' inside.

'You get slim,' said Millie. 'Cow.'

She took the rest of the paperwork and sank into the sofa. The Toblerone was visible in the plastic duty-free bag. It stood no chance. Three triangles of it were in her mouth when the doorbell rang. She staggered to the intercom and picked up the receiver with sticky fingers.

'Mm?'

'Shall I take that Toblerone off you?' It was Harry.

'You can't. I'm just about to get in the bath.' Millie replaced the intercom with a crash.

She sat back on the sofa and gnawed through another triangle.

The phone rang and she listened to her answer message: 'Hi. This is Millie.' Then there was a cough. 'Sorry. Do please leave a message after the noise.'

She should change that recording. A cough was not welcoming as part of a greeting.

'Hi, Millie. Er, it's Al here. Got your number from . . . well, from your telephone. Actually, it was written on it. I'm thinking you might need a . . . check of your fuse box by now. I can . . . get a good price for a new one. Or check the old one if you want it to be checked through . . . and give you a certificate. Yeah, my number is . . .'

Millie took stock. In just over two weeks – since the evening at the Bolt Whole – she'd gone from someone whose house was about to be repossessed to someone who had been offered £20,000 if they lost three stone. Not only that, she'd become a magnet for men who either wanted to brush her décolletage with a small feather or fix her fuse box. These were definitely reasons to be positive.

But nonetheless the negatives still outweighed the positives, by some margin. She was still broke and fat, and her house would be repossessed if she didn't lose the weight . . . She needed help.

She picked up a letter from Harry's highlighted pile. It was from the bank. Harry had highlighted most of it in pink.

'Nasty,' she said, and closed her eyes.

She called Florence to thank her for the lift again and fix the Tough Titty Supper Club thing. Florence was subdued. The kittens were poorly.

'Thank you for collecting me, Florence. I really appreciate it.'

'That's fine. You'd do it for me.'

They both knew this wasn't true.

'Sorry I was a bit distracted.'

'It's jet lag. No worries.'

'So when is the next Tough Titty thing?'

'Tomorrow.'

'Tomorrow? That's a Saturday?'

'Yeah, Saturdays are a high-energy night apparently. The best night to have a dynamic but supportive gathering, because it's not a Sunday nor is it a weekday.'

'Incredible,' said Millie.

'I'll tell Joan and Pat you're coming.'

'Pat?'

'The leader of Tough Titty.'

'The leader?' Millie didn't like the sound of Pat.

'Bring some cash for the raffle. Have a nice bath and relax. Bye.'

Did she smell now as well? Actually, she did, but money was more pressing than travel odour. She went over to her desk and started writing a column about mother-daughter bonding. She'd write it on spec and hope Esther would put it straight into the magazine without even reading it. She'd need the extra £300 to fund three weeks of QwickCash interest payments, or at least one, and have some left over for bills.

Suddenly, an email pinged out at her and made her jump. It was from Papua New Guinea. She knew Mary's email off

by heart and it wasn't from her. It was probably the hotel
wanting to charge her for the stolen flannel or . . .

It was from Eugene.

Dear Mommy,
Did you arrive safe? I think of your orbs and it make me
remember you. I not tell Mary about our moments. I
come to England soon. I have a love of peace and green.

Millie had to read it twice. This was serious. She would
have to let Eugene down gently, in case he thought . . .
Well, if he thought he was part of the family – such as it
was. The hand-hovering would have to remain a secret.
She had to protect her child. She wasn't sure what 'orbs'
were, but it didn't sound hopeful . . . Mary should never
be told about the key-ring thing either.

EIGHT

AFFIRMATION 8:
'I healthily connect with other thin women and share their pain about being teeny tiny'

SATURDAY 22 MARCH

Harry had underlined the courtesy introductory card from Barrington Bailiffs with the pink highlighter. It was hard to guess what a Barrington Bailiffs professional might consider valuable. Her car was a definite target. Would they leave her the beaded back cushion? But if she could get some cash to the loan shark, they'd have to call off Barrington.

Millie planned to drive herself to the Tough Titty Supper Club on 'high-energy Saturday' to celebrate the fact that at this point she still had her car and valued it as a luxury item worth having. She would eat nothing during the day ahead and drink only water.

Unusually, Esther had invited Millie to watch her have lunch on her first full day back. In spite of the jet lag, she would meet her and deliver a hurriedly written column at the same time. At least she'd managed to cobble 300 entirely fictional words about a mother-daughter bonding experience in the New Forest that could pass as an informed travel piece. Esther must have engineered the meeting as an opportunity to check up on her weight loss. Millie would turn Esther's suspicions to her advantage and get herself another fee. She mustn't be a victim.

Millie had already written a list to empower herself for high-energy Saturday. She expected it would be tiring.

Write column about mother-daughter bonding. Give to Esther. Ask for immediate cash.

Take water tablets. Drink water. Take more tablets. Meet Esther for lunch. Nil by mouth.

Take back plates for refund. Use cash for petrol and parking, plus Tough Titty raffle if compulsory.

So after the lunch she would get a cash refund on four oversized and unwanted plates from Anthropologie before pitching up to the sisterhood supper. The plates had been a Christmas present from her mother, with the gift receipt still in the bag. For some reason, her mother had chosen four monstrously large dinner plates with four sets of pink copper knives and forks that were also unduly large.

She knew her mother had always thought Millie to be a 'big eater', but these plates were closer to tea trays.

So this was the plan: prise a cheque off Esther at the lunch, get the cash back from the returned plates and then find a free personal trainer from the Tough Titty Supper Club – all without eating a morsel.

*

'Have you lost *anything*?' Esther asked Millie, peering at her over her glasses.

Millie slipped the hurriedly written mother-daughter bonding article on top of Esther's side plate and tapped it excitedly. She had put it in a plastic folder.

'Anything at all?' Esther repeated, ignoring the folder.

'Oh, do you mean weight-wise?' said Millie.

'I do, since that is the assumed currency we are all using for this campaign.'

Millie realized Esther was being dry. It made her look and sound like a female MP trying to get attention and making herself unpopular.

'I think,' began Millie, 'it was the change of climate that slowed my metabolism by the end of the trip, but I'm really ready to get going now.' She smiled at Esther and looked at the folder meaningfully.

'And what happened at the start?'

'Well, I lost a lot. A huge amount. But I put most of it back on on the plane. And on the night before I left. And some of the airports. I wish I'd taken a picture of me, Esther, because I was tucking my shirt into my jeans for the first two days. It was a great trip, though, in every regard, and when I got back, I missed Mary so much I had to write this article about mother-daughter bonding on holiday because I thought it would be perfect for your readers. Our readers,' Millie corrected. 'I really missed writing,' she added.

'Thing is, Millie, we're not on target, are we? Kleinne Fett have suddenly said they need to see evidence of your loss on Monday or they may pull the campaign.'

'Monday? I thought it was Thursday,' said Millie, imme-diately fearful.

The waiter came over. Esther ordered an omelette and salad with Prosccco. Millie felt hungry.

'It was, but now it's Monday. They've brought it forward.'

Esther sighed. She tried to get a better look at Millie, who was relieved to be sitting down and half hidden by the table.

'I think this piece will really inspire readers to bond with their daughters, Esther. It was the first thing I wrote when I got back last night. I just had to write it. Even though the holiday I'm remembering actually took place a few years ago,' said Millie, mindful of the fact that Mary had been in Papua New Guinea for the last year. She didn't want to be quizzed on its content, especially as it was entirely made up.

Esther looked depressed but wrote out a cheque for Millie, who was just about to say more about the entirely fictional holiday when Esther's phone rang.

'I'm going to have to take it, Millie. It's them.'

'Who?'

'Very Medical.' The very words now sent a chill. Those two skinny sisters were her guilty conscience.

'Good luck.' She knew Esther would have to spin the news that while all was well, it wasn't quite as well as hoped.

Millie took the cheque and quickly put it in her bag. Then she swallowed a Kleinne Fett horse pill to prove to Esther that she hadn't forgotten to take them, which she had, and five flavoursome citrus water tablets. There was a slight question mark over what to do with the omelette and the Prosecco, which Esther had barely touched, but she would sit with them.

*

Driving down Regent Street was proving a challenge for Millie. A learner bus was straddling the bus lane as well as the road. A cab driver overtook her and shook his head at Millie as if this were her fault.

'Arsehole,' shouted Millie at him as the effects of five 'waterfall' tablets sprang into action.

The plate shop appeared to have been moved by someone. Funny how a shop could just disappear. She was sure it was a few down from Hamleys. As she was looking, she started to ruminate that Esther hadn't been thrilled to see her at the lunch meeting. Not even mildly curious about her trip. And the fact that she wanted Millie to book herself a colonic as soon as possible made her think that Esther didn't have a whole lot of confidence in her ability to do the job.

Millie suddenly saw where the shop was, in her rear mirror. She'd have to do a U-ey. She was nothing if not fast. She was on a mission. Empty the bladder, return four oversized plates, then hit the supper club. Perhaps she could park on a double yellow outside the shop. Maybe do one of those half-up-on-the-pavement jobbies so people would think she was consulting the A–Z. No, she'd turn left into Warwick Street, park outside the Pret A Manger and use their loo. She was losing the ability to think laterally or forwardly. Plates or bladder? Park, plates or bladder? Bladder and park? Buy a Shewee? Perhaps there was a Millets. No, she couldn't walk straight, and anyway, Covent Garden was too far.

Suddenly, the sight of flashing blue lights in her mirror distracted her. This could not be meant for her. Who had done something silly? Was there a pickpocket on the loose? A stolen car? She didn't care. She looked around for other road users who might have attracted their interest. These lights were persistent.

Shite. And she'd had most of one glass of Prosecco, which was Esther's. Two if you counted the second one, which she'd ordered while Esther was outside on the phone. But she wasn't drunk. The remains of Esther's full-fat cheese omelette would have soaked up any alcohol. Gruyère was quite a proud cheese in its rich calorie content. She wouldn't have eaten it, but Esther had taken ages on that phone call on the pavement, leaving the omelette unattended. She didn't blame her. The sisters weren't very bright and would need lots of convincing. Millie could see Esther waving her arms around dramatically on the pavement while she manipulated and spun.

Eventually, Esther had returned to the table, drunk from her almost empty glass with relief and announced she'd managed to delay Millie's first proposed weigh-in by a few more days until Millie could shift some pounds. Any pounds in fact. Millie knew Esther to be too shrewd to commit to a date without assessing Millie's weight loss beforehand. Hence this lunch viewing on her first day back. Millie didn't mind, as long as she got paid for the extra column. The need for cash was as great as the need to lose. And at least they'd ended up with a plan. It had been agreed that two days, or even five, to lose half a stone was not doable (without surgery), but moving it forward to eight days (gaining several more days of loss), *might* be, at a severe pinch. In fact, it was their only hope. If they could all meet on 30 March instead, they might stand a chance. In fact, 30 March might prove to be her lucky day.

It was now clear the police car with the blue light

display really was intended for her. They were right up her jacksie and staring. Millie stopped abruptly in the middle of the road. If they ran into her, it would be their fault. That was the law. But they pulled up alongside her. She electronically plunged the passenger window and smiled across at the two policemen in an enquiring way. Millie knew not to say, 'Yes, can I help you?' because this could be interpreted as assertive.

'Could you pull over, madam?' the policeman in the passenger seat asked. He was Scottish. It would be tricky to assess his background and how much he would despise her for sounding middle class.

'What, into the bus lane?' Millie called out of her window, incredulous that she was being asked to break the law.

The young policeman nodded.

'Yes, please, madam.'

Millie disliked him, and he disliked her. She could tell. Even at this early stage.

She pulled over into the bus lane. Then both of the uniformed men leaped out. The non-Scottish one adjusted his trouser area, perhaps because they had been sitting down for quite a long time. Then they both simultaneously started speaking into their walkie-talkies, all the while avoiding her eye, which made her feel lonely and exposed. Whole families were staring at her as they piled into Hamleys, who were having a spring sale and attracting loads of custom. Perhaps it was half-term. It was certainly their busy time. Millie could hear a crackled vocal confirmation of her address and postcode in both machines.

Millie stood on the pavement and tried not to look guilty.

'Do you have your driving licence on you, madam?' said Scottish.

Millie patted her jacket.

'No, sorry.'

'Do you have your insurance documents?'

She patted the same pockets.

'Not on me, no. I've got an invoice to my magazine. It's called the *Good Woman*. Do you know it? I do the "Lovely Things" column, if you want to check me out.'

The man blowing bubbles outside Hamleys's door looked fascinated. He had swapped the bubble-blower for his mobile and was taking some pictures.

'Do you know why we've stopped you, madam?'

'Er . . .' Millie knew there was a right answer to this, but she couldn't remember what it might be. She tried a short answer with an upward inflection. 'Not sure?'

Her ploy appeared to pass unnoticed. She was having no impact on her inquisitors. They were simply asking their set of questions and had now moved on to the next one.

'Where have you come from?' The first one hadn't moved, but she noticed he was wearing rubbery black round-toed boots.

Everything felt unreal.

'Where have I come from?'

'Yes, madam.' Still no movement.

'Er, Clapham. A restaurant.'

'Which restaurant?' asked Non-Scottish. He obviously felt it was time to join in and took out a pen.

'Er, it was a cafe.'

'Called?'

'Well, more restaurant, actually.'

'Name?'

'The Boiled Egg and Soldier, I think.'

'And have we been drinking, madam?'

'No. One Prosecco only.'

'One?'

'One, yes.'

'At the Boiled Egg and Soldier, you say, was it?'

'There's a wine menu for the nannies. Yes.'

The second policeman nodded. He was a Londoner. He didn't smile. But he had puffed himself up at the word 'Prosecco'. A small audience had gathered with the bubble man and were also taking pictures.

'Would you like to sit in the back of the car, madam?' asked Scottish. He had a mole on his neck. But she didn't feel sorry for him. Millie noticed they both had the same rubbery round-toed shoes. These must be compulsory police footwear. Practical, yet unfortunately childish in appearance.

'Um . . .' Millie peered through the window into the back seat. It looked a bit grubby. 'Great, thanks, cheers.'

Millie assumed it had been a quiet day for them and they were both quite pleased to have ensnared a middle-class woman who had admitted to alcohol consumption.

'Right. What's going to happen now is . . .' The second PC with the pen began talking very slowly.

Millie braced herself for an arrest. She would text Florence that she'd been unable to attend the high-energy Tough Titty supper due to her being unpredictably arrested. But her bag was in her own car, and her phone was in the side pocket.

'Could I just get my bag?' Millie's voice was sharp.

The Scottish one with the mole said, 'I'll get it,' clearly

pleased that she had allowed herself to show irritation, as this meant he could be stricter with her.

The other one ushered her into the back seat. He sat next to her. As if she might escape and run into Hamleys and hide among the family puzzles and flying robots. Her bladder was reaching its limit and she was sitting in the back of a boys' vehicle. A towel might not go amiss.

'Yes. What's going to happen is, we are going to get a colleague to drop off a breath-testing kit. That will take . . .' he paused, 'approximately twenty-five minutes.'

Millie nodded. Twenty-five minutes.

'And then we can get you tested. Obviously, having driven through two red lights, we need to be sure you are aware of your actions and the risk you pose to other pedestrians and drivers.'

Millie nodded. Two red lights. Extraordinary. She would now be silent.

Scottish, who Millie wanted to call Moley, came back with her bag but kept it with him in the front seat. Possibly wary of the risk of her accessing a weapon of choice and spraying them with mace while locating the cocaine she'd been carrying in her housewife's purse.

'The phone is in the front pocket?'

PC number one rummaged clumsily.

'Side pocket. Sorry.'

He found the phone and looked at it before handing it over.

She took it in silence.

'And my glasses are in the front pocket. No, other side pocket. Sorry.'

He found her glasses and handed them over with less interest.

No one spoke. In desperation she asked the one with the mole in the front, 'Could you pass my book? It's in my bag.'

He rummaged again and picked out the book. It was a paperback. A Scandinavian translation about an older woman who lived in a home. She'd bought it at the airport by mistake. It was still in her bag.

'I think I've read that.' He turned it over expertly.

'Have you?'

Millie took it and pretended to read the first chapter while they waited for the colleague (who appeared to be in no rush) to arrive with the test tube and probe apparatus, or whatever it was they would be shoving down her gob.

On two occasions the walkie-talkie sprang into life with a very old female voice saying, 'Where did you say you were again?' Clearly her two young PCs were not top of the list for assistance or respect.

Finally, the kit arrived in another panda car. Suddenly nervous, Millie found herself saying, 'I get asthma,' in a small and scared way, as if this gave her some sort of immunity.

She was ignored.

'So you need to cup your mouth over the tube—'

Millie had to interrupt.

'What does "cup" mean?' She knew people cupped a breast, but cupping a tube? It sounded dirty and deviant. She was now in such a state nothing made sense.

'Just cup your mouth over the tube.' If the young PC had an idea how rude this sounded to Millie's ears, he didn't show it.

Millie cupped. She breathed. They watched.

After a few seconds Scottish with the Mole announced

very loudly, 'You have *passed.*' No congratulations or certificates were issued, but she had passed.

Millie said nothing, but she hurriedly got out of the car, was handed her bag and walked back to her own vehicle.

A quick glance at Anthropologie told her it was now closing. Girls in brightly coloured sweaters and biker boots were locking the doors. The bubble-blower had disappeared and she had now wasted more than half an hour.

The Tough Titty event was being held in a slightly faded but still trendy members' club on one of those roads off the Embankment and behind the Savoy Hotel. The paintwork was a bit 1990s, but there were blue lights embedded in the stairs, which Millie felt still gave it a bit of West End verve. The walls leading down to the bar had been covered with leather patches, which was either very good or very bad. Millie didn't know. But she knew the exposed brickwork in the bar itself was correct, even if it was hung with three large canvases of fir cones. There was hardly anyone interesting-looking in the bar, just a few suited young men with laptops. The real noise was coming out of what must be Tough Titty's allocated supper room.

Florence was already seated at a table full of very chatty but well-dressed women, and of course sitting smugly close to Joan Le Measurer. Florence and Joan waved at her as she walked in. This was the second time Florence had waved at her like that in less than two days. Flustered and still with her coat on, Millie stared grimly back. She hadn't been willing to surrender it to the surly Romanian at the reception area just outside the bar. A pound to retrieve it from a rickety coat rail placed in the middle of the mezzanine was a pound too far in current circs.

Either no one had been told how to work the dimmers on the lights or else Tough Titty actually preferred brightly lit rooms in the evening, but it was bright to the point of strip lighting. Joan Le Measurer looked very luminous due to the whiteness of her silk top, which was bouncing off the white tablecloth, which was bouncing off the lights and back onto her. But then Millie remembered Joan had also told her she was a believer in 'light attracting light', so perhaps that explained it.

At the end of the room, a stick-thin short-haired blonde was fussing over a table where a pair of women's sparkly silver shoes were displayed on a glass cake stand along with raffle tickets and other cheap-looking tombola-type prizes. Balsamic vinegar and hair conditioner were not worth the investment in the raffle ticket. The woman waved purposefully at Millie with a Tough Titty kind of smile. With veneers like that, Millie would also be smiling, if only to make sure she got value for money. She must be Pat – founder and high priestess of the Tough Titty lodge.

Millie didn't quite know where to sit or what to do. She would have joined Florence and Joan's table, but there were no spaces. Each seat was occupied by women wearing the same kind of figure-hugging Lycra cocktail dress. The older ones looked young, and the younger ones looked corporate, but they all looked genetically related in some way. Slim, blonde and lip-heavy.

'I'm Pat.' The leader left the table of Tough Titty trophies and strode towards her.

Florence got up from the table to make the introduction. Joan waved from her seat, wiser and more restrained.

'You must be Millie,' said Pat.

'Yes.'

'This is Millie,' added Florence.

'Hi, I'm Millie,' said Millie, suddenly nervous at the thin woman staring at her.

'Well done for getting here, Millie!' exclaimed Florence.

'You won't believe where I've been,' she said to Florence abruptly. She needed to share her tale of humiliation immediately, but Pat had other ideas.

'Can I take your coat?' she asked.

'Can I keep it on me?'

'No, let me take it,' said Pat firmly. She must have an arrangement with the Romanian upstairs.

At this, a woman shot across the room and said, 'I'll take it, shall I, Pat? I'm going upstairs anyway.' She was the only woman in the room to have hair that wasn't at least twelve shades of blonde. The combination of pink hair and a red dress made her look quite bohemian compared to the sea of women uniformly encased in dark stretch fabric with identical pale hair.

Since she had been ganged up on, the coat had to be surrendered to the crimson woman, who draped it over her arm like a sick child before disappearing upstairs with her prize.

Millie was now very keen to sit down. The water tablets seemed to be working on a long cycle. She'd need to locate the powder room, as she was sure it would be referred to by Pat.

'So Florence tells me you write a column,' said Pat, who was leaning to one side like a stork.

'Just for the *Good Woman* magazine. I do the problem

page, and sometimes the odd piece for *The Times*.' This wasn't true, but it might lead to being given a chair.

'I love the *Good Woman*! In fact, we've got a budding columnist on one of the tables tonight, haven't we, Florence? She couldn't come last week,' said Pat.

'We have,' nodded Florence, and glanced excitedly around the room.

Millie sensed Florence had no idea who the budding columnist might be.

'I'll put you together with Ingrid. She's from the Wirral but staying over this time. Easier with trains.' Pat leaned in to speak to the air between them. 'Don't say anything but Ingrid's won the Tough Titty Newcomer Slipper.'

Florence slowly mouthed, 'Wow,' with barely contained wonder.

'There she is,' said Pat, spotting Ingrid sitting at what looked like the least popular table with several empty chairs. There were quiet people looking at their apps either side of her.

'Great,' said Millie, almost running over to the half-full table to join Ingrid from the Wirral.

Pat and Florence followed her, to make sure she didn't introduce herself to anyone without supervision.

This must be what Florence meant by networking. But what would Millie get out of being seated next to the budding columnist from the Wirral who was staying over?

When they got to the quiet table, Florence took Millie's arm to raise it above her head and shook it at Pat as if she were a referee giving Millie a yellow card.

'Millie's also a celebrity, Pat,' said Florence. 'And she knows quite a few people on the shopping channel.'

Millie was embarrassed.

'Does she, now?' Pat was pleased.

Millie raised her free arm up in defence.

'The shopping channel's not exactly celebrity based, Pat.' She looked apologetic, but Florence was having none of it.

'Kelly Hoppen's a celebrity. She's on the shopping channel,' Florence announced.

'And you write for *The Times*,' Pat reminded Millie, impressed.

'Kelly Hoppen's hardly ever on in person. They just did her bedwear when I was there,' said Millie defensively. 'But it wasn't my section.'

'Which shopping channel did you do?' asked Pat.

'QVC 2. Kitchen wardrobe.' Millie didn't really like to recall those days of stroking plastic utensils twenty times a minute in order to get a sale.

Pat nodded and looked at Ingrid from the Wirral with a gleam in her eye.

'Ingrid, this is Millie.'

Millie nodded at Ingrid.

'Hi,' she said apologetically.

A woman with a ponytail and thick glasses smiled back. Millie noticed the veneers. The club should be renamed the Terrific Teeth Club. Ingrid had also broken free from Tough Titty dress code to add a faux-leather jacket on top of the regulation tight corporate dress in one colour. The ponytail and the pebble glasses combined with the leather gave a whisper of lady-boy mystique. A sort of Gok Wan for the Midlands.

'But the thing is, Pat' – Florence was determined to get the next bit of information out – 'Millie's also heading up this celebrity weight-loss campaign,' she said, looking at Millie as if to say, 'Go on – tell everyone.'

'Yes, I am, Pat,' she said.

'You don't need to lose weight!' said Pat with a sincerity that was almost convincing. Millie was clearly the fattest woman in the room.

'It's going to be massive!' added Florence.

'Which celebrity are you doing it with?'

Florence jumped in again.

'Well, Millie is the main one, obviously, and we think it might be Tessa Keltz or a Farton sister, don't we, Millie?'

'In the American campaign it's an Osmond,' added Millie, feeling surprised that she had been moved to impress this thin, bespectacled woman from the Wirral.

Pat excused herself to ready the prizes at the slipper table, and Florence returned to her table. Joan offered up another little serene seated wave.

The cold starter had already been set on each placemat. This would be a challenge. Millie loved pastry. She could do it raw if need be. Millie introduced herself quickly and enquired if Ingrid liked pastry as much as she did. Ingrid said she liked it, but she didn't like it raw. All the women told Millie they were going to eat everything that was put in front of them, especially as they'd paid for it. Millie wondered how they all remained so stick-thin in that case.

'I just starve for two days afterwards,' Ingrid explained. The other women agreed that extreme starvation was part of their temperament, which usually went with being high achievers and perfectionists.

Another extreme activity the women had in common was an addiction to serial online dating. Millie was then given a thumbnail description of the agencies available – in case she might want to try her hand. Match.com was like Wetherspoons, where you got loads of servings at a knock-down price. Soulmates was like the cafe in the British Library apparently, and Tinder was an app you used on your phone where you had to say 'yes' or 'no' to images of body parts. Out of these options Tinder seemed to be the most popular with the table, but Ingrid wouldn't endorse its suitability for the older dater. Millie acknowledged her caution.

'What does your company do, Ingrid?' asked Millie, beginning to get the hang of the Tough Titty signature networking method.

'Sex toys.'

'Interesting. What's the company called?'

'Sex Toys.'

'Cool.' Millie thought this might be a good one-word response. Modern but crisply non-committal. She looked with relief to see a bottle of white and a bottle of red wine in the centre of the table. Every one had been given the same, so these must be included.

'Shall I?' The women nodded. Millie unscrewed the bottle of white. 'Might as well,' she said as she poured herself a full glass.

Ingrid took the bottle from her and distributed the rest round the table. In a few seconds the bottle had been completely emptied. This was depressing.

Millie decided to read the menu out to her table in order to involve herself.

'Well, girls, we seem to be looking at a mushroom puff strudel, followed by a lamb hotpot with potato gratin, followed by "death by chocolate" chocolate mousse.'

Millie's heart sank. She'd have to eat it. Of course she would. This meant she'd have consumed a Toblerone, the remains of a Gruyère cheese omelette, which Esther must have noticed and not said anything about, which was worse than if she had, and now a three-course meal, all through no fault of her own. When would she start to lose? This was her first full day back and she was one pound fatter than when she left for Papua New Guinea. She had twelve days of failed weight loss to make up for, and eleven more weeks to crack the whole thing.

No one else seemed to be made anxious by the presence of the strudels. After ten minutes of pastry anxiety and forced conversation, during which Millie's fingers were itching to at least touch the spare strudels, Pat tapped an empty glass with a knife. She obviously didn't drink. Too thin and taut. She was standing at the popular table.

'Ladies! Thank you! Yes, hellooo. Welcome to another Tough Titty supper. We've got some amazing ladies here tonight, including a few newbies.' Pat flared her veneers at Millie, who was now sitting on her hands. 'But before we welcome our guest speaker, who I know you're all going to love, let's go round the room and say who we are and what we do.'

Millie felt a familiar jolt of adrenalin and fear. She would have to speak out loud. Her heart sank even more. The orating had begun anticlockwise. If she'd gone first, the starters wouldn't have been such a challenge, but there was a lot of listening to be done in front of the pastry before it was her turn. The women ranged from those who'd just got out of a bad marriage/bad debt/bad climbing accident to women who felt a need to 'monetize' helping others with various business schemes. It was coming up to Millie's turn. She absented herself for a dash to the powder room in case the nerves combined badly with the water tablets. Somebody had rather carelessly left a bottle of house white next to one of the basins and a glass. Since everyone else had now started on the red, she wouldn't even have to share her lucky find. She poured herself a glass, drank it and carried the bottle and glass back to the table.

Back in the supper room, a woman in a green bobble dress was sharing her dream about rolling out her 'Crochet Your Way Happy' scheme in Northern Ireland. Millie wondered if people might do a fair bit of crochet work already in Northern Ireland and might not need to be made happy by it, but she still tried to be supportive of the Tough Titty's collective, where women made life better for others and got paid for it.

As the crochet scheme continued, Millie lapsed into worrying about Eugene and what he had or hadn't done to her with his key-ring feather in the garage. She ate the outer case of a spare strudel and drank the misappropriated wine to help manage these thoughts.

And then it was Millie's turn. Perhaps it was the drama of being exposed as a criminal in front of Hamleys, or the jet lag, or the extra wine, but something stabbed at her heart when she stood up.

'Hi. My name is Millie—' she began.

'And you are . . . ?' interrupted Pat knowingly, with the pearly-toothed smile.

'Oh yes. I am a Tough Titty virgin,' Millie said obligingly.

Everyone laughed knowingly and warmly, even though this joke had been made before with the other virgin, the woman in the green bobble dress.

'And not only am I a Tough Titty virgin and also rather fat . . .'

There were supportive murmurings of 'You're not fat' and 'You're womanly.' Millie could see Joan Le Measurer looking at her very intently from her very white, glowy space on the popular table.

'Well, anyway, I've just been to see my daughter in Papua New Guinea . . .'

Appreciative murmurings came from the supportive Tough Titty ladies who did not compete but helped each other instead.

'And she's doing OK, but you know, sometimes I do worry I've kind of kept her quite young for her age and . . . I mean, she's very bright, very clever. She got a first at Durham . . .'

Someone on Millie's table was heard to ask their neighbour, 'A first what?' which might have been a joke, though Millie couldn't be sure, but most women just looked supportive, although slightly less so now, since Millie had been a little bit boastful, which wasn't really what Tough Titty women did.

'And she's fallen for this chap over there called Eugene.' Millie now drained the last of the stolen wine.

Everyone murmured, 'Eugene,' appreciatively to show their continued interest, which set Millie off.

'Yes, Eugene. And I know he's small and tubby and possibly related to a distant generation of cannibals . . .'

There was confusion as the women wondered if they had heard correctly. And the supportive purring went a bit quiet.

'But he's opened up a rather unusual reaction in my . . . well, my you-know-where . . . my female area, my womanhood, my silver bowl of preciousness . . . and I just wondered, with you all being supportive and thin and tied in to the same amount of Botox, which is really effective, actually. Well, I wondered whether you had any advice for someone like me who's, well, not had any . . . intervention for' – Millie counted on one hand – 'eight . . . no, wait . . . for quite a while, actually. And I was wondering if anyone might have a family friend or brother who might . . . you know, start me off again . . . because that might, and I'm only saying might, be why I'm so drawn to chocolate, and the thing is, I chose a Toblerone to eat this morning and I wanted to know if the Tough Titty thinking considers that to be a metaphor for a penis and a longing for one . . . Sorry to say that word . . . here, Pat. But I'm lonely.'

Millie found herself giving out a single and rather ugly sob. She couldn't believe she'd just said this about herself. She wasn't even drunk. Well, she was a bit drunk now, but not overly drunk. Just slurring. A thought dawned on her. She'd have to get a taxi. No one would want to give her a lift home now. She was a disgrace.

'Sorry. It's just that you're all so supportive, and you're all amazing Tough Titties, thank you.' Millie was now seated.

There was a short silence before Pat said, 'Wow, Millie! Lots to chat about there, I guess. So! I suggest the rest of us make a start on the strudel, shall we, before we hear from Pam, who's going to share some quite revelatory findings about colour and the power of attraction . . . because what are we, ladies?' She looked around as joyfully as she could to reclaim the confused energy.

Millie heard someone on her table whisper, 'TMI,' to

her neighbour. She knew Pat would have to work hard at getting her Tough Titty ladies back on message. She felt responsible, but it was too late.

'What are we, ladies? We . . .' Pat started them off.

There was a chorus of 'We're Tough Titty women.' Then there was a crunch of cutlery and the awkward moment passed. Joan and Florence were deep in discussion. The hennaed lady who liked coats offered her strudel up to Millie. She'd taken up one of the spare seats at the table.

'Here. I'm Anne. You enjoy it. How many is that you've actually had now, Millie?' she asked with interest.

'Er . . . six?' Millie was guessing.

Anne nodded.

'That's the equivalent of three metres of puff pastry rolled out. Same length as half your small intestine.'

'Gosh.' This was impressive.

'Maybe have a look at male sportswear online? Apart from the obvious pleasure at what's inside a Speedo, the Lycra works surprisingly well on a female beer belly. Try it.' Anne tapped her nose.

Across on the popular table, Florence and Joan were engaged in an intense exchange with a tall woman. Even when seated, Millie could see that the woman's shoulders came up to Joan's earrings. This would make her almost a giant, if she was ever to stand up. Perhaps that was why she hadn't.

Millie shook an empty bottle of house white wine on the table. It had been empty for a long time.

'Oh, sorry,' said Millie, pretending to be surprised.

Luckily, the woman to the right of Ingrid fell for it and said, 'I'll get another one. The ex is paying! Let's have a red, though.'

Millie hated red.

She was working out whether she could get over her hatred when Joan wound her dainty way towards her. It was as if she sensed Millie's unhappiness. Ingrid looked impressed that Millie had given their table a visitor, especially as Joan was very white and glowy.

'May I sit here, ladies? Now, Millie, Florence and I have been plotting.'

'I thought it looked intense.' Millie was quite proud to have been the centre of attention in a good way this time.

'We have, and here's the result! Tada!'

Joan threw down a business card, which stood out on Millie's very clean plate.

'We've found you a personal trainer who will give you free sessions if you mention her in the *Good Woman*.'

Ingrid seemed to become animated at the attention Millie was getting from Joan. While Tough Titty was supportive to all comers, it seemed to be important to align yourself with winners. This was what NLP was all about, apparently. Millie had been briefed on the merits of copying people who copy other people already. A lot of aligning and copying was necessary in order to get to the top.

'Millie, you could mention that in *The Times* as well.'

Joan gave Millie her serene smile.

'I gather Papua New Guinea was quite an emotional time for you.'

Joan looked concerned, which made Millie want to cry.

'It was, Joan, yes.'

'Do you want Jon and me to come and make some minor adjustments in your house? You could need your south sorting.'

'Well, maybe you could tell me what to do over the phone and I'll do it myself. I'm a bit strapped for funds.'

'Of course, Millie. You'll be fine for now if you put a crystal under your bed and maybe give some gifts to your neighbour. Is there anything you're proud of that you could hang on the wall?'

Millie would not do the middle one, but took Ingrid's pen and jotted down the other two instructions on one of the many business cards that had been placed hopefully around the table. Joan was still thinking.

'I don't suppose your shed could be moved, could it?'

'I'll check.'

Millie was being polite. She knew it couldn't be done without a bulldozer. It was made of brick.

Joan waved back at her popular table. She pointed to Millie and then put her thumb up. The very tall woman returned the thumb-up sign and mimed that they would do some running together. She did this by getting up from her chair to demonstrate some elaborate running moves. Millie nodded back, embarrassed. The woman really was very tall indeed. Maybe she did the long jump as well.

'That's Adrienne,' said Joan. 'She's also a psycho-nutritionist. Job done, methinks.' Then Joan winked at Millie and returned to her table.

Ingrid suggested that they'd just been visited by an angel. Perhaps they had.

Millie was grateful to Joan. She really was the 'door-opener to change', which is what it said on her leaflet. Joan had left several of these on the table.

Anne slipped back into the vacant seat just as Pam began her talk on colour and the power of attraction.

NINE

~

SUNDAY 23 MARCH

Millie did not want to wake up. She was rerunning the scene with Eugene at the garage in her head. She started at the moment when Eugene gave her the brown-paper bag to open. She then extended this detail to build in a fantasy moment where his little hand had reached inside her blouse to seek out her breast and then pull it out of her bra so that it fell huge and plump, free to hang loose in the breeze of the garage forecourt, nipple forced into a monstrous pout by the sharp wind, his lips bearing down on her breast and his tongue searching and – something annoying was pecking at Millie's face. It was Vernon. Millie made herself wake up properly. Vernon was licking her face. She screamed at him. Vernon leaped off the bed with an offended yelp. She was now fully awake and very guilty. Perhaps she should remove the crystal from under the bed to deactivate herself. She could also hear the phone ringing.

'Ergh. Hello?'

'Everything all right your end?' asked Esther.

'Yes, why?'

'Good. Because I've booked you an appointment at the All White Clinic at ten.'

'Teeth whitening? Because, um, you might not know this, Esther – actually, it's quite private – but I've got veneers on my upper front ones. I had them done ages ago, so you might not realize they're veneers. In fact, they're really quite small, not like today's fashion for white bricks.'

Millie was reminded of the teeth displayed by the Tough Titty women. Altogether bigger, better, bolder . . .

'I'm talking about colonic irrigation. Nowhere near your teeth. It's off the King's Road.'

Esther went on to share her worrying news that the Very Medical girls were now looking forward to the first test weigh-in (with complimentary coffee and possibly croissants, which would be reserved for Esther and Ernst, the MD of Kleinne Fett), in the Double Tree Hilton near Victoria. The girls had cleared their diary for a whole morning and would of course be bringing their state-of-the-art German scales with them.

Sadly, no one from Very Medical could be available on their new suggested date of 30 March and the sisters had insisted on reverting to the original meeting, Thursday 27 March, which was four days from now. This was disastrous, but could, Esther decided, still give them a fighting chance to shed some pounds and get back in the game. Esther stated for the umpteenth time that Millie would have to weigh eleven stone thirteen pounds on 27 March and she had four days to lose seven pounds. Millie didn't dare mention that she'd actually put on a pound – she couldn't face any more maths.

'So I'll be weighed then, will I?' Millie had made notes of these requirements on a notepad by her bed, in which she was supposed to recall her nightmares.

'Very much so.' Esther was adamant about this. 'And make sure you get rid of any foot calluses. That can throw it. I notice you wear those Clarks sandals a lot.'

'They're Birkenstocks, actually. But I can wear my Uggs?'

'If you must. Take them off for the weigh-in. So I suggest you book a course of five and do two of them on the morning of the meet-and-weigh.'

'That might be quite tight, if we're meeting in the morning. Will they give me a break in between bouts?' Millie had never had a colonic before. Neither, she suspected, had Esther.

'Yes, or just ask for an extra-long one. I would. One of the minor princesses goes there, so I know it's top hole. The older one with the scarf.'

'Which princess is that?'

'Oh, Magdana or Marina or Alexandra? You know the one – dark glasses, K shoes? The Duchess of Stoke or something. Works with monkeys. Or lions.'

'Will she be there?'

'No idea. And get as many supplements and what have you while you're there as well. Detox teas, herbs, the lot. We've got to get things moving. It's lose now or lose out.' Esther sounded pleased with her new slogan.

Harry's pink-highlighted warnings had finally got through to Millie. She had no choice other than to earn this money.

'And . . . will I be expected to pay for that?'

'It's not a charity. Even princesses pay, I'd imagine.'

'OK, it's just . . .'

'I gave you a cheque yesterday for your bonding column.'

'Great. Yes. So . . . I'd better get myself washed!'

'Whatever works for you. But let me know how it goes. Within reason.'

Millie suddenly realized that payment for the four sessions and an extra-long one at the end might be difficult. Esther's cheque had not been banked and she was too scared to risk her credit card.

Harry was patently over the moon to see Millie on his front doorstep wearing a dressing gown and Ugg boots. His face shone with childlike pleasure. Millie tried hard not to look disgusted at this joy. It made her feel responsible for his happiness.

'Millie! Did you miss me? I've still got your keys.'

'I can't lie. No. And post them back, but only when I'm out.' His pleasure in reading her poems to Florence was becoming an issue the more she thought about it. What had happened in the tent at guide camp aged twelve should stay in the tent forever.

'Look, I've got an appointment on the King's Road in an hour . . .'

'Cromwell?'

'No.'

'Oh, the Brompton?'

'No, the King's Road.'

'On a Sunday?'

'Yes. The world still turns, Harry. Even on the Sabbath.'

'Fancy a biscuit and a pot of tea?'

Harry knew how to tempt Millie. She wavered.

'Er, no. Not today.'

'Come in, though? It's nippy.' Harry looked at her chest hopefully.

'I'm fine. I've got to go to the All White Clinic.'

'Brain scan?'

'Colonic.'

'Is that private?'

'I'm going to have to pay.'

'What about a home enema? I could help.'

'Harry, I need to borrow £270 from someone.'

Harry looked genuinely worried. He reached out and gripped Millie's wrists. She wanted to struggle but didn't dare, until she'd managed to borrow some money off him.

'I've seen your bank statements. The overdraft is up to its limit, so how can you pay whoever it is back, Millie?'

'I will when Esther's cheque clears, or when I sell my mother's engagement ring on eBay – if she's still got it.' Millie freed a hand to wave the cheque from Esther as proof. 'Look, I've got money. It's just short term. It's a cheque from Esther. From the magazine.'

Harry took the cheque. He put his glasses on to read it.

'Post-dated for next Tuesday.'

'Really?' Millie looked at the date. Harry was right. 'Could you offer me a cash advance till next week?'

Harry was enjoying his sudden power. Millie wanted to make this short-lived, but she needed the extra for the colonics and had run out of options. Four sessions at fifty pounds and the last extra-long session at seventy . . . She'd researched it.

'What about Florence?'

'She collected me from Heathrow. I can't ask her for anything else.'

'Can I come in with you?'

'No.'

'Can I sit outside?'

'Can I have cash for all five?'

'Can I sit outside?'

Millie thought this through for a second.

'Yes.'

The All White Clinic was carefully designed to be an oasis of calm, as well it might, given the turbulence going on behind closed cubicle doors. Tibetan wind chimes hung across the glass door, and incense sticks smoked gently from ceramic holders.

Harry looked out of place in his duffel coat and stretch leisure trousers, possibly because they were red, or possibly because he was old. The All White receptionist was wearing a white high-necked overall and very pale lipstick. The effect was so pale Millie wondered if she might be anaemic. Maybe she got colonics on the house and was iron-depleted.

The receptionist looked at them passively. She must be too weak to react to humans, thought Millie. The basement was very white, and the lack of colour may have psychologically removed any socializing behaviours. There were white walls, with a white wooden floor and white boxes of creams and potions on the white display shelves. White fairy lights lay in a snakelike fashion across the shelving. But the receptionist's passivity ended abruptly when she noticed Harry.

They were not the usual colonic clientele.

'I'm Roma. Can I help you?'

'Yes, Roma. I have an appointment for ten.'

'Sessions?'

'O'clock.'

'Both of you?'

Roma must know this was unlikely.

'He's just my driver.'

'Would you like a seat or to come back?' Roma looked at Harry. She nodded to emphasize this last option.

'I'll sit, thank you, miss,' said Harry.

Harry was in his element. He was out of the house and on a colonic outing with Millie. Better than the garden centre any day. And almost as if they were sharing a life together.

Harry sat on the green felt sofa and stared hard at everything. It was certainly bright white in here. Roma scrolled down her screen. Apart from the discreet sounds of calling curlews, it was very quiet. Suddenly, the peace was interrupted with the sound of human coughing and a lavatory flushing. No one came out of the lavatory until a second flush had been made.

Harry laughed.

'That old trick,' he said to no one in particular.

Roma addressed Millie. 'You will be with Anthea. She will call you.'

A tall woman hurried out of the lavatory and directed her gaze towards the door. She had a chignon, a camel-hair cape and dark glasses. She was carrying suede gloves and was so keen to get out of the building without having to acknowledge anyone she dropped a glove in her haste.

'See you tomorrow, ma'am,' said Roma, and bowed

reverently at the tall, highly coiffed middle-aged woman who was now squatting to retrieve the glove.

The woman was forced into whispering a soft 'good morning' before she righted herself and slid out of the building.

Millie walked over to examine the All White Clinic products, which were lit cleverly to make them sparkle in the recess of a shelf unit. She picked up a box of vitamin-type pills, which had been emptied for fear of theft.

'Hey, Millie,' Harry called urgently from the green sofa. He was reading the price list. Perhaps he had changed his mind about paying. Men were very conservative when it came to paying for things.

'Yes,' said Millie quietly, walking quickly over to him to set an example of the preferred speaking tone.

'What's brown and sticky?'

Millie didn't reply.

'A stick.'

Millie returned to the shelf unit in case she'd missed a beauty item with something actually in it.

'Millie!' he called again.

She went back – a prisoner to his whims, for this short period of time.

'Yes, Harry?' she whispered.

'I call my dog Pharaoh. Why? I'll tell you – he leaves pyramids wherever he goes.'

Millie stared at Harry. Then she did something she had never done before. She pinched him quite hard on the arm.

Because Roma had put headphones on, she didn't hear the colonicist rushing over to the desk to grab the clipboard with a list of her next appointments.

Millie thought Anthea's crew cut to be a challenging

choice of hairstyle for a colonicist and at odds with the gentle birdsong that echoed the clinic's ethos of 'gentle force'.

The standard-issue white clinic tunic was reassuring, but her Dr Martens were less so. These smacked of tree-festivals and individuality. A pair of soft leather clogs would have been more reassuring. Anthea was going to have sole access to her behind; very few people could claim that privilege. Millie was suddenly gripped with fear. Her bottom bore the scars from Eugene's cushion. Would it look like she had fleas? She imagined it would also bear pain badly – like the rest of her.

'Do you want to come with me, then?' Anthea looked at Millie without much interest. This wasn't a question; it was an order. Anthea blew her nose on a Kleenex and put it back in her tunic pocket while holding out the other hand to usher Millie into a dark and dimly lit corridor. Millie began to follow but turned back to look at Harry with real fear in her eyes.

She could see him well up. All Harry ever wanted was for Millie to need him, and at this moment in time she did.

'Sure you don't need me to come in, Mill?'

Roma had taken off her headphones to hear this.

'Don't let him! He's the driver!'

The cubicle was dark, which was a blessing. Neither of them would want to be able to have a good view of anything for the next hour. It smelt quite sweet, which had worrying connotations, but maybe they just used a different type of joss stick in the chambers. There was an en-suite lavvy next to a see-through barrel, a funnel and a pipe that Millie could only assume to be quite key.

'Right, so put your clothes here – knickers, tights, the lot – and here's your gown, but that's optional. I'll be out here if you want me.'

Very slowly Millie removed her clothes and wondered which way round the paper smock was supposed to go.

She waited. And waited.

Eventually, Anthea knocked on the door while opening it simultaneously.

'That's the wrong way, my love.' She took the paper overall off and bade Millie slip her arms through the arm-holes. 'Gap at the back, dear.'

'Oh.' What else was there to say?

'So up you pop . . .'

'Here?'

Millie was having difficulty following directions. She'd now had a closer view of the industrial-sized Pyrex cylinder at the foot of the couch. Chernobyl sprang to mind.

'Have you had one of these before?' asked Anthea routinely.

'No.'

'You'll not have had a coffee one?'

'I've had a coffee, thanks.'

'In a colonic?'

'Not in the clinic.' Roma had been remiss. She'd not been offered a beverage whatsoever.

'But in a colonic?' persisted Anthea.

Millie was struggling. Perhaps she should give up using words.

'I'll put the coffee in for your first one, just to speed things up.'

It appeared that Anthea intended to pour a steaming cafetière of black coffee into an industrial tube.

'We want to see results today, don't we?'

Millie wasn't sure she wanted to see anything.

'Over to the side for me. Bend your knees.'

'Like this?' Millie found she couldn't bend her knees. They had gone into lockdown.

'More.'

Humming to cover any sense of failure, Anthea deftly hauled Millie over manually.

'Aw, you'll love it, Millie. It might be a bit . . .' Anthea paused.

Millie braced herself.

'Brutal?'

'Uncomfortable. But these are truly the best things you can do for your body.'

'Right.'

'Next to sex!'

'Mm.' Millie was studying flecks of something on the wall. She didn't want to look too closely, but she didn't want to look anywhere else.

Anthea was clearly an open person, while Millie had never felt more closed. Or the need to be.

The machine had started to make a noise.

'We'll start off like this. Then you can go on your back,' said Anthea, as if that might be a real treat for Millie to look forward to.

Millie was aware that a pipe – not a million miles from the one attached to her Henry hoover at home, but rather troublingly transparent – would be utilized any minute now. She was curious to understand how the pipe would remain attached to her bottom if she lay on top of it, perhaps squashing it and hence preventing the flow of movement, but didn't want to ask anything too technical. Anthea had done this before. Other bottoms had no doubt been attached with equal success and effectiveness.

There followed a few gurgling sounds from the Chernobyl nuclear plant/barrel.

'Let me know if it becomes too much,' said Anthea.

'Yes!' said Millie.

'We haven't started,' said Anthea, annoyed.

'I know. I mean, yes, I'll let you know.'

'Oh right,' Anthea laughed. 'We get all sorts in here.' She tapped her affectionately on one cheek. This was very unsettling.

'And has the . . . ? Do you use the same pipe for everyone?' Millie asked as conversationally as she could.

'All plastics are disposed of by the council, Millie,' said Anthea reassuringly, before unceremoniously whipping the pipe up into Millie's nethers. She was now officially attached. This act had been thankfully brisk and surprisingly warm, which didn't make it pleasant.

The hydraulic pumping action whirred into action.

Millie said, 'Ow.'

'What?' asked Anthea.

'Nothing.'

There was more pumping and more impact. Millie decided that 'Ow' didn't work as an instruction. She went for a very loud 'Shit!' which caused the machine to switch off and the contractions to cease for a few glorious moments of calm.

As Millie lay there being pummelled and listening to Anthea's political moral compass and why she'd joined Greenpeace, she kept thinking of the good this was doing.

And also that she'd just met two people who liked Greenpeace. Perhaps this was a sign that natural waste and Greenpeace went together.

'Are you fond of Pinot Noir, then?' asked Anthea conversationally.

'Not as a rule, no.' Then she suddenly stopped. 'Oh, you mean . . . Can you see?' Blimey, this was quick. She'd only had that one at Tough Titty out of desperation after she'd been gifted the extra Sauvignon in the ladies'.

'I can, yes. All sorts. There's stuff from six months ago in here. You like your choccy, don't you?'

This was now getting to feel like *The Generation Game*. What else had been up there? Teasmade, picnic hamper, cuddly toy . . . ?

Anthea suggested Millie might like to take a break.

'I'd be just as happy to call it a day altogether if I may?' suggested Millie.

Suddenly, the prospect of having Harry in the waiting room felt very agreeable.

'I'd not be doing my job if I let you out.'

Millie noted Anthea sneak a look at the door. This was clearly non-negotiable. Anthea would barricade her in if it came to it.

'Why don't you sit on the loo while I make some notes?'

'OK.'

This had all started to feel so surreal that Millie went along with it. What would Anthea write about? Would she be writing about her personality or her stools?

The sit on the loo was a revelation. It was like an oil spill gushing forth into the sea and she could see why it had to be en suite.

The second half of the session was every bit as painful as the first. Perhaps she'd ask for one without a gallon of coffee in it next time. At least it had achieved some gassy sounds, which meant progress and seemed to make Anthea happy. Millie soon learned to stop covering the noises with a little 'Oh dear' or 'Whoopsie' until it felt almost conspiratorial and the machine and the connection pipe had nothing to do with either of them.

There were only a couple of desirable foodstuffs that Millie should even be contemplating putting in her mouth from now on, said Anthea. Millie waited. Whatever these food items were, she would buy and eat them.

They were organic lettuce and spirulina powder.

Luckily, Anthea had the powder, tea and extra pills in stock. She would leave a starter pack at the desk for when Millie booked her next session. There'd be no discount, she was afraid, as their sale offers had just run out.

'So when are you coming again, Millie?'

'Er, tomorrow.'

'How much do you want to lose?'

'Eight pounds. By Thursday.'

Anthea sucked her teeth.

'In four days?'

'It's that or I could go to prison.'

Anthea didn't question these consequences. She was a professional.

'Well, in that case I'll mark you down as high priority.'

Millie didn't bother to question what this might mean.

'You sit on the loo again in here to finish off. And there's one in reception if you haven't quite finished off here, as it were. And there's a McDonald's if you get caught on the King's Road.'

This explained why the cape woman had been caught short. The body obviously kept thinking it was being hoovered out even after nozzle removal.

Millie worried how Harry and she would manage the post-colonic downtime. She felt a bit bashful coming out into the reception area knowing that he knew what she'd just had done. She needed him to pay for quite a lot of stuff and didn't want to frighten him off by being too demanding.

But Millie knew she'd never been very good at manipulating men. Her mother had suggested she could do worse than learn how to 'put the man first' in her relationship if she was to 'avoid ending up a divorcee', but Millie had never quite got the hang of it.

In any case, Millie had always known divorce would be her path. She'd been taught at school how to do 'thumb-reading' by her best friend, which was similar to palm-reading but using the thumb. Two lines on the right thumb meant the owner would have just one child and one divorce. The friend told Millie that this fate had been decided by her ancestors, so there was no real surprise when Trevor left.

She knew that Trevor would be the man she would marry as soon as she saw him. They were at an *All About Pasta* book launch and someone had tipped her off that Trevor liked her. This helped matters along considerably, but she was also at the peak of her career. Working for QVC 2 as a writer/presenter in the gadget division, while moonlighting with 'real-life' stories for *Family Circle* that could both shock and inspire, had filled her with confidence. And because she knew the divorce would happen at some point, the blow wasn't as harsh when it came. She had a lot to thank her thumb for.

Over the years she had learned to expect little and do without. This was why her reaction to Eugene had been so long in coming and so exquisite, and so sad. He had woken her up, but unless Al could take up the conch, she'd be better off sleeping again.

'Harry, I really need your help.' Harry had joined two seats together to make a day bed while he waited. He'd had a nice chat with three other colonic hopefuls, one of whom was a man.

'So, Harry, if you could just loan me the money to pay for the sessions and a few essential supplements . . . Maybe pay with your card and I'll pay you back.'

Anthea had very swiftly packed up a large box containing her detox pack, which consisted of pills, a sachet of herbs and five litres of All White Clinic own-brand H_2O. It had already been placed on the reception desk.

'I've given you an instruction sheet, which essentially means no carbs,' said Anthea, patting the box affectionately.

'No carbs,' Millie repeated, feeling suddenly very bereaved and sad.

'Can you make sure she reads the instructions, driver?' Roma had removed her headphones to take Harry's money.

'I will, yes, madam,' said Harry with great authority, adding, 'And I shall be on hand to make sure of it.' He handed over his credit card, making certain Millie saw him do it, and made a great fuss of checking his receipt.

'Now, Millie, just to say I won't be in tomorrow,' said Anthea as she consulted her clipboard.

Millie was depressed. She'd got quite fond of Anthea. They'd been close.

*

Millie had allowed Harry into her house, but only because he insisted on carrying the water and the detox box and had paid over £300, which included the All White Clinic's own-brand water and supplements. She was just working out how to get rid of him when her stomach made a loud noise and startled them both. Vernon left the room.

'How are you feeling, Mills?' Harry asked as he unpacked the contents of the box and smoothed out the 'Post-Colonic Diet for Life' instruction sheet rather pointedly.

'A bit drained, actually.'

'Maybe have a lie-down?'

'Good idea.'

'Shall I get you a towel?'

Millie gritted her teeth and ushered Harry to the door.

'Thank you so much for the loan. I'll drop the cheque by next week.'

'I'll see you tomorrow, then,' said Harry.

'Why?'

'For your session.'

'I thought you were just coming to the first one.'

'I need to see your progress. That will be my payment. As well as the cheque.'

They were on the doorstep. There was another rumble. She pushed him out of the door as she rushed back inside.

The diet sheet had suggested that all foodstuffs should be removed from the fridge and larder. She didn't have a larder, but she did have a lot of food elsewhere, dotted around the house. She wished she'd done this before the colonic. The feel of her family pack of Cheddar made her waver, but she managed to put it into the black bin bag, along with various soups and sauces, icing sugar and peanut butter, among other things. Then she hauled the bag out to the bin at the end of the front garden.

She said, 'Goodbye, my friends,' and went inside to open and close the fridge door – just to see what the experience would be like for her when it was empty. It felt like someone else's fridge. Wrong. It no longer held the promise of comfort and general grazing activity. Worse, there was still a lingering aroma of dairy.

Joan Le Measurer had emailed to ask if there was any news on the shed front. Perhaps Al would know about moving a shed. This would mean getting in touch, and he might suggest eating some food. Even smelling someone who was on solids would be a challenge. She would simply have to hole up in her own home for the next four days and lose weight. She saddled up onto her Nordic track and very, very slowly began to pedal. There was a slight concern her teeth might now fall out through lack of use, but she'd just have to cross that bridge.

Suddenly, she saw Harry rummaging through her bin.

In spite of her weakness, Millie managed to dismount the Nordic and shouted at Harry from the porch, 'What the hell are you doing? That's my property.'

'Just taking these tins out. For the homeless.'

Millie closed her eyes and pointed at a packet of biscuits.

'Harry, you don't know how hard that was for me.'

'Don't worry. Bin men come tomorrow. All gone. You get inside and lose that weight!'

Millie would have kept a midnight vigil over her tins from her bedroom window, mourning their loss, but broke away to take a very welcome and desperately needed Skype session with Mary.

Millie readied herself. She tonged her hair, applied the new blue-black mascara and christened her new Viva Glam lipstick that had almost gone to Florence in the confusion over her duty-free spoils. She was very glad it hadn't. A new lipstick would draw a line over the past and usher in renewed energy and verve. It was her war-paint – a symbol of intent. Men did test drives; women did lipstick. She wasn't being competitive. She just wanted to set an example of the best facial style for her daughter all those miles away. Perhaps it might influence Mary to come round to her mother's way of presenting herself. She may be fat, but if people looked at her from the collar-bone up, she was fine – which is why this new Skype thing rather suited her.

Also, Eugene might be passing by and wanting to say a few words.

There was so much she wanted to know. Only some of which she could ask Mary. She assumed there had been no bombing or it would have been on the World Service. Maybe he just met up with some activists and talked about trees for the day. She might write a poem about men who offered their womenfolk erotic talismans out-side a garage.

Mary looked unusually energized on screen. This may have been because she was smiling or because she had washed her hair and it sprang out from either side of her face in a light and airy way. Soft and crinkled, which was almost pretty. The same old vest, Millie noticed, but at least Mary looked animated. Millie would have hated it if the anxious look had greeted her.

'I've got some news, Mum.'

Millie arranged her face to look pleased at whatever

was to be shared. As usual Mary was halfway down the screen.

'Wonderful! What is it?'

'I think I've got Richenda suspended.' Mary leaned forward and looked up for extra impact.

'That's fantastic, darling!' Millie was genuinely delighted. 'Tell me everything.' Maybe Eugene had bought Mary a lucky lady key ring as well. Should she declare hers? If he'd blown up the Parliament on the International Day of Forests, Mary would have mentioned that first, so at least they were all off the hook on that one.

'I'll just tell you about Richenda if that's OK, Mum. I've got a treasure hunt in five.'

'Of course, of course, crack on.'

This was what came with adult children. They gave with one hand and took away with the other, but anything was better than pining over her surrendered biscuits. And Mary looked cheerful, which bode well. Millie wondered if she could bring up the subject of the key-ring gift without it sounding loaded in any way. If Mary had been given one as well, then she'd be pleased for her.

The story about Richenda was a bit complicated, so Millie knew she had to concentrate. Apparently Richenda stole Mary's memory stick containing her original thesis, in which she'd used blood samples and DNA from two villages to conclude that, although the villages were separate, they had the same ancestry. Richenda pretended she'd invented this methodology herself and pitched it to her team leader as a way of linking period synchronicity and vulnerability to malaria. He was very impressed with it, and it was only when Mary overheard her work being read out to a visiting sponsor that she realized her thesis had been stolen.

'Told you!' exclaimed Millie in fury. 'Bad apple.'

Luckily, Mary could quickly prove it was hers by calling a group meeting to stage a big showdown using the reveal of the memory stick as shocking evidence.

'How dramatic!' exclaimed Millie, clapping her hands. 'How damning! How wonderful.'

'Actually, it was very traumatic, Mum.'

'Of course. Awful.'

'What would you have done?' Mary asked defensively.

'The same. I'd have done absolutely the same,' said Millie quickly. 'Well done, you. Genius. Who was at the showdown?'

'Everyone.'

'Everyone?'

'Not Eugene or his dad, because they're just backers for the research side.'

'Yes.' Millie nodded knowingly at Mary, but was a little dispirited. She sat in silence.

'Pardon, Mum?' asked Mary, peering at the screen.

'I was wondering how you all are. That's fantastic. So Richenda's been sacked, I assume?'

'Well, she's very good at being sorry, so who knows?'

'That's no good. Your work could have been discredited. I told you she was trouble. She should be expelled and shamed.'

'I know, I know. I should listen to you more.'

'I love you so much, and your hair looks fab.' Millie was interested to see Mary was wearing it half up and half down.

'You too. Oh. New lipstick?'

'What's wrong with it?'

'Nothing . . . Anyway, just thought you'd like to know.'

'I'm so pleased. So will you get that published?'

'Just need to make some new links with the periods and the conferences that are coming up. That's what Richenda was trying to do with my stuff.'

'Awful girl. And so unattractive.'

'Then I've got to show my tutor. I might have to come back.'

'And when might that be?'

There was a distant shout from outside the hut.

Millie could hear 'Coeeeeeeeeeeee, babieee.' It was Eugene. Had to be.

'I'm doing a treasure hunt. Lots of gear to take across the ravine.'

'Who's giving you a lift?' Millie smiled brightly.

'I'm not getting a lift! There are no roads in the forest, or can't you remember?'

'Helping you, then?'

'Coming! Love you.'

'Who? Oh, you too.' Millie waved at a blank screen.

Mary had looked particularly lovely today, but there was no one to tell this to, so she checked her email to stop herself from crying. She had been contacted by Sweaty Betty, John Lewis and someone called Cardio Monkey, which turned out to be from Adrienne, the giantess from the Tough Titty Supper Club.

Dearest Millie,
It was a true honour to be introduced to you by Dr Joan Le Measurer last night. I adore that woman.

Please fill in the sample food diary attached and let
me know when we can start our adventure. I'm very
flexible (and double-jointed!).
Your servant in health,
Adrienne

Millie immediately emailed back.

Dear Adrienne (and servant in health),
This is my typical day as from tomorrow:
Breakfast: water
Mid-morning snack: spirulina with water
Lunch: lettuce with water
Supper: lettuce and spirulina avec water
Bedtime snack: water
So may we begin five days from now, after a purging
situation has ended? I may be too weak to move until
then. I'd be honoured also.
Best,
Millie

'I am so hungry,' said Millie to Vernon, who had forgiven
Millie her stomach upset and was back in the room. 'So
hungry.'
They both licked their lips in sync.

TEN

AFFIRMATION 10:
'My body is an empowering energy of gas –
a sacred tool for room-clearing'

WEDNESDAY 26 MARCH

After the initial session Millie had decided 'to let Harry go' in his role as colonic chaperone after his insensitive tin-salvaging for the homeless. The irritation he caused could easily tip her into the newsagent's, and while she acknowledged she was indebted to have secured him as a financial sponsor, she remained repulsed by him in every other way. Reactive comfort-eating was a huge risk. She would make the trips solo and ban herself from shops.

Florence had recently volunteered her services in a new Pets Need Vets charity shop to wean herself off the kittens and was loving it. She had given Millie a velour onesie to simplify her wardrobe during her colonic confinement. This was a surprise gift but nonetheless appreciated. All she had to do was stay put at home, contained in animal print, only going out to get emptied and then coming home again.

The day before the first weigh-in, having suffered four

days of nil-by-mouth with lettuce, Millie found herself ruminating on what Hitler's daily food diary might have been. The findings could be a game-changer for getting a column commissioned – she might even pitch to *Vanity Fair* – but proving historical evidence might be problematic. As Millie lay in her bed, weak and hungry, she pondered, Would Adolf have started his day with a sausage? Followed with breads and cheese before being buoyed up with marble cake for elevenses and perhaps a Vienna schnitzel and dumplings for his evening meal? Or would he have snacked on pumpernickel (no yeast) and stuck to pickled veg throughout the day? Perhaps she'd ask Esther about writing a hypothetical food diary column using historical figures. People should be stretched . . .

'You're mad,' said Esther, who had come over with some bottled water, which she kept to herself.

'What do you mean?'

'That you're mad. Hitler was a vegetarian.'

'Not all the time, surely?'

'It's mad to even consider writing such a thing.'

'Mad is quite a serious accusation.' Millie refilled her own glass of water from the tap. She was up for a debate and preferably a quarrel. 'I could take that personally, Esther.'

Self-denial was making her very cross with everyone, especially Esther.

'OK, not mad but eccentric,' Esther relented, sensing a fight. 'Outside the circle of normality.' Millie noticed her slide her chair back from the table and glance at the door.

'But surely it's an interesting idea?' insisted Millie, rubbing a berry lipsalve over her top lip so she could lick it off in front of Esther. Berry lip balm contained calories, and illicit but flagrant consumption in front of Esther felt empowering.

Esther surveyed Millie's kitchen. The fridge had masking tape round it and there'd been an attempt to stretch cling film over the hob, though that hadn't quite clung. It swayed gently in the morning breeze. A large china jug of water sat on the kitchen table between them.

Millie knew Esther's mind was on her commission from Kleinne Fett. In fact, the more Millie thought about the contract, which she still hadn't read, the more suspicious she became. And although she allowed that starvation of essential vitamins to the brain might be setting off these doubts, it did beg the question if Esther was so good at championing the best terms for Millie, wouldn't she be just as adept at manipulating commission for her own benefit? After all, Esther was a businesswoman and not a friend. Not even slightly. Millie hadn't liked the way she had asked for the bill at the Boiled Egg and Soldier. And she rarely said, 'Thank you.' It was as if gratitude were a sign of weakness. Millie decided she really should have a look at the contract but was too exhausted to find her glasses.

'And pumpernickel has quite a following in the Home Counties,' said Millie. She wasn't giving up.

Esther folded her hands together.

'Millie, this is a no-brainer.'

Millie hated this expression but would have hated anything Esther said at this moment in her tight, empty, hungry existence.

'I can't allow you to write about Hitler's food diary. No one would read it,' said Esther, adding, 'And the people who might are not my readers.'

'Even as an "as if"?' pressed Millie. 'What he *might* have eaten if roasted boar had been in season?'

'No.'

'It's a proven fact that lack of food causes an altered personality state. I'm exploring the notion that lack of carbs causes evil acts.'

'We don't do Hitler stories, Millie, and nor does anyone else. Normal.'

Millie thought for a second.

'Maybe the chancellor, then? The correlation between a full stomach and rational decision-making.' Millie was so hungry that arguing with Esther was her only outlet. It was the only thing that could take her mind off starvation and lack of sweetness to put in her mouth.

'Too oblique.'

'Do you even know what a rational decision is, Esther?'

Millie's stomach growled loudly. They both waited for it to pass.

'Pardon.'

'Granted,' said Esther, as if she were the Queen.

'For instance, having one's stomach emptied for fiscal gain – that is, the fiscal gain of both me and you – would you say that is rational?'

Millie could see Esther was wary of her new snippiness but was trying to make allowances given their arrangement.

'Yes. I would. It is. If one stands to gain more than one might lose, then the decision is entirely rational.' Esther got up to leave.

Millie could see she wasn't being nice, but she needed to be indulged. It was her right.

'Why not move right away from the Hitler angle and compile a list of "me time" activities?' suggested Esther.

'Do you mean me time with food?' Millie was interested. Was this an extra commission?

'Without food,' corrected Esther.

'Great idea. "Me Time Without Food".' Another article on top of the bonding. Yes, please.

'That won't be the title, Millie. Just "Me Time".'

'On its own . . . More water, Esther?' Millie felt almost celebratory. An extra commission meant £300 in the bank. Result.

'Lovely, thanks. And lovely jug. Is that from Divertimenti? I've got a cream version like that. Oh. Sorry to say "cream".'

'Don't worry. I'm not myself, as you may have gathered. Any news on Tessa Keltz?' Millie stood up to show how pleasant she could be, but felt dizzy and gripped the chair.

'Lack of blood sugar,' nodded Esther without moving. 'Tessa's people are still keen apparently.'

'That's good. Only one more day before normality.'

'What do you mean?' Esther's voice became sharp.

'Before the meeting tomorrow, I meant.'

Esther looked relieved.

'Yes, because after then it's only . . . Hang on, let's get a figure.' Esther took out her phone to calculate. 'If all goes well tomorrow, it's probably another two and a half stone to go.'

Millie stared back. Miserable. Two and a half stone. The weight of a toddler, or a shed.

'But at least we'll be in the game.'

'We will.'

'Right! Better see if my wayward son's turned up. He said he might. I want to get the oven on in case he wants a ready meal. Macaroni cheese always makes a home smell cosy, doesn't it? Oh sorry, Millie. Have you booked the double-whammy one for tomorrow?'

Millie had got as far as the fridge. If she leaned on it, she could appear to be adopting a standing position.

'Anthea's doing it. Thank God. The other one was awful. She was supposed to have a mentor from the Prince's Trust to supervise her technique, but they never sent anyone. She shouldn't be left alone with clients. She's rough but shy at the same time, which is a bad combo, believe me. I should ask for a discount, but I don't want to knock her confidence.'

'Right!' said Esther briskly. 'I'll book us an Addison Lee both ways. I expect they'll be drinking, so I'll have to show willing.'

'Who?'

'The Germans – the Kleinne Fett people – are coming, remember. Just to put a face to a name. They know you work for the magazine, but they want to see you. In the flesh, as it were. Bring some empty pill packets, won't you?'

'OK.' Millie was doubtful.

'You'll be fine. You've lost loads. I can even see your chin. I never knew you had one like that! We're on message! It's just that our starting point was quite . . . far off before.'

'Yes.'

'Best not talk about Hitler with Ernst.' Esther was rummaging about for her car keys, repeating herself while her head was inside her huge shoulder bag.

'Why?'

'He's German.'

'Doesn't make him related, though, does it?' Millie still wanted an argument.

'Is it time for your lettuce?'

'No.'

'Big day tomorrow,' Esther said again, slightly at a loss. Then they both smiled at each other. Millie's boss wasn't an ogre. Just dishonest and a bit superficial. How else would she have maintained her editorship for so long? She was probably worried about Nathan, who didn't seem to like his life, and the daughter-in-law and grandchildren, including the step-grandchild no one ever mentioned. Millie should have compassion. She had it easy compared to Esther. At least Mary was clever and going places. It would just be good to know who with, and when. Meanwhile Millie was working on her Al think-dreams. She tried to imagine him dressed in a calico toga.

THURSDAY 27 MARCH

Anthea was determined to extract every last inch of waste from Millie's body with thirty extra minutes of devoted, bonus douching. And while Millie and Esther were grateful, as every extraction helped, it also made them late. The pre-booked Addison Lee car had to go on to another job and was replaced in a hurry by a parcel car, which didn't have quite the same finesse as a limousine people carrier.

Esther was still seething when their parcel car swept up outside the Double Tree Hilton in Victoria. She gruffly offered Millie an arm to lean on as they began to make their way inside. Millie managed a slight wave at the Very

Medical sisters, who could be seen peering anxiously through a window, waiting for them. Lucy immediately backed off from the window to plunge the cafetière as an aggressive greeting. They must be very late.

Terri remained at the window and indicated with a lot of frantic pointing that they should both hurry up and get inside. Millie had spotted a plate of biscuits on the coffee table behind them. She would sit as close to these as she could.

'No, don't get up,' said Esther. No one had got up.

But Very Medical PR had, for once, shown what Esther would describe as emotional intelligence in booking the more formal London surroundings. The reserved seating and loaded-up tray of coffee and biscuits would look far more impressive for a couple of German entrepreneurs than the purple unit in a Chiswick warehouse.

However, the German couple were seated on the very edge of the two armchairs and looked in need of rescue.

Lucy had just finished pouring herself a coffee, and smoothed her skirt as she sat down. She was clearly not used to skirt wear and this was very short. She sipped daintily and then put the cup down on the table, away from the saucer. All four individuals looked apprehensive and doubtful. No one else had been poured any coffee.

The Kleinne Fett man had tightly cropped sandy hair and wore a felt blazer over tweed trousers. The woman had a neat perm and wore a suit with an edelweiss brooch clipped at her throat. They wore almost matching lace-up shoes. Millie thought the Kleinne Fett couple looked very strange and wasn't surprised that a few people at a business meeting on an adjacent table were staring a little.

Esther shook off her fake-fur three-quarter-length

jacket, laid it with a flourish on the arm of the reserved sofa and looked brightly at the foursome.

Millie hoped Ernst liked Rive Gauche, because Esther was drenched in it. She had already warned Millie she'd be anticipating the need to take charge socially, and the perfume was to be used as her secret weapon.

'I'm Esther! Editor of the *Good Woman* magazine and campaign coordinator.' Esther smiled warmly at the man wearing a Tyrolean blazer. Adding, 'UK readership twenty-nine thousand but huge in Dubai.'

Esther waited for recognition. There was none, from anyone, not even the Very Medical girls, who were just staring, so she continued brightly, 'And this, hiding in the raincoat, is your special lady! Your Kleinne Fett guinea pig, Millie!'

Esther gestured at Millie, who then shook hands with the couple in the armchairs. They didn't get up for her either, but Ernst's grip was predictably vice-like. The woman's less so, but still painful. Millie assumed the couple would be wanting to assess her body and quickly sat down to make it difficult for them. She felt very weak. It had been an early start and Anthea had done her worst.

Lucy took this lead from Esther and felt confident enough to state, 'We are Very Medical PR.'

'We all know that, dear,' said Esther dismissively, but Lucy had obviously been inspired by Esther and wanted to experiment with a bit more leadership behaviour. She pulled her skirt down over her knees again to appear more professional and attempted a rather late introduction with a wave of her arm.

'And these, Esther, are the two MDs of Kleinne Fett. They are German.'

The man now stood up for Esther, which Millie put down to Esther's proud cleavage reveal and soft woollen day dress. It was commanding. Esther was not concerned with the odd tiny bulge here and there. In fact, she wore them with pride. Millie felt Lucy could learn a lot from Esther's professional wardrobe today. Losing the skating skirt would be a good first step.

He clicked his heels and said, 'How do you do, madam? I'm Ernst Schmidt, and this is my business partner, Lulu Ebenstein.'

Esther returned their handshake without wincing. Millie thought she might have been superficially bruised. She'd take a look when she had a minute.

'Lulu? As in the pop star Lulu?' Esther believed in ice-breakers. 'Which pop star?' asked Ernst.

'Lulu. The pop star?' said Esther, slightly less confidently.

'Married to Maurice Gibb the hairdresser,' said Lucy, who decided she should now shake the hand of Ernst and Lulu as well since Esther had done so.

'She means married to a Bee Gee,' corrected Terri, who began making the rounds with the handshaking as well. The Germans shook each hand back, slightly baffled, as they had already met and must have been seated together for some time.

'We are not musicians,' said Lulu. 'Ernst is not, and I am not.'

'Absolutely. Nor are we. Millie, do you want to take off your coat? Put it here next to mine.'

Millie had placed herself dangerously close to the biscuits and she knew Esther had spotted this.

Terri looked up from the scales that she was busily linking up to a portable printer with a long lead. It seemed like a lot of equipment for a simple weigh-in, but at least Terri wasn't groping her this time.

'Or you could give it to the waiter,' Terri suggested. 'He might hang it up for you.'

'I'm all right, thank you, Terri.'

She planned to keep the raincoat on her body until the last minute. Another gift from Florence. Her new job at Pets Need Vets was proving to be quite handy. This particular raincoat had belonged to a man who'd rather unusually choked on a hair in a glass of milk and died. His wife blamed herself. Millie and Florence agreed these were shocking circumstances but unforeseen and therefore the widow should not blame herself or her hair if it was hers.

'So how is it all going with the campaign, Ernst and Lulu?' Esther swiftly picked up the plate of Duchy Originals and told them these biscuits were made exclusively by the royal family. Millie knew she was only doing this to move them out of her eye line.

Ernst appreciated this initiative. He was a great admirer of the Windsors, he told Esther, and almost smiled as he bit sharply into the shortbread. It made a soft popping sound. He kept his eyes on Esther as he crunched evenly. Millie didn't know how long she could cope with other people's crunching. It sounded louder than she remembered. But her stomach did feel flatter as a result of all the internal plumbing. She had been stroking it under the coat and enjoying a new absence of flesh.

'In fact, we don't really know how the campaign is going at all. Our agendas are here, as you can see.'

Ernst tapped some pieces of paper on the table. Millie could read the points from the sofa: 'Who is the celebrity?

What is the non-celebrity's weight loss? Twitter issue?'

Millie was surprised they were interested in Twitter. This seemed a bit modern for a couple who wore Tyrolean jackets and lace-up shoes.

But it was obvious to Millie that Ernst liked what he saw when he looked at Esther. She was a large, confident woman who said things and took control. Millie felt sorry for Lulu, who looked a little plain and introverted in contrast. She had now put on some glasses to open her briefcase, which was on her lap. She was more midwife than business-woman. Millie was sure Esther had noted that.

'Really, Ernst? Well, I'm sure we can put that right this morning. It's always so much better to meet in person and get to grips with the issues. Are you staying over?'

Ernst crossed his legs and settled back in his chair.

'We are, Esther. For one night. We have a client in Bays-water. We might meet with them, but we don't know how it's going to go here.' He looked over at Lucy and frowned slightly.

Esther caught this look and laid a hand on his arm.

'Anything you need to know, Ernst, anything at all can be sorted today. I promise. That's why we're here. Millie is raring to go, aren't you, Millie?'

Millie nodded and tried to look eager. Ernst seemed particularly affected with Esther's hexagonal-patterned jersey wrap-over dress, and even allowed himself a moment of pleasure with the fabric.

'May I?' He leaned forward and gently caressed Esther's sleeve. 'Is that viscose? My brother owns a fabric factory in Düsseldorf. They also make circus tents.'

'Do they? Well, I got this from Jaeger, who mostly do garments.' She smiled, punctuating her pleasure with a tiny bit of lip-licking. Millie had seen Esther do that at the office when she was being persuasive. It was supposed to be non-judgemental and open. Millie couldn't believe how quickly the two of them had connected. Over a shared interest in fabric.

'I will mention it. Jaeger is a German name. My brother may know one of them.' Ernst smiled, revealing tiny, even teeth.

Millie glanced across at Lulu, to see if she minded about this instant chemistry with Esther, but Lulu was wrestling with the combination lock on her leather brief-case and breathing heavily.

Millie wanted the meeting either to begin or end. If it was this awkward now, it could only get worse.

At last Lulu had success with the padlock on her doc-tor's bag, having reluctantly followed Terri's suggestion of trying a combination of '1234 – in that order', and the lock sprang open.

'*Ja*. We wanted to show you this, ladies.' Lulu fished out an iPad and located a page before looking closely at Millie.

She passed the iPad to Ernst, who nodded gravely. He handed it to Esther, who looked at it for a few seconds. She looked puzzled. Then she looked alarmed. The silent passing was too much for Lucy, who almost snatched the iPad from Esther. Lucy looked at the page, shook her head with disbelief, before passing it to Terri, who was still busy and passed it straight on to Millie.

Millie took it and gasped.

The page on the iPad revealed a twitpic of Millie blow-ing into the breathalyser outside Hamleys with the two policemen. There was a caption: '*Good Woman* magazine columnist reaches new high.' Underneath was a re-tweet by @NathanGoodWMag, @Gayuk and @Toyboy11.

'I can explain this,' said Millie.

'Of course we can!' Esther grabbed the iPad as if taking it back would eradicate the photo.

Terri had finished with her electrical work.

'Let's see?' she said.

'No need,' said Esther quickly.

But Terri prised the iPad off her.

'What's going on?' She looked at the image expertly. 'You have to look at the history, Esther.' She pressed the screen to show a new page. 'See?'

It didn't take long to learn that Esther's son was friends with @Toyboy11, who blew bubbles outside Hamleys. And as Terri scrolled further down, she was able to surmise the situation for Esther's benefit.

'Basically, Esther, @Toyboy11 overheard Millie saying she was a columnist with the *Good Woman* and thinks Nathan might like to see what his colleague gets up to in her free time.'

In spite of being half starved and emptied, Millie realized the breathalyser picture might need explaining.

Their Kleinne Fett guinea pig had been depicted on social media as a drink-driver, and Esther had been alerted to the fact her son might be gay via the same means. Millie had the grace to feel a bit responsible.

'But he's married, you see, Ernst?' Esther was in shock and had turned to Ernst. 'And he likes cars.' She shrugged her shoulders dramatically, as if this explained any anomaly.

'He does love cars, Ernst,' agreed Millie. 'Which is another reason I've always thought it a waste that he does

"Lovely Things" with me, when he could be working with cars in another magazine. What do you think?'

Esther looked quite hot suddenly. Ernst had noticed this as well. He looked as if he might put a protective arm around Esther's shoulders, maybe to get another feel of the viscose, but he restrained himself. Probably out of respect for Kleinne Fett's conduct abroad.

Millie decided to take the lead. It was her turn.

'Shall we get me weighed now, guys? I can explain, but basically it was a publicity campaign for the magazine. It's called "seeding".'

'Yes,' said Esther. 'It was. It is.' She was using a tissue to wipe her hands.

'We were building an outreach strategy to attract a younger demographic,' said Millie. She reluctantly removed the raincoat. 'I volunteered to front it, didn't I, Esther?'

'She did. It's all about magazine covers, Ernst. Which we have to take very seriously. Market research shows time and time again that young people like men in uniform mixing with a celebrity, no matter how minor,' said Esther, who then found herself pausing with concern as Millie began to unpeel her clothes in full view of the busy foyer. A waiter came over to their table and went away again.

'We were going for the pop-up shock tactic,' continued Millie, who was now down to the Spanx Open-Bust Mid-Thigh Bodysuit. If she talked quickly, she might move things forward swiftly.

'To reach a new readership,' added Esther.

'But sadly not many people re-tweeted that image, so we're abandoning that approach for now, aren't we, Esther?'

'Have done already,' she agreed firmly.

'Do you want these off as well, guys?' asked Millie, pointing at her newly purchased flesh-covered 'shape-wear'.

'By the way, sorry about the screen,' said Lucy in an apologetic voice.

'What screen?' asked Millie, looking around.

'Apparently there was a mix-up.' Lucy looked at Terri significantly.

'I did order it,' said Terri defensively.

'Ernst,' asked Esther, 'what do you think, Spanx on or off? You're the important ones.'

Lulu answered, 'Off,' at the same time as Ernst said, 'On.'

'Screw it – just do it!' said Millie. She was on a mission to get this over with – and there were no shortcuts.

'Millie, are you sure you want to? I mean, the Spanx can only weigh, well . . . less than an eyelash probably. Oh. OK, then. By all means.'

Millie had already started to peel down the top half of the new, impressively robust Open-Bust Mid-Thigh Body-suit. Mercifully, the bra could stay on – she just needed to rid herself of the heavy industrial fabric securing her stomach.

'Go for it,' said Esther, nodding stoically, trying to keep up.

Millie was sweating. With one almighty tug, she wrenched the shape-wear over her thighs with such force her knickers came off at the same time. Before Millie could reverse proceedings, the two garments had fallen at her feet – inextricably intertwined.

'Ready when you are,' said Millie, looking in dismay at her interconnected underwear on the floor. She zoned out.

She had to. She dissolved into a state of nothingness where she could feel nothing. Perhaps she was dead.

But Millie's bravery drew gentle but awed applause from the breakfast party nearby. The soft clapping brought her awareness back into the room, and when she opened her eyes, she noticed Ernst and Lulu looking back at her, horrified. Lulu had swapped glasses to get a better view. Ernst's mouth was ever so slightly ajar. Esther insisted they took another Duchy biscuit each.

Terri suddenly jumped up from her calculations with excitement. She looked at Millie for the first time on the scales.

'Oh, Millie, I think you've got something attached.' She stepped closer. 'Oh sorry. You haven't. That's just . . . you.' Terri stepped back awkwardly. She tried not to look surprised, which she clearly was.

Terry steadied herself as she began her work. 'Right, ladies and gentleman. The start weight was . . .' She looked nervously at her file.

Esther stood up as well, as did Ernst.

'For God's sake, Terri! Millie was twelve stone six. She was monstrously overweight. Hurry up. She'll be getting cold.'

'Thanks, Esther,' said Millie. At least one person was on her side. She tried not to look at the table who had clapped her.

'Just underlining your progress, Millie,' Esther said brightly. She leaned in to Ernst. 'With the undoubted assistance of the Kleinne Fett herbal supplements, of course! In fact, we'll need a second batch of pills soon, girls. We've practically run out. Haven't we, Millie?'

Millie wondered if Esther had forgotten she was not

dressed. She didn't want to risk bending down to retrieve her pants, but she wondered how long she could remain upright with her hand covering her modesty. It was quite a stretch.

Terri would not be hurried. She flicked some pages.

'Two and a half weeks ago, on the start date of 10 March, Millie was . . . twelve stone six. And now she's . . .' Terri looked at the dial and started counting on her fingers.

They all waited.

'Eleven stone thirteen!'

'Wow. That's a whole stone gone,' said Millie loudly in wonder.

She looked around for her coat, which had been hung up by the solicitous waiter. One of the businessmen from the power meeting left his table, gallantly removed his jacket and placed it over Millie's shoulders. Millie curtseyed with relief and tied it around her waist.

Lulu coughed.

'*Entschuldigung Sie, bitte*, but that is not a whole stone lost.'

'It is. I'm now in the elevens,' said Millie.

The concerned waiter hurried back with Millie's coat and, having gently untied it, returned the jacket to the businessman.

'That's a stone down. Get used to it, Lu.'

There was a silence.

'So can I . . .' Millie asked, 'go and get dressed properly?'

'But of course,' nodded Ernst.

Millie grabbed a sugar lump and sped off to the ladies'.

*

Millie was on a high. The official loss of seven pounds over the two and a half weeks had given her optimism, but eight pounds lost in five days made her positively euphoric. She might even make an effort to look a bit stunning tonight, she wasn't sure.

That evening Florence and Millie were back at the Bolt Whole. Their usual window seat. Millie had changed into an extra-large black T-shirt, which she wore over her usual black skirt, but on this occasion without the customary protective jacket. This was Millie's ready-for-the-beach look.

'I can see you've gone down a bit,' said Florence proudly.

Millie breathed in.

'Can you?'

Millie had polished off a margarita in three short sucks of her straw. She had now decided that the sour taste was caused by a lack of sugar, which suited her current needs. It was just a pity she had to drink quite so many to stay hydrated. Florence was predictably still nursing an almost full tumbler of Baileys.

'Can you really see any difference, Florence?' Millie stood up.

'Tell you what, it's a great start.' Florence looked approving.

Millie wasn't happy with this reply.

'It's been a nightmare, Florence. I don't know why I agreed to it. Why did I?'

'Because your house was going to be repossessed if you didn't,' Florence said.

'But also for health reasons.' Millie decided to sound pious. 'I mean, I *was* overweight.'

'That's true. You are.'

'Was, yes.'

'Either way, it's good to face that, Millie.'

'Which I've done.'

'And did you see what came out during the colonic? Amelia wants to know. She's thinking of having one done with her mates.'

'I didn't look. It's old meat mostly.'

Millie sat down again and breathed out. She was agitated.

'Nuts? While you finish that?' Millie looked at Florence's glass.

'Best not,' said Florence. 'When do you get paid?'

Millie looked defensive.

'I've got enough cash for nuts, Florence. I wasn't fishing.'

'I'm sure you have – I was just thinking maybe we shouldn't eat more.'

So they both agreed to deny themselves nuts out of respect to the Kleinne Fett cheque, which Millie had been assured would arrive in two weeks' time. By then she would have been dieting for a full month.

They settled back in the booth feeling slightly pleased with themselves, the weigh-in becoming more distant with every suck on Millie's straw.

Florence was being sanguine.

'In a way, Millie, I think this first weigh-in has just been sneaked in to check that you're losing weight.'

'Which I am,' said Millie quickly.

'Yes, you are. Now. And you've had a hell of a shock today. No one could have predicted your underwear sticking together.'

Florence suddenly became hysterical. Millie waited for it to pass.

'Sorry.' Florence composed herself.

'It's fine.' Millie was hurt. She'd walled off her feelings and now here was Florence of all people laughing at her. She needed to reclaim some self-respect. And defend her unusual circumstances. 'Thing is, Florence, I should get paid £6,666 every month for three months, but because I asked for an advance to go to Papua New Guinea, they gave me £2,000 up front, which means my first cheque's going to be less.'

'The one you'll be getting in two weeks?'

Millie was too depressed to note how diligently Florence had been following her financial crisis. The money wouldn't be enough. Out of what she would now be owed she still had to pay the mortgage and the QwickCash interest. The post-dated cheque for the mother-daughter bonding article wouldn't be cleared till next weekend, and the new 'Me Time' column had only just been submitted. More importantly, she'd be needing to get the drinks in.

Florence twirled her glass of Baileys. Only a tiny bit left. Actually, Florence should get the next round, for being cruel.

'So, do you think Amelia would like the experience of a colonic?'

Millie had just felt her waistband. It was now loose. She cheered up again.

'I wouldn't recommend it to anyone under thirty. They might still be growing.'

'I'll tell her.'

Florence twirled her glass again. The ice cubes chinked. She put it down on the table.

'Actually, I got a call from Esther just now.'

Millie had sensed Florence was building up to something. The hysteria over the underwear-sticking was out of character. She was hiding something.

'Esther?'

'Yeah.'

'How did she get your number?'

'She got me at Pets Need Vets.'

'How did she know you worked there?'

'You told her I gave you the raincoat from there.'

But Florence still looked guilty. This made it worse. Millie braced herself to feel let down over Florence's lack of loyalty. Feeling pain in advance often lessened the blow when it came.

'What did she say?'

'She wants to be organized about your weight.'

'Don't we all.'

'She offered me the job of being a paid-up supervisor of your weight-loss campaign.'

'Really?'

'And I said I couldn't let down Pets Need Vets in any case.'

'It's not a proper job.'

'Actually, Pets Need Vets are a credited and growing retail charity outlet, Millie. They're looking for an ambassador—'

'The other job, where you have to be a weight supervisor.'

'Oh yeah. And she said she'd pay me on retainer. I just thought I ought to tell you.' Florence looked like she was hoping for praise. Millie wouldn't give it.

'That's just to make it sound like a proper job.'

Millie looked at Florence.

'Oh. I said no.'

'Good.'

'I couldn't possibly take any money to help you.'

'No.'

'So she asked if I'd do it anyway.'

'Sneaky.'

'So if she holds any meeting and asks Joan to attend in her new post as "spiritual mentor", I should go along as well, I thought?'

'So, how does Esther know Joan?' Millie was jealous now. Millie had mentally appointed Joan her third-best friend after the energy-clearing, and Florence was already her second best. Esther would never get rated, as she was her boss. But she didn't want them all meeting up behind her back.

'I introduced them. Esther was looking for a spiritual mentor on the team, so I thought of Joan.'

'And is Joan getting paid?'

'She's building a website, so . . . she might need to earn some extra . . .' Florence shrugged.

Millie stared into her empty glass. The musicologist might have got quicker at making the drinks, but size seemed to be the problem now. Millie looked over at the bar, where the girl was pointing her pencil in the air, humming and then writing things down importantly.

'I think I might have to mention about portion size,' said Millie, looking at her almost empty glass. 'She needs to know. I'm not just thinking about me. I'm thinking of other customers.'

'She might give you some more if you say that.'

'Yes. I know.'

'But that will be like having another drink.' Florence looked worried.

Millie wondered if Florence was going to become strict and boring, now that she was an unpaid supervisor of the campaign.

'It will be like having a correctly sized first drink,' assured Millie. She wanted to relish every precious second of being light-headed before they returned to the subject of money and sums.

'But then you might have another one, you see, and we said we were only having one to celebrate, didn't we?'

'Florence, I think we should just be mindful about living in the moment.'

'OK. I'm OK with that.'

'Let's not worry about the future. Or the past. It's what's happening now that's important.'

'Agreed.'

They sat in silence, neither of them quite sure what there was to discuss that was current.

'I'll just go and correct my portion now.' As she stood up, Millie turned to say, 'I don't mind about the secret campaign. Honestly. I'm up for it. Thanks for telling me.'

At the bar, Millie smiled at the musicologist and showed her the empty glass.

'We never got your name last time . . .'

'It's Cara. That was my first day when you came in. I wasn't telling people then.'

'Understood. So, Cara, I've been on a health kick since we were last in.'

'My mum does that. Sometimes.'

'Does she? So, this margarita seemed a bit smaller than last time.'

'That's the right size. You must have had a bigger one before.'

'OK. Bung me another one in there, will you?'

Millie changed her mind. She couldn't stomach further lime-squeezing and messing about with mean measurements. It would take too long. She was thinner and emptied and needed to get full again quickly or she might faint.

'Actually, tell you what – I'll just have a house white, shall I?'

'It's up to you. Do you want one?'

'Go on, then.'

Millie held out her cocktail glass. Cara took it and swapped it for a wine glass. Then she found an open bottle of wine and emptied it. Millie looked at the new glass. The wine had not come up to the top.

'Do you want me to open another bottle?'

'No. OK, then. Actually, no, I'm fine.'

Millie placed a precious five-pound note on the bar, took a decent gulp, shoved some coinage into the jelly beans dispenser, ate a handful and went back to her seat.

Millie felt better. She'd had one margarita, a few slugs of wine and sugar from the beans. She was drunk. For the first time in her life she was a lightweight.

She leaned back on the banquette to embrace the feeling fully. She had missed the benefits of this benign poison. The oblivion, the bonhomie. Florence was such a nice friend. Everything felt rosy and possible and nice again when they were out together. She'd neglected her with all this weight-loss pressure.

'Tell me about Jack.'

'Tell me about Eugene.'
They laughed.

Millie began describing her trip, assuming Florence would know lots of things about the Papua New Guinean infrastructure, and the fact it had been a protectorate and had problems with illegal logging and mosquitoes and that Eugene wanted to stop corruption and protect the forest and was a member of the VPL pressure group.

Once Florence had been convinced about the authenticity of the VPL, she announced that Eugene sounded very interesting indeed.

Millie then put together an account of the long drive back to the airport and asked Florence what she thought about the key-ring incident, and if she felt it had been intended as a sexual overture. Florence felt very sure the licking had been intended as sexual. She seemed certain of this.

Millie wanted to be shocked by Florence's assertion that Eugene had been flirting outrageously, but felt secretly rather pleased, and not a little excited by having to revisit the memory. The fact that anyone, anyone at all, had found her attractive and the fact that the two of them were now discussing it on their night out made her feel almost a bit wanton – but not because of Eugene. More ... well, she didn't know, but it had something to do with her silver bowl. And after all, Florence was an expert in this area.

Florence insisted on being given a physical description of Eugene, including height, chest and 'the rest'. And then she winked rather alarmingly, which reminded Millie of a dirty old man, which wasn't ideal. The implant had a lot to answer for. Millie would only say he was 'stocky' and 'not unusually tall'. She didn't want to encourage lewdness. Her silver bowl shut down protectively.

'Like a personal trainer?'

'Almost,' said Millie, non-committal.

'Like the ones in that cheaper gym at Forest Hill?' pressed Florence, who was now Googling 'Papua New Guinean men' on her iPad. 'Is he more Costa Rican or Peruvian, would you say?'

'He's more Mexican without being Mexican. Only shorter.' Millie wanted to bring Florence's research enquiries to a close.

'That could work,' she said, adding appreciatively, 'Nice.'

'Mm. Well, anyway . . .'

'So back to the key ring.' Florence's eyes looked suddenly keen. She didn't want Millie to lose interest. 'Did he use it to touch your . . .' She fondled her own breasts to illustrate her enquiry. Florence needed to calm down.

Then Millie had a thought.

'Florence, have you just had a top-up?'

Florence looked at her drink.

'Of testosterone?'

She had. Florence had just come from the smart new Lady Harman wing at their surgery, where she had been topped up. If Millie had known, she would have delayed their night out. The implant might need a settling-in time.

'Right.' Millie eyed her friend warily. 'Florence, do you think you're able to be objective right now?'

'What do you mean?'

'With all that new testosterone rattling around?'

'Of course I can.'

'Because I've been quite affected by the key ring. It's not just titillation. I mean, I was quite taken aback when he did it, because . . . I wasn't *asking* to be given a key ring – as useful as they are – and why dangle it up and down my chest area like that?'

'Because he fancies you.' Florence was adamant.

Millie knew she still shouldn't be feeling any pleasure at Florence's diagnosis, but a compliment went a long way. Harry's didn't count due to the questionable sanity factor.

Perhaps if she played Al's answering-machine message over and over again at the *same time* as visualizing the key-ring moment with Eugene, she might be able to transfer some lust and keep her integrity. But she still needed Florence to hear the rest of the story. Especially if more compliments could be wrung from it. She deserved them. A few hours ago she had been almost naked in a public hotel lounge. She needed her self-esteem rebuilding.

Predictably, Florence could hardly contain her excitement when Millie described the hand-hovering section and the unusual breathing noises.

'It was probably some sort of healing technique, don't you think?'

'Healing?' Florence said. 'No. That's not healing, Millie.'

She sensed Florence had a new respect for her, and rather enjoyed the fact.

'Drink, then?' Florence was suddenly perky.

'I certainly will, yes. What happened with Jack?' she asked, and then regretted it. A reply would delay the drink. She should have asked this when Florence came back with the order.

'He said we had to get married or that was it.'

'Marry you? Why?'

'He couldn't get over me being with the Belgian.'

'Is he anti-Europe?'

'He was jealous.'

'Oh. Yes. Of course.'

'And then he got upset and said he wanted to get married or end it.'

Millie took out her purse. Florence took the hint and stood up.

'And get some peanuts with the wine, will you? To cheer us up?' said Millie. She'd had no protein in five days. At least peanuts were small.

Millie sank back into the banquette. She was pleased to hear that Florence wasn't quite as on top of things on the man front as she thought.

The loss of weight had given Millie new hope that she could look and feel normal, and now here was a bit of schadenfreude to give her an extra boost. Other people's unhappiness was great for morale.

Florence returned with a bowl of pistachios.

'These are more slimming, I thought.'

'Good choice.'

Millie tore into them, scattering shells across the table. The glass of wine was half full. Florence must be monitoring.

'I'll get Joan to call you and chase up Adrienne in the morning.' Florence nodded at the glass in a guilty way.

Millie changed the subject.

'So, do you miss Jack? If it's over? You must do.'

'Well—' began Florence.

'Enough about me,' Millie interrupted, and burped

quietly. The acid in the margarita tended to repeat on an empty stomach.

'Are you OK about him?' Millie persevered.

'I'm all right,' said Florence, as if she had come to terms with her lot. 'I knew it wasn't going anywhere.'

'Did he say that?'

'No, but I did. I couldn't offer him what he deserves. He's thirty-six.'

'Thirty-three, I thought you said? Maybe you can stay friends?'

'He says he can't. Too painful. Even for a cuddle.'

'How do you know?'

'I asked.'

'Maybe it's meant to be?' Millie knew Florence would like this phrase.

Florence smiled fondly. 'Yes. And the kittens wouldn't be enough for him in the long run.'

'The cats?' Millie knew she should sound sympathetic, but really, only people with a special calling would be able to handle those cats. 'Have you heard from the Belgian?' she asked.

'No.'

'Well, Brussels isn't exactly practical, is it?' said Millie, trying to help.

'Nor is your daughter's boyfriend fancying you.'

Millie looked shocked. Had Florence been turned by Esther?

'But I don't fancy him.'

Florence raised her eyebrows.

'Really I don't.'

'Of course not.'

But Millie was slightly worried Florence would mention

Eugene to Amelia, who might put it on Facebook. She'd become wary of Facebook. She wasn't sure how it worked, but from what she gathered, it could be very dangerous. Apparently there was already some Facebook interest. Most of Mary's old school friends – not that she had many – were rather intrigued by the series of photos that had been uploaded of Mary with a tiny tribal man and a rather odd middle parting.

'Anyway, there's someone I quite like at Pets Need Vets. He's only in on a Thursday, but he's nice.'

'What's he like?'

'Quite . . .' Florence searched for the right word, 'simple.'

'Carpenter or vegetarian?'

'I mean he's . . . a pure kind of soul.'

'Good luck with that.'

Cara sauntered over to their window table.

'Can we have a –' Millie looked at Florence, who looked stern. Millie knew she wasn't going to be allowed any more to drink – 'candle, please?'

'Sure. And another wine for you, Millie?'

'Another one? Is that wise on an empty stomach?' said Florence, worried.

'No, she's all right. She had the jelly beans in the machine.'

'I did.' Millie nodded and stretched to relieve some worrying indigestion.

'Goodness,' said Florence.

'What?' said Millie defensively, and pulled down her top. She may have exposed some of her reduced midriff by mistake.

'Hello, ladies.'

Al looked different to how she had remembered him.

There was a cream jacket she hadn't seen before over a T-shirt.

'I saw you two through the window,' he said proudly.

Did Al want a prize? Millie felt slightly uncomfortable, which was disappointing. She was supposed to be fancying Al, but he looked too overjoyed to see them. It was too keen. She wasn't used to being adored. It made her awkward.

'I hope you didn't go home and change on our account?' She didn't like the jacket.

'I did.' Al smiled. This was the wrong answer.

Florence looked apologetically at Al.

'Millie's just lost a lot of weight.' Florence waved a hand at Millie, as if to explain.

'Has she?' Al looked at Millie carefully.

Millie was outraged.

'Yes. I've lost eight pounds in five days! Can't you see?'

Millie lifted up her T-shirt very quickly and then down again. She regretted this immediately, but the weight loss had been hard won and she needed it to be noticed. Florence was frowning.

'Can I get anyone anything?' asked Cara, who had appeared with a miniature handheld vacuum cleaner. The pistachios were everywhere. She started hoovering. It made a subdued buzzy noise.

Al was still looking excited, which scared Millie.

'Sorry, Cara – can we help?' asked Millie.

Either Cara couldn't hear or she was ignoring them.

Millie liked Cara. She looked arty. She might even read her one of the early poems.

'Wine?' Al looked at her glass.

Millie nodded. Happiness had been restored.

'With actual peanuts this time, pleeeease.'

Al nodded but smiled at Millie again.

'Where are your tools?' she said, trying to sound like Florence in happier times.

'In the van. I'm using it as a temporary home.' Al set off to the bar.

Millie stopped him. 'Why?' A van didn't sound very satisfactory as a base, if things were to move up a gear.

'My ex chucked me out of the spare room so Stan said I could stay at his, but his wife started putting bin liners on their sofa, and I opted for the van.'

'Why?'

Al raised his eyebrows. 'It was a hint. They need the space, Stan says.'

'But why bin liners?'

'Back in a mo. I need a drink.'

'Oooo, get you!' said Millie to Al's back as he walked off. She knew she was showing off, but she felt like it. She'd lost weight. Loads of weight. It was fine.

'I think you should weigh yourself when you get home, Millie. You need to keep at it,' said Florence urgently.

'Haven't got any scales.'

'Esther will be upset.'

'She should buy me some, then.'

'About us drinking tonight.'

'Esther doesn't have to know about tonight. She'll be with the Germans,' said Millie.

'But you can't afford to blow it, can you?' said Florence in a worried voice. 'Remember you're under contract to keep losing?'

'Look, Florence, as long as I get my first cheque in two weeks' time – because they only pay me monthly, remember – I've actually got six more weeks from now until the next weigh-in, haven't I!'

Millie was pleased to have reminded herself of this sudden freedom. Florence looked doubtful.

'So surely I've earned myself a bit of leeway for the odd pistachio in the interim.'

Florence took out her childlike pink phone and pressed the calculator.

'How much will you have to have lost by the next weigh-in, in six weeks, if you're eleven stone thirteen now?'

'I have to be down to ten stone six. Nathan was going to do another mind map for me, but I begged Esther to stop him. I hope she has, otherwise it's psychological bullying.'

Millie found Florence's hand on her arm to stop her spiralling.

'How many pounds?'

Millie sighed.

'I need a loss of twenty-one pounds in six weeks.'

They both looked glum.

'Fancy another drink?'

'I'm a bit strapped for cash, actually, Florence, until the next—'

'Cheque. Yes.'

'Yes.'

'Maybe you shouldn't drink any more, Millie. I'm not being mean, but you've still got to wait for two weeks for your fat cheque and lose another two and a half stone in total after that, so you can't afford any slip-ups – every mouthful counts.'

Millie didn't like the way her earning had been called a 'fat cheque'. She was also depressed at the thoroughness of what must have been Esther's excellent briefing notes to her campaign team.

Millie closed her eyes and visualized a glass of wine and offered up an affirmation. 'The more wine I drink, the better I am. Life is good.' It worked. Within seconds Al came back with a tray. On it was a glass of wine, a Baileys for Florence, a beer, a bowl of peanuts and a large lit candle. She should do this more often.

Millie stood up to get at the wine quickly, but keeled forward and lobbed the candle straight onto Al's jacket. The jacket got singed. Nothing serious, but a definite singe. The tray was fine. They all looked at the singe mark, rather sobered.

'It's new. It's fine,' said Al.

Millie was mortified.

'You actually chose it?'

Al handed out the drinks.

'Thank you, Al,' said Florence and Millie obediently and at the same time.

'Shall I take her home, Florence?' Maybe Al was shy, but he seemed to be using Florence as a go-between. This was often a sign of attraction, thought Millie.

'Might be a good idea. Can you drop me off first?' said Florence. 'I've left the kittens alone.'

'Me first,' said Millie.

'No, me,' said Florence. 'I'm really worried about the kittens, Millie, and Jack's not there anymore, remember?' Florence looked as if she was going to cry. Even through her drunk haze Millie could see that Florence might be getting upset. Millie would have to look after Florence. This was sensitive of her. Florence would thank her in the morning.

'OK, Al, here's what we do: we all take Florence back to hers and pick up the kittens; then Florence and the kittens get back in your van; then you drop me back at mine; then you drop Florence and the kittens back at hers . . .' She'd forgotten what alcohol did for you. It made everything clearer – a prism of light, imbued with logic.

'That's a plan,' said Al, looking uncertain again.

Al brought the van round to exactly where they were standing. As Al fussed about, dusting off a mattress that lined the floor of the back of the van, he said, 'Lucky for you two I like a challenge.'

'We don't mind. As long as we get home!' replied Millie, looking doubtfully at this van that appeared to have no seats in the back. It would be awkward for Florence to get in and out. And she was cold. She wasn't sure if she was going to like being slim if you couldn't go out at night without shivering.

Al set off quite slowly. He looked at the rear mirror.

'You all right back there, Florence?'

Millie turned her head round to show concern for her friend, but immediately felt sick, so she turned back and held on to the dashboard. She spoke from this slightly crouched position facing forwards.

'Yes, you all right, Florence?'

'Fine! I see you read the *Week*, Al.' Florence had got over her wobble about Jack and was making the best of being crouched on a mattress with a pile of newspapers and magazines.

'I do, yes.'

'And the *Lancet*. Impressive. And . . . Oh.' Florence sounded shocked at what she had discovered next.

'Is it a rude one?' asked Millie from the front. For some reason she wanted to humiliate Al because he liked her and she knew that she could. She put it down to the conflicting feelings caused by her trip. She didn't like herself for doing it. He was only being nice. Very nice.

'I use them for cleaning my shoes.'

'We believe you, Al. Thousands wouldn't.' Millie suddenly sounded like Florence when she was being all lewd from her topped-up implant. She needed to get some air. She tried to open the window but opened the door instead.

'Whoops!'

Al slammed on the brakes.

'You going to be sick, love?' he asked.

'Gosh, no. I'm never sick.'

'Just say if you are and I'll stop.'

Once they'd set off again, Millie wound the window down as low as it would go using the correct handle. Blasts of air shot through the van, landing with force on Florence in the back. Millie felt slightly better for it in the front. Florence used the men's mags to shield her from the full blast.

'Ooooo!' exclaimed Florence after a few minutes.

'Sure you're OK?' asked Al.

'Just a bit shocked,' said Florence.

They travelled like this for a while, Florence intently reading from a collection of porn magazines, and Millie hanging on to the dashboard.

*

As soon as they pulled up at Florence's flat, Florence leaned forward to get out and tapped Millie on the shoulder. But she was too drunk to respond, slumped as she was against the passenger door. Florence turned herself round to crawl rather inelegantly out of the back door as Al guided her out. While they waited for her to collect the cats, Millie closed her eyes so she didn't have to say anything to Al, who had got back into the driving seat and was watching her.

'Here we are!' said Florence, waving her cat basket through the window. Millie pretended to wake up. Memories of Eugene and the hammock came to mind. Why was she always having to pretend to be asleep or to wake up?

'Are we there?' asked Millie.

'Just got the kittens,' said Florence. 'Can you budge? Save Al getting out this time, won't it?'

They drove on, with the kittens eating their supper hungrily in the back.

Florence suddenly leaned forward.

'Sorry – I can't remember why I'm here and not there.'

'So you can supervise my weight loss at all times when I'm at risk.'

'Oh yes.'

'And report back to Esther we only had water.'

'I can't lie, Millie.'

'Joking!' said Millie.

Millie took a sideways glance at Al. He didn't look too bad in the cream jacket now. It did trigger a distant memory of a head waiter in the Mandarin Hotel at a travel drinks party for the magazine, but it could be worse. It could have been a reefer jacket with gold buttons.

Al caught the glance and smiled back. Millie sensed he was assessing his chances and wondering how long they could leave Florence in the van talking to the kittens while she made him a tea.

Al carried Millie into her house. She didn't really need carrying, but she let him, since he'd taken the initiative and she didn't want to quibble about suddenly being hoisted aloft without being asked. She lay passive, like a sack of hops in his arms, just to see what it felt like. If Eugene had tried this, they wouldn't be very high off the ground. As it was, she hadn't had to walk at all, her legs swinging from quite some height in fact, and now she could be leaned up against the porch while he searched through her huge bag to locate her front door key. It was good to be comparing the two men and making Al the winner this time.

'It's on a special ring,' said Millie, 'a very, very, very special ring.' Adding emotionally, 'Al, it's really special. If I ever lost it, I'd be . . . Well, I don't know what I'd do quite frankly.'

'You wouldn't be able to get into your house and you'd have to sleep in my van,' said Al, adding, 'With me.'

Millie ignored this. She was too worried.

'Please say you've found her.'

As Al rummaged deep in the bag, they were both blinded by a bright light. Harry leaped out carrying a Davy lamp and everything suddenly felt all Christmassy. Then Millie realized Harry must have switched the fairy-ring installation outside his house to flashing mode. Millie's garden was now sprinkled with intermittent slices of green and pink.

'If I can see your shaved head, Al, you must be able to find the key. Where is it?'

'You all right, Millie love?' asked Harry, peering from under his lamp in a worried way. Al was taken aback at this propriety.

'Fine, thanks, Harry,' called Millie, for once grateful for the intrusion. 'Al, this is my neighbour. He lives next door.'

Al nodded at Harry and continued with his search for the keys.

'Got it!' He finally located the key ring. He thrust it into the lock and picked Millie up again to continue the fireman's lift into the house, which he was rather enjoying doing.

'That's Harry,' said Millie from upside down. 'He loves me.' From this position, she could see Harry walking down the path toward Al's van.

Al emptied her onto the sofa. She couldn't move. She'd had virtually no food for five days and a lot of alcohol in the last five hours.

'Come here,' she ordered.

Al joined her on the sofa. They sat together in the semi-darkness. Very, very slowly, so that she might not notice, Al put his arm around her shoulder. It was done quite carefully. Presumably he didn't want her to know he'd done it, in case she didn't want him to, but at least the arm would be there if she did want it. Millie knew it was there but didn't react. She felt she ought to ask Al a bit about himself since he'd got her back in one piece, but not too much in case she got bored. She needed to get the image of Eugene staring down at her with his hovering hand out of her mind. Al was her chance.

She sighed and turned slightly. As Millie shut her eyes,

she sensed a persistent yet seductive licking of her fingers. She froze. It had been years since her fingers had been given this kind of attention. She couldn't help feeling aroused in spite of the surprise of it. But the most elevating thing about the sensation was that thoughts of Eugene and his key-ring licking receded. This new reaction was all about Al . . . She almost gave in to it, but had to stop herself. She was too drunk. She might tell Al about Eugene.

Then, as if Al sensed this, the licking stopped as abruptly as it had started. She leaned back and closed her eyes and concentrated on stopping the room spinning.

After a few minutes Al cleared his throat and said in a voice full of barely controlled excitement, 'That's lovely, Millie. Really lovely.'

Millie's eyes had become adjusted to the dark and she could just make out Vernon sitting on top of the sofa. Al had the same expression on his face as the one she'd seen when she flashed her stomach at him. Poor man.

'Al, I hate to tell you this, but Vernon's been quite lonely recently – he's been on his own a lot.'

'Vernon?'

'Vernon! Stop it now. Al doesn't want you licking him, do you, Al?'

'Er, no.' Al and Vernon eyeballed each other.

Millie pushed herself up as best she could.

'I'm knackered. Sorry to be rude, but have you ever had a colonic, Al?'

'Probably not.'

Al was backing himself out into the hall.

'It leaves you pretty drained – I'm not myself. Where are you going?'

'Better get back to Florence.'

'Florence, sorry . . . Sorry, wait, can you put the light on? I can't find the kettle.'

In her drunken state Millie felt a compulsion to tell Al all about Eugene. She couldn't be sure, but Al might be very attracted to her, and that made her think about Eugene and the involuntary urges, even though she had now achieved a replacement urge, which was at least a move in the right direction. But she should really tell him. It was only fair.

'I really like you, Al,' began Millie.

'You should have said . . . earlier. It's a bit late.'

Millie wasn't quite sure what Al meant by this.

'Have you, er, got any tea towels of any description?'

'Yes. I have, thanks. Quite a few. And I'm sorry. I just feel . . .' Millie started to cry. She was drunk, and possibly aroused. Or not. But laden with guilt. What would she say to Mary about Eugene? After all, her daughter was the most important person in her life. What if Eugene told Mary about his feelings for her mother? She'd lose Mary forever. But Mary was young. And once she'd ditched the camouflage trousers and started being a bit of a government hotty for world diseases, surely she'd have other, better chances at love.

'I'm crying, Al. I don't know if you can see that, but I'm crying quite a lot now.'

'Are you? Yeah, so better be off just in case Florence might need the loo.'

Al let himself out and rushed outside to the van. Millie followed after him. But she stopped when she saw Harry, who was now leaning on the van door and feeding the kittens some of Vernon's catnip.

ELEVEN

AFFIRMATION 11:

'I thank my higher power for making my personal trainer get stuck in traffic'

FRIDAY 28 MARCH

Millie had worked out that the effective key to losing weight, so far, was through emission. She would now swap the emission of waste matter to the emission of body sweat. This was what Adrienne, the personal trainer from CardioMonkey.com, was here to encourage. She was to arrive at nine, when Millie was to be all ready to be sweated into further weight loss. This was not something to look forward to. Millie was disappointed to see her at the door. She was on time.

Adrienne had cycled over from Mill Hill to get to Millie's house. She balanced the lightweight bike on one finger before leaning it against Millie's hatstand in the hall. She was wearing silvery trainers and black Lycra all over her body, even her neck. The costume felt slightly sci-fi. Perhaps the silver was to inspire leaping.

After some pleasantries – such as 'God, you're thin'

from Millie and 'Just a water, thanks' from Adrienne – they got down to business.

'So let's have your food diary.' Adrienne looked keen and shiny.

They were seated at the table in the kitchen. The masking tape round the fridge had been removed and a dirty saucepan with the remains of some cheesy carbonara sat on the hob.

'Well, I've only just started eating solids, so haven't had time to build up a food portfolio for you as yet.'

Adrienne's face fell with disappointment. Millie knew she had been feeble and had failed already. But keeping a food diary was not really her thing. It was what obsessive-compulsive people did on TV documentaries in which the voiceover kept recapping what had happened in case people lost the thread.

Adrienne looked very masculine. It wasn't just the height or the broad shoulders; it was something about the neck, or the hands. Millie wondered if there was anything she ought to know. Not that she was interested. And she knew she'd have to give Adrienne a chance. This was, after all, a lifeline. The next weigh-in was six weeks away. She had to prove she could lose at least twenty-one pounds by then.

'And what were you eating before you were on the lettuce, spirulina and water combo?' Adrienne smiled, but there was determination in her piercing blue eyes.

She was ready to make careful notes in a posh leather-bound book.

'Everything.'

'Everything?'

'Yes.'

'Portion size?'

'Large.'

'And –' Adrienne put the ballpoint down and pressed her hands together as she leaned forward and stared intently into Millie's face – 'don't take this the wrong way, but would you say you have a problem?'

'I would, yes.'

Adrienne sat back, relieved.

'Good, because that's half the battle, isn't it?'

'What's the other half?'

'Discipline.'

'Am I going to like you?'

'I hope so.'

Adrienne then whipped open her waterproof rucksack and produced a blood pressure machine as one might produce a rabbit from a hat.

'Just to be sure.'

'Of . . . ?' asked Millie.

'That you're normal.'

'I can help you there. I'm not.'

Adrienne laughed but not with her eyes.

'Normal enough, then,' she said firmly.

'For . . . ?'

'A run.'

'A run?'

'We can build up to it.' Adrienne put her hand on Millie's shoulder and looked deeply into her eyes. 'You're very tense.'

'You're very close.' Millie pulled away. 'I think I've got an issue about being touched.'

Adrienne nodded and crouched down to look up at

Millie, who sensed this was Adrienne trying to pull low status on purpose. Clever again.

'So would it be OK with you –' Adrienne was speaking to Millie as if she was a very volatile patient – 'if I touched your arm for a few seconds while I attach the blood pressure pack to it? Would that be OK for you?'

'It would, yes. Fine. Go ahead.' Millie surrendered up her arm.

The blood pressure results were normal.

'Are you sure?'

'Entirely. You're a hundred and ten over seventy.'

This was depressing. There was no reason why she wouldn't have to go for a run now.

'Is there a park near you?' asked Adrienne.

'No,' said Millie.

Adrienne looked at her. 'Actually, I Googled it and there's quite a big one at the end of your road.'

'Oh yes. It's at the end of the road. Quite big.'

Adrienne had bought Millie a tracksuit to wear for the session. Predictably, Harry was fascinated to see Millie in her borrowed sportswear as they left the house for the practice run.

'Don't speak to that man,' hissed Millie.

Harry raced down his path to be parallel and stopped where the gates met in the adjoining wall.

'Howdy.' Harry looked appreciatively at Millie. 'Nice headwear.'

Millie had also been loaned a cap, which needed getting used to due to its small size. Both women looked stoically ahead, ignoring him.

Harry whistled softly nevertheless.

Once they were in the park, Millie was dismayed to

spot some people she knew. Someone she was acquainted with from the magazine was walking a small dog and waved in surprise at the sight of Millie in a tiny cap and an Olympic-style running outfit. Millie pulled the cap over her eyes. This was going to be excruciating. Adrienne's Lycra vest top had the words 'Personal Trainer' in gold letters emblazoned across both sides so Millie couldn't even pretend she was out jogging with a friend.

'Let's trot, shall we?' said Adrienne.

'I'm OK like this, actually.' Millie had seen Cara walking towards them with headphones wearing baggy sports gear. She looked cool, while Millie felt overdressed in her borrowed designer tracksuit.

'Could we not trot until I'm more familiar with being outside?'

She didn't want Cara telling Al she'd seen Millie trotting with a trainer in the park. She was slightly miffed he'd left her while she was crying. But then she knew men didn't like emotion. It reminded them of their mothers and triggered a fight-or-flight response.

'Come on. Like this.' Adrienne picked up her feet in their silver trainers and began to trot.

Millie said she'd have a go at doing it, but only when Cara was safely past them.

The trot was doable for a few more minutes, until they came to a gradient.

'Why have we stopped?' asked Adrienne. Her sports gloves had air vents for when her hands might sweat.

'It's a gradient, Adrienne. There'd be no point.' Millie was now puffing hard from the trot. She hoped she was sweating as well, so she'd look exhausted and generally spent when Joan Le Measurer came round for the check-up.

'OK, let's do some thrusts.'

Millie looked around nervously.

'Together?'

Adrienne rushed off to bagsy an empty park bench and claimed it triumphantly.

'Over here.'

They sat on the bench. This felt agreeable.

'Are all your family tall as well?' Millie asked, keen to keep her there for as long as possible without having to do anything.

But Adrienne was lowering herself down from a sitting position and pushing herself up again and then repeating the action.

'Go on. You do it.'

Millie tried, but it hurt too much. She tried again and then said, 'Nope,' and shook her head. There was something wrong with her. She couldn't thrust.

Adrienne suggested they trot back home. They'd been out for forty-five minutes. This was unprecedented. As she tried to keep up with Adrienne's trot, Millie saw two men walking by the other way. They were sharing a lead attached to a tiny chihuahua. It was Nathan and Bubble Boy from Hamleys. The park was fast proving itself a dangerous place to be if you wanted to avoid people. Fortunately, each pair had passed the other by the time Nathan had realized who was under the cap.

'Come on,' said Millie. 'Race you back.'

Millie, for the first time in her life, was actually running. Adrienne looked smug.

And Millie was pleased she'd spotted Nathan. She wasn't sure how yet, but the discovery that Nathan and Bubble Boy were sharing an improbably small dog could surely be turned to her advantage. Perhaps if Esther knew, she would be less inclined to spoon-feed him the magazine columns that should rightfully be hers.

As they huffed back up the path to her house, Adrienne said, 'It's been a privilege, Millie.'

'Has it? I'm glad.'

'There's something I have to tell you, Millie.'

'Yes?' Millie could barely speak from lack of oxygen. It was probably about hidden expenses and fees. She'd have to tell Adrienne she couldn't afford her after all. This may be the last time she would ever run with a personal trainer. She'd have to pretend to be sorry.

Adrienne seemed to be hesitating.

'I want you to know I am pansexual.'

Predictably, Harry was watering his hanging basket at this point in the adjacent porch, and for once both neighbours were speechless at the same time.

'She means bi-curious,' said Harry out of the corner of his mouth, giving both their geraniums a generous zest of plant enhancer. '"Pan" stands for "omni", meaning "all". I knew a pan who was in love with his car.'

Luckily, Adrienne was already inside and Millie shut the door.

TWELVE

~

AFFIRMATION 12:
'I am what I eat. Today I am a bean'

As far as Millie was concerned, the whole sweaty, unpleasant business was behind her until the next session, which would be horribly soon. She was now officially in the tutelage of a pansexual. She'd have to ask Mary what a pansexual was the next time they Skyped. It sounded as if it might originate from Skyros.

Adrienne seemed to be taking an inordinately long time to zip up her Day-Glo cycling cardy and leave. Joan Le Measurer was due shortly and she didn't want to rush her first snack before lunch.

Millie would have zipped the turtleneck up herself but didn't want to come across as overfamiliar. Instead she went for a hand-on-the-back-with-steering gesture. This was only effective if one didn't shove. It was a delicate balance.

The back steer went for nothing. Adrienne affectionately hooked on to Millie's steering arm to ask if she might just share something else with her before she left.

'Shoot,' said Millie in reply. She wanted to keep her

vocabulary to the minimum. They had progressed to the bike. Millie tapped the seat.

Adrienne took a deep breath and asked Millie if she might be interested to learn that she had 'attachment issues'.

'Attachment issues,' Millie repeated slowly. 'You mean like stalking your clients?' She would have to open a tin of something soon. She was weak from the trot.

'No. It's more that I over-identify with my clients as we establish a way to work together and at the beginning of a relationship.'

'Scary,' said Millie.

'And then it finds a natural level. I just wanted to share that now, in case you felt alarmed by any of the techniques I've used so far.'

'I'm up for most things, as you will have noticed. Maybe not carrying weights in a rucksack.'

Adrienne assured her the issues had been easy to work through on a retreat course in Glastonbury that Millie might consider attending at a later date. Sport and self-analysis had paved the way for her recent kettlebell qualification. Millie hadn't a clue what was being said, but thanked her for her honesty and tapped the bike again, a bit harder than before.

The tapping worked. Adrienne's parting words were, 'You see? If I can do it, you can do it, Millie. I know you can. It's all about discipline. I mean, I never thought I would ever work with the public and look at me now.'

Millie didn't have much to go on about where Adrienne had come from and where she was going. And without a drink or a snack in her hand, the inclination to find out more shrank quite significantly. This so far was a very light relationship. And it was one she wasn't keen to deepen. As long as Adrienne was prepared to turn up and train her for no money, she'd be trained – as unpleasant as it had already proved itself to be.

Finally Adrienne lifted the micro mountain bike out of the door on her double-jointed middle finger and turned back to smile from the path. Millie managed a smile in return, but some trust had gone.

Joan Le Measurer was running a few minutes late. Millie replied to her text with a single 'x', as she had been taught to do by Mary. It was what you did when you didn't know what to say but didn't want to be caught out avoiding a response.

Luckily for Millie, a pack of baked beans had escaped the culling of her pantry food. She ate two tins. It was these or die. She threw the empty tins into the recycling bin. They missed.

Joan arrived with a large crinkled paper bag. She offered two apologies. The first apology was that she was five past midday, as she'd been held up.

'No problem at all,' said Millie with honesty.

The second apology came via Joan from Jon, who was away for a few weeks studying silence at the Silent Community as part of his MBA. He'd broken his silence to send Millie some reflections for her weight loss.

'I've not got them yet.' Millie was suspicious.

'He's been reflecting from his end.'

'How could he do that if he is being silent?' Millie wanted to know.

'It was a text, to me. Usually there's an embargo on texts as well, but . . .' Joan trailed off, using an expansive hand gesture that made Millie feel she ought to feel very touched by his effort.

'I'm amazed he felt me worthy of breaking a text embargo. Wow.' Millie was obligingly impressed.

Joan rattled the paper bag.

'Look what I've got in here!'

Millie peered inside. The bag contained a pair of grimy second-hand scales.

Millie wondered when Joan was going to admit that she was now a fully paid-up member of Esther's fat-busting Stasi Commission. Maybe she was going to keep it a secret. Millie enjoyed the power that this knowledge gave her and sat quietly judging Joan. People, it seemed, were flawed. Even spiritual ones.

'Now, where shall I place them?' Joan hauled the scales out of the bag and carried them around the kitchen as if they were a precious sheep's carcass. They were also in need of a serious wipe-down. If Millie wanted to catch a verruca, here was her chance.

'Esther said you'll need to weigh yourself in the same place every morning. For accuracy, given the vagaries of water retention, so . . .' Joan seemed still to be searching for a feng shui-friendly location. Esther? So Joan had given herself away already.

'Esther?' asked Millie.

Joan looked guilty, but only for a moment.

'I dropped in to see Florence at Pets Need Vets and met Esther, who was there at the same time. Aren't they perfect?' Joan put her hand over the stained bit on the rubber part of the scales as if to hide it. 'Anyway, Esther said they had your name on them.'

'Esther?' repeated Millie, giving Joan another chance to reveal her new job.

'She paid for them.'

'Fifty pence well spent.' Millie had checked the price tag.

'She was bringing in a box of things for the shop.'

'What things?'

'Some DVDs . . . I think they were the son's, actually.'

'Nathan?'

'Yes, I think so.'

'And did she also mention how useless he is, and how he shouldn't be working for a women's magazine?' Millie asked pleasantly.

'Esther's not sure what's going on there.' Joan managed to make this reply sound very knowing, which Millie found rather overfamiliar for such a new friend.

Joan rested the scales for a few seconds on the kitchen table. They had left a tidemark of grime on her paisley silk tunic top. Millie wouldn't tell her. She was feeling squeezed out of her social group even though Esther wasn't a friend and she couldn't call Florence and Joan a 'group'.

'And there's lovely stuff for the home as well. They've just commissioned these wicker coasters from the Somali community.'

'I wouldn't allow a wicker coaster in the house, Joan. My mother might like some, though – for her girl Friday perhaps, or the warden, if the girl Friday's got any taste.'

Joan really needed to put the scales down. They looked like they were hurting. She was standing by the French doors, just where the tins of baked beans had landed.

Joan looked at the tins and then at Millie. 'Do we think this is a cry for help?'

'No. I don't, Joan. In the bin if you will, please. Oh sorry – you can't. You're encumbered. I'll do it.'

'No, no. I can do it,' Joan insisted. She placed the heavy-duty industrial scales by the door with a groan and threw the tins in the bin.

'So let's talk about your diet, then, shall we?' Joan had changed to business mode with great speed. 'You've only just started on controlled solids?'

Millie looked suspiciously at Joan.

'How do you know that?'

'Esther told me.'

'And why would she tell you that?' Millie asked.

'She had a wonderful night out at Westfield with Ernst last night apparently.'

'Ernst and Lulu?'

'She didn't mention a Lulu, but they both ate at Jamie Oliver's restaurant and the service was incredible, she said.'

'Ernst would like incredible service.'

Millie could see Joan was building up to her diet pitch by appearing conversational and inclusive. It was depressingly transparent.

'And Ernst gave Esther a *diet* sheet, which she kindly emailed to me this morning.' Joan pulled a sheet of A4 from her back pocket.

'Did he?'

'Yes, and Esther asked me to give it to you this morning. I thought we could bless it with a stone.'

'Another one? How many stones can one person have without them cancelling each other out?'

'This stone is diet-specific, so there'd be no conflict.'

Joan produced a brown stone from her other pocket. It had been in a velvet pouch, which gave it slightly more glamour than a pebble.

'This is a sardonyx. Can you say that? *Sardonyx*.'

'I think I can, Joan. *Sardonyx*.'

'Excellent. And this sardonyx stone is the embodiment of discipline and strength of character. What's not to like?'

'The colour?'

'That's the blended orange carnelian. You'll need a blend.'

'Why?' Millie asked. How long was Joan going to be banging about in her kitchen?

'It improves your close relationships.'

Millie suddenly quite liked the fact that it was a blend. She picked up the stone.

'Joan, can I just ask you something?'

'Anything.'

'Is Esther paying you?'

'No.'

'Really?'

'I'm also keen to make the difference to your campaign.'

'So she is paying you?'

'A nominal fee. But my skills are worth it, wouldn't you say?'

Joan had Millie on this one. They both knew Millie's life had completely and utterly changed since being feng-shuied. She owed Joan, and shouldn't begrudge her a cut of Esther's cut of Millie's cut. Now it was out in the open, Millie could stomach it.

'I would, Joan. My life has changed completely since you released the dead baby from my ceiling.'

'There we are, then.' Joan smiled triumphantly and with some relief. 'We all had a brainstorm as to how I might be able to spur you on. I'm on a two-week trial.'

'Thank you,' said Millie.

'I just want to help,' said Joan.

'You already have, Joan. Without you and Jon, I'd still have a dead woman circling the ceiling with her baby, wouldn't I?'

'Has that gone now? Have you heard anything? Any scratching noises? Flickering lights?'

Millie had experienced regular light dimming, but that was to do with her fuse box.

'It's all gone, Joan. There's nothing. Not a peep. Mind you, I hadn't sensed anything before you made your visit, had I?'

'But it was very much here.'

'It was. And then, when I went to Papua New Guinea, I had another totally complete chi-releasing experience, so if you'd like to hear about that?'

'Shall we go over the diet now?' asked Joan. This was a statement. She placed the diet sheet on the kitchen table and tapped it twice.

'Yes,' Millie said meekly, and placed the stone on the piece of paper and braced herself to hear about a food menu with hardly anything in it.

'Ah, how could I forget?' Joan reached into her neat little handbag and took out three packets of Kleinne Fett herbal pills and placed them on the table.

They both assessed the rows of massive brown capsules

individually encased in hard plastic. They looked like huge contact lenses. She ought to give one a go in front of Joan, if she could get it down without gagging. She'd managed to avoid taking any thus far.

Millie popped one out of its case and swallowed. It took a whole glass of water to get rid of it. Surely these needed to be sized according to an average throat. And Ernst's diet sheet was quite odd as well. Breakfasts required a bowl of sauerkraut with half a grapefruit. Lunch allowed an egg or up to six. Supper involved the other half of the same grapefruit and vegetable soup. Snacks could be any number of gherkins, which should help in feeling psychologically unrestricted.

'Doable?' Joan was smiling.

'Sure.' Millie could feel herself zoning out. A sharp reminder of the Spanx incident came into view. She had to try the diet. She was trapped. 'Thank you, Joan.'

'I bought you a starter pack of food, to up the ante.'

Joan fished out a Sainsbury's bag, which had been in the crinkly paper bag. She unloaded eggs, gherkins, a grapefruit, a beetroot, a swede and a receipt onto the table. She smoothed the receipt out in a careful way.

'I'm assuming you have onions?'

'Why?'

'I just did.'

'Alas no.'

'Never mind. Adrienne's seeing you again tomorrow?'

'She is, yes.' Joan would know this. She was in the inner circle now.

'Esther's arranging a half-page promotion feature, so don't be surprised if Adrienne takes some pictures of you in the park.'

'I'll ask her to take them after I've lost a bit.'

'Good call. I'll tell Esther you're asking Adrienne to hold. And always have your gherkin after your session. Never before.'

'I'm not going to take any chances, Joan. I'm seven or eight pounds down from my start weight. Well, I was yesterday morning.' Millie crossed her fingers, remembering vaguely the later part of the previous night.

'You're in good hands, I must say, Millie. Adrienne's got some great results with the Tough Titty ladies in the past.'

'Pat's very thin. How often does she train?'

'She doesn't.'

'Why?'

'She'd die. She's got an aneurysm.'

'Ah. Anyway, we did a trot together this morning.'

'A trot?'

'That's less than a run but more than a walk, Joan.'

'For how long?'

'Ages.'

'So, Millie, you now need to lose three and a half pounds a week in order to be ten stone six in six weeks. Two of those weeks are my responsibility. I want us to get close, share our thoughts and get into each other's psyche, if that's OK with you.'

'Be my guest, Joan. My door is always open.'

'So how did you find Tough Titty last Saturday?'

'In what way?'

'What did you think about the colour therapist?'

'Mediocre?'

'That was her first session, Millie.' Joan looked hurt. 'And she's a widow,' she added gravely.

'Sorry. But I liked Ingrid, the sex-toy person, on my table. She was nice.' Millie didn't want to cross the Tough Titty code, where dentally matched entrepreneurial women with jobs she'd never heard of supported each other with such gusto.

'Ah yes! That reminds me!'

'But I wouldn't go down the sex-toy route personally, Joan. In fact, I was going to tell you about a life-changing experience – about a special someone I met in Papua New Guinea. Someone who has made me rethink my life.'

'Yup?' Joan was opening up her neat little handbag. 'You mentioned this at Tough Titty, didn't you? Doesn't your daughter live there?'

'Yes, and he's very special.'

'You have a son over there as well?'

'No, I don't have a son, Joan.' With a sinking feeling Millie began to suspect that Joan might actually be . . . quite ordinary. And what was she doing with a vibrator? How very suburban.

Joan waved the box in Millie's face.

'I wouldn't need anything like that, Joan. I believe in the existence of love to drive physical union . . . I don't think you can manufacture desire . . . with a gadget.'

Millie surprised herself with her purity, but Joan wasn't listening. She was taking things out of a box.

'This will take pounds off you. Think of the calories saved.'

Joan held out a cylindrical tool that, when pressed, vibrated.

'A . . . Rabbit?'

'Where's your glasses, Millie?'

'In the car. Why?'

'Can you see?'

'Yes. What is it?'

'It's a HapiFork.'

Millie didn't quite know what to say. Joan pressed a button on the handle and they watched the fork light up and vibrate.

'Does it speak?'

'It vibrates. It comes with an app, but I'm looking into that on the App Store. The main thing is you use this for all your eating needs.'

'Which won't be very much.'

'No, but it tells you if you eat too quickly, which you mustn't do. If you eat fast, you absorb more calories. I bet you come from a family of fast eaters, don't you?'

This was true – mealtimes had always passed by in a flash – but Millie didn't feel like telling Joan that. It was slightly shaming.

'No. So what happens?'

'It vibrates. Which tells you to slow down.'

'OK.'

'And it's portable. This here HapiFork is the answer to your prayers, Millie.'

'I might have to beg to differ there, Joan, if I may.'

'Why not road-test a gherkin before you pre-judge?' Joan cut a gherkin in half and shook it about invitingly.

'OK.' Millie bit into it and chewed. It was bitter and unpleasant.

Joan's phone vibrated. She checked it.

'Sorry – can I take that while you eat?'

'Who is it?' Millie was annoyed. She was getting used to bespoke attention and didn't like it when it was taken away.

'Might be a client. Sorry.'

Millie waited for Joan to listen to the voice message. It was on speakerphone. An organic vegetable company were warning all their customers not to expect broccoli this week. They had various options to make up for this omission. A list of vegetables followed.

'Sorry. Continue.'

'It might be quite a palaver having to cart that around whenever I go out. I don't like to think when I eat. I just want to . . . you know . . . do it blind, without a vibrating utensil telling me what to do.'

This was when Joan had what she liked to call a light-bulb moment.

'You know what, Millie. I think you've put your finger on it!'

'Thanks.'

Millie saw it coming. Here was the perfect link for Joan to make with the diet.

'If we can crack why you emotionally eat, and when you do it, we'll nail the diet! Excited?'

'Sort of,' said Millie.

'I think you should talk about this with Adrienne when you trot tomorrow.'

'Why?'

'Because she's a specialist in emotional eating. That's how she got the Tough Titty women to shed three stone between them.'

'Between how many?'

'Five.'

'That's not that much each.'

Joan tried again.

'OK, if you lose weight at three and a half pounds a week, and get some more money in the bank . . .'

'Yes?'

'You'll feel better. And ready for the next weigh-in, which is 9 May. Lots to think about.' Joan picked up the HapiFork and the receipt.

'The 9th? That's six weeks away,' said Millie. She had almost forgotten. Wine did that.

'Whatever! Let's just have a go with the other half of the gherkin.' Joan made this sound like great fun.

Millie took the HapiFork, pierced a quarter of the gherkin· and started chewing normally. The fork went wild.

'Is it supposed to do that?'

'Yes.'

Millie slowed her chewing down to avoid the annoying little weasel sound in her mouth. And in this way Millie discovered very quickly that slow eating was very, very tedious.

'So, Joan, how much do I owe you?' Her second snack of the day had now been consumed.

'The fork is free. No, really it is.'

'I meant for the food.'

'Fifteen pounds. I think it says on the receipt, doesn't it?' Joan pretended to be surprised she was still holding it.

Millie handed Joan the last twenty-pound note from her purse. Joan handed two pounds back as change and clicked her purse shut quickly as if to close the subject. Millie had been robbed of three pounds. Maybe that was Joan's spiritual commission. She'd let it go, to bank up some karma.

'Actually, Joan . . .'

'Yes?'

'I've got a slight emotional problem that may be affecting the eating. Maybe you can emote a spiritual clearing?'

'Is there a main theme to get us in the zone? It might have to be quite general.' Joan looked at her watch.

'OK. Um . . . it's about the conflict of emotion when your daughter's boyfriend compliments you.'

'You?' Joan asked, surprised.

'Yes?' Millie was defensive.

'Millie, a conflict of emotions is more to do with indigestion from eating too fast. We all do it at times. And some people even confuse physical pain with lust. Jon's a big one for that!'

Millie wasn't surprised to hear that about Jon.

'But I tell you what, Millie,' said Joan.

'What?'

'Put those crystals under your bed and I promise you'll restore your chi to its rightful home. Good luck for the rest of the day, then!' Joan was really leaving.

'Are you off?' said Millie. She was annoyed that her mentor hadn't been moved to advise her more caringly.

'Esther said she's popping in on Sunday to see what a difference three days' worth of extreme training will do to you, without any pressure, of course.'

'Always nice to have guests, Joan. As I said, my door's always open.' Millie would hit Esther with the Nathan chihuahua sighting and see if she could derail her. Getting paid for the 'Me Time' column would be a nice gesture as well, on Esther's part. She'd drop in a hard copy later to make the point.

'Shall we just weigh you on these scales?'

'No need. I know I've lost.'

Joan looked serious. She swallowed.

'You were seen in the Bolt Whole last night, Millie.'

Millie suddenly felt afraid.

'By who?'

'Florence mentioned it to Esther and me, but we're not judging.'

It was Millie's turn to look at her watch.

'Bye, then.'

SUNDAY 30 MARCH

Millie was prepared for Esther's Sunday check-up visit. She'd eaten nothing except three carrots and another gherkin. She'd used the fork and made sure it looked sufficiently smeary as proof, should any member of the Stasi Commission wish to check.

Esther looked very stern, as she bustled into the kitchen. Millie didn't offer her any water. After Esther's next announcement Millie was glad she hadn't. In the light of her findings about three nights ago, Esther thought it the right time to reveal her fiscal motivational plan.

'For every pound you don't lose—' began Esther.

'Can I just say, that's quite negative already, Esther. I tend to avoid speaking in negative terms when I'm trying to change my behaviour. Affirmations have to be in the present tense and always positive.'

'For every pound you *don't* lose, I keep twenty pounds of your fee, and for every pound you *put on*, I get a hundred.'

'That's extremely negative.'

'It's in the contract.'

'Where?'

'In the small print.'

Millie hadn't read any size of print in the contract, so accepted this to be true.

'Fair enough, Esther,' she said meekly. 'And any news on Nathan? Because I think I saw him when I was out trotting the other day.'

'Really?' Esther looked worried.

'Yes. I wasn't sure if I should say anything.'

'It's better to know.'

'He was with a chihuahua.'

'A chihuahua?'

'And a man. With a really long scarf.'

This did the trick. Esther sank into a kitchen chair and revealed how upset she'd been about Nathan's 'other' life and how stupid she'd felt about not knowing his 'other side'. The fact that everyone else in the office appeared to have known made her feel foolish. Did Millie know? Millie was too self-obsessed to be interested, but decided her disinterest wouldn't help her cause.

'Well, there seemed little point in mentioning anything, Esther. I mean, what people do and with whom is really their own business, isn't it?'

'It is, Millie,' she agreed, and blew her nose vigorously.

'But I suppose the only thing that's really changed for you is that you might worry it's unfair to immerse Nathan in a very female world, one that is so . . . *accessory-led* when he might be much happier looking inside bonnets. Of cars. Or writing about dogs perhaps now, of course?'

Esther nodded and seemed to consider this as a possibility, which was promising. Then she moved away from

Nathan and began talking in detail about her time with Ernst in Westfield after the weigh-in. Apparently Ernst had helped her over the first shockwave about Nathan and had been very attentive when they had the steak cooked at the table at Jamie Oliver's. It forged a special moment between them – especially with the tender way he tucked the serviette in for her – but he was back in Munich now, sadly, leaving her to deal with the news afresh. Nathan had left a note saying he'd be back after taking some 'time out to reflect', but as yet she didn't have an address.

Millie wondered if it might be helpful for Esther to know that the man with the long scarf and the chihuahua was also the bubble-blowing man who had been outside Hamleys and had outed the *Good Woman* on Twitter. She decided against it.

'Actually, Esther . . .'

'What?'

'How about I edit the "Lovely Things" column for now exclusively, until we find out what Nathan really wants to do with his talents and skill set?'

Esther made a vague sort of affirmative sound followed by a cough, which wasn't as reassuring as Millie would have liked.

Nevertheless Millie announced that she would weigh herself in front of Esther. This would be as an act of trust, and recognition of the fiscal motivational plan, which had not been mentioned until now and was hidden in the contract.

Esther was pleased.

'Excellent. Well, now, it's Sunday, and I know you were eleven stone thirteen on Thursday, so let's see where we are at now, shall we?'

Millie stood on the scales. She was eleven stone thirteen.

Esther pursed her lips and shook her head slightly. Any
vulnerability about Nathan's welfare evaporated and
Millie braced herself for punishment.

'You haven't lost?'

'Seemingly not. But I have maintained, which is positive.'

'This will invoke the twenty-pound penalty, you see.'

Millie looked at the floor.

Esther repeated that as already stated, for every pound
Millie had not lost, she would be obliged to withhold
twenty pounds. For this reason, Esther told Millie, she
would have to take twenty pounds. But out of respect for
Millie's debt predicament, she would only extract this
penalty by deducting from Millie's pending 'Me Time'
payment.

God gave and She took away. And She also put the
boot in. Apparently Ernst had contacted Esther with a
breakthrough suggestion of his own. Due to Millie's
uneven weight loss, and to ensure he would get a return
on his investment, Ernst wanted a rider added into the
contract.

'A rider?'

'An additional clause that states you have to lose a certain amount at a certain rate.'

'But what if I lose six pounds one week and nothing
the next?'

'Well, I'm not sure. Possibly you might be taken off the
programme.'

'Really?' Life just kept getting worse.

'Ernst wants me to guarantee you'll lose at a rate of at

least three pounds per week as a safety net. We can sort the minutiae out at the end.'

'What minutiae?'

Esther said she'd get back to Millie on that.

'So I'll be looking forward to a cheque for £280, then?' This was all Millie could think of to say – her wages had now been docked, as well as having a rider and some minutiae hanging over her head.

She realized with a sinking heart that with all the pressure of the colonics, the weigh-in and the cost of the new Spanx shape-wear, she'd missed an interest payment to QwickCash. This meant she would have to pay a penalty fee to them using her already penalized wage . . . On top of that, the mortgage was due in a week. The minutiae had better be small.

'Can we stop for a minute?'

'When we get to that tree.'

'Where? What tree?'

Adrienne was full of tricks like this to keep her moving. Millie prayed for the moment the session would cease. It was still Sunday. She should be watching TV. In half an hour, Millie told herself, Adrienne may well be dead from over exposure to running. Five more minutes and Adrienne will be run over by a runaway buggy. Soon, very soon she will get cramp and be taken away in an ambulance.

Since this was the third training session, Adrienne felt more familiar and, once they were back at the house, went into the kitchen, on the pretext of getting a glass of water, and said to Millie, 'So, I hear you have a conundrum about emotional conflicts – fancy sharing?'

'Who told you?'

'The committee,' answered Adrienne.

'Who's the committee?'

Adrienne was drinking a lot of water. But she was sweating a lot. Millie had yet to move beyond a few tiny beads.

'Who makes up the committee, did you say, Adrienne?'

Adrienne counted on her double-jointed fingers.

'There's Esther, Joan, me and Florence – but she's not being paid, of course – and Harry.'

'Harry?' Millie might have known he'd be involved.

'Is he the weird man we saw on the doorstep?'

'Sadly yes, and what about you?'

'What about me?'

'Are you getting paid?'

'Your weight loss will be my gift.'

'And if that doesn't happen, let's say . . . ?'

'A double-page spread in the *Good Woman* when you reach your target,' said Adrienne.

'And if the target isn't quite reached?' asked Millie.

They looked at each other. Millie knew she would have to find yet more money. No such thing as a free run . . .

THIRTEEN

AFFIRMATION 13:
'I am non-judgemental of my own poetry —
even though I may be alone in that regard'

FRIDAY 4 APRIL

Millie appeared to be in a mild trance at the kitchen table. Florence was seated opposite in Mary's usual chair. She snapped her fingers.

'Just do it, Millie.'

'I can't.'

Millie had been on Ernst's Kraut-tastic Diet for a week. Even her skin smelled of cabbage now, and the house had a definite whiff of indoor rabbit.

'You have to.'

'But it's so . . .'

'You *have* to.'

'Why?'

'Adrienne said you've got to do it every day.'

'That's just her being overly pansexual. Ignore it.'

Florence got up and marched towards the scales.

'This is ridiculous.'

'Don't touch them!' Millie ordered.

'Why?'

'They mustn't be moved. It's their position. Don't touch them.' Millie was feeling unusually protective about her possessions. The night before, she'd listened to a rather chilling message, left by a high-pitched bailiff from the West Country. Barrington Bailiffs would be coming to list her valuables next Monday. If she didn't let them in for any reason, the police would be called.

Millie was scared. She'd missed the deadline of her QwickCash loan by a few days, so not only was she going to be charged fifty pounds but she was going to be fleeced by the bailiffs as well. And while the mother-daughter bonding cheque had paid back a quarter of Harry's fees, and got him off her back (the thought of him being anywhere near it disgusted her), it had been too late.

'You need to confront the weight, Millie. Just do it.'

'I do. Yes.' Millie couldn't bring herself to move. What if the bailiffs broke one of her legs, as their message seemed to imply? There'd be no more trotting.

'You've got two months left to lose two and a half stone. The next weigh-in is five weeks away,' said Florence helpfully.

They both looked at the scales. Millie wanted to scream. She didn't want to step on those grubby scales again. The usual way to deal with this kind of pain had always been to drink or eat, but now, without recourse to either of those, she'd been forced into rediscovering her poetry. It was Harry and Florence's fault for so rudely helping themselves to her private anthology, but now she was almost grateful.

'I wrote a sonnet late last night. It's a way to release some of my . . . you know, pressure stuff.'

'You should try surfing YouTube. That's what I do.'

Millie ignored this. 'Shall I get it?' She didn't want to share about the bailiffs just yet. The shock was too recent. But reading out a poem would be an agreeable release.

'Maybe not now. We need to do this.'

'OK. Actually, you might not like it.'

'Is it like the one Harry showed me?' Florence had bent down to squat by the scales as an act of encouragement. Millie wished she'd get up.

'No.'

'I only like the ones you wrote about the netball girl, and the ones at guide camp. Come on, just step on the scales. We can do a sonnet after.' Florence checked her watch. 'If it's a short one.'

'OK. Yes.' Millie hadn't moved.

'You will have lost weight, Millie. You don't have to be frightened.'

'How do you know?'

'Because you've been training for a week solidly and you're on gherkins.'

'And eggs,' added Millie.

'Sounds nice.'

'Not with gherkins.'

Millie had now done several sessions with Adrienne without cancelling any of them, eaten twenty gherkins, two jars of sauerkraut, countless eggs and much soup. She had also been forced to run sideways, which although different from trotting, did not make her feel like a lithe marine, as Adrienne had promised.

'You've got to do it.'

'I know.'

'It's just you and me here.'

Adrienne had given Millie a notebook to record her weight loss, although weight gain had to be recorded as well.

In the exercise book Adrienne had written, 'Start weight?' Underneath she had written, 'Feelings?' and then underneath that she'd written, 'Water?' with a drawing of a glass, which she had to tick several times. Underneath the tick section was written, 'Forbidden foods?' with an image of a gargoyle crossed out.

'OK, I'll do it.'

'Good, because then—'

'I'll feel like a failure?' asked Millie. She liked to try and pre-empt Adrienne's rhetoric.

'You'll know where you stand,' said Florence firmly.

Millie slipped out of her slippers and stepped onto the scales. She didn't look down. She knew it was going to be bad.

'Don't look yet, Florence.'

'I'm not.'

'Until I say.'

'Just do it.'

'Don't tell Joan.' Millie knew Florence would tell Joan, but it felt good to say it.

'Of course not.'

'Or Esther.' Millie knew Joan would tell Esther.

'God, no.'

'Or Adrienne.'

Florence shook her head but didn't speak.

Millie repeated, 'Or Adrienne?'

'You just write it in the book for Adrienne.'

'OK.' Millie braced herself.

'Now!'

They both looked down. She was eleven stone and eight pounds.

'That's good,' said Florence.

'How is it good?' asked Millie.

'These scales only go up to twelve and a half. Binge-drinking hadn't been invented in the 1950s because people went to milk bars – that's why they all had smaller scales.'

Millie wished Florence would stop rambling.

'Hang on a minute. I'm eleven stone eight?' she asked.

'Brilliant.' Florence clapped.

'That's only five pounds off since the weigh-in, which was eight days ago.'

'That's amazing, Millie!'

But Millie wasn't happy. She was full of resentment about all the denial she'd suffered and all the trotting she'd been put through and wanted more extreme results.

'I should have lost more. I've been on gherkins and trotting non-stop.'

Florence was looking thoughtful. 'Millie, I was thinking . . . did you do anything with Al while I was in the van?' Florence was chewing her lip with concern.

'No.'

'Food-wise?' Florence didn't believe Millie.

'Oh, er, no. I don't think so.'

'No bacon butty?'

'No.'

'Jack and I always had those after we had . . . a session . . . to replenish our protein.' Florence was not giving up.

'I can assure you there was no butty situation, Florence.' Millie decided to look offended.

Then she remembered. After Al had left, and she had stopped crying, she had discovered a batter mix ideally suited for Yorkshire puddings that had been missed during the throwing-out session . . .

She immediately confessed. The batter had provided for about twenty very small pancakes, which Florence said would have added at least two pounds. And even if the pancakes had been made and consumed over a week ago, they might still be a causal factor of the low loss.

Who could Millie blame for the sabotage apart from herself? Her mother had always been there for her, as had her father. There were no unpleasant background circumstances, no violent outbursts and no secrets of criminality as far as she knew. But somewhere at the back of her being was the vague memory of loss. Funny how all the bad stuff came up and bit you when you were ashamed of yourself. And what should she do with her confused, shameful, guilty, *fluttery* feelings for Eugene? Apart from eat things to send them away, or eat things to fill her emptiness? Eating had always been part of her solution, which was now putting her further and further in debt. This was a new and cruel twist. Esther had offered a way out, but even now the habitual self-sabotage was revving up, getting ready to spoil things. She was still in debt, she was still fat, and she was now also sexually all over the place. Which was very toxic.

Her teenage anthology book was still in the hall – Harry hadn't put it back in the filing cabinet where he found it – and there was a smaller notebook tucked inside that she'd have to reread . . .

Millie wrote, 'Eleven stone eight pounds', in Adrienne's food diary, and under 'Feelings?' she wrote, 'Despair', before adding three ticks in the 'Water?' section.

'I think Al's quite keen on you. In a genuine way.'

'What other way is there?'

'My lorry driver?' Millie knew Florence wanted to cheer her up with a nice sharing of her sexual activities, post-implant, but that was in the old days. Before Millie had journeyed to deeper pastures herself . . .

'Oh yes,' said Millie without her usual enthusiasm. 'It's just, you know, Eugene started me off on a bit of a journey of arousal.'

'Didn't you say Eugene studied accountancy?'

'Yes, but he's a very touchy-feely one. Which is rare.'

'But he's over there, and Al's over here. In the Bolt Whole, isn't he?'

'So?'

'So why don't you drop in for a water and just see if you can work up an interest for him? That's the way to move on. Works for me.' Florence drained a glass of water and slammed it back on the table. 'And anyway, fancying someone will help the weight loss,' she added.

'Should I put in about the pancakes?' asked Millie.

'It's done now. I wouldn't.'

Florence suddenly looked upset. She'd seen a text.

'Are you OK, Florence?'

'I just got a text from Jack, that's all.' Florence was looking resigned and upset at the same time.

'Oh.'

'He's met someone.' Florence was trying to be casual.

'You said yourself it wasn't going anywhere, didn't you?' Millie said helpfully.

'But he was such a good lover. I've never had that before. Always making sure about me.'

'Yeah, I know what you mean.'

Florence looked at Millie.

'Did you and Eugene *actually* have sex?'

'I don't want you telling Amelia.'

'It would do her good. She's very judgemental about the implant, and I'm really liking that guy at Pets Need Vets.'

'The simple one?'

'He's Polish.'

'Didn't take you long?'

'You've got to move on, and I knew it wasn't going anywhere with Jack.' Even as Florence spoke the sentence, she went from sad and down to buoyant in one easy gear change. Millie was getting increasingly jealous of Florence's overriding optimism.

'That's got to be the implant talking. I should get one.'

'You might not be eligible. You have to be very depleted. And being suicidal helps . . . So did you, then?'

'We had a sexing of sorts,' Millie admitted.

'Phone sex?'

'Not entirely.' Millie wasn't sure what this was.

'So you didn't.'

'No.'

Florence nodded.

'Do you want to see my HapiFork, Florence? It vibrates,' added Millie.

'Next time? I'm sure it's amazing.' Florence was now late for her shift.

'Sure. Thanks for being here.' Millie was miffed that Florence had been less than enthusiastic about her poems and now the fork.

'No worries.'

'Don't say about the weight to Esther. I'm going to crack it this week.'

'I know you will.'

Millie gave her friend an awkward hug and slipped a few of the loose pages from her sonnet collection – 'Young Adult' section – into Florence's bag. Florence thanked her. 'I'll come out with you.'

Harry saw them and hurried down the path.

As they got into their respective cars, Florence called out, 'Where you off to?'

'The Bolt Whole,' replied Millie.

As Millie started the engine, she could hear him ask Florence, 'Did she say the Bolt Whole? It's lunchtime – danger.'

She could see him run back into his house from her rear mirror.

The Bolt Whole was empty as usual, except for two tables pushed together by a yummy mummies' lunch club. They had hemmed themselves in with a pushchair configuration that blocked access to their table as well as the lavatories. The mummies all appeared to be equally fervent and annoying, and Millie immediately regretted her decision to drop in. She felt conspicuous for not having a buggy. And grateful.

Cara was transferring plates of food from the dumb waiter onto the tables. Millie had never seen her so concentrated and quiet before. It didn't suit her.

It seemed there was a problem with the order. One yummy mummy had asked for a pâté and been given quiche. These were women who got easily piqued. The kind to entice a sense of injustice out of each other and stay outraged together. Cara didn't seem particularly concerned.

Millie sat up at the bar and poured herself a glass of water from a jug. This would be free, she assumed. Al wasn't anywhere to be seen, which put paid to Florence's idea of redirecting her floating desire onto him. But it would give her a chance to read the smaller poetry notebook, which she was now ready to do. If she could tap into her younger self, she might understand what really made her who she was, and learn what she cared about, and maybe unlock whatever it was that Adrienne said was locked. All this might finally enable her to lose the weight and who knows . . . get laid? Run the magazine? Find peace?

All she really wanted was to find someone to go to the cinema with – this would be just fine.

The small notebook was covered in a film of glossy Fablon, and the word 'Anthology' was written in fountain pen across a sticky label, which was placed at an angle on the cover. She flicked through. There was the poem called 'Netball Captain Not Listening'; another was called 'Pain Again'. Millie felt the rush of teenage anguish as if it were yesterday. In fact, the anguish yesterday was almost identical – except she felt it when she was running in the park with Adrienne and all down her legs. It was also unfortunate the rejected plate with the quiche was placed near her nose. How could anyone reject a quiche Lorraine? Cara shouted at someone below-stairs to put some 'pâté on a plate pronto'.

'Busy today?' Millie asked unnecessarily.

'Mummy lunch club.' Cara gestured to the table of women breastfeeding and one quite plain woman wearing very large earphones and reading a Kindle.

'What's wrong with this?' Millie tapped the quiche to feel its texture.

'They wanted a pâté.'

'So who's having this, then?' Millie needed to know. A quiche without a home made her anxious.

'No one. The chef got it wrong and put out a quiche. He's new, Millie.' At least Cara recognized her. Probably for questioning portion size.

'Is Al in today?' Millie could smell the cheese.

The dumb waiter rattled up from the kitchen with a plate of pâté. Cara took it over to the wronged customer.

This left Millie an unguarded moment alone with the quiche. She patted the top of it again and felt herself salivate. She might bark at it if it wasn't removed.

'Yeah, he's just on his tea break,' Cara said as she returned.

Millie eyed the quiche with regret as Cara took it over to the dumb waiter. Should she have asked to take it off Cara's hands? They watched its journey down to an unseen kitchen.

She'd just been given a lucky escape from 250 calories. Millie decided to go to the loo to reflect on the positive outcome of her visit. Maybe an affirmation was nigh. She climbed off her favourite stool and dodged the buggies.

When Millie came back, Cara was looking at her differently. It was as if Millie had changed from harmless fat woman to harmless fat woman with a bit of edge. Then with a sense of dread Millie realized that Cara had picked up the notebook and, worse, had clearly been reading it.

'That's my notebook you've got there, Cara.'

'It's so old!'

'Yeah, well, so am I.'

'But these are great.' Cara seemed sincere, which was half nice and half worrying.

'Are they? Well, I haven't had the chance to look at them, actually, so can I . . . ?' She held out her hand.

'Hang on a sec, Millie.' Cara ducked down behind the bar and produced her guitar.

This was unexpected. She wasn't ready for the high-pitched wailing and nor, she suspected, were the yummy mummies. If they couldn't cope with an erroneous quiche, they wouldn't be able to stomach Cara's torch singing, as heartfelt as it clearly was.

Cara dramatically struck a chord. A baby cried instantly. The mother gave it an olive to suck on.

'Everyone all right for drinks and stuff?' asked Cara.

The mummies assured Cara they were fine. The longer they could stay in the Bolt Whole without having to buy drinks, the better, but Millie had things to do. She started to gather her things together and then realized with a sick jolt that Cara had taken her Fablon-covered notebook and propped it up against the water jug.

Cara started strumming in earnest. She looked over to the women.

'Words from the Bolt Whole,' she announced theatrically.

They murmured encouragement such as 'Lovely' and 'Go for it.' Millie wanted to leave quite badly now. Cara was reading from her book. She broke into an infectious rap and the mummies clapped – clearly familiar with music and movement workshops of any kind.

Your arms are strong, your aim is high,
Your legs so taut, I yearn, I sigh.
You lead the team and let them see
You're there for them, but what of me?

One of the mummies hadn't noticed her breast had become unplugged from the baby at the end of it. Millie was hoping one of the other mothers would slot it back in when she felt a nudge on her shoulder. Al had brushed past her with his tool bag. She leaped off the stool to try and grab the notebook, which was now unguarded, and nearly fell in her panic. Al caught her. He was very close to her. She recovered herself.

'Thank you, Al! Thank you, Cara!' Millie said. 'I'll have that back now, shall I?'

The mummies clapped, thinking it was over, but Cara had other ideas. She held the book away with one hand and said, 'I haven't finished.' She continued:

I watch for you at morning prayers.
You are the cause of all my tears.
Nicola Bennett, netball captain of the A team, upper
   sixth, I love you.

One of the mothers called over to Cara, 'Did you write that?'

Cara replied, 'Not the words I didn't. She did those,' and pointed at Millie.

'That was called' – she checked the notebook – '"Netball Captain Not Listening".'

Millie went over to retrieve the book.

'Well, anyway . . .' She held her hand out, but Cara kept hold of the notebook.

Al was staring at her.

'Blimey, Millie, I had no idea. A word mistress! You should go on *BGT*. With a pen and paper – they haven't had one of those, have they?'

'So shall I take that off you now, Cara?'

'I'll hang on to it and play around with it. I'm a rapper.'

'I thought you were a student.'

'I do that as well, when there's time.'

Millie wanted to leap over the bar and grab her notebook, but knew she couldn't without a chair. And it would look desperate.

'I might check with the owner about running a poetry slam night. Interested?'

'I'll just take my book back if I may?'

'I'll work on it over the weekend. You can have it back then,' she said firmly.

Millie wanted to say, 'Oh no, you don't, young lady,' but couldn't in case it made her sound old in front of Al.

Suddenly, Stan appeared with a ladder.

Millie was flustered. She wanted to leave, but she was caged in by the buggies and now the ladder and two large men with lots of tools. It was all going wrong.

Cara was pleased to see Stan.

'When are the lights going to be finished? The boss asked me to ask. He wants it for a wedding.'

'Not long now, Cara. A week, tops,' said Stan.

'So . . . you like netball, Millie?' asked Al conversationally.

Stan gave Al an old-fashioned look.

'Not really.'

'I used to play badminton.' This wasn't very manly. A thin racket with a flimsy shuttlecock was almost as asexual as chess, as an indoor sport. But she needed to find a hook to move her off the food addiction, so it was worth persevering. She took a deep breath for courage.

'But I was wondering, Al, if we should meet after work?' Millie turned round and there, in a pair of nasty running shorts, was Harry, wielding a thermos of soup.

'Nice to see you again, sir,' Harry said to Al without meaning it at all. Harry put an arm around Millie proprietorially.

The mothers were staring. She was so embarrassed she let him lead her out through the jungle of baby equipment. She was mortified.

'Will you be wanting a blanket, Mill? You might feel the cold with only a gherkin inside you.'

She snatched the thermos and downed the soup in two gulps.

'How did you get here?'

'I ran.'

'Right, so you can run back again. I've got to get to work to get paid.'

Half an hour later Esther hurried out from her partitioned unit in the open-plan office to greet Millie like a long-lost friend. Millie was suspicious. This was not the behaviour of someone who'd been recruiting a committee of Millie's personal acquaintances to act as informers. She smiled back.

'How are you finding Adrienne? I hear she's wonderful.'

'She's all right, Esther. "Wonderful" might be pushing it . . . Any update about Nathan and his "time out" situation?'

'Not as yet.'

'How odd, to just up and leave. And what about the children? Poor things.'

Esther wasn't going to be drawn on her son. Millie knew that businesswomen like Esther didn't cry twice within a short time frame, and certainly not in front of the same person.

'Their mother is coping admirably. I biked over an HD TV this afternoon.'

'How lovely. Did it fit on the bike?'

'It was small. I thought they could do with one.'

'Everyone could. Lucky them to have such a caring granny and step-granny. Is the teenager capable of watching a small TV?'

'I don't know her capabilities, Millie. I'm just relieved she's loved.'

'Indeed.'

Esther looked at Millie's midriff and gave it a pinch, which was sudden and intrusive.

'How are you feeling?'

'I felt that.'

'Any lighter?'

'Any movement on the cheque front for "Me Time"?'

With the pressure of her mortgage and still no sign of the 'Me Time' fee that afternoon, Millie found an anger and a voice she never knew she had. They were in the park as usual when Millie suddenly screamed at Adrienne, 'Stop, damn you! I *hate* this.'

Adrienne stopped.

Millie said, 'Do you mind if I say something?'

'I don't mind at all.'

'You might after I've said it.'

'Training is about taking risks. I do it every day.'

'OK. Well, I think I've become allergic to you.'

Adrienne nodded but looked hurt, which was to be expected.

'It's everything, really. I mean, I can't even stand the sight of your bicycle.'

'OK. That's quite personal, but OK. It's probably associative anxiety.'

'And it would really help me if you didn't speak when I'm out of breath. Which is all the time.'

'I see where you're coming from.'

'I don't think you do.'

'Let's work this out while we trot forward to that bin over there.'

'There isn't a bin over there.'

'There is. Round the corner.'

'I'm not trotting anywhere unless I can see a bin before I trot.'

'The bench.'

Millie could see the bench. She'd done many a thrust on it.

'You said bin.'

'I meant bench.'

'Too late. I've been tricked. I need to say this now. From a stationary position.'

'OK, Millie.' Adrienne looked concerned.

'Right, because I can't be out of breath and listen to you at the same time, and I can't wear headphones because that makes us look as if we've had an argument and I'm not talking to you, and yes, I may well be losing weight, but I can't stand sauerkraut, because it's so bitter and brown and depressing, and I hate sauerkraut more than I hate you, which is quite a lot at this moment in my sad, screwed-up life. Sorry.'

Adrienne thought for a moment.

'Two things here.'

'Yeah?' Millie was shaking. She didn't like confrontations.

'I will agree to be silent *if* you canter for me.'

'What's that?'

'A canter is faster than a trot.'

'I'm not going sideways.'

'No.'

'So when I canter, you won't speak?'

'Agreed. And the second thing is, I can find you an alternative to sauerkraut that tastes nice.'

'What will Esther say?'

'It's still in the cabbage family.'

'OK.'

But the trade-off worked. Adrienne held back on some of her favourite Hindu teachings – such as 'Truth is like a surgery. It hurts, but it cures' – and Millie raised her game to a mild canter for ten minutes before collapsing.

MONDAY 7 APRIL TO WEDNESDAY 9 APRIL

Adrienne decided that as it was ten days since Millie's first weigh-in, she should try something new to 'flick the switch' of emotional change. She arrived with a huge industrial piece of equipment. It had travelled with her on her back from Mill Hill. The new system was called a Diffuser and took up the length and breadth of Millie's work surface. This was not an imposition, as Millie no longer engaged in food preparation other than to boil an egg.

Adrienne sliced a cabbage and placed the slices inside the industrial tumbler and told Millie to open it the next morning. The cabbage had to be specially diffused overnight so that it would no longer look like cabbage.

Millie felt she was witnessing a miracle of metamorphosis in the life of a vegetable. Overnight the cabbage slices had emerged frazzled into cabbage crisp look-a-likes. Millie was in cabbage heaven. In just a few hours she could eat crisps and ditch the vinegarized mush. Adrienne was the first pansexual she'd ever met who could turn sauerkraut into crisps. Millie felt confident that the cabbage crisps were going to really help her hit her target in a month's time. This new crunch facility made her feel that it would be doable.

She was right. Two days later, on the Wednesday, Millie had lost two pounds. She'd even managed to weigh herself unsupervised and felt confident enough to keep her stud earrings on while she did it. Eleven stone six pounds was a result.

She called Esther to tell her the good news, who was so thrilled she decided Millie should be bought a non-edible but decorative gift to mark the moment.

'Do you want to tell Ernst?' asked Millie, wondering what kind of jewellery would be coming her way.

'Let's wait till the second weighing session on 9 May,'

had been Esther's reply, taking great care as usual to mention the date. 'Then we'll have five weeks to lose the final stone!'

Millie felt hopeless. This would be impossible unless she was sawn in half.

FOURTEEN

~

'Gosh, thank you.'

Millie had been presented with a recipe holder as the congratulation gift by Florence, but paid for by Esther. This apparently was one of the least offensive homeware items Florence had been able to cherry-pick from Pets Need Vets that morning. 'Although everything had its merits,' said Florence, keen not to appear critical of her own stock.

'I'm speechless. Why, thank you,' said Millie as if they were all on the set of *The Golden Girls*.

'Congratulations!' said Florence, thrilled at the latest weight loss. The unused Divertimenti recipe holder would, she said, be an ideal accessory to showcase the weight loss.

Millie tried to show interest in the infant cats that had accompanied Florence. There must have been a regression on Florence's part, thought Millie. They were getting far too big to be carted about. But she mustn't judge. Too much. Vernon was sat very still and very close to them and Florence was keeping a wary eye on the cage. They both knew

Vernon could turn. Vernon had wandered into a neighbour's garden a few years ago and head-butted a hedgehog into a quick death, so they all knew what he was capable of.

Joan arrived shortly afterwards for a 'spiritual-mentoring catch-up', asking 'if that was OK with everyone' as she walked into the kitchen. Joan didn't wait for a reply as she was addressing the spirit world, allowing a quick conspiratorial wave to Florence before taking a seat in Mary's chair.

'I've lost seven pounds since the first weigh-in, Joan – I'm eleven stone six.'

'No!'

Millie pretended not to see Joan wink at Florence, which meant she'd obviously been told the news beforehand.

Florence showed her the recipe holder.

'Perfect, Millie,' said Joan. 'The universe needs to know you are trying.'

'And Adrienne,' added Florence. 'She'll be thrilled as well.'

'Actually, guys, I just need to update the stats. If it's going to be in the public gaze,' said Millie importantly as she removed her weight-loss book from its new lectern and started to write in it.

She wrote carefully in the book, before sliding it across the table to Joan, who read out loud.

'10 March, total start weight (before Adrienne) 12st 6. Feelings? Surprise.

'27 March (after 5 days of colonics), 11st 13. Feelings? Dizzy and weak.'

Joan raised her eyebrows but nodded her approval. Not to be outdone, Florence took the book from Joan.

'30 March (3 days with Adrienne), 11st 13. No loss. Feelings? Despair.

'9 April (13 days with Adrienne), 11st 6. Seven-pound loss. Feelings? Psychotic and hungry.'

Millie would have added, 'And scarily rampant with desire,' but wasn't sure if these were entirely food-triggered emotions and therefore might not count.

Florence crossed out where Millie had written, 'Negligible amount of batter,' under 'Forbidden foods?'

'Why don't you write "Happy" instead of "Hungry", so it looks more upbeat?' asked Florence. 'And do you realize something, Millie?'

'Realize what?' Millie was so hungry she could hardly realize anything.

'You're totally on target – you've been on this for a month and you've lost a stone!'

'I don't think she wants to get complacent, do you, Millie?' said Joan, ever conscious of her role as official spiritual mentor.

'There's no chance of complacency, Joan. Not with the prospect of an open prison sentence.'

'What?' Florence was shocked.

'Why?' Joan was suddenly worried. Millie knew this was because a client with a prison record wouldn't look good on her website.

Millie took a sip of water and paused dramatically.

'The bailiffs came round on Monday to list my valuables, and they told me if I didn't let them in, they'd get the police.'

'What did you do?' Florence was alarmed.

'I let them in. I'd already given my valuables to Harry.'

Both women looked shocked.

'They only come round if you fall behind on your payments, and since the loan shark just doubled mine to keep me in debt, the bailiffs came to reccie my items.' There was some relief in saying it out loud.

'You can't go to prison.' Florence looked shocked.

'Bailiffs can't take things that you need,' said Joan firmly.

'You'd have to eat white bread in prison, wouldn't you?' said Florence.

'And they can't take anything belonging to someone else, Millie.' Joan seemed to know a lot about this.

'Oh. I only got Harry to harbour my valuables. He's not keeping them.'

'Just say all your stuff's been donated by a friend,' said Florence.

'Well, it has been, Florence. Pets Need Vets has homed and clothed me like no other.'

'Do you believe in guardian angels, Millie?' said Joan thoughtfully, tracing the wood of the recipe holder with her healing forefinger.

'No.'

'I do,' said Florence.

'You don't,' said Millie.

'Part of me does.'

'Which part?'

'The part that gives me hope.'

'How do you know hope comes from a guardian angel?'

'Because I swapped my day at Pets Need Vets to coincide with the Polish guy, which has made me hopeful.'

Millie was easily agitated, being hungry all the time. She didn't have the patience to hear about Florence's Polish crush.

'Can I offer anyone a mug of tap?'

'No, thank you, Millie.' Joan produced a small bottle from her pannier and sipped it.

'I'll have one if it's going,' said Florence. 'I love tap.'

Millie held a mug under the tap and placed it reverently down on the table.

Florence cradled her mug and they both sipped appreciatively.

'Not being funny, but I'm worried about Harry with your valuables,' she said.

'I'm not. They wouldn't fit.'

'But don't you think you should warn him he might be committing a crime if the bailiffs decide they want them? Is that allowed? They might arrest him if they find out he's got your stuff.'

'Harry said he'd lay down his life for me and I took him at his word. It would be rude not to.'

'Well, if you're both aware of the risk, I suppose that's OK.' Florence still looked concerned.

'I've got no choice. I've seen them on TV. They talk about you in a derogatory way in their van, while they're still being filmed, and then they try and get a shot of the victim going out to her bin with something innocuous like a piece of fish and try and make it look like she's sponging off the State by saying, "Well, she can clearly afford fish, so why does she owe millions to her creditors?"'

There was a brief silence. Millie was still outraged. The women let her fester for a few seconds.

'So anyway, let's focus on the achievements, shall we? Five pounds is the weight of a five-pound bag of sugar, and so far you've lost fourteen pounds, which is—'

'Almost three five-pound bags of sugar.'

'Exactly! You should give a talk at the next Tough Titty. She should, shouldn't she, Joan?' Florence wanted everyone to stay excited.

'Well, at least I can do up my cardigan now.' Millie eagerly demonstrated this new ability, which unfortunately proved premature.

'So we're four weeks into the campaign now, aren't we?' Joan took out her calculator.

'Four whole weeks? Really? Where did they go?' asked Millie in a panic. She had wasted the time.

'You were in Papua New Guinea for just over a week of the four, so you can't count that,' said Florence loyally.

'That was at least four days of the squirts and yet I came back a pound heavier! So baffling.'

Joan pursed her lips. Florence copied.

But that wasn't the real reason Millie was depressed about the week away with Mary. She knew she had short-changed her daughter. She'd forgotten to deliver the hair tongs, which had formed the central axis for the whole trip. She had failed to deliver maternal guidance and she had very possibly ruined the sweet and innocent burgeoning love affair between Mary, a trusted research scientist, and Eugene, a potential political leader of men.

'Then there was the recovering from Papua New Guinea, which took about three days,' reminded Florence loyally, to make up for snitching to Joan.

'In the Bolt Whole,' added Joan pointedly.

'With *Florence*,' countered Millie.

'Who didn't drink much,' qualified Florence, who'd decided to swap sides again.

Joan pressed on with her calculations.

'We all seem a bit tetchy today.'

'Could be lack of food?' said Millie.

'Just going to release some chi.' Joan tapped her calculator fondly. 'It's looking good, Millie. You've got nine weeks to lose only . . . two stone!'

'What?' This was impossible. Millie went to the sofa where she and Al had experienced Vernon's tonguing and threw herself down. She felt defeated. The denial would be never-ending. Nine weeks was a life sentence. Whatever was slowly being lost from her body she was also losing from her brain. She wanted to bite down into a large bap of white bread.

'How do you conjure a guardian angel, Joan?'

'You can't. They just know when they're needed.'

'I could put out some sherry.'

The committee remembered their roles suddenly.

'You haven't got any sherry in the house, have you?' Florence asked.

'No.' Millie almost believed this herself.

'Let me clap the corners for you instead.' Joan sprang into action and clapped the corners of the kitchen with gusto. Florence came over and sat with Millie on the sofa, united in their reaction to Joan's unwavering commitment to feng shui and all its possibilities. They both thought she looked a bit silly.

*

Later that afternoon Millie was leaning in to the computer screen, eager to catch sight of as much of Mary as possible. She had a generous view of her torso. And noticed she was wearing that same vest top again, but she'd like to get at least some of her face, with maybe a bit of hair. Was that a plait she was wearing? That was new. It looked rather childish. Was she regressing?

'Can you crouch down a little? I can't see you, darling.'

'That better?'

'Much,' her mother lied.

'So it's all go this end – since you left, actually.'

'Has there been an official complaint about Richenda?' Millie needed to know that everyone knew her daughter was not only a brilliant scientist but, more importantly, incapable of wrongdoing. The shadow of shoplifting five years ago needed to be replaced with global notoriety and good works.

'She's on leave. I've got the hut to myself. It's amazing.'

The Richenda outrage had clearly lessened in significance since they last spoke, but then the young could forgive each other quickly. Millie had forgotten that. She, on the other hand, liked to harbour a grudge. It came with having a slow metabolism.

'I hope they tell her tutor she's a cheat at whatever technical establishment she comes from.'

'The Bournemouth University.'

'So what happened?'

'Well . . .'

Millie could see Mary's face break into a smile. Mary's smiles were rare and worth noting.

'Yes? Tell me?' Millie felt huge love for Mary today, which was all very inconvenient. She didn't want to feel too much love, because it couldn't be returned – not with all the stuff going on in Mary's important life.

'Well, I heard this morning that my research . . . Got that? *My* research, Mum.'

'Yes?'

'Might be used in the World Health Organization conference.'

'But that's amazing. How did they know about it? That's such an endorsement . . . I'm speechless, and thank God Richenda's not there to steal your thunder this time . . .'

Millie missed the fact that Mary had taken a few seconds to drop out of sight and take a sip of tea. She waded in with a new question.

'So did Eugene hook up with the VPL people after he dropped me off?'

'What do you mean?' Mary's voice was sharp.

Millie realized her mistake and regretted the question instantly. Mothers were supposed to be grateful to be told news. They should have the grace to receive it with fascinated interest, unquestioning support and let it settle, rather than probe so quickly for their own sad agenda.

'There was the International Day of Forests, wasn't there? Which was concerning me.'

'It was fine! Eugene's cousins made a human pyramid so he could get to see some of the speeches.' Here was that tortoise look again, peering round the screen in hurt confusion. Millie sat back in her chair trying to look warmly in control, but she knew she was losing it. She'd have to work hard to get back up to speed.

'Well, I just wanted to know that there was no bomb. Was there?'

'No. It was perfectly peaceful. Why are you talking about Eugene?'

'I'm just checking how you're feeling, darling. About him.'

'Because he's short.'

'Because he's your boyfriend.'

'Oh, I'm not sure about that actually now, Mum.'

'Really?' This was good news.

'He's so jealous about Michael.'

'Michael the tutor from Durham?'

'Yes! Obviously the tutor from Durham! And I can't keep hiding what I'm doing from Eugene.'

'What are you hiding?'

'Don't you start.'

'No, I meant what research are you hiding?'

'I know what you meant.'

'Do you?'

There was an awkward silence between them. Millie had lost track of what she meant and what Mary meant and who was hiding more. It looked like Mary was weighing up whether to continue the conversation. But Millie knew if she flounced off, she'd have to pick up from where she left off another time, which was not so convenient when one was in a Third World country, and she probably wanted more praise about her research.

'It's not about you,' was all Mary would say.

'Of course it isn't, darling! So who's going to hear the research first? I mean, what happens? That's so amazing!'

'Yes, so my tutor—'

'The one from Durham?' Millie needed to focus. Neither of them wanted any slip-ups.

'Of course the one from Durham. Where else? I'm talking about my course tutor.'

'Yes, and he's . . .' Millie prayed for a short second and then it came to her. 'Michael?'

'Michael Morris. Exactly. With the glasses. So Michael wrote to the research guy here, who you met.'

Millie nodded. Another test. She couldn't remember anyone's name from the settlement. There'd been a lot of research personnel who would have been told about her violent explosion in Mary's hut, and she'd rather avoided eye contact with anyone after that – all of which hindered recall.

'Oh yes, I remember him.'

'Graham.'

'Graham. Was he the kind man who offered me his Imodium and a towel?'

'Yes – don't worry, I washed it.'

'Oh God.' More mortification.

'Well, Michael's got this sudden funding from the Medical Research Council and will give a percentage of it to Graham over here if they use my data for global conferences like the one coming up for the World Health Organization.'

'Wow. So many "if"s.' This sounded wrong. 'Which is such a strong position to be in, Mary. So many possibilities for so many people using your data.'

'I think they want to use my research methods mostly, and use how I've noted the local resources and set up my lab testing – that kind of stuff.'

'They would do, yes. That makes sense.' Millie nodded.

'So I'm coming back.'

'What?'

'I'm coming back.'

'What?'

'What do you mean, what?'

'With Eugene? Will he be coming?' She'd done it again, and just when she'd gained a bit of leverage.

'Why?'

'On all those planes? Help you carry bags and whatnot.' This was silly and they both knew it.

'I've never needed anyone to carry bags.'

'I know, and that's what makes me so proud of you, apart from the other things.'

The tortoise eyes swivelled, scanning the screen for signs of distress.

'How are you, Mum? Are you OK?'

'I lost fourteen pounds.'

'Money?'

'Is that a joke?'

'No? Why?' Mary looked defensive.

'I've lost fourteen pounds in weight. Can you see cheekbones?'

'Where?' Mary seemed genuinely puzzled.

The Skype call had not been one of their better ones. Change was afoot and she needed to be ready. Millie took the hidden sherry bottle from under the sink and poured some into an eggcup. Prior to this moment sherry had been the unfortunate drink of choice at the Silver Lining Care Village in Hythe, where her mother now lived – and was only drunk to be sociable with the Camber Sands Singers, who came to offer a medley of arias on a Sunday afternoon. Today it was her absolute favourite.

She'd put the bottle in the fridge and try it with ice next time. Joy.

THURSDAY 10 APRIL

Adrienne and Millie were walking back to Millie's house at what Adrienne described as a brisk pace. Millie called it rushing. Millie was in a relatively good mood because the cantering was over and so far no one on the weight committee appeared to have discovered her sherry bottle.

She'd meant to get Mary's definition of a pansexual, but they'd got side-tracked with the malaria and Mary's pending visit. She wasn't clear if Eugene might come at the last minute. The spare room had an Argos clothes rail and a Swiss ball, which wasn't very inviting. Or would Eugene sleep in Mary's room? It was directly above hers. She would be able to hear their every sigh and whisper, which was alarming. Such thoughts had to be banished.

Millie smiled at Adrienne and then quickly regretted it because Adrienne smiled back at her. A smiling trainer wasn't really something one wanted to encourage. They might take it as a sign that the client was actually enjoying themselves. But she was relieved to be away from the park and to have respite from having to look at a sea of determined-looking people in tracksuits running in unbearable pain.

Luckily, they had reached the house and she could get rid of Adrienne and resume her life.

Typically, Harry had timed his heavy-duty garden work on the front lawn to coincide with their return from the park. He was busy mixing some cement to sink a sundial into the grass next to his son et lumière water feature. He excitedly waved a trowel at them as they walked up the path.

'Look ahead,' said Millie out of the corner of her mouth to Adrienne, as had become customary.

When they were parallel with each other, Harry looked at Millie and saluted with the trowel. The sun was out, Harry was bare-chested, and today's yoga pants were bright orange.

'Looking good, I have to say, Millie.'

Adrienne couldn't resist the compliment. Millie was a source of great pride to her.

'Isn't she! We lost five pounds last week, Harry – that's fourteen pounds so far.'

'Snap! We lost five pounds the week before, didn't we, Millie? With my colonics.'

'Do you do colonics?'

'I pay for them.'

'You said you'd be OK if I paid you back the last bit later? I should get the Kleinne Fett cheque this week.' Millie looked vexed. Harry winked at them both.

'Do you want to see my sundial?'

Harry had been practising. Now that he was sure of their attention, he quickly jumped behind the plinth to cast his shadow of a large phallus onto a rather crude sundial face. There were other images interspersed round the clock face that, from a distance, could pass as Hogarth caricatures, but closer up resembled crude figurines with saucy appendages.

'When the sun casts a shadow over the cyclops, a woman comes out of hiding and shows her—'

'Thank you, Harry. Rushing past now.'

Millie gave Adrienne an encouraging shove forward, as she appeared to be wavering.

She whispered, 'It's not clever or original, Adrienne. I've seen these in Homebase. Ignore him.'

Adrienne turned to Harry and said, 'I'm sorry, Harry. My client has asked me not to comment, and she is my priority.'

'Snap again.'

.

In the kitchen, the two women competed to see who could finish a full mug of tap water first. Millie won. She knew Adrienne had let her.

'I heard that you wrote some heart-rending poems when you were in the guides, Millie. Could I perhaps hear even a little bit of the poem?' Adrienne asked in her coaxing way.

'So do all the fat committee know about those?'

'We're only sharing our information to find the best way to help you. If I knew what turned you on, I could stop the desire to eat, you see.'

'It's already stopped. My feelings about gherkins are dead. I've closed down. I'm going mad.'

'And I can stop you going mad.'

'How?'

'The power of empathy. It's my specialty. Ask the other Tough Titty ladies about my programme. I need to know what drives you, Millie. What presses your buttons?'

'My buttons haven't been pressed for a long time, Adrienne, except for once quite recently.'

Adrienne was dangerously close to the fridge. With horror Millie saw the tragedy unfold in slow motion.

'Let's just remind ourselves what's going on with your diet, Millie. I'm sure we can vary it.'

Adrienne opened the fridge and surveyed the contents before closing the door quietly. Millie dared hope she might have missed the sherry bottle nestling in the side where the eggs and butter used to be and the fridge de-odorant now was.

'I see you already have varied it.'

Millie looked away in shame, but still wasn't entirely sure she'd been rumbled. She played for time.

'How?'

'The Sherry Diet?'

Adrienne opened the door again and placed the half-full sherry bottle on the table. Millie acted surprised.

'Oh, that sherry. Yeah.'

It was a sweet Harveys Bristol Cream.

'There's not much left. Do you want to finish it?'

'Seriously?'

'Yes, go ahead, drink it.'

Millie took the bottle and was about to swig from it, when Adrienne said, 'That's 136 calories per glass, eight glasses in half a bottle, totalling 1,088 calories – more than a day's worth of food and guaranteed to add three pounds to your weight status, but go ahead if you want to set us back another week from your target. It's up to you. Enjoy.'

Millie stared at her.

'Oh, do what you will with it.' Millie felt like a tragic Shakespearean heroine defeated in battle and in love.

Adrienne took the sherry, uncorked it and poured it down the kitchen sink. It made a glugging noise, which was slightly embarrassing for both of them. When it was empty, Adrienne turned and held her arms out to Millie.

'If you can make yourself humble, you can win the war.'

'I'm not interested in being humble. Ever.'

'You would be if it helped you lose weight.'

'And I hate you. That was a vile act.'

'You gave me permission.'

'You forced me.'

'Listen. The sherry has shown us something. It's a sign we need to go raw.'

'I'm not eating anything raw that has a face. Or hooves.'

'I'll keep it green. I'll bring a selection of irresistible samples over tomorrow.'

'You can't. It's my canter-free day tomorrow. I've booked it.'

'I have to set you up with a week's food.'

'But I won't be in.'

'OK. I'll leave it with Harry in a freezer box. He can drop it round.'

'Please don't involve Harry. I'll pop back at midday from my important day job.'

Adrienne walked over to her and put both her hands on Millie's shoulders. She looked at her intently with those cold, searching blue eyes. She'd put some blue liner inside the lids, which made her eyes look smaller, but Millie wouldn't tell her that. Let her make her own mistakes. She'd just wasted some perfectly good sherry.

'I knew this was going to happen, luckily.'

'Did Joan get a tip-off via the spirit world?'

'I knew the cabbage was going to get to you sooner or later. Don't feel guilty. It's about low blood flow.'

'So it's just my blood?'

'But we can fix it. I've booked you into a workshop tomorrow to get it increased.'

'Where?'

'Finchley. A wonderful couple I know run it.'

'But it's my day *off* from cantering.'

'You won't be cantering.'

'What kind of workshop is it?'

'It's called "Tantric Sex", but don't let the name mislead you.'

Millie was speechless. How could she not be misled? A tantric-sex workshop could only be comprised of tantric sex in a workshop. What else could its constituent parts be made of?

'Does Esther know?'

'Yes. She's in complete agreement.'

'She's not doing it with Ernst, is she? At the same time? I don't think I could stomach that.'

'No! It's just you and whoever you want to take with you.'

'Can't I go on my own?'

'It's a couples-only thing. They have to work in pairs.'

'Maybe they could lend me somebody's other half whose other half didn't show up?'

'It's not policy.'

'Sounds very strict.'

'They use a pairing formula to get the pulse up. Once it's up, I promise you'll be burning more fat. It's fixed like a thermostat.'

'Who shall I take, then?'

'Harry?'

'Is that a joke? Don't answer.' Millie looked at the sofa. 'Al's an electrician. He might come.'

'Sparks may fly.'

Millie didn't like it when Adrienne made jokes. In fact, she hated her all the time now.

Millie called Al on his mobile. Stan answered.

'Al's phone.'

'Hi, Stan. It's a bit last minute, but can you ask Al if he's free to go to an evening class tomorrow for a metabolic workshop?'

'Ask him yourself, Millie.'

There was a bit of muffled noise and she could hear Stan say to Al, 'It's her. Tell her you can't go. She wants you to go to an evening class.'

'Hi, Millie?' Al was breathless.

'Tell Stan I heard that, Al, would you? So can you come? It's a class,' said Millie.

'So what is it again, then?'

Millie sensed she was going to have to sell it a bit more.

'It's just a tantric evening class. To do with getting the pulse up.'

Al repeated in a muffled voice to Stan, 'It's a get-your-pulse-up class, Stan.' Then to Millie he said, 'Is that round here?'

Before she could reply, she heard Stan in the background.

'Why doesn't she do a spin class like everyone else who's a big bird? They get to sit down as well.'

Millie didn't like Stan. But she needed someone to go with.

'I'll be there, Millie. Look forward to it. Text me the address,' said Al with restrained excitement.

FRIDAY 11 APRIL

The day of the tantric workshop was later called Foul Friday by Millie. After a gruelling canter with squats in the morning – Adrienne had 'popped round to surprise her' after all – Millie went straight on to the *Good Woman* office only to be told she had to assemble her 'Lovely Things' column in four hours to meet a deadline that had been brought forward because Esther had forgotten to tell her the original one. Esther was still distracted by Nathan's disappearance, as well as needing to be available for Ernst's requests from Munich to 'face-chat', and as a result she was becoming forgetful.

Millie had recently discovered her new power over Esther. She had taken Esther aside one afternoon at work and very quietly explained her position. She wasn't blaming Esther directly, she had said in a troubled voice, but by not being given enough commissions at the magazine, she was now being placed at risk of uncontrollable nocturnal binge-eating, which was jeopardizing her weight loss. Esther was worried.

Millie added, 'Don't take it personally or anything, but I really think if you gave me more work, I might lose more weight, as I won't be comfort-eating in my sleep, which I do when I'm upset.'

Millie resented Esther profiteering from her weight loss – and felt more than justified with a little blackmail.

This was how Millie came to be under pressure in a

jewellery shop in Hackney, setting up a photo shoot for the magazine still looking rather sweaty from her morning squats. The owner thought Millie was a jogger needing directions and had to be convinced she was a proper journalist before allowing her to take any photos of his merchandise. Millie hurriedly took photos on the office camera of the handmade necklaces of broken bits of porcelain and silver welded together and wrote up her column in the office before racing up to Finchley for the tantric session. She was so rushed she didn't have time to think too much about what she was doing, but in the back of her mind she did start to wonder why she was driving herself, voluntarily, to a couples-only tantric-sex workshop on her own.

It wasn't until she was halfway up the Finchley Road that Millie realized she'd left her mobile in the jeweller's.

The Alhambra Centre was to be found in a white-painted coach house that nestled discreetly off the main road. A quick sniff under the armpits told her that she had been pushed very hard in the park that morning, but here she now was – ready to have her pulse raised again. She hoped Al wouldn't read too much into it or mind her slightly rum aroma.

The word 'tantric' might be misleading, but she hoped he'd be fine about knuckling down and getting his pulse raised and set like a thermostat, as Adrienne had promised. And anyway, who else could she pair up with? It was Al or Harry.

At least she was becoming more open to suggestions from the fat team. She would allow them their profit and concentrate on her loss. It was Friday and she was still eleven stone six. She needed to be nine stone six in two months' time. Not out of the woods, but at least she was in the park, as Adrienne might say.

So Millie arrived reconciled to the hard work that lay ahead. This was when Foul Friday really began to be foul. In the doorway of the coach house was a familiar figure . . .

Harry looked a little uncertain as Millie drew her car up and parked. For a second she considered driving straight into him, but stopped herself. She parked and then repeatedly banged her head on the steering wheel instead.

'I know what you might be thinking, Millie,' Harry shouted through the closed window.

She reluctantly allowed herself to be coaxed out of the car and gently patted on the back as she held on to the bonnet.

'How could you?!'

'Al came round in a jitter just over an hour ago.'

'Why?' Millie looked up.

'He said he couldn't get you on your phone, and nor, funnily enough, could I.'

'That's because my phone's in the jeweller's. Idiot.' Millie spat this out.

Harry explained that there had been a small fire at the Bolt Whole and that Stan was away in Leeds with the van. Al was being put under pressure to sort the wiring before the owner came back. His wiring might have been the cause of a minor explosion.

'That's just an excuse!' said Millie. 'Anyway, why are *you* here?' This could not be happening. Harry? Tantric sex? Finchley? This was beyond her worst nightmare. What if he sneaked in some senior yoga moves? What if he proposed?

Millie knew she couldn't do it. She couldn't sit cross-legged with Harry in a tantric evening class that neither of them had been to before without some form of sedation. It was sheer madness.

'I can't do this with you, Harry. It's out of the question.'

'I can understand that, Millie, but Esther had a word with me, which changes things.'

'How?'

'So, the class officially comes under the contractual auspices of the Kleinne Fett weight-campaign requirements. If you don't do it with me tonight, Esther said she'd have to deduct a sum from your next instalment, because you'd be reneging on the agreement whereby you agree to burn calories as a show of commitment.'

Harry tried to appear a bit shamefaced to be the bearer of this bad news, but failed because he was too excited about being Millie's plus-one.

Millie knew that Esther would stop at nothing to earn her commission. She would have no qualms about humiliating her if it kept them all on target.

'Hi!' The voice was warm and female.

A plump redhead in an Indian tunic and baggy trousers came out to greet them.

Millie straightened up from the bonnet and wiped the tear-wet hair from her eyes.

'You must be Millie. Everyone else is here. Come up – we've got herbal or builder's, so there's something for everyone!'

Millie and Harry stared at the woman. She did not look like a tantric person at all. The large glasses and painter's smock made her look more like she might run an adult education institute where they did a lot of the arts subjects.

'I'm Kahina,' the woman told them with a Glaswegian burr, 'and yes, it does mean "warrior princess" if you were wondering.'

Kahina shook their hands warmly and led them inside. She patted Millie on the back for extra reassurance. Millie shuddered at her touch.

Harry whispered in Millie's ear as they mounted the stairs, 'Al didn't want to let you down. He asked me personally to stand in for him. Just imagine I'm Al.'

Millie screwed her face up in disgust. Her ear felt soiled where he'd whispered in it. This wouldn't work for her.

'Well, at least you'll get your pulse raised. He said he didn't know what else to do.'

There could be no backing out. Kahina led them into a sparsely furnished sitting room. A group of four introverted-looking couples in loose clothes were sitting on beanbags sipping mugs of tea in silence.

The leaflets on the coffee table said, 'Intimate couples evening, 11 April.' Most people had one of these in their hands. Millie began to worry she might have holes in her socks. A swathe of silky material undulated beneath a circle of twinkling mauve candles in the middle of the floor. Little camping seats had been placed invitingly round the candles.

Kahina was now sitting cross-legged next to a chubby man who, they soon learned, was called Ray. The first task, once balanced on the little stool, was to go round the circle and say something positive about their partner. Millie froze. She just needed to get her pulse up, that was all, and then get it set on a thermostat for future, optimum weight loss. People were offering up some strange facts about their partners. One pair said they were first cousins, which gave Millie hope that she might not be the only platonic member of a pair. This was dashed later when Millie caught them snogging in the tea break.

When it came to Millie's turn, she said, 'Hi. This is my neighbour and he . . .' Harry was looking at her intently. 'He has a sundial that attracts a lot of interest. Mostly when the sun's out, obviously.' Everyone nodded, which was a relief. She'd have hated it if they had shaken their heads in disbelief.

Harry said, 'This is Millie and I love the way she walks.' He then spoilt it by adjusting his testicles immediately after he'd spoken, which made people look suspiciously at him even though they continued to clap.

'People are staring,' whispered Millie, disgusted.

'Why?' Harry whispered back, interested.

Millie ignored him.

Foul Friday got worse. For the next exercise, each partner had to face their partner, close their eyes and imagine they were seeing each other for the first time and offer a compliment. Kahina walked around the room to listen in and nod. Millie knew there would be no escape.

Harry's compliment was, 'Nicely shaped eyebrows.'

Millie was struck dumb. Kahina was hovering on hand to help any couples who were floundering. She rushed over at this hesitation.

'Are you stuck?'

'I am,' said Millie. 'Sorry. I seem to have channelled a painful French trip to Dieppe when I was fifteen.'

Kahina nodded understandingly.

'Don't push it. If it doesn't come, move on to something else. A childhood birthday party perhaps?'

Millie's failure prompted a general chat whereby Kahina told the group that people went on their courses for many reasons. She looked pointedly at Millie. 'Either because they feel they've become too busy with life to just "be" with each other or perhaps it's to pop back a bit of "sparkle" or even to combat a bad body image.' At this point the whole group looked at Millie with kindness. 'Increasing the blood flow to the brain is the only way to unstick you, unpick you and unzip you.'

Nervous laughter followed. No one had said 'tantric' yet. Perhaps 'unzip' was getting them close.

The compliment section resumed. Harry was very comfortable with this. While he listed her qualities, Millie switched off and focused on a wall tapestry of a knight. She shut her eyes. This had been a warm-up. Kahina and Ray stood up, adjusting their loose clothing in case any bits could be seen, and addressed the room. Ray spoke for the first time. Millie was surprised to hear a Midwest drawl.

He said, 'You know something amazing? Intimacy can also mean "into me", you see.'

After this revelation he invited the pairs to stroke each other's hair. Kahina warned this was to be just a 'gentle stroke' rather than scalp-buffing, which elicited a small laugh from the group. As Harry didn't have much to play with, Millie successfully negotiated a pass on this exercise.

Kahina and Ray then moved into the 'workshop straddle'.

'You'll all need to get down on the floor for this one,' Ray explained as he did so himself. Kahina lowered herself, cracking a few joints on the way down.

She began talking the group through this manoeuvre.

'Either the female can have her legs over his or he can have his over hers. Or – surprise! – you can have one of each on top, as we are doing.'

No one moved.

'And straddle!' announced Kahina to get the group started.

Millie was officially in a very dark place now. Even the colonic, at its deepest point, was preferable to straddling Harry. She knew she needed a shower because of the stressful day, and held her breath so she wouldn't have to draw any conclusions, adverse or otherwise, about Harry's state of hygiene. Ignorance was bliss.

A drumming CD was now playing through the speakers and became louder. Perhaps this was the preamble to the pulse raise and soon they could all go home. Each pair was to stand up from their straddle and do a bit of gentle stamping if so inclined. Kahina suggested individuals might want to verbalize. Millie suggested she wouldn't, and told Harry to keep anything verbal to himself.

From the new standing position, Harry got busy trying to align his behind with Millie's, to adopt Kahina and Ray's back-to-back position. They had to give up due to the height discrepancy, and waited till the group were on to the next exercise.

Then came the moment they thought they might have all been waiting for.

'The tantric concept,' Kahina explained, 'is really another way to describe weaving.'

Person A was to stand to the side of person B and put their hand on the base of B's spine. They were both to breathe deeply together. A was to put their hand up and down B's 'genital space area', and A and B were then asked to swap. That was the weaving part done.

Kahina and Ray then did a bigger, bolder, more confident weave, which got them very hot and panting in a forced and embarrassing way. The group copied them. Even Millie found her pulse raised, and could almost forget the fact that Harry and she had their hands on each other's bits. Although not completely.

For the next ten minutes the room was awash with highly raised pulses and panting and drumming until finally Kahina and Ray looked at each other's third eye and bowed. Their work was done. Ray sneaked a couple of what Millie assumed to be blood pressure pills into his mouth. Kahina patted him affectionately on the head. She wondered if Kahina would be quite so affectionate if Ray suddenly keeled over and died from a heart attack.

An old speaker was tucked in the corner with a large handheld microphone balanced on it next to a box of tissues. Kahina grabbed it to begin a wind-down speech. Xylophone music played softly under her words. The section repeated itself on a loop.

Kahina walked round the room and whispered, 'You can be what you are. You are what you can be.'

Millie wondered if anyone ever asked her to clarify what the riddles might mean, but was beginning to feel too drowsy for a debate.

Ray took his cue from Kahina and led people into the centre of the room and encouraged each person to fall, one by one, into a collective heap. He was surprisingly forceful. Blankets from the side were thrown over each person to keep everyone 'held'. A grubby pillow landed on Millie's face, and she chucked it off in Harry's direction. Millie could feel her hair being stroked by one of the cousins and Harry's sockless foot rubbing up her calf. There was no escape. She was trapped by the sheer number of other bodies. As the xylophone played on, a soporific trance descended on all parties. Millie's head began to loll on Harry's chest.

Kahina carried on with her soft clucking. 'You are all open beings. When you are with others, you can be open or closed. You can dance the tears of joy or sadness, but know this: you have now been opened.'

Whether she had been opened or closed, one thing was for certain: Millie felt thinner. She must have shed two pounds in sweat alone.

FIFTEEN

AFFIRMATION 15:
'You are beautiful. No really, you are.
Believe that, and you will believe anything'

SATURDAY 12 APRIL

'Ten more, please. *Really* push this time.' Adrienne was staring at Millie's rear like a concerned midwife. 'Come on, Millie – you can do it.'

'I *am* pushing, funnily enough.' Millie was especially cross. She'd lost one pound. She was eleven stone five. She knew this because she'd weighed herself when she'd got back from Finchley. All that panting with Harry just to see off a meagre pound.

A jogger with a double buggy whizzed past, offering a cursory nod of acknowledgement to Millie's plank position attached to the bench. Millie spat at him mentally. His wife would be having a facial or a macaroon lesson. She was being made to genuflect to a bench.

'Millie?' Adrienne squatted down to deliver her warning. 'The more you hang on to your emotions, the more the fat just sits on your tummy.' Adrienne prodded Millie's stomach with her index finger. It sank in quite far.

'I thought we could take some photos of you for the next weigh-in. That's a month away, isn't it, on 9 May?' Adrienne said, trying to appear casual.

'Could you not do that, please?' Millie was feeling very sensitive today. She'd nearly cancelled her weekend session and needed a bit more respect from Adrienne, especially on a Saturday, when she would see people in restaurants drinking wine on the way home.

'Sure.' Adrienne withdrew the double-jointed finger and made it do a forward somersault to show she wasn't offended.

'But if you lose a stone, we can do the article as a teaser with just some bullet points about how you lost the weight and then end with a "will she, won't she do it?" tag line. The readers will be hooked, Esther thought. With me in it as well. If that's OK?'

'It's all about you anyway.' Millie rolled over onto the grass. She screwed her face up to demonstrate the agony and the effort of the exhausted athlete.

'Millie, your emotions are stored in your stomach,' said Adrienne, and rolled her back again to haul one leg over her shoulder.

But Millie said, 'You said emotional eating's in the mind.'

'I said you can *control* your *mind*. Change legs,' said Adrienne as Millie allowed her other leg to be wrenched out of its socket. 'You see, the fat gets *stored* in the *midriff*. The older you get, the more it sits. Last five, Millie.'

'Could you not be such a doom-monger?'

'Three weeks ago you wouldn't have been able to say that, Millie.'

'I would, actually.' Millie felt duty-bound to correct yet another lie.

'You couldn't talk *and* exercise when we started, could you? And you haven't used your spray today either! That's a result!'

'I left it at home.' Millie was pleased to be able to spoil Adrienne's bubble of optimism. It was her only pleasure this morning. Any other day she may well have marvelled at the fact that she could now trot and talk without collapsing in a heap, but today she was traumatized. Millie wanted to be left alone in a dark room to recover from the Harry pairing.

'The more TV you watch, the more fat lands on your stomach, you see.'

'That's just stupid. That's like saying . . .' Millie couldn't follow through with an example at this precise moment.

'It's empirically proven.'

'Then I'm an exception to the rule.'

'If we can reduce the *stress* in your life, we can reduce the *fat* – I promise. You can get up now. Good job. High five.'

'I'm all right, thanks,' said Millie, and refused to high-five her torturer. She readjusted her scrunchie in a sulk.

As they walked rapidly back to the house together, Adrienne looked at Millie with affection and love.

'You should think about going back next Friday. Your thermostat will thank you.'

'If I think about it, I won't go.'

Millie winced at the memory of Harry astride her legs and looking eager as he pulsed.

'So, apart from the raised pulse rate, which is amazing

by the way, and really made a difference to your energy, what else would you say you got out of it?'

'Humiliation?'

'And?'

'Isn't that enough? Don't pry.'

'OK, let me ask you something else . . .'

'Can't it wait? There's a small swatch of nori and chopped carrots waiting for me at home that I need to assemble before I pass out.'

'Do you think you're ready?'

'Who wouldn't be? I'm starving.'

'You're ready to go raw. You wouldn't have been before. But once you're raw, all the humiliation in the world – your words, not mine – will be worth it and you'll never hit the sherry again. Trust me.'

'Why did you say "sherry"?' Millie was pleased to notice a flicker of uncertainty cross Adrienne's face.

'Because the sherry is a thing of the past.'

'So why did you say it? You've just put me on a raw food diet. You've just filled my fridge with boxes of cut-up root crops and a jug of miso tincture that smells of damp nappies as if that's a nice thing. And *then* you said the word "sherry"?'

Millie had been very unsettled by the sherry incident and they both knew Adrienne had made an error in referring to it. Adrienne needed to up her game. She put her hand on Millie's elbow to stop her walking. She looked very grave.

'Millie, I understand your feelings about the sherry. I get that. But you've got just over eight weeks to shift nearly two stone.'

It was Millie's turn to look grave. She nodded.

'So! You need to let go of the anger.'

'OK. How?'

'This is what you do. You say, "I forgive you." Do that with me. Let's just do it here.'

'What, here?' Millie looked around nervously. They were outside the newsagent's.

'Say, "I forgive you. I love you. I'm sorry. I thank you."'

'All of that?'

'Yes.'

'In which order?'

'Any order. Just say it. Look into my eyes and say it.'

Millie looked around to make sure the coast was clear of anyone she knew – and also of anyone she didn't know – and had a go.

'I forgive you. I, er, I love you. I'm sorry. And what was the last one? Oh yes. I thank you.'

'Again!' instructed Adrienne.

Millie repeated the mantra. Adrienne was now sporting a beatific smile, the kind of manic grin that came from drugs or madness . . . which in Millie's view was dispro-portionate to her achievement.

'See? It attracts good energy! Feel better?'

Millie nodded, which seemed easier than a lie.

'If you can forgive those around you, you cut the stress and reduce the bulge.'

'I'll forgive Al on Monday, OK? I need a day off.'

'Perfect.'

They'd rounded the corner. Since Friday Harry had moved his rotary clothesline onto the front lawn. This was so he could time his washing to coincide with Millie's arrivals and departures.

'What about Harry? That would shift a lot of—'
'Rome wasn't built in a day. Walk on.'

MONDAY 14 APRIL

Millie called Al to suggest they meet at the Bolt Whole to carry out the forgiveness plan. She also thanked him for the five-page letter, which she figured must have taken him all afternoon. Al told her it had taken him all day.

Al's essay, which had been posted through her door, left Millie in no doubt about the extent of his contrition or valiant attempt at joined-up lettering. He ended with a plea: 'Believe me, if I could turn back time and rewire the narrow-beam spotlights behind the deer's head from green to red rather than red to green, then Millie, I would have.'

For now, Al's wish to turn back time and rewire the Bolt Whole would have to be parked. She had other, more achievable, goals to see to. Her next task was to forgive Al *spiritually*, to shift some fat *physically*, and then maybe, once she was thin, attraction would follow. And if Millie could really make herself attracted to Al, it would pave the way for a new life. One where she was not fat, not in debt and had a bloke to go to the cinema with.

More worryingly, she had less than four weeks before the next weigh-in, on 9 May. She needed to have lost a stone to liberate the next £6,666. With that money (minus Esther's precious 15 per cent) she could knock the loan shark on the head, sort the house and get her roots done in a salon and stop colouring in with a wax crayon. The deadline for repayment of the double interest to the loan shark was two days ago, on 12 April, so she was due another penalty. Unless the money was in from Kleinne Fett, the bailiffs would have no qualms about emptying her house without notice.

It was just a shame the next Tough Titty Supper Club's debate evening wasn't sooner, because she could have done with some support in this area. Pat's email was full of promise. A visiting speaker was going to debate the statement 'Ladies, beware of making men happy.' The second speaker would then ask, 'Silencing of women? No thank you. Discuss.' Pat had added in at the bottom of the email, 'Tough Titty members are asked to remain for *both* talks out of courtesy. Q and A compulsory.'

More worryingly, Millie had recently received an email from Eugene telling her that Mary had gone off him and asking if he could see a photo of Millie's orbs as a souvenir. These were, in her opinion, her breasts, which would confirm his inappropriate interest. Eugene's request would have been a good area to bring up with the supportive Tough Titty ladies. Or perhaps she could raise it with Al without spoiling what they had. Either way, the orb request remained unsettling and needed tackling. And more important surely was Mary's welfare. If she had gone off him, what was going through her mind? Millie needed to be there for her.

After Al's wiring emergency, the Bolt Whole looked as if it had been given some kind of makeover. One wall had been so smoke-damaged someone had been inspired to draw graffiti on the black surface in pink and green. Millie was so taken with it she began writing an article about the wall in her head. She'd call it a 'happy accident' since the smoke-stained exposed brickwork transformed the Bolt Whole's ethos of 'suburban try-hard' into confident 'industrial design'. She would force Esther to devote two pages of the magazine to feature the wall and include a whole range of designer wallpaper to complement it.

The window seat had remained intact, although it looked slightly damp. It must have taken a hit from the fire extinguisher. Millie might sit on it later with Al. She hoped the forgiveness exercise wasn't going to take too long.

Cara seemed unusually pleased to see Millie.

'Hey, babe,' she said.

Millie looked behind her. No, this greeting was meant for her. And she was going to get that notebook back if it killed her.

'Hey,' Millie replied.

'So you heard about the fire?'

'I did. Any fatalities?'

'No one's come forward as yet.'

Cara handed her a bowl of olives. Millie handed them straight back.

'There were real flames, but I localized them, luckily.'

'That was brave.'

'Not really. Just used a damp cloth and a squirt of foam.'

'Clever you.'

'And then I got Al to come and sort it.'

'Quite right. He caused it, so he should fix it.'

'I didn't tell Farzin.'

'Who's he?' Millie did not know a Farzin, but she

wasn't going to spend too much time on a person she didn't know. She needed her poetry back.

'The owner.'

'I expect he'll love that wall now. It's really got character.'

Cara was surprised but pleased.

'I might feature it in my magazine. The one I write for.'

'Cool. And there was me panicking! I said, "Al, the Bolt Whole's on fire. It's your fault – get over here."'

'Understandably.'

'But he said he was going to a tantric workshop.'

'Yes.'

'And then when he said it was with you, I thought he was joking.'

'I did ask him, actually. It's part of my diet plan.'

Cara stared at her.

'I might tell my mum. Is it like ceroc?'

Millie didn't want to talk about the tantric workshop with Cara. Or anyone. She was still in shock and really wanted her poems back.

'A bit of a departure, if I'm honest, but not entirely wasted as an investment in cardiovascular empowerment. So where's my notebook, Cara?' Millie needed to get the business sorted before Al arrived.

'It's in my bag.'

'Where's your bag? I'll get it.'

'It's right here. Do you want to see something on my iPad?'

'Maybe after you give me the book.'

'Just have a listen. Go on.' Cara looked so excited Millie couldn't resist. And she didn't want to appear any duller than she felt.

Cara's iPad cover reminded Millie of young people, and Mary. She experienced a pang. Mary had the same one, with signs of the galaxy on it. It had been a birthday present. Perhaps one day, when they were all relaxed, she might tell Mary about her confused feelings, and they would laugh about it together. No, she wouldn't do that at all. Ever. If Mary found out about the key-ring-licking moment, or the more recent request to see her orbs, she would disown her. She didn't want to die alone in a care village.

Cara placed one earpiece in Millie's ear and one in her own. Millie put on her reading glasses and began looking at murky footage of Cara sitting on a stool with her guitar. She could hear a build-up of rhythms and chanting and much drumming. Millie had never heard anything like it. Then she recognized the words.

> *Your arms are strong, your aim is high,*
> *Your legs so taut, I yearn, I sigh.*
> *You lead the team and let them see*
> *You're there for them, but what of me?*
> *I watch for you at morning prayers.*
> *You are the cause of all my tears.*

> *Nicola Bennett, netball captain of the A team, upper*
> *sixth, I love you.*

Millie was speechless. Her teenage poem had been used in a rap. The YouTube clip showed Cara, dressed in black pencil jeans and a wool hat, rapping for all she was worth about Nicola Bennett. Cara was very proud to tell Millie that 'Netball Captain Not Listening' was also being seen as a message of the third wave of feminism from a small, recently formed group in the south-west.

Millie was on the fourth viewing when Al arrived, still wearing the singed cream jacket and holding out a small bedding plant.

It looked as if Al had been rehearsing a speech for Millie. He was mouthing some words. When he got close enough to them, Cara and Millie both heard him say, 'Millie, my letter may have said too much, but you might like to know that I grew up on a farm.' He stopped, as the two women were so obviously engrossed in watching something on YouTube.

Cara held out the bowl of olives to Al as she had done to Millie. Millie could see they were on good terms.

'Evening, both. No, thanks, Cara – just had my tea.'

He put the plant on the bar counter next to the olives.

'Where did you go?' asked Cara. She took out her earpiece. Millie quickly filched it so she could have a better listen of her poem. It sounded very impassioned the way Cara did it.

'Just down the road. Nearly burned my mouth off with their soup. Might tell them next time.'

Al looked in a bit of pain around his mouth. It was certainly red.

'I would,' Cara agreed, 'or at least threaten to sue.'

Millie wished they'd be quiet. She'd taken to shaking her head back and forth as she'd seen Cara do in the clip. She caught sight of Al looking at her, expectantly. Reluctantly, she took out both earpieces to give him proper attention. All the excitement of 'Netball Captain Not Listening' had made her forget the forgiveness challenge.

'Hi, Al! How are you?' Millie was in shock. If Nicola

Bennett ever knew this was on YouTube . . . What if she had children to protect? No, that would be unlikely.

'I'm well. I brought you this to say sorry.' Al picked up the plant from the bar and held it out again.

Cara said quietly to Al, 'Take it out of the . . .' She nodded at the bag.

Al took the mean-looking flowerless shrub out of its flimsy bag.

'Thanks, Al.' Millie didn't think a cactus was the kind of plant you smelt a lot, so she just put it back on the bar. 'I might have to put it in the garden if it's got spikes. I'll check with Joan.'

'Is Joan your daughter?'

'No. Spiritual diet mentor.'

Al did not appear to recognize the title and asked, 'What are you watching?'

'"Netball Captain Not Listening,"' said Cara, as if that were sufficient.

'Rap version,' added Millie and flicked her hair.

'Have a look,' said Cara.

Al looked at the rap clip. He was impressed. But Millie knew he would be. She was sure Al liked art; it was just he hadn't been given the right opportunities to appreciate it.

'Netball's having a real comeback, isn't it?'

'I need to forgive you,' said Millie.

Al looked happy about this.

'No need, Millie.'

'I need to say, "I thank you. I forgive you. I love you," and what else?' Millie wondered if she'd left anything out.

Al looked overwhelmed.

'No need, Millie.'

'I'm sorry.'

'I mean it, Millie. There's no need.'

'No. I knew there was one more thing I had to say . . . which is, "I'm sorry."'

'Oh. You've got nothing to be sorry for. It was me.'

'No. Me. I'm sorry. I thank you. I forgive you. I love you. So shall we leave it at that?'

'I'm happy to. If you are. It's quite unexpected.'

'I really, really forgive you.'

'Good.'

'No, I mean, I really, really, really, really, really . . .' Millie had to force herself to snap out of it before she put herself into a trance. Trevor used to get most put out whenever Millie froze during a row and became inert. 'I forgive you.'

'Yes, that's fine, then. No harm done.' Al decided to take charge. 'Would you like to go for a walk?'

'Not really, Al. My muscles are knackered.'

'Did they work you hard at the workshop?'

'I'd rather not talk about it, Al. I had to take *Harry*, remember?' Millie said the name 'Harry' with so much venom she even surprised herself. 'But I forgive you. Obviously.'

'Yeah, got that, thanks . . . Shall I take you home?' Al was concerned.

'I've got my car.'

'I've got my van. We could go for a cup of tea.'

'I'd have to have a tincture of miso.'

'Do you know where they do that?'

'Yes.'

'Where?'

'My house.'

'I'll come with you and walk back.'

'As long as you know you're forgiven, do you?'

'I do.'

'Light-bulb moment, guys,' announced Cara. She raised her hand theatrically.

The others waited.

'Do you want to be patrons of the first "Words From the Bolt Whole" poetry slam session?'

'Not unless I get my notebook back.'

'It's actually at home.'

'You said it was here,' said Millie.

'I'll text you. Have I got your number?' asked Cara.

'I can give it to you.' Al stepped forward with pride. 'I've got Millie's number.'

He tried to make this look suggestive with a wink. Millie decided not to pick up on it. She couldn't rush things.

It was dark when Millie and Al got back to Millie's house to take the tincture. There had been a delay. She had run out of petrol, which she'd told Al had never happened to her before. He would have to hitch a lift back to his van, drive to a garage, fill his can up with petrol and then drive back to her car.

Millie assured Al she would be better off waiting in the van. She'd done too much exercise already. And it would give her time to get to know the World Service, which was one of those things she'd always intended to do, and here, oddly enough, was her chance. But once Al had left her, she forced herself to read Esther's contract for the first time. She'd asked for a copy to be forwarded to her iPad. Ever since the bailiffs, Millie was making a new effort to read all printed matter, no matter how hostile, and had set everything up electronically.

She began making notes, but she gave up after the third reading of the same sentence. It was too depressing. She needed to be ten stone six on 9 May, which was three and a half weeks away. More importantly, she needed to get the rest of her first instalment off Kleinne Fett or Qwick-Cash would triple her repayments. She offered up a precautionary money affirmation to the universe: 'In this moment I have all that I need.' Adding a 'namaste' for extra punch. And logged into her bank account.

A miracle. The money was in. Even without Esther's commission, it was enough to cover the mortgage, the extra loans and some bills. But this sent Millie into another panic – if she didn't lose the weight in the next three and a half weeks, she'd have to pay it all back and be worse off than before.

The only empowering action available, given that she was currently stationary and trapped inside a vehicle, was to rip into the citrus laxatives bought for an emergency such as this one. She chewed a few. And then a few more until she'd finished the packet. They tasted like pear drops. As the minutes passed, Millie prepared herself for the fact that she was now going to have sex for the first time in years by way of a thank you to this kind man who liked too many takeaways for his own good. And perhaps unwisely, she had just consumed very nearly a whole packet of laxatives.

Millie turned to Al and hugged him. They were in the hall. She gave it a few seconds to test a reaction before she pulled away. There had been a small surge in the silver bowl area. It was as if her body was greeting a long-lost friend who had popped back recently and was now making a return visit. There was a slight sparking in her abdomen, and a release of endorphins she usually associated with the licking of icing on a ring doughnut. At least the body was responding. On the other hand, it could be hunger, which would not be helpful. Al had been some time and Adrienne had told her hunger could inhibit her natural serotonin levels and desire. But that might have been a trick to make her do more push-ups. As they walked hand in hand towards the kitchen, Millie began to explain to Al that in her opinion it was only fair to share how anxious she was about any potential intimacy, but, and she wanted to emphasize the 'but', she also wanted him to know about the recent attentions she had received from a man overseas called Eugene, who also knew her daughter, Mary, very intimately, and that she had become aroused by him, but only fleetingly.

She only stopped speaking when they both heard a noise from the kitchen.

Al sharply instructed Millie to turn off the hall light. She did so. Through the window at the back of the house they could see a flashing torch and a pair of hands feeling their way across the windowpane.

'Who's there?' said Al masterfully.

If it was a burglar, the chances of a reply were slight, but Millie was glad she wasn't alone.

The French doors were immediately unlocked.

'I heard a noise,' said Harry.

Millie turned on the lights. Harry was standing in a

towelling dressing gown jangling the ring of Millie's house keys, which he'd never posted back.

There was an outraged yelp from the floor. They all looked down and there on the carpet was a rather annoyed-looking Mary encased in a sleeping bag.

Before anyone could say anything, Millie let out a restrained moan.

'It's only me, Mum. No need to freak.'

Millie looked around to see if Eugene had accompanied Mary, but the sight of her child suddenly reacted badly with the citrus lozenges.

'Excuse me,' Millie said, and buckled slightly. Al and Harry rushed forward to envelop her as she groaned again.

Millie broke free and headed left to the downstairs loo.

'Not again, Mother!' screamed Mary. 'What is wrong with you? Is it me?'

Millie came back into the kitchen looking flushed but upright.

'I think it was a number of things,' she began conversationally.

Mary's hair was not looking its best and she looked very cross to have been so rudely awoken. She must have been on a lot of aeroplanes and Millie felt very sorry for her. She had been asleep and was now sitting up at the table, in her usual chair, looking a bit bewildered. Harry gallantly took off his towelling dressing gown and draped it around her before she could refuse. This was kind. Mary's vest and shorts were quite minimal attire for a family gathering. This left Harry naked apart from his trim boxers, which prompted Al to take off his puffa jacket and give it to Harry.

'Tea, anyone?' suggested Al.

'There isn't any,' replied Mary. 'I found something that smells like the sea if anyone wants it as a hot drink?'

Millie walked as normally as she could over to the kettle.

'Miso flakes or fig tea? Digestive beverages suggested by my trainer.' Millie was keen to be sociable with her liquids.

Al turned to Mary, who was looking wide-eyed with tiredness. He shook her hand.

'Pleased to meet you, Mary. I'm Al.'

Mary nodded slowly.

'We bought you an ashtray in the market. I'm Mary.'

'Damn, I forgot to give it to you, Al.' Millie felt rather awkward. She'd forgotten where she'd put it. There was also an unusual amount of body in the room. These weren't ideal circumstances to introduce Mary to a possible new male friend of her mother's.

'What did you bring me back, Mills?' asked Harry as he got up from the sofa with enthusiasm, Al's jacket swinging open and free just short of his navel. It was almost endearing that Harry embraced life equally passionately whether he was clothed, unclothed or in Al's clothes. 'I think the Toblerone got lost in translation by all accounts.' He winked at Mary. 'You know what she's like with the choccy, bless her.'

Millie went off him quickly. Did Harry have to shame her so cheerfully? How could he profess to love her and do that?

Mary raised her eyes to heaven at the sight of Harry's torso. Millie took charge.

'Harry, can I ask what you were doing in my garden just now with my keys? Can I offer you a housecoat?'

'I heard a noise, Millie. I felt it to be my duty to check.' Harry looked reproachfully at Al and Millie. 'I won't be needing a housecoat, Millie.'

'Where were you, Mum?' asked Mary. She was still cross.

'On a dual carriageway waiting for a can of petrol.'

Millie suddenly came to her senses. Her daughter was home.

'Mary! Welcome home! I wish you'd told me you were coming. You're here!'

Millie went to give Mary a hug, which Mary allowed for a few seconds.

'Is it for the research meeting? How exciting! Tell me everything. Mary's going to be big in overseas development, Al, and yes, I'm very proud!'

She went forward for another hug, which Mary nearly returned, and then she pushed her mother away.

'What were you talking to Al about on the way in?'

'Why were you on the floor in the dark?' Millie countered. Had Mary heard anything about Eugene? This would be very difficult.

'Because Michael's allergic to Vernon.'

'Michael?'

'Michael Morris. He's in my room. Vernon doesn't go in the bedrooms, does he?'

'He didn't until Harry looked after him. Now Vernon seems to go everywhere.'

'He's a lot happier for it, Millie. Can't you tell?' asked Harry gently.

'I don't spend too much time with Vernon, to be honest. Where is he?'

A male scream from upstairs told them where Vernon might be.

Everyone rushed out into the hall. A thirty-year-old man in a pair of pyjamas was peering down at them, gripping the banister. He was having difficulty breathing and was scratching his arms, which were covered in a rash.

'Mary,' the man gasped, 'I think perhaps your mother's cat *had* been in your room.' He waved weakly at the group and gasped again.

Mortified, Millie sprang into action – as best as she could.

'Harry! Get Vernon out of Mary's room. Michael, I'll get you my asthma spray. Hang on. I'm so sorry!'

Harry called out to Vernon, who seemed pleased to see him amid all the chaos, before disappearing under Mary's bed. Michael was concentrating on his next breath while putting on his glasses.

Once Millie had given Michael her asthma spray and he'd taken several deep puffs, he began to breathe more normally. Harry coaxed Vernon out from under the bed and then wrapped him in a towel for some reason that no one could quite fathom but were too panicked to ask. It was an emergency.

Millie was contrite.

'I'm so sorry, Michael. How do you do? I think we might have met in Durham once maybe. Can I just say that Vernon's never been in Mary's room ever?'

Mary looked accusingly at her mother.

'Did you put him in there?'

'I never put him anywhere. Why would I do that?'

'I don't know. Why would you?' Mary looked at her mother for so long Millie had to look away. Had she heard her preamble with Al?

'It must be since Harry's had him. He's trained him to be curious and sly –' Millie glared at Harry – 'like his temporary carer.'

'How do you do, Millie? I heard a lot about you from Mary.'

Michael looked more relaxed now that he could actually breathe and had put on a T-shirt.

Michael gave Millie a firm handshake, which she rather enjoyed. Here was a man who was suitable and well brought up and not weird in any way. So far. Millie thought he had a kind face. Intelligent – especially with the glasses. Neat and not too obtrusive.

'He hasn't heard anything about you, Mum. I've hardly mentioned you at all, actually.' Mary looked sullen and small.

'I'll get some calamine lotion for you, Michael.'

'I'm sure I'll be all right. But thank you. I hope you're OK with our sudden visit? We've got a big day tomorrow.'

'Really big, Mum. So we need to rest.' Millie was aware Mary was still accusing her of cat-poisoning her tutor.

'What are you doing tomorrow? Is it the malaria conference? Gosh, that must be very important. For you both. I'm so sorry about Vernon.' Millie felt she should demonstrate her hosting skills by asking lots of key questions. She liked Michael.

'The university got an urgent call from the Overseas

Development team last week, and then I got hold of Mary and said, "We need your data!"'

'For the World Health Organization conference. I might be speaking!' Mary was too excited to be too mean for long.

'It's all a bit vague, but we need to be there. These chances don't come twice.' Michael seemed excited as well, but in a more composed way.

'God, no. If at all! Wow. And the . . .' Millie was struggling to understand and sound intelligent, 'the conference is when?'

Millie loved this new energy in her house. And it had nothing to do with food or arousal.

'Well, we need to be at Westminster at nine.'

'In the morning? Yes, obviously.' Millie looked around for some inspiration. Everyone seemed to be expecting her to sort out the chaos Vernon had caused.

Harry came to the rescue.

'Tell you what, Mill. If Al takes Vernon to his place, and I take you to mine, Michael – I'm only next door – then we've all got a fighting chance of sleeping before tomorrow.'

No one could find anything wrong with this plan.

Harry loved to be needed.

'You can stay at mine tonight, sir.' He put an arm around Michael's shoulders.

'That would be very kind.' Michael didn't seem to mind being slightly cradled. He was too relieved.

'Excellent plan, then!' Millie clapped. Harry had saved her. Unnerving but nevertheless timely.

Michael smiled shyly at all of them.

'I have to say a few minutes ago I thought my dreams were going to evaporate in a crippling attack of asthma! I'll just get my stuff.'

He turned to go upstairs. Mary followed him.

'I'll take Vernon with me, then. Have you got a cat box?' Al looked resigned to a night in the van with a cat. At least they weren't strangers.

'Somewhere. I'll find it. Do you mind, Al?' Millie asked.

'No.' Al wasn't convincing.

Millie smiled at him. Al really was very kind.

Michael came downstairs carrying a large briefcase. Mary put her hand on his arm. 'You can leave that here, Michael.'

He shyly removed a toothbrush from the pocket.

'Perfect. I'll be round at eight, then?'

'Brilliant.' Mary smiled back, and Millie thought she looked as pretty as she always did when she was being nice.

There was something in the way they looked at each other. Millie couldn't be sure. Vernon had been dispatched with Al in a dusty cat box with two tins of tuna. She would find out. Harry and Michael disappeared next door while Millie and Mary got ready for bed, for the second time in Mary's case.

With everybody out of the house at last, Millie felt safe to take off her blue-black mascara. Mary was sitting on the bath and working her way through a box of Celebrations chocolates she'd bought in duty free. Sweet wrappers were scattered on the floor. Millie disapproved of this behaviour but was too scared to say anything parental in case Mary took the sweets away.

'It's a really big meeting.'

'How big?' Millie was now plastering a generous dollop of Crème de la Mer onto her neck. She'd eaten one mini Bounty, one mini Topic and was after a plain chocolate slab.

'Well, first there's a drug company who wants to look at the data over coffee. Oh my God, it's going to be so exciting.'

'What is?' Millie was also excited. She stole another mini Bounty.

'Coffee in the House of Commons? Hello? So we do the posh drug company before we do the *lunch* at the Overseas Development Institute and meet this MP who's giving this paper on making it a safer world.'

'You're making it a safer world.'

'No, he is. That's his paper.'

'Amazing.'

'I wish Michael didn't have that rash.'

'It will be gone by tomorrow. I gave him my spray.'

'Really? Thank you, Mum.'

'What are you going to wear?'

'Clean jeans. I packed some.'

'Can't you use some of your old clothes if it's going to be on the news?'

'Like a girlie girl, you mean?'

'No, but someone who doesn't look like they've just finished cleaning the latrines.'

They laughed. For the first time in ages. Mary offered her mother the box of chocolates and shook it at her.

There were three each. Millie ate them quickly and without pleasure, knowing that whatever she'd lost would now have come back. Worse, Mary had brought gin into the house. Mixed blessings.

SIXTEEN

⌒

AFFIRMATION 16:
'I am building my social circle slowly.
Soon I will involve people'

TUESDAY 15 APRIL

As Millie stepped on the dreaded scales, she was forced to observe that even five sachets of citrus fructose laxatives couldn't quite counter the effects of a few gins and a handful of Celebrations the night before. She'd put on two pounds, making her eleven stone seven, which would mean hiding from Esther, who would doubtless charge her £200 for the unfortunate gain. There were now three and a half weeks left to the next weigh-in.

But Mary deserved a normal breakfast.

She put on an apron to celebrate Mary's homecoming and to prove to Michael that she had one. It had been at the back of the airing cupboard with a few other items of household linen her mother had palmed off on her before upgrading to Hythe. But the apron, thought Millie, should now get an airing. She tied herself into the cherry-themed baking pinny. It felt odd and not just because it had 'Queen of the Kitchen' embroidered across the gingham.

It felt sacrilegious to be celebrating a kitchen when for the past few weeks she'd been emptying it of all food.

Michael Morris would be used to a normal kitchen, perfumed with toast and percolating coffee, and serenaded with the authority of Radio 4 . . . She liked his sandy-coloured hair and neat beard. The hair wasn't cropped like Ernst. He was normal. Even his glasses were understated. And she had to face it, a fridge sprinkled with miso flakes, miso tinctures and nuked root vegetables did not scream normal.

She had to find a breakfast from somewhere and make the kitchen smell warm and toasty and welcoming. It was a quarter past seven. They were leaving to start their very important day at eight. Millie grabbed her keys and drove as speedily as she dared towards Sainsbury's. Mary was her life. She had to do this and get back in time to dress the kitchen without them guessing the lengths she had gone to. Given the early hour, Millie didn't think one of the empty disabled spots would begrudge her a quick loan.

Once inside, Millie felt herself fall at the first hurdle. The artificial air of freshly baked bread hit her as soon as she rushed past the buckets of rubber plants and reduced fruit. She couldn't fight it. This wasn't about Mary anymore. It was about her. She had to get to the bakery at the back of the store: she needed to consume dough urgently. Even a sliced Mighty White would be acceptable. The cash she was using for bread would probably cost her three pounds in weight, which would equal a £300 fine from Esther, but she didn't care. Her nostrils were alive. She would starve again tomorrow. There was time to shed eighteen pounds in three and a half weeks. Millie broke into a trot and a canter as she had been trained to do by Adrienne and bought twenty calories in credit. Adrienne would be proud. Perhaps if she took home a half-cooked French stick, she wouldn't be tempted to tear into it in the car. On the other hand, if she could happily tackle raw pastry, she knew she could gnaw her way through a semi-baked French stick.

Her lack of control in the aisles showed how much she'd depended on the support of Florence and Adrienne, who'd delivered food to her door. As Millie piled her basket with bread variants, the early-bird Easter eggs on the opposite aisle caught her eye. She swiped two large ones and rushed to the till. Her mission accomplished, she arrived home to find Mary and Michael seated at the kitchen table deep in an important conversation.

They made a nice tableau, thought Millie – heads bent together and full of the same purpose. She felt a twinge of jealousy, which was quickly supplanted by the need to inject a breakfast smell into the kitchen. She hoped Mary hadn't gone on to her emails. It was all going so well. No one needed a jangly reminder about Eugene.

'Morning!' cried Millie cheerfully, revealing only a slight undertone of nervousness. 'Don't mind me.'

Michael removed his glasses and stood up politely.

'No. Don't get up.' She hauled the toaster out of its hiding place and shoved some crumpets in it before she'd removed her coat.

'You look lovely, Mary.'

Mary had taken her mother's advice and plundered her teenage wardrobe for the conference. Millie thought she looked surprisingly fashionable in a blazer teamed with a pair of gym shorts worn over a pair of her mother's support tights.

'Why are you wearing Granny's apron?' asked Mary.

'Because I might make a roast later if you two were thinking of supper.'

'A roast?' Mary looked puzzled. Her mother had never made a roast.

'Or a cake, if Michael's got a sweet tooth. A lemon drizzle?'

'My mother's a writer, Michael,' Mary said as if to explain away this eccentricity.

Michael nodded.

'A food writer?'

Millie felt flattered at Michael's attention. Al wouldn't have made such a connection. But then Al had just sheltered her cat – she shouldn't be so disloyal.

'I write for the *Good Woman*. It's a women's magazine.'

'Of sorts,' added Mary. She wanted to be proud of her mother, but she couldn't quite manage it.

'We're big in Dubai. Sixty thousand readers and rising.'

'Really?' Michael seemed to be genuinely interested in everything anyone said, but then he was an anthropology person as well as a tutor in global awareness, so he would be – if she could remember her conversation with Mary in the bathroom last night. The gin had made things a bit hazy, but she remembered Mary admitting she quite liked Michael's height. Neither of them had mentioned Eugene.

'There's a sizeable Somalian community in Dubai, isn't there?' asked Michael.

'Is there?' Millie had no idea. 'Actually, Michael, they sell a lot of their craft-ware in my friend's shop.'

Millie chose to omit the name of the shop.

'And will you both be wanting to –' Millie had to force herself to say the word – '*eat* . . . when you come back?'

Mary glanced at Michael.

'Shall we text you after the conference, Mum?'

Millie could see that Mary had no intention of spending too much time with her mother.

'Gosh, yes. Don't worry about me. This is the least important part of your stay. So exciting about meeting the minister who's making the world safer. I think I've seen him on television. Grey hair and glasses.'

'That's everyone in the Cabinet,' said Mary smugly.

Millie forgave her. After all, she had a new man to show off to at her expense. Let her do it.

'True. Yes.' Millie forced the crumpets out of the toaster by shaking it upside down but realized there was no butter. She arranged the Scotch pancakes on a plate to alternate with the crumpets and placed it casually on the table.

'Mary, have you got your uni paper packed?' asked Michael.

'I have, Michael.' Mary was twinkling at him.

'She's very efficient,' said Millie, a little possessively.

'I know,' said Michael. 'I want GlaxoSmithKline to see her early work – as backup for the Young Scientist Awards shortlist.'

'You've only got one shot at it, haven't you – good thinking. And how was it at Harry's, Michael? Comfy? Or scary?'

'Comfy.' Millie could see he felt this was the right answer.

'He's a summer naturist, but apart from an injunction

order, there's little we can do . . . Hot water this morning for you, Michael? I seem to have run out of Barleycup. Do you like Barleycup? Otherwise, I've only got fig tea, which no one seems to like, do they?'

'I've never had it, to be honest.'

'I only ask because if you'd tasted Barleycup first, it's a great way of appreciating the water after.'

'Perfect!'

Millie poured hot water into their mugs. There was an awkward pause. He was probably very aware and grateful that Millie had loaned him her asthma spray, which would tie them together forever. The fact that she'd said he could keep it as a spare might have gone beyond, she hoped.

'Harry's very spiritual, isn't he?' said Michael.

'Are you thinking about his yoga bottoms, because if you are, don't let those fool you.'

Millie uttered this last sentence to herself but partly to see if the young people were listening. They weren't. She was hung-over and ravenous, which had been triggered by the bread. Mary and Michael, on the other hand, were busy working out how much research material they should reveal and what kind of malaria data could be turned into a sound bite that would link them personally to the research without undermining the drugs company. They didn't want the MP ripping off their hard work either – it was all a bit delicate by the sounds of things. So much so they might decide to stay in a hotel and work it all out the next night between themselves, and she could be left in peace to finish the gin.

*

The young people had gone, taking with them an encouraging amount of luggage. By midday Millie sank onto the sofa and assessed the new height of her stomach. She was glad Mary couldn't see her doing this. And she was glad she seemed so happy with Michael, even though it meant she'd have to get used to sharing her all over again with someone else. Her stomach had definitely risen. She was measuring it with an old ruler she'd found in a vase of dead biros. The stomach had grown into a peak, fermenting, she assumed, from the cheap yeast used in the semi-cooked French stick she'd eaten in the car. Florence rang. She wanted to drop round for a chat.

'You can, but I'm not in great shape,' warned Millie. The ruler showed that her stomach was now at eight inches tall.

'You can manage the tap yourself, can't you?' Millie was too depressed to get up again having let Florence in. She sank back with horrified fascination at the rapid growth of her midriff. It had bounced up into a ball shape.

Florence poured them both a mug of water and told Millie the reason for her visit was to report on a secret meeting.

Millie sat up and tried to forget about the unwelcome phantom pregnancy.

'Who was there?'

'Everyone.'

'OK.' Millie nodded. 'Hit me.'

Florence took out a pad of notes to refer to and shook her head. Esther had been on FaceTime with Ernst and had learned a few new and very worrying facts.

'He's married?'

'No.'

'He's gone bankrupt?'

This wasn't the problem as far as Florence was aware. Apparently he'd booked his flight to the UK for the penultimate weigh-in, but would cancel the flight *and the fee* if Millie didn't demonstrate progress by adhering to the new rider.

'I'm on it! Jeez. I'm losing as we speak.'

They both looked at the ball stomach. Florence looked doubtful.

'Ernst wants to know you've taken his rider on board.'

'So anal,' said Millie. 'I'd never heard of a rider till recently. Now it's all anyone talks about.'

Florence, as ever, was fully briefed.

'Esther said you need to have lost a stone before the next meeting, on 9 May, which is three and a half weeks away.'

'I know that,' said Millie.

'But did you know you've got to lose at least three pounds for the next three weeks or you won't be on target?'

'Don't say "rider" again, please. Anyway, who's going to check my Rider Rating? Is he going to fly over and gauge the actual rate of my loss? That's against my human rights. I lose when I choose.'

Florence shrugged.

'I'm just the messenger. But Esther said unless you lose at the rate required, you'll be chucked off the campaign and have to hand back £6,666 to Ernst as well as Esther's commission.' Florence checked her notes. 'I think she let you off her commission for your advance, didn't she?'

'So generous,' said Millie.

'But there's a lot at stake here, Millie,' said Florence, checking her notes again.

'You mean Adrienne's double-page thing in the magazine might not go ahead? And what about Joan? What's she going to be denied due to my refusal to lose at the precise rate of a laboratory mouse?'

'She's got a new website to pay for, hasn't she, and she was on an unpaid two-week trial as your mentor,' Florence reminded Millie diligently.

In spite of the unpleasantness at being talked about, Millie remembered her manners and thanked Florence for being so loyal as a friend and asked for more information gleaned from the meeting. Florence was relieved to unburden what she could remember, and referred to her notes when she needed to. Apparently Ernst was worried there still wasn't a celebrity on board. He'd been hoping for a member of the royal family. Then Esther had shared that she knew Eamonn Holmes on a personal front, and although not royal or female, he might fit the bill in every other regard, and might do it if the wife agreed. There was also an outside chance Cilla Black might agree to a fat suit for the photo shoot, but this was of course just an option at this stage.

'A fat suit?' Millie was amazed. Things must be desperate.

'To be fair, I think she's got worries about Nathan,' said Florence.

'Haven't we all. He's a talentless git. Living off my earnings.'

It appeared that Nathan had taken a lot of Esther's

private money from a personal account and was now in Spain spending it. Esther was worried because she needed to pay her team, keep the magazine going and keep Ernst on message. In Florence's humble opinion there might be some chemistry between them.

'Yeah, I'd noticed that. Ages ago.' Millie's stomach had gone down. She could see over it now. This was promising.

'And then Esther told everyone she didn't think your willpower was quite there, and what did we all think.'

'What did you all think?'

'Adrienne said she dreams about you.'

'And?' Millie stood up to stretch and wondered if she should try downward dog position. She decided against it.

'That she wants you to go back to the tantric class next Friday.'

'I don't discuss that.' Millie slumped back on the sofa. 'Ever.'

'Fair enough,' said Florence. 'Then she asked if any of us knew a doctor, and none of us did, and that's when Adrienne said she'd do a gastric band.'

'Were you all drinking?'

'Esther got us all a skinny latte.'

'Adrienne insert a gastric band? You're mad.'

'I agree. And Joan said they'd ask for medical qualifications for that kind of interventionist work, but Adrienne said she was trained in gastric band hypnotherapy.'

'Is she?' Millie finished the water in her mug and held it out for Florence to refill.

'Apparently. She studied at the Gastric Gift Clinic.' Florence took the mug and refilled it slightly huffily.

'Where's that?' She remained doubtful.

'Marbella, but her accreditations are recognized across most of Europe. I asked if it worked and we all agreed it's going to be a combination of everything, isn't it, so that's where we are at now.'

Florence handed her the full mug of water.

'Where?' Millie had got lost.

'You and I are going to have a virtual band fitted by Adrienne – virtually.'

Florence nodded and sat next to Millie on the sofa. She seemed tired with all the reportage about Adrienne.

'OK . . .' Millie wasn't convinced. 'You as well?'

'Yes, and then Esther said we all had to go on this intense retreat in the country somewhere – for free. It'll get publicity for Ernst.'

'Wait a minute. We're going on a retreat now?'

'Yes. In Glastonbury. Some of the buildings are on a ley line apparently.'

'Why are we going on a retreat?'

'So you'll be denied your food triggers, while we all die of boredom.'

'Is that the plan?'

'Yes. Then she asked what weight you were, which is what I've got to tell her now.'

'Look at the book.'

Florence stood up. She looked even more tired now.

'You've got to be ten stone six by the next weigh-in, which is the 9th, which is twenty-four days from now. Oh, I forgot.'

'What?'

'Adrienne told Esther there'd been a glitch – that you should be eleven stone six, but that you had an emergency relapse with some sherry. So you might now be eleven stone seven or eight, and that's when Esther had a tantrum and said you'd ruin us all, and then she and I had a row.'

'Really?'

'Yes, and I told her to calm down, and she said I was Miss Goody Two Shoes because I wasn't being paid, and I said, "Well, if you don't think I should be here, then I've got places to be." And then Joan told me to stay, and then Esther told me to stay because I was your best friend.'

Millie didn't correct Florence on this.

'And then I told Esther that Mary was really clever and might be coming over for a conference about world malaria and Esther got a bit annoyed and didn't believe me, and then I told her Mary was a postgraduate research scientist in vaginal hygiene.'

'In what?'

'Is that wrong?' Florence looked surprised. Millie didn't have to feel guilty about Amelia now.

'Yes, but never mind. Thanks for sticking up for me.'

'And then she admitted that Nathan was a failure even if Mary wasn't – and I think she was jealous.'

'God, what didn't happen at this meeting?'

'And the upshot is, we've got to get you hypnotized by Adrienne and get you processed mentally on this retreat before 9 May. Ernst is going to be there but not Lulu because, Esther thinks, she's got ME.'

'Conveniently for Esther.'

Florence nodded.

Millie measured her stomach with the ruler again. It had gone down another inch.

WEDNESDAY 16 APRIL TO SATURDAY 19 APRIL

And this was how Millie came to be reclining in her darkened sitting room with Florence and a smell of ether. She was being told she was going into a deep sleep. Millie was relaxed on one chair with her feet propped up on some magazines, and Florence was on another.

Before they began the virtual gastric band programme, Adrienne asked both women to sign a contract saying that they trusted what was going to happen and that they were in agreement about everything. They were, so they signed.

Adrienne said the process would take four days. This seemed longer than a usual operation, but who were they to question her? She'd been trained in Marbella, after all. Even so, Millie struggled with the belief aspect.

She asked, 'Jumping ahead, Adrienne, can a virtual rubber tourniquet round my stomach really solve years of eating without one?'

'Yes,' said Adrienne. 'Do you trust me?'

Florence said she did. Millie was wise to this and had learned to avoid answering.

'I'll be using a mix of NLP, which encourages you to feel more positive, and CBT, which stops you being negative.'

'Are you going to tell us what those stand for, like "WTF"? Which you might know, of course.'

'No, I don't know that one,' said Adrienne.

'OK. Crack on.' Millie wanted to get a chicken in the fridge before Mary came back. When she'd return was all up in the air, given the attention her paper seemed to have received from the World Health Organization. *Newsnight* was keeping it back as a strand to chime with a 'Disease with Frontiers' talk hosted by the United Nations in Brussels.

'So, there's a difference between what you want and what you need, isn't there?'

Adrienne was sitting on a small chair with a clipboard of notes and what looked like a car radio. Millie assumed this was to be used for special effects of some kind.

Millie and Florence looked back pleasantly. They were enjoying the rest.

'OK. You might want a large glass of sherry.'

'Can we not do sherry?' asked Millie.

'OK, you might want a large glass of gin.'

'Or gin, yes.' Millie was thinking of the leftovers in the airing cupboard.

'OK, you might want some salted cashews, but do you *need* them?'

Florence answered correctly, 'No.'

Millie answered, 'Yes,' and then changed it to 'No.'

'What are your goals, ladies?' Adrienne put her head to one side.

'To get the money, get solvent, find love and not be judged harshly by my peers or by my daughter. And to have someone to go to the cinema with.'

'Mine's to look good in jeans,' said Florence simply.

Adrienne made quick notes on these areas. She then asked each of them to describe which flowers they liked and what kind of sacred place they preferred. This took some time because Millie liked a nice beach with a clifftop and stone steps, while Florence liked a pretty garden with a sunken rose patch and lush space to spread out for picnics and maybe a game of boules.

Once a setting had been agreed upon that was mutually acceptable (a rose garden, set back from a beach, under a cliff, with a sparkling stream trickling gently), they were asked to feel free to go 'under', to the accompaniment of various smells and orchestral music. Adrienne had been trained how to use the car radio, which was in fact a laptop that activated sounds of the sea, birdsong and hospital corridors. There were also bottles of various smells that needed to be opened and closed at key moments to correspond with the vocalized hypnotic journeying. Adrienne only messed up once, Millie decided, when the smell of disinfectant came out at the same moment they were reaching a beach from a series of cobbled steps.

Each session began with the same lecture. They were both told that they would have numerous thoughts during the course of each day, some positive, logical and helpful, and others that were less than helpful.

Florence always nodded at this, while Millie nodded off. But on the third day of being told the same information they both went under.

This was where Millie learned she should press the pause button before she had a 'carb spiral'. In her semi-conscious state, Millie was asked to make a mental inventory of the current carb risk in the kitchen. The Scotch pancakes had been binned, Michael had been forced to put two crumpets in his briefcase, and Millie had only eaten the remaining four. On the last day, the day of the operation, Adrienne brought with her a carrier bag of instruments and tubs of lard.

They were asked to feel the lard. This was what four

crumpets amounted to, which was a bit close to home. Adrienne suggested Millie sleep with the test tube of fat under her pillow as a reminder. Perhaps she had revealed more about other areas than was decent. This was the trouble with mind work. One didn't know quite what was going in or out.

With a crescendo of music and sounds of hospital clicks and clacks, the virtual band was fitted. One each. Adrienne took them on a final journey as this was carried out. There was a smell of anaesthetic, a scraping of a scalpel and some squashy sounds while the tummies were tied up from inside.

'So how do you feel?' asked Adrienne when they came round.

Florence said, 'Full.'

Millie said, 'Hungry.'

This was the only time Millie had ever seen Adrienne look as if she might hit her.

She corrected herself. 'Full. I meant full.'

Perhaps it was the fact that Millie knew she was going to go under the virtual knife and be saved that had made her brave enough to weigh herself on the first day of the four-day hypnosis plan.

They were back in the kitchen staring at the scales.

'Do you think the band weighs anything?' asked Millie. 'No.'

Millie had asked if Florence wanted to go first, which was really only a tactic to delay her own moment of horrible truth, and Florence declined. She told her she didn't want to compete. The only reason for having the band was to squeeze into a new pair of jeans so Aaron the Polish volunteer might be interested.

Millie stepped on the scales for the umpteenth time with a sense of dread. She was eleven stone eight. She was not surprised, just very, very sad.

Finally Florence broke the silence. Adrienne was due any minute and she didn't want Millie in a sulk and spoiling it for both of them.

'Were there any other foods you ate last week that you can't remember? Apart from the sherry mishap.'

'There were, yes.'

Millie nearly told her about the gin and the crumpets and the two chocolate eggs that she'd accidentally on purpose left in the car and had come out in her dressing gown to reclaim. She could see Harry watching her eat them both from his bedroom window. She didn't care that they were both experiencing mutual arousal in their very different ways. The eggs were magnificent. And she couldn't remember the last time she'd enjoyed the envelope of extra buttons so acutely. It was almost worth suffering the consequences for the few short minutes it took to consume them.

But given the seriousness of the shared operation ahead, Millie decided to keep this information to herself.

SUNDAY 20 APRIL

After the band had been 'in place' for a day, Millie agreed to meet Adrienne for a Sunday session to let her check that it hadn't 'dislodged itself'.

After their usual sulky session in the park, Adrienne

begged Millie's permission to witness a weigh-in. Permission was granted, as Millie had been very busy with the citrus laxatives and carrots since Mary and Michael had left for Durham.

In light of the success of the conference, the dean of Durham had invited Mary to open a small room – with her name on it – in the anthropology faculty. Also, they'd been sent a generous per-diem travel allowance, and they were planning to sample the full English, with complimentary biscuits, in first class.

'Don't worry, Millie, I'll make sure the letters on the door aren't too garish,' Michael had said as he'd carried both their bags to the taxi.

'Thank you, Michael,' said Millie, as she waved them off. She felt quite optimistic. Mary would now have her name written on a university door, in subtle lettering, and Millie had reason to hope that she'd got herself back in the game. And she had. The scales now read eleven stone four.

Millie was over the moon. Adrienne was perplexed.

'So you were eleven stone eight on the 4th, and now you're eleven stone four on the . . .' Adrienne paused to count on her extraordinary fingers, '20th? That's over two weeks and only four pounds lost, Millie.'

'It's been a busy time for my body. Four pounds down. Let's be thankful and full of praise.'

'Millie, d'you want me to bring some smoothies for the next week, before we go to the retreat? To work as a partner to the gastric band. Your stomach might psychologically reject solids.'

'OK,' said Millie. Adrienne was taking her belief in the power of the virtual band quite near the edge, but she didn't say anything.

'And I think we should seasonally adjust the weight-loss book.'

'Lie?' Millie was shocked at Adrienne.

'No. But I think you should write you were eleven stone four *last* Monday instead of today and that you have plateaued since then.'

'What difference does that make? I'm still eleven stone four today.'

'Esther will be happy. She can tell Ernst you are losing at the correct rate – about three pounds a week.'

'But you said I plateaued?'

'That comes under the same banner,' said Adrienne quickly, adding, 'If Esther's happy, we can all enjoy the retreat. Are you looking forward?'

'Mostly I am.' But there was a lot Millie needed to attend to. She wanted to write a column about the feature wall at the Bolt Whole to give Cara some money for transforming her netball poem. She needed to take Al out for a hot water to thank him for cat-sitting. She also wanted to book a personal-shopping session in Harvey Nics with Mary to help the transition from 'geek with no idea' to 'celebrity young scientist'. The list went on, but the team were poised for this retreat and she had no choice but to join them, since she was the reason they were all going.

FRIDAY 25 APRIL TO WEDNESDAY 7 MAY

Millie met the other women in a car park in Catford, where they were to catch a coach to the retreat. No one was to take their own cars, to prevent escape or trips to an off-licence.

Millie wasn't sure what to expect from thirteen days removed from society. Unlucky for some, no doubt. Esther informed everyone from her seat at the front of the coach that she had pulled some strings for them all to have a good time on a limited budget. In other words, there was no need for passports and not to expect a pool. Millie was seated at the back of the coach. Florence and Joan were in the middle, looking at different types of storage solution on Joan's iPad. Adrienne was on her own, plugged into a self-help tape.

The driver warned his passengers he'd need a cigarette and a pie at the Little Chef that would be coming up in a few miles. They could get out and stretch their legs if they wanted, but he'd be taking his legally required twenty minutes for a fag break. It seemed a bit antisocial to remain on the coach, so Millie stood in the vestibule area. She bought some sugar-free gum that might whiten her teeth to be at least a bit like the Tough Titty ladies.

When the driver decided he'd safely digested his meal, they all climbed back on board for the last leg of the journey. The coach drove straight through the town of Castle Cary and then stopped at an unassuming gate in a wall on a country road. The women were told to get their own luggage out of the hold, without any help from the driver, who had to pause for a legal cigarette break. After a bit of a struggle with wheelies and hand luggage, they found themselves in a cobbled courtyard with a fountain and huge wind chimes. Millie seemed to be the only member of the team not excited by being sniffed at in the groin area by two rather hyper dogs.

The front door of the house was open, and a woman in a dressing gown showed them into a sitting room without speaking, except to tell them that letting people in wasn't really her job. The room smelt musky. Bowls of potpourri had gathered dust and had a few dead flies mixed in. The walls had been painted orange over bobble wallpaper, giving a marbling effect like the inside of someone's brain. It reminded Millie of the Finchley premises. Naked figurines lined the windowsills. The style was homely, earthy, with, as far as Millie was concerned, a worrying hint of sexual openness and paganism. She didn't like the way the clay horned goddess was sitting on the fireplace.

After a few awkward moments of nothing happening at all, during which people pretended to look at the self-help books but really wanted to go home again, Kahina swept in. Millie wasn't surprised to see her. The self-help fraternity evidently looked after each other, and Adrienne was clearly on a commission of some kind – just as they all were. This time Kahina was wearing a bright floral day dress with court shoes but with the same beaming, determinedly wide, open smile. Adrienne and Kahina exchanged a very long embrace. They stood together, holding each other without moving, while everyone else looked on with fixed smiles.

Florence decided to break the moment by saying, 'Well, anyway . . .' and the two women pulled apart.

Kahina eyeballed everyone in turn and said dramatically, 'Welcome to Dana!' No one called Dana entered the room, making it clear that 'Dana' was the name of the retreat.

Dana meant 'giving' in Buddhism. Kahina pronounced this 'Booodizm'. Joan and Adrienne nodded, keen to identify themselves as the ones who knew this. Millie, Esther and Florence didn't.

Kahina gave Millie an extra-sincere smile and bow. As if they were friends.

Millie felt obliged to acknowledge their previous acquaintance by saying, 'Is Ray here?' and hoped that he wasn't.

Kahina laughed confidently. She was impressively confident, thought Millie. She was confident of Ray, confident of herself, confident that she could have an orgasm in front of quiet strangers with her 'central relationship' and confident that everyone loved the salivating dogs as much as she did. Confident, but not necessarily likeable. But, being so confident, this would of course not matter.

Kahina suggested that everyone might like to put their hands on their heart chakras and visualize twelve petals on a flower. It took quite a long time for everyone to be sure they'd done the full twelve.

Having established they were all breathing as one, Kahina told them a little bit about her own narrative and the origin of Dana. They were welcome to go off and make tea in the kitchen for themselves at any point. Everyone departed immediately, leaving Kahina alone with her narrative, as yet untold and unheard. Even Adrienne came out in search of sustenance. Millie was there first, and showed Florence and Joan the padlocks on the food cupboards in horror.

Florence whispered to Joan, 'There must be a pub in the town that does food.'

'I heard that,' said Millie, feeling betrayed and depressed.

'Sorry,' said Florence, realizing she'd broken rank within minutes of the retreat. She smiled, helpless but still trying to look encouraging. Millie shrugged huffily and stuffed three teabags in a mug, adding five chunks of ginger because someone had left them out on a saucer.

When they returned for Kahina's narrative, they learned that Kahina had been quite a mover and a shaker in London and had worked in a top office and lived in Chelsea in her previous life. In fact, the job was so high-powered, Kahina told them quietly, that one year she had been given tickets to Ascot by her boss.

Everyone nodded. This was high-powered. But after a vision telling her to buy sacred land, which Kahina had experienced on the Heath while walking her beloved dogs, she was soon shown a piece of paper by her central relationship life partner, Ray. The piece of paper, it turned out, had information on it that told her the house they were all in now was for sale – and she knew it was a sign.

'Was the piece of paper from an estate agent with a list of properties on it?' asked Millie.

Kahina confirmed that it was.

'And what was the main attraction for you?'

'Well, look around, Millie!' Kahina waved an expansive arm to indicate the self-help books, the varied figurines and the view into the courtyard with barking dogs, who were attacking a piece of terry towelling.

'Are we on a ley line here, Kahina?' asked Joan gently.

Kahina looked defensive.

'This room is. Mostly.'

Joan said, 'I think my mature student's in a retreat down the road.'

'Is he?' Kahina was not interested.

'It's called the Silent Community. Do you know it?' Joan assumed everyone would be interested in where Jon might be.

'No. And I wouldn't normally meet any of its residents.' Kahina's answer was brief, demonstrating she wasn't going to give any more attention to the other building, which straddled the ley line more fulsomely.

She went on to suggest they all wash up their own mugs out of respect for the community and have a nap before the complimentary vortex session. Benita or Will would collect them and take them to the outhouses for their individual treatments. Some of them might be asleep, but the rules of the retreat stated they would be woken up for all treatments due to the 'tight turnaround'.

The treatment outhouses were accessed via a wet room, which had not been finished. It wasn't yet wet, but had a few waterproof tiles piled up on the floor in readiness. The beige whirlpool looked promising, but had a lawnmower and a saw stowed in it currently. This had to be squeezed past before accessing the row of treatment huts. They were tiny and called 'Candida', 'Merriment' and 'Touchet'. Millie was told to go to Candida, which was the last cubicle along. She took a peek inside Merriment and spotted a hatstand covered with murky-looking towels and a washing-up bowl sitting on the small bed. A thing that looked a bit like a tickling stick or possibly a riding whip with bells on lay next to it. Touchet had a sign saying it was 'occupied' and that one should 'walk quietly'.

Benita welcomed her inside Candida and they danced round each other so Benita could squeeze past and wait outside while Millie got undressed. Benita advised it would be better to get up onto the water bed herself, as she couldn't risk her back. Millie duly clambered onto a wobbly mattress that undulated with warm water and placed a threadbare stamp of a towel over herself while she waited for Benita to step back inside tactfully.

The heat from Benita's hands shot through Millie and unplugged energies in a similar way to when Eugene's hands had hovered over her in the hotel room. Perhaps they were both vortex-trained.

This was either disturbing or a huge coincidence. Millie decided it was disturbing. Was Millie so prone to being ignited by strangers? It made her look rather a lightweight and desperate. She hoped the masseurs didn't share the reactions of their clients. It would be so humiliating to be known as the one guest who climaxed easily with just the touch of a fingernail and a hot towel.

But Benita went in for a similar high-pitched sucking in and blowing out of air too that she'd heard from Eugene in the hotel room, so there had to be an overlap.

At the end of the session Millie asked Benita what the funny noise had been. It can't have been the air extractor, or could it? Benita told her she had sucked bad energy out of Millie and sent it off to another land. Millie hoped the land wasn't anywhere near Durham. She wanted the best for her child and didn't want to jinx anything. When Millie asked her more questions about the origin of the treatment itself, Benita confided that anyone could practise the vortex method as long as they possessed basic healing powers. Vortex was becoming very effective in releasing repressed libidinal energies and was used a lot in Utah with Mormons and non-Mormons alike.

'It is like the Bowen technique, where the healer touches you, then goes away and leaves you, then comes back and touches you again, until you release yourself with an inner impulse,' explained Benita.

'Oh, I think I've got déjà vu,' said Millie slowly.

This was what had happened to Millie in the hotel room.

'It's particularly good for opening the womb chakra,' nodded Benita. Then she whispered to Millie, 'I think you have had a little release? No?'

'I had one very similar in Papua New Guinea recently, with a family friend of my daughter, actually, who is also a man,' replied Millie, yanking on her Ugg boots. 'It was involuntary. And quite small. Thank you, Benita. That was very nice. Thank you.'

When the women all came together in the evening for their mountain of salad, they agreed that their energies had been universally unblocked by the vortex method. Joan seemed to have been particularly affected by experiencing what she described as a 'minor epiphany' and looked unusually tousled.

Kahina gave an evening talk called 'How Will You Know the Truth?' before bedtime in the orange room, which took place at nine thirty. Millie had to wait for an hour and a half for the answer. Finally it came: 'The answer will be on a billboard or in a passing comment or even a road sign.'

Feeling very cheated at the paucity of clues, Millie still slept the best night of her life, having been released.

The boxes for gratuities were placed in the front hall and residents were encouraged to make entirely voluntary donations to their favourite therapists. Each resident had their own glass box for each worker, labelled, 'Millie's

Tips for Benita,' or, 'Millie's Tips for Kahina,' and so on. Millie had real concerns about leaving her boxes empty, which was exacerbated by the growing hunger and the ongoing worry about debt. On day three she hit on the idea of writing a grateful limerick for each worker after a massage. She folded these up and placed them in her boxes. Her boxes became fuller than everyone else's, but they were also the only ones without any money in. Benita, Will and Kahina became slightly more distant to Millie as the limericks mounted up but the money still didn't appear. Millie in turn became more paranoid. On day six Benita's massage had dwindled to a mere prod and a stroke before she left the hut altogether to have a fag and call her mother in Spain. Finally, Millie was saved by Florence, who lent her twenty pounds. This at least ensured some decent vortex release for the last few days. Millie was sorely grateful.

But overall, a routine of soaked grains and linseed upon rising, legume salads at midday and mixed pulses in the evening kept everyone understimulated and emotionally vacant. People sat in the day room staring into space with nothing to say to one another because they were so hungry.

If it weren't for the vortex massages, and inspirational DVDs, including one about the perils of mercury fillings, Millie would have asked for asylum at the Silent Community down the road. But apart from a sudden burst of Tourette's at the dogs when she thought no one could hear, she got through it. She had never been so hungry in her life, but there were no food triggers, as there was no food. The cupboards were padlocked, and her meals were weighed out to the letter of Kahina's law.

Joan escaped to see Jon on the second evening and must have enjoyed a pub supper because she arranged to meet him there with the rest of the group every night for the remainder of the retreat. Millie was allowed to join them as long as she sat in the children's play area with a book and no food. The Silent Community, Jon mimed, brought with it mixed blessings. Jon had completed his tax return, designed a yacht and finished his paper for the MBA, but he'd struggled with the experience. He felt he'd been ostracized by the other guests, even though no one spoke. There was fellowship in silence apparently, but he'd still felt rather left out psychologically. Some of the guests took the tension out on the tennis court, but it was difficult to keep track of the score, as no one could say what it was.

'Maybe they liked your yacht but couldn't say,' suggested Millie on an early evening walk into town.

Jon nodded vigorously, which was one of the two gestures of communication available to him. The second one was to put his finger to his lips, which earned him the occasional free cider. The effort to keep their outings secret from Kahina gave them all a special bond – although much of Millie's time had to be spent reading or looking at crystals in shop windows to occupy herself while the others drank in the pub.

During their stay Very Medical emailed both Esther and Ernst in great excitement to say that they might have secured a slot at the back of *OK!* magazine, where a celebrity had to be photographed reading a cocktail menu with another less-high-profile showbiz person or – at a push – a close personal friend from outside the business altogether as long as they weren't ugly. A few other provisos still had to be sorted. Namely if the cocktail could be made to look like a glass of water, and if Millie could 'pass' as a close personal friend of the celebrity. It would be a case of putting the right celebrity into the mix. Esther replied that any celebrity would be handy, as time was running out. She was determined to provide Ernst with at least one example of journalistic reportage, to showcase Millie's emotional journey for his product.

Esther arranged a photo call. The women were required to gather round the fountain in Dana's courtyard wearing pyjamas. The theme was to be 'sleepovers, girl bonding and healing'. Millie had only brought a nightdress and had to be put in Esther's tartans, which were too long and too tight. Esther wore her backup satin pair, which looked very alluring. The healing aspect of the image was represented by Benita and Will, who were hurriedly given white chef's jackets from the pub, so they could look like clinicians instead of hippies.

Esther wanted to create an Annie Leibovitz *Life Through a Lens* sort of feel, with everyone jumping and looking released in a spontaneous sort of way. On the count of three everyone was to jump and look released at the same time. The rain hadn't stopped since they'd arrived, making the release hard to communicate after several attempts on the slippery cobbles. Kahina assured them that Varuna, the Hindu god of water, was ensuring social cohesion for the group. Benita and Will had to join fingers and make a tower shape to create the shape of an upside-down vortex through which the cherub on the fountain would sow his seed.

*

Kahina gave Millie a one-on-one empowerment session in the orange room on the last night. Rather generously, Florence had given Millie five pounds to offer up as a tip, which seemed to ensure Kahina's renewed enthusiasm to get behind Millie's eating issues. Rose petals had been placed in tiny jam jars around the room. Millie thought they were strawberries and got momentarily depressed when she discovered she couldn't eat them. Adrienne was allowed to sit in and take notes for this session. Millie's eating stemmed from being blocked by fear. Otherwise known as 'false evidence appearing real'. Adrienne wrote this in big letters at the back of Millie's weight-loss book, which gave her something to do while she observed. Millie was to imagine the fear as a black tower, and every time the thought of a carbohydrate came into her mind, she was to topple the tower.

Millie wasn't convinced; she'd rather eat half a baguette and leave the tower intact, although she had to admit that the feel of her flatter stomach was giving a cautious new sense of hope.

SEVENTEEN

〜

AFFIRMATION 17:
'Just for today I am finding boredom in all things'

In spite of the Tourette's that had frightened the dogs and made some of the guests in dressing gowns write a note of complaint about Millie to Kahina, the campaign team agreed Millie's imprisonment had been worth it. She'd successfully lost weight and been released via the vortex method, as had they all. It looked as if the campaign team would now get paid. And some of them would now orgasm in a new and impulse-driven way, which they all agreed was a positive by-product.

Jon had finished 500 hours of silence and bagsied a lift on the coach. He took turns at sitting next to everyone and shared all the different things that had been on his mind while he'd been silent. Millie suggested to Joan that if she'd just met him for the first time, she'd think he was an extrovert. Joan nodded.

'Personally, I prefer him quiet,' she whispered to Millie on the way to the Sanilav, while Jon was enjoying a stint with Adrienne at the front.

Millie spent most of the journey sitting next to Florence, who was very relieved to be going home. She'd been commuting via train, cab and Tube to Pets Need Vets, and to check on the cats, who she feared would have forgotten her and become devoted to Harry. Florence admitted to Millie it had been hard to come away without the cats, but she felt her loyalty to Millie was more important, and at least Aaron had shown a bit of interest. He'd asked her to bring back a sprinkling of sacred earth for his kitchen herb garden.

When Millie arrived at the retreat, she was eleven stone two, having lost another two pounds in the five days after her Sunday session with Adrienne. For thirteen days she'd been kept alive on seeds, major salads and one abseiling challenge, when everyone refused to go down the side of a cliff on a rope. Kahina was very apologetic about the group's feebleness and told the Outward Bound ex-marine that this had never happened before. He took it very badly and it was all rather awkward until he got paid.

They arrived home two days before Millie's Friday weigh-in. Millie ripped off her leisure outfit and stood on the scales. She was ten stone ten.

She was supposed to be ten stone seven, if she was adhering to the recent rider regime, but surely this would be good enough. She felt tiny. Her cardigan not only did up with ease, it hung off her. She might even branch out with a belt over a jumper and be like the kind of person she used to despise.

THURSDAY 8 MAY

It was decided that the Bolt Whole would be the best venue for the penultimate weigh-in. It would certainly be local. If the weight loss was good – and it would be, given the dangling cardigan – Millie suggested Esther could show Ernst the delights of South London afterwards. Being a fabric man, he might like to come back and admire her double-lined curtains with the tassel trim. While Esther wasn't sure if either of them was quite ready for that, she did reveal they'd been in constant touch on FaceTime, which Millie already knew about because Florence had told her. Millie wondered if it was time for Esther to switch things up a notch. She assured Esther that magic could happen in the Bolt Whole.

But the day before the weigh-in, Esther called Millie in a panic. She was having a crisis, which put Millie in a particularly good mood. She liked it when Esther was upset and vulnerable. Esther wanted flowers and background music in the Bolt Whole. Could that be arranged? She'd do it herself, but had just got a call from Nathan's ex, who was threatening to take the children to Costa Rica, and she didn't want her grandchildren growing up Spanish or poor. It was just wretched timing. She really wanted to create a great impression for Ernst. To prove the English team could do it. But she didn't want urchin-like State-dependent grandchildren.

'Any news on the celebrity?' asked Millie.

'No.'

'Very Medical?'

'I've given them a later arrival time, so they'll miss the meeting. How's your eating going? Any cravings?'

'Fine.'

'What was that?' Esther heard a crunch.

'Nothing.'

'I heard some mastication.'

'Oh, that was a carrot.'

'OK, then. Thanks for doing this.'

'No worries.' Millie ended the call and dipped her carrot in a jar of mayonnaise.

Millie had been intending to pop into the Bolt Whole to find Al and make amends about making him bed down with Vernon. She also wanted to see Cara again. Or anyone really. The quietness of the retreat had made her long for human voices and incidental background noise. The first thing she'd done when she'd got home was ask Harry to mow his lawn so she could hear something loud and annoying.

'Hi, babe,' said Millie.

It was lunchtime. Cara was busy serving platters of falafel wraps. The yummy mummies were installed at their usual table. This time the mummies gave her a wave of recognition. Millie acknowledged them with a shy nod. She could hear murmurings. 'It's the poet, look!'

Cara looked pleased to see Millie.

'Where have you been? Al's missed you.'

'Glastonbury,' said Millie, feeling lucky that this was both true and cool at the same time.

'A gig?'

'A retreat. So, my notebook, please?'

Millie tucked her cardigan inside her skirt. Then she took it out again. She liked doing this.

Cara was ready. She handed it over.

'I loved "Balls Off", by the way.'

For some reason Millie wasn't scared about being outed for her adolescent yearnings. If the words meant something to modern-day feminists, she was glad.

'They were written a long time ago, but I'm glad you find them . . . useful.'

The yummy mummies looked especially pleased to see Cara and Millie together. A few more members had joined the lunch group as word had got out about Words From the Bolt Whole. Millie had got herself a rep as a poet apparently. Cara was an up-and-coming rap artist and worth catching before she got discovered.

'Do you want to just give this a quick listen?'

Before Millie could say anything, Cara pulled on her woolly hat and took up a rapping position, which meant a sort of crouching-down look. She started clapping and jigging.

'You were my idol, baby, and although I wasn't yours,
I took a shine to your brother, baby,
Even though he had these spots.
I left a note for your brother, baby,
In a tin in Highgate Woods.
I said I'd like to meet him, baby,
And told him all my thoughts.
And when he found the note, my baby,
When he knew it came from me,
Your brother turned all nasty, baby,
And said, "Balls off," to me.
What does "Balls off" even mean? I hate him and you.'

The rhythm was so powerful a mother with an exposed breast clambered onto the counter. She was the same mother whose baby had become unplugged from the nipple at the previous gathering. Millie backed away slightly. The mother sensed this and urged her to join her in some

Zumba moves. Millie went along with it, but only to avoid a scene with someone who was clearly postnatal. Cara weaved in and out of this stomping ensemble, encouraging a group rap and ending with a climactic power salute at the end.

Cara was so high from the music she gave Millie a falafel wrap and herself a pint of lager.

'I shouldn't be having this,' said Millie, tucking in. 'Right, what was I here for?' she said with a mouth full of falafel and sweet chilli sauce. 'Oh yes, tomorrow's weigh-in meeting. Esther wants flowers and music.'

FRIDAY 9 MAY

'You look pale,' said Cara the next morning. 'Is that make-up?'

'No. It's skin with a hangover,' said Millie. The free falafel had triggered several follow-up glasses of wine as well as peanuts, gin and jelly beans. She was now dreading today's weigh-in. She hated herself. She would have worn her sunglasses if she could find them.

She suspected Mary might have taken them, given her daughter's startling rise to becoming the 'new face' of young science. At least Mary was now miles away in Durham with the sensible and quietly attractive tutor, thus freeing Millie from the tyranny of having to cook wholesome food on the off-chance they might want to eat some with her.

However, before she left, Mary had found time to leave a copy of the *New Scientist* on the kitchen table with an accusatory Post-it note on top, which hurt.

'How could you miss this?' it said. 'See photo. See email. If you need to get in touch for any reason, try my new agent, Emma. Here's her mobile.'

There were no kisses. And Mary had an agent called Emma now? The photo showed Mary looking very young in her school blazer talking to the deputy prime minister or someone who looked as if he might know the deputy prime minister. The pride Millie felt was quickly replaced by dread as she rushed to read Mary's email and find out just how much she had missed of her daughter's life. Millie had tried to call Mary before she went to the retreat, but was too depressed about going away to starve in exile to say too much on an answering machine.

But seemingly she'd been so neglectful her own daughter had to email a clip of herself on the news to keep her in the loop. This was indeed a new low in parenting. But that said, Millie couldn't help but be impressed with how cool Mary looked in the magazine – and how incredibly clear and unfussy she was on camera when she talked about how she'd researched ways to eradicate malaria.

And there was more. Mary's tight little email also informed her mother that the new minister from the Department for International Development was being filmed as part of a documentary about his own rise within Westminster and decided he needed Mary to be filmed with him talking about her work in Papua New Guinea. His interest in Mary would help him 'tell his story' apparently. If she'd been consulted, Millie would have warned Mary not to be exploited, as her involvement was surely just to make the new minister look good, but no one had asked her. Because she hadn't been there. One way or another, her daughter, Mary Rose Tucker, had become the new face of young science overnight, and she had missed it all. Mary was going to be found a role in a think tank attached to Civitas. Meanwhile, Millie had been staring into nothing at a weight-loss retreat.

Esther arrived in a flurry. She had squeezed herself inside a cream lace dress and shiny nude shoes.

'Too much?' she asked Millie, smoothing down the lace and patting her freshly pinned chignon nervously.

'Just enough,' said Millie.

'So have you lost?'

'I have, and also I think it was done within the new rider remit.' Millie added this before Esther could ask.

'Shall we have a quick check?' Esther unpacked some rather smart, thin scales.

'Let's not. Let's just leave it till he comes.' Millie smiled, but she was nervous.

'Of course. You look much thinner today anyway, and pale, Millie. Which also helps. So Ernst is on his way, and I told the girls we were meeting at twelve. Look.'

Esther showed Millie the bogus email she'd sent to herself about the meeting time to prove to Very Medical they had received the right time as far as Esther was concerned.

'Will that work?'

Esther waved Millie's worries away.

'Everything can be blamed on the internet or traffic as long as one doesn't get bogged down with whys and wherefores.'

Esther had become very cross with the Very Medical girls. It was time to play a bit dirty. Millie was tempted to remind Esther how much she'd sung their praises at the start, but was too depressed about her wine relapse.

The whole axis of the campaign had been scuppered. Very Medical had clearly messed up, but Esther was tied into them. Their only hope was to entice an even mildly overweight celebrity to endorse the pills. But celebrities weren't fat like they used to be, and nor did they like to be associated with non-celebrities. Millie's credentials as an ex-QVC 2 presenter and occasional columnist just didn't cut it.

Esther's best trump card, she'd told Millie, was a promise from Tessa Keltz's agent that the star would offer an endorsement if she could meet Millie first to vet her, which might be a problem. Tessa might not find Millie acceptable. The Fartons had been interested, but it needed to chime with a tour they were doing next year – if they were still talking. Cilla Black's people had put the phone down at the suggestion of the fat suit. Someone was tracking Jo Brand, who was last rumoured to be car-rallying in Brazil.

A lot of spin would be needed today, but Esther assured Millie she was prepared. She'd just brought the scales from Currys and sneaked them discreetly under the table. The main thing was to wow Ernst with their verve, commitment and professionalism. Hence the chignon.

Esther and Millie told Cara she'd done a good job with the flowers. Fake ivy and poppies were entwined across the bar; the Bolt Whole had never looked more like a May Day festival.

Millie was almost pleased to see Al, who had come in early to make sure the lights would sparkle safely out of the deer's head and that nothing electrical could go awry. A spare extinguisher had been placed by the door. Every single light effect that had been sourced and installed was lit and bouncing in sync to the music. All in all, the Bolt Whole couldn't have looked brighter.

As far as Esther was concerned, Millie had lost weight and she wasn't worried about the outcome of this weigh-in. She had personally initiated and supervised hour upon hour of Millie's non-eating time at the retreat – and was now eagerly preparing to pocket her profit.

'What were you before we went to Dana?'

'Eleven stone two.'

'You're bound to be down now.'

'What if I'm not?'

'Any variables can be blamed on water retention. Or maybe an ulcer?' Esther seemed pleased. 'They can weigh extra.'

'OK.'

Al was trying to catch Millie's eye, but she was too anxious wondering about what an ulcer might feel like, and the fact that Mary thought she was a bad mother. It was going to take a lot of work to claw back their relationship. She had missed her daughter on the news, which was shocking.

At last Ernst arrived. Esther fawned over him and was relieved at his pleasure about the venue. He seemed particularly enchanted with the deer with the flashing eyes.

'Perhaps you shoot deer, do you? In the mountains.' Esther was jabbering slightly. Millie was quiet.

'Lulu sends her apologies,' said Ernst as he kissed Esther's hand and bowed.

Millie knew she was secretly thrilled Lulu couldn't make it. Esther presented Ernst with a scarf donated from Pets Need Vets to give Lulu, which had been treated to a spritz of Febreze. The scarf originally came from Liberty, so she knew Ernst would be impressed.

Millie could sense Ernst was wary of her. She knew he wanted to see her skeletal. If she could prove that her weight loss was doing what he wanted, in his increasingly anal way – allowing for a rogue ulcer – he might even force himself to offer her a smile.

'Any news on the celebrity, Esther?' Ernst was straight to business.

'Well, actually, yes, there is!'

They were all seated at a table. Millie was sitting especially upright to show off her decreased stomach. Esther crossed her legs twice and leaned forward to pour Ernst a coffee from Cara's retro industrial tin jug. This had the effect she wanted. Ernst dropped his fountain pen in a fluster and had to bend down to pick it up. Millie could see how much more Ernst had become attracted to this handsome woman in lace. She assumed Esther must have gone to a lingerie shop and got herself some stick-on nipples. She'd never seen her look like this naturally. If it was a marketing ploy, it was working. If Millie hadn't been so central to the meeting, she would have felt very slightly in the way.

Ernst listened to Esther's list of possible celebrities but was set on enlisting a member of the royal family. This would tap the 'high-end' requirement. Their American counterpart had just recruited a Republican senator in place of the Osmond, and Ernst felt a royal would match this nicely. He wasn't familiar with Tessa Keltz, although he conceded the name could be German. Esther assured Ernst that Tessa was a household name, but they could both tell he was brooding at the lack of celebrity endorsement thus far.

'You seem worried?' Esther enquired with a provocative pat of the hair and another little thrust of her stick-ons.

'We have donated a lot of the budget to this end and we need delivery of the goods,' Ernst explained to her sternly, in spite of his pleasure.

Suddenly, Millie had an idea. She recalled the woman with the dark glasses at the All White Clinic. That had to be the Princess of Stowe or wherever. It was just a pity she didn't know her real name.

'I know a princess, actually,' Millie blurted.

'Which princess?' asked Ernst sharply.

'Princess Magdana?' Millie mumbled. 'I met her recently on an irrigation course. She might be up for it.' Millie immediately regretted saying this.

Esther looked cross at Millie's lie. It had just popped out and now Esther would have to get them out of it. Unfortunately, Ernst was looking very pleased indeed.

'Yes, I want her.'

'Or Tessa, if she bites?'

'The princess, *bitte*, is better. Esther . . .'

Esther glared at Millie. She retrieved the scales from under the table. Cara and Al made themselves scarce. Cara turned up the Caribbean salsa. The lights flashed in time to the beat.

Esther said, 'Oh dear. The Very Medical ladies must be held up somewhere. It's quite a schlep from the suburbs! So shall we just weigh Millie now? Let's not bother with all the tributaries and arteries measurements for today!'

Ernst agreed. Esther laid out the very small scales. Millie ripped off her dress as she had become used to doing and stood on them. This time everyone was too intent on the outcome to look at her body. Except Al, who was arranging himself on a ladder to adjust the antlers and get himself a good view.

EIGHTEEN

AFFIRMATION 18:
'I love my diet pill doctor more than my cat, and she's OK with that and I'm OK with the pills'

Esther, Ernst and Millie peered down to read the verdict. The scales showed ten stone thirteen.

Esther said, 'Get off,' and shook the scales. 'Get on.'

It was the same reading.

'This doesn't make sense. She must have lost more than seven pounds in weeks of starvation?' Esther was almost shouting this. A piece of hair had escaped from the chignon and she looked a little wild. In her panic, Esther forgot whose side she was on and appealed to Ernst. 'I mean, this is a piddly two pounds a week. She was supposed to be losing at least three pounds to get her to ten stone six.'

'Indeed, my dear. The correct result would be guaranteed if she had followed my rider request of losing at least three pounds every week. You see, if Millie was ten stone six today, she would have proved to us all that she had been observing it correctly and losing at the regular rate, but as it is . . .' Ernst shrugged his shoulders. He looked a broken man. This was awful. Millie felt dreadful.

Millie stepped off the scales and waited for instructions. She folded her arms across her stomach.

'I think we might be losing sight of the main picture here. Millie has lost.' Esther had pulled herself together.

'But not to the Kleinne Fett rider template, alas.' Ernst shook his head slowly.

'Millie, can you step up on here again, please?' Millie had seen Esther fiddle with the knob, but it had been done so blatantly no one seemed to notice. This must be how Mary had got away with shoplifting for so long.

Millie stepped on again. It read ten stone ten.

'You see, Ernst, this proves she has kept to your rider – that's a loss of seventeen pounds from the last weigh-in, because on 27 March, she was eleven stone thirteen, weren't you, Millie, so that's a stone and three pounds lost, which equals *more* than two pounds per week lost over six weeks – give or take a burgeoning ulcer that might be growing, but we don't want to worry you with that today, do we, Millie?'

'Did you do something to the scales, Esther?' Ernst looked confused and a little suspicious.

'No?'

'Excuse me, Esther, but doesn't the rider say it's got to be a three-pound-a-week loss, not two?' asked Millie.

She was slowly coming to understand the whole rider thing and the maths . . . Perhaps she had succumbed to the indoctrination of her immediate environment.

Esther coughed over Millie's last few words and said, 'And now some coffee for all is in order, I think!' She glared at Millie.

'Are you sure you did not twiddle?' Ernst was frowning.

'I think you would have noticed, Ernst! No. I'm just making sure we get the right details for us to move forward. Millie, do get dressed, dear.'

Ernst didn't look convinced, but Millie felt they were in with a chance. She regretted her interruption, but the rider clause had got to her. At least Esther was being impressive with her number-crunching. Perhaps Ernst could be encouraged away from it and just celebrate the loss. Surely as long as she got to the goal by the end she should get the money. He was just being picky, which was more a reflection of his anxiety. In any case, if Very Medical had done their job, Ernst wouldn't have been allowed to come up with this new ruling midway into a campaign.

Millie ruminated on these developments and forgot to get dressed.

'Do get dressed, Millie. Unless you want to stay like that, of course?'

Millie stayed as she was. She decided she was fed up with being told what to do, and anyway, she felt very light today.

'That's a significant loss, Ernst.' Esther smiled.

'But not within the terms of the redefined contract, Esther,' said Ernst, and smiled back. He had small, ferrety teeth.

Millie lost interest. This was stuff for the big boys. She just hoped Esther could handle herself.

'It's a loss.' Esther looked at him seductively. She stroked her décolletage. Ernst had to look away. Millie could see he was getting aroused. He placed his papers over his lap.

'So, shall I take the cheque off you now? And then we can have a sloe gin. On me, Ernst.'

'I cannot give you the full instalment of £6,666, Esther. I can only go up to 66 per cent of this amount, which would be £4,444.'

It occurred to Millie that to the uninitiated, it might sound as if Ernst had a stutter.

'Do you play poker, Ernst?' Esther asked playfully.

'Why?' Ernst wasn't giving anything away. He must do, thought Millie.

Esther assessed him, narrowing her eyes. Millie wondered what she was going to come up with now. Esther's hands were going lower and lower . . . Millie yawned. If they needed a room, Esther's Victorian semi wasn't very far.

Suddenly, there was a shout from Al.

'Oh my God, Millie, you've gone viral!'

'Where?' shouted Esther.

Al was shaking his head.

'Millie, come and look at YouTube!'

Cara turned the screen of her iPad to face them so Esther and Millie could get a proper view. Perhaps Cara was trying to save her. If so, she had done the opposite. First, she gave her the falafel wrap, and now a final kick in the stomach. This would be the end of Millie's association with Kleinne Fett, and any hope of saving her home . . .

Cara spoke up.

'"Balls Off" has got a hundred thousand hits.'

The clip showed Cara doing the 'Balls Off' rap with the mummy on the bar top clapping. It was the one who had the breast free. Her friend must have put it on YouTube straight afterwards. Millie appeared to have her mouth wide open singing, but unfortunately it looked like she was in the direct line of milk flow.

Al was bouncing from one foot to the other with obvious pride.

Esther and Millie watched the clip in amazement. As soon as Esther could work out what was going on, she rushed to stand in front of the screen to obscure Ernst's view, but Ernst was enjoying the rhythm and appeared still to be dealing with an excitement of his own and hadn't looked up to see any of it.

He closed his eyes and tapped his hands on the table in time to the rap.

'Again, *bitte*.'

Cara played it for Ernst again.

'I want Princess Magdana,' said Ernst firmly.

Esther suggested Ernst might have been misled in this subject matter, and then wondered if Millie would like to go to the ladies' with her to 'check something' and possibly put her clothes on at the same time.

Once they locked the door in the ladies', Esther swung round to Millie.

'I don't know what to think. What was that?'

'It's just Cara being a feminist war poet or something. She got hold of my poetry – don't ask. It's all got a bit out of hand, to be honest.'

'But the breast milk? What's Ernst going to think?'

'It was a yummy mummy's milk, not mine.'

'I know it was a yummy mummy, but what was she doing there?'

'She just got overexcited about the rap and happened to be lactating.'

Esther didn't know what to say. Millie decided to go on the attack.

'Did you twiddle the knob, Esther?'

'Of course I did.'

Now they both had things to hide. They went out to face Ernst. Cara had poured him some sloe gin and he was looking more relaxed. No one seemed to notice that Millie had not bothered to get dressed.

'So I can pay you 66 per cent of the fee,' said Ernst. This gave Esther and Millie hope. They were still in the game.

'Shall we make that 80 per cent of the instalment, bringing it to a nice £5,333?' Esther knocked back a glass and refilled Ernst's. She held the bottle out to Millie and then remembered. She put it quickly back on the table.

'I can do £4,666 at 70 per cent. And I will give you that remaining 30 per cent in five weeks' time if you make the target of nine stone six on 10 June as well as the final £6,666.'

'OK, that's wonderful, Ernst, and so clear.'

Ernst wrote out a cheque and blew on it before he handed it over. Esther blew on it as well. They shared a look. Millie sensed Esther's curtains might be given a viewing.

At twelve o'clock on the dot the Very Medical girls walked through the door carrying their equipment and looking very corporate. This immediately changed to suspicion as it became evident the meeting was clearly at an end.

Cara called out, 'Hi. Can I help you?'

'Yes. We're here for the Kleinne Fett meeting.'

'Is it still going?' Cara asked Esther.

'We're here to meet our client, thank you,' said Terri patronizingly, and walked over to Ernst to shake his hand. At least they had learned from Esther how to greet clients, thought Millie. But that might be it.

'We were so worried. What happened, ladies?' Esther looked concerned.

'You said twelve?'

'Ten.'

'Twelve.'

'Let me check. How strange.' Esther held out her iPad for them to see the email she had sent to herself and then closed the cover before the girls looked too closely.

Millie was impressed.

'That's so odd.' Lucy looked at Millie suspiciously.

'Must be your end,' said Esther with a hand on Ernst's back to propel him to the door.

'But have you lost weight, Millie?' asked Terri.

'I have.' Millie nodded. 'Quite a lot, actually.' Millie thought a smirk might be apposite as well.

The girls assessed Millie. Terri went up and pinched her waist as she had done on their first meeting. She clearly felt this was her job.

'So shall I get dressed now?'

'Should she get dressed, Ernst?' asked Esther.

'Yes, by all means.' Ernst had put on his cravat.

'I'll email you the figures, but it's a big loss. Any luck with the celebrity? So Ernst can be reassured.'

Esther knew she could get them on this. The women looked sheepish.

'It's building momentum.'

'We're working with Lesley Joseph on another project.'

'And the connection with Lesley Joseph and Kleinne Fett is . . . ?' asked Esther. She shook her head and looked at Ernst as if to say, 'You see?'

'So! I want the princess, please.' Ernst nodded at Millie since the princess was her contact.

Millie hurriedly pulled on her clothes while she wondered what to do. How was she going to track the woman? She could hardly put a shout-out on Twitter.

Esther took Ernst's arm.

'Ernst, shall we use your few precious hours in London to celebrate our success? I thought we'd start with fabrics locally and then move on to trims in Soho.'

SATURDAY 10 MAY

The next day was a Saturday. Millie was eating a carrot on the sofa. Four more were lined up on her lap. She was making notes, looking at Harry's pink-highlighted sheets and trying to do some calculations.

She now had £4,666, minus Esther's £700 cut. Cow. Millie had underlined 'cow' twice. This left her with a clear £3,966, which, it turned out, was enough to pay her mortgage for the month and pay off QwickCash, who would have to take the bailiffs off the job so they could apply their award-winning ways elsewhere. Major result.

It was a milestone. It made all the pain worthwhile. She should be celebrating with a glass of fizzy water. However, Millie was still unsettled. Even though a big burden had been lifted, she wasn't quite right. This must be what people meant when they said, 'Money isn't everything.'

There was still a lot to worry about. She knew there was something else very bad that was going to come up and bite her; she just couldn't quite put her finger on it.

Then it all kicked off. Her mother was on the phone. Julie, the girl Friday, said, 'Hi, Miss Tucker. Julie here.

Your mother wants to know, is it you on YouTube with
the lactating mother?'

'Who's asking, Julie?' Millie asked unnecessarily, and to
make the point that it might be nice for her mother to call
direct on occasion.

'Your mother.'

'Oh, um, yes, but it's all got a bit out of hand. Why not
pass her over?'

Millie could hear a muffled discussion in the background. The girl Friday came back on the phone.

'Audrey wants to know why you did it, because your
daughter is here and they're both very upset.'

'Mary's with Granny? What on earth for?'

Mary came on the phone.

'How could you do this, Mum?'

'Do what?' But Millie knew what was coming. This
was what the bad feeling had been about. She had
blanked it out because she knew it was so bad.

'Mum, why are you on YouTube with a lactating
woman? Can you explain? I just want to understand.'

'It wasn't me.' Millie felt like a child.

'Is it a fake? Because if it is, I can tell my agent.'

'I wrote the poem years ago and then Cara made it into
a rap.'

'It's on all sorts of dodgy sites now with your name on it.'

'I didn't know that.'

'And any link with me could be damaging for my brand.'

'It wasn't supposed to happen like that.'

'You're in a bar with a woman doing semi-lesbian
dance moves!'

Millie could hear her mother shout, 'Unbelievable,'
from her day bed.

'I'm going to have to disown you.'

'Why?'

'I might be on the cover of the *New Scientist*.'

'That's wonderful.'

'But I can't have baggage – that's what Emma says, and Granny agrees, don't you, Granny?'

Millie could hear her mother say, 'It's the *New Scientist*! What were you thinking, Millie?'

Millie began to respond with a heartfelt defence. How she was mortified she missed Mary on the news, and how this really hurt her the most. When she paused for breath, she noticed there was no one on the other end.

Millie telephoned Florence immediately. 'Can you come over?'

'Of course.'

Florence arrived with Joan.

'I thought Joan might help.'

Joan had come prepared. She smiled softly and lit her smudge sticks to wave in all the dark corners of trapped energy.

'This might be a long job, Millie.'

And then for the first time in years Millie cried properly. A major type of heaving crying that made the crying she'd done with Al look like hay fever. She sobbed.

'I've lost my daughter. I missed seeing her on the news. I'm still fat. I hate carrots. I'm so alone. My mother thinks I'm a bad mother. Which is true . . .'

Florence sprang towards the kettle.

'You're not a bad mother, Millie.'

'I am. You can't say I'm not. I'm dysfunctional. I don't

do presents at Easter anymore, no one sits round my table and has interesting conversations, and Mary wears khaki all the time . . .'

Joan leaned in with a smudge stick.

'Excuse me,' she said softly, and darted away.

'I should have persuaded Trevor to stay. I should have tried cricket or had sex with my shoes on. I should have done something different. I should have been normal . . .'

'Sheila's mother was a bad mother. Remember her? Always in the velour tennis cardy?'

This stopped Millie slightly in her tracks.

'Tennis skirt, Florence. She wore it to school so the fathers would look.'

Joan saw this as an opportunity to sneak a Kleenex under her hand to Millie as if Florence shouldn't see what she was handing over.

'Thanks.' Millie blew her nose thoroughly and held her hand out for another one. Joan was busy and missed it.

There was a knock at the door.

'You go. If it's Harry, tell him I still hate him even if he has persuaded Michael Morris he's some kind of yogi prophet. He's not. I know better.'

Florence came into the kitchen looking rather panicked.

She mouthed at Millie, 'I think it must be Eugene. What shall I do?'

Millie panicked. 'Can you say I'm out, Florence? No, say I'm on holiday. No, say I'm at my calligraphy class.'

'Have you joined one?' said Joan.

'No. Where is he? I could sneak out the back.'

'I left him on the doorstep.'

'Did you shut the door?'

'I can't remember.'

'Momma!'

'Too late. Oh my God.' Millie smoothed her hair and tried to look happy.

Suddenly, the short man from Papua New Guinea tumbled into her kitchen.

He held out his arms to her and she walked awkwardly into them, being mindful about the Bowen technique and what practitioners could do to their subjects.

Florence stared at Eugene and whispered, 'I see what you mean.'

'About what?' Millie hissed back.

But Florence and Joan quietly picked up their bags and let themselves out. Some of the more troublesome corners would have to wait.

'I'll be back to smudge-stick your upstairs,' whispered Joan, 'when you're . . . you know . . . more sorted.'

As Millie held Eugene for the first time, she was reminded quite acutely of their height difference. He really did only come up to her armpits, and Millie was a short five foot three in slippers. As he nestled beneath her collarbone, she stared over his head at the fireplace in a state of shock. She was not feeling the same ring-doughnut surge she had felt with Al. There was also an overwhelming smell of garlic and basil, which hadn't been present in the hotel room.

Millie pulled back first. So far nothing bad had happened. They were just two people greeting each other, one of whom had probably just consumed a pizza.

Eugene looked at Millie for a long time. She looked away. Apart from the shock and the rush of adrenalin, she now had to face the fact that Eugene had turned up unannounced, with or without Mary knowing. There was a lot to find out. Also, he was level with the top of the fireplace, which did not make matters any easier.

'Does Mary know you are here?'

'She is not replying, Momma.'

'Well, she's got a lot on. Did you see her on the news?'

'I did, Momma.'

'I didn't, I'm afraid. I'm a bad momma.'

'You are not fatty now.'

'Thank you.'

'I like you fatty.'

'Sod's law, then, isn't it.'

Millie looked around for inspiration. She was out of her depth. He'd arrived with a small suitcase on wheels and a jaunty beach bag. She felt less in awe of him and more distant, but also responsible. Was it the luggage that had done that? Was he intending to stay?

'So, Eugene, can I offer you a glass of water or a fig tea, perhaps?'

'Everything, Momma.'

'Rightio.'

Millie went to the kettle. Eugene followed close behind.

'I love Mary.'

'Me too.'

'I love you too.' He was really very close. She could smell the garlic.

'Mm.' Millie tried to sound non-committal as she busily banged about with mugs and fig teabags.

'And I love my country.'

'Yes.' This was more promising. Perhaps they could just get back to politics and all would be well. Somehow.

It wasn't easy to deal with these new feelings. She knew

with a sudden sadness and relief that Eugene was just someone rather strange. And sweet. He had been there at the right time to arouse a very dormant desire in her when she was at her most vulnerable. But now Eugene seemed to feel very at home. Maybe she should call Al . . .

'You see?' Eugene went to his suitcase. He took out a ukulele, which was a surprise.

'Thank you, Eugene. You shouldn't have.'

'It is for me.'

'Oh.'

Very gently and very beautifully, Eugene began to play and sing.

'See, Mommy, this is a calypso song.' He then un-ashamedly burst into verse, which made no sense at all.

'Very jolly, Eugene. Shall I put your mug here for you? It's hot.'

'We use calypso songs to get our message out.'

Perhaps Eugene *was* a terrorist. She should have asked Florence to stay to get her opinion. And Joan.

'I sing the words our government doesn't want its en-emies to hear.' Eugene drained his mug appreciatively and held it out for a refill. Millie took it, but wasn't sure she liked serving him. She could see how Mary might have had problems.

'And I've been meaning to ask – is the government building still standing in Port Moresby?'

'It is, Momma.'

'Good. I was worried.'

'I need to see Mary, Momma.'

'Don't we all, Eugene. As I said, she's tied up with the malaria message and, er, Michael.'

'Michael Morris?' Eugene nodded and looked very sad. Millie felt sorry for him.

'And how's the VPL coming along? Any news there?' She gave him a glass of water while she made more fig tea. She'd be pleased to get rid of it.

'Oh yes.' Eugene stopped strumming abruptly. It was as if he remembered his purpose.

'I need to know what Mary is doing and who she is working for. Because a lot of people who pay her are ones who are bad.'

'Like who?' asked Millie.

Eugene stood up as if he were at a public meeting.

'The drug companies who bribe Papua New Guinean government to buy their drugs to make them rich. That is dirty money – it goes to politicians who buy weapons to keep power over the good people of our country with no voice. Our Arab Spring has come. We must be ready.'

'Of course you must. The more unrest, the cheaper the flights – worked for China, I notice. So many more people have done the wall now.'

'But, Momma, you are colluding.' Eugene looked troubled.

'Am I? How?'

'The more my VPL fight to stop the logging and keep the forest, the more you encourage Mary to study swamp life to bring her status. Her status is at the cost of my trees.'

'She needs swamps to study malaria so she can cure it!'

'We need trees to preserve the planet, Momma! Which would you choose, Mary's status or the planet?'

'Er . . . well, you've got me there. Obviously we'll be needing a planet in the long run.'

Eugene sat down exhausted but triumphant. Millie didn't want to let him win outright.

'But we still need to cure disease, Eugene . . . Anyway, next time she gets in touch, I promise to mention your concerns again. Tea?'

'Yes, Momma. I have to warn her. Her sponsor is my enemy.'

'I thought your father sponsored the settlement.'

'He is tyres, Momma.'

'You'll have to go through her agent. She's called Emma.'

'We want a democracy, Momma. And that is my gift. I give my accountancy skills to arm my people – the VPL can have wealth, to overthrow dictatorship.'

'That is so sensible, Eugene, and I don't care what anyone says – financial stability is the way forward. I should know.'

'I have taught the party bookkeeping. It makes sense, Momma.'

'And what is it you've got, Eugene? Is it a diploma in bookkeeping? Or is it a BSc? Either way, it's what they call a "transferable skill", don't they?'

The conversation was taking a very formal turn.

'And also I learn vortex.'

'What?'

Eugene looked at Millie from under his long lashes.

'It is famous for healers. I go to Glastonbury and . . .' Eugene licked his fingers. Millie shuddered. 'It is like the Bowen, but with more . . . energy.' He gave her a tiny little smile.

'I don't believe it! Did you work with Benita?'

'Benita. Spanish lady? Yes, she is good.'

'She gets better with a tip, I noticed.'

'True. But vortex is only powerful in the right hands.'

'Clearly. I can't fault either of you on that one.' Millie smiled at the memory.

'I also teach the VPL the energy so they can be good to the weak.'

'Amazing, Eugene.'

Millie was slowly coming to terms with the fact that her 'release' could be explained by a number of elements. Not only had she been in Papua New Guinea in the heat, trying to diet and feeling vulnerable, but she had at the same time been exposed to a system of healing, and it was especially good to hear him say it. She allowed that she had felt an attraction, but there were also a lot of extenuating circumstances that explained it. She was feeling better by the second.

'So can I just ask again – just to be clear, are you a terrorist?'

'Papua New Guinea is tied into Europe, so I have to make sure we have a power that works for us.'

'Same! You don't want Brussels telling you what the size of an egg should be, do you? A lot of people here don't like that either.'

'Our parliament is weak, so the minority are getting stronger. It is like Arab Spring, yes? We have to fight. But who do we fight and why?'

'I've forgotten, but it's a good question. Mary might know more than me on that side.'

'I am here with my calypso. I was here to see my aunt and do my business and to see my lovely Mary and then I notice "Balls Off" got ten thousand hits. You want to get your rapper to sing my message? We blow the world, Momma.'

'Slightly more hits than that, actually. I think it was a hundred thousand. But the thing is, Mary's quite upset with me at the moment . . . so I have to lie low now.'

'I love Mary.'

'As do I.'

'Let's sleep, Momma.' Eugene yawned, giving Millie the full benefit of his garlic-infused breath.

He held out his hand to her. She took it and felt the charge that she had in the hotel room. She dropped her hand immediately. No. Not again.

Millie showed Eugene the sofa and crept off to bed to cry. There was a lot to cry about. It had all been to do with vortex. She had almost betrayed her daughter due to a Bowen-technique-type reflex; she had missed her on the news; Eugene only wanted to use her unwanted notoriety on YouTube to get his message across . . . and she was still not thin enough.

SUNDAY 11 MAY

Adrienne came round for Sunday-morning training. Millie let her in as usual and she marched into the kitchen full of purpose. 'Right, we've got to be nine stone six in four and a half weeks. We can do it, Millie. Oh!' Adrienne had spotted Eugene in a dressing gown giving a salute to the sun.

'Oh,' she called. 'Millie, come quickly. There's a person in your back garden.'

'Hello, ma'am.' Eugene came inside through the French

doors. He looked at Adrienne and held out his hand. Adrienne took it, then turned on her heel.

'I'll meet you outside, Millie. Sorry.'

As they began their trot, Adrienne ran on ahead in a sulk. Millie waited at the usual bench for her to come back to orchestrate the thrusts.

'Please don't worry, Adrienne. There's nothing going on.'

'But it might change things.'

'How?'

'Between you and me.'

'In what way? He's just a house guest.'

'Well, he's also a man.'

'Yes?'

'You know.'

'There's nothing going on. He's my daughter's boy-friend or was, and please don't sulk.'

'I'm not.'

'You are.'

'Not.'

'Having a male house guest shouldn't stop us from trotting.'

When Millie got back, Eugene had left a note saying he was going to visit one of his aunties in Knightsbridge and asking if he could leave his small bag with the wheels. Millie wheeled it out into the hall. She didn't think it would be right to have it in the kitchen as a reminder of the charge she'd felt at Eugene's touch earlier. Healers moved in mysterious ways, and her house was especially sensitive to energies, as the whole dead-baby-in-the-cornices episode had proved.

She'd had no word from Mary and decided to start writing a modern-day sonnet under a pseudonym, for the

Poetry Society, about a woman wearing Spanx control wear, as a metaphor for capitulation under male oppression – just to see if she could. Then she would set up the Bolt Whole's feature-wall piece for a double page in the *Good Woman*. She had to keep going. The comments she'd received as the 'Balls Off' rap gained notoriety were quite fruity. Predictably, Esther wanted some glory from it. She put out a joint statement from the *Good Woman* thanking readers for their support and stating that earnings made from YouTube, if any, would go to a good cause, as yet unnamed.

Millie emailed Esther suggesting her mother's Hythe care village might be a popular charity. She needed to make a gesture to her mother, who wasn't taking any calls until further notice. Julie, the girl Friday, told Millie that Mrs Tucker was currently 'baffled and disappointed' and would get in touch with her daughter when these feelings had subsided. There was little point until then.

But Millie was now feeling hungrier than she had ever been in her life. There was a new ache about Mary that never left her and another slightly different ache from seeing Eugene again, even though she wasn't quite sure what it stemmed from. Perhaps it was because he was so young, so committed to changing the world that it made her feel old and so without possibilities. Without hope for the future there was nothing. She'd sunk into one of those black moments. She was still in debt with bills, still too fat and still not very successful at work. How dare he turn up and make her feel so useless and have the cheek to want a slice of her unwanted glory as an ex-poet?

She'd had enough. Adrienne had weighed her. Still ten stone thirteen. In a fit of despondency, Millie Googled 'diet doctors who sell drugs'.

She needed to do something different. Something radical and on the edge. Something that didn't involve guilt, pain, self-flagellation and failure . . .

She was going to shift this last stone with amphetamines, and no one was going to stop her.

MONDAY 12 MAY TO MONDAY 2 JUNE

The diet clinic was in Harley Street, which seemed unlikely, since the price for a week's supply of pills was eminently affordable, unless she'd misunderstood the decimal point again. Two Middle European female receptionists broke off from their Middle European conversation and seemed very pleased to see Millie. They must like strangers, thought Millie, as she was told to go straight in to see the doctor. She had to walk past a bowl of shiny green apples in the waiting area. But she would not sneak a free apple. She felt cured already. Such was the power of suggestion.

The female doctor wore a jaunty skirt that was half-kilt, half-skirt. She smiled at her, confident in the knowledge that her pills would stem Millie's gluttony. Apart from a simple diet sheet, which Millie could take away with her, it was to be a case of pills, water and protein. And an injection in her bottom if she would like one.

'Go on, then,' said Millie.

She just couldn't believe how easy it had all been. You just walked past the apples, without eating any, and got given a fix. She did ask the receptionists what had gone into her derriere, as an afterthought.

'Oh, just some vitamins,' one said cheerily.

'OK, then, marvellous,' said Millie happily.

During the session the doctor had held up a tin of tuna for Millie to look at, as an example of the kind of foodstuff Millie would be allowed on the new protein-only weight regime. The tin had been on her desk, but now she turned it round so Millie could get a decent feel for it. She thought it might easier for Millie to buy one of these tins, now she'd seen this one. Suggestibility was clearly the name of the game. The doctor also told her to reduce her coffee intake if she got palpitations.

'I'm used to miso tincture, so there's no danger of that.'

The doctor nodded and took her blood pressure. Normal. She loved the sound of this word. All Millie ever wanted to be was normal.

She was happier than she had been for ages. Now it was out with the vegetables and in with the chicken or tin of tuna. The only other area to think about, the doctor said quickly, was to stop the pills if she felt suicidal.

'Will do,' nodded Millie excitedly. Death by amphetamines still sounded preferable to death by 'failing to lose a stone and succeeding in losing one's house'.

Armed with a tub of blue pills, Millie stopped off in Sainsbury's to buy as much chicken as she could fit into her bag. Cooked and sliced would do her. These babies were the new black. Chicken and pills. The trip also proved she could shop on her own without recourse to flapjacks. With her very full protein-only basket she walked defiantly past the Kit Kats that had been placed on a little shelf in front of the newspapers. Not even a second glance. The shackles of her weight-campaign friendships were beginning to loosen and it felt good.

Millie took a pill as soon as she got home and remained alert till four in the morning. While she was watching

Britain's Best Bakery and a riveting Bronze Age *Time Team* special, she idly looked at the label on the tub – 'Best taken upon rising', so she took another one when she woke up. The combination of taking two pills so close together gave Millie a big surge of energy. She decided to run round the park. This was unprecedented. This was what fit people did who didn't have fat arms and torsos. They got up and ran somewhere immediately without moaning. Now she was one of them.

The voluntary running took place three mornings in a row for the following three days. Millie told Adrienne in a jaunty text that she was going to 'fly solo' for a while. Adrienne immediately phoned back, but Millie didn't answer. Never before had she felt so callous and uncaring about others. It was very freeing. Adrienne texted that she was 'saddened' by Millie's sudden decision, when they were really so near their goal, but would check back within a week. She wasn't giving up on her friend. On the third day Millie overtook the jogger with the double buggy. These pills were great. She had no desire for food. Newsagents were no longer off limits. She could walk in and walk out of such a shop without so much as a glance at nougat.

Nor did she harbour the dull aches of guilt about Mary, or her mother, or her friends, who she now didn't need – she was superwoman and self-sufficient, and as long as she had her pills, she could do this thing alone. The lady doctor was very pleased with her progress and said as much when Millie offered up the other buttock for her second vitamin burst. Millie had lost half a stone in a week. On the 9th she'd been ten stone thirteen, and now a week later, Friday 16 May, she was ten stone six. She would do it. There were only fourteen pounds to shift before D-Day; 10 June would set her free. The doctor smiled even more the following week when she lost another five pounds: on the 23rd Millie reached ten stone one.

Her mind was in overdrive and she had to keep finding new activities to feed her overstimulated brain. One of these was to drive down to Hythe and back while waiting for the fridge to defrost. Harry had been persuaded to pay for the petrol, which meant he had to come as well. He insisted on sitting in the front, which was annoying, but once she got into her stride about her plans for a cat house, a clothes sale and very possibly a sewing club for local professionals, they'd arrived. Her mother soon forgave the YouTube debacle when she saw the amount of tidying Millie wanted to achieve for her in half an hour. Millie had shown no interest in the care village till now, viewing her mother's recent house purchase to be the cause of her financial problems. But now there was so much filing and sorting to do, Millie didn't know why she hadn't come down earlier. Harry and her mother did fall silent when Millie asked for her mother's toothbrush to zap the slight mould in the grouting of the walk-in shower unit. It was only when Millie suggested filing her mother's sweater drawer in order of colour that her mother begged her to stop and asked Harry to take her away. He led her away, still talking, to the car.

On the next drop-in to the diet clinic, the doctor enquired if everything was all right with Millie. She replied that things had never been better. Her mother's tiles had been stripped of mould and were now gleaming, and her Spanx sonnet for the Poetry Society had been highly commended, and would be published on the website. The doctor was pleased for her on both counts, and then asked if Millie had experienced any 'side effects relating to the pills'. Millie stated quite adamantly that there had been none whatsoever, save for a slight over-familiarity with chicken, which was why she'd swapped to tuna in brine for the time being.

Millie found herself keen to share other exciting details with the diet doctor about her daughter, who was making new waves in the world of science and had just gone back to Papua New Guinea for a few days to close up her research project before returning to Durham. The project had received so much attention that her handsome tutor, Michael Morris, whom the doctor might know, suggested she base herself in the UK and simply commute, but Millie was sure there were other reasons for Michael to keep Mary close. Millie looked significantly at the doctor at this point, before explaining that Mary had said her farewells to Eugene, who was a terribly short Papua New Guinean prince to whom Mary had once been attached and who Millie thought she fancied, but then didn't, and that Eugene was now calling Millie twice a day from his aunt's house, where he was now staying, to share his grief. This was safer than having him lodge in her house to act it all out in calypso, and what did the doctor think about sharing a house with such a man? The doctor said she might have to give it some thought, so Millie carried on talking while she came up with something.

There had also been talk of Mary taking Millie to the House of Commons for tea to meet her new friend, the minister from the Department for International Development, but Millie wasn't holding her breath for that one: the notoriety on YouTube hadn't quite yet disappeared. Esther had received an enquiry at the magazine suggesting

Millie might wish to work with some NCT groups in a 'Breast Is Best' campaign. The doctor now looked like she was rather enjoying herself and asked if Millie considered herself a 'crazy lady'. Millie didn't but went on to explain the latest problem, which was that in spite of the offer of a free advert in the *Good Woman*, the All White Clinic refused to give out the identity or contact details of the princess who had enjoyed their colonic services, which had rather scuppered their celebrity chances for the PR campaign. Having listened attentively to all these areas, the doctor suggested halving the dose for next week.

Millie replied that for her money, the dose was just right.

At the end of the grouting week on Friday 30th, with five more days of pill-taking under her belt, Millie invited Esther, Florence, Joan and Adrienne to witness a public weigh-in at her home the following day. She wanted to see what it felt like to be confident about stepping onto the scales in front of her campaign group. And also to see what they might make of her new-look dungarees, bought from New Look. She had bought some patent leather Dr Martens from Pets Need Vets to go with them and felt her ensemble reminiscent of the 1980s, when she had been able to get boyfriends and not eat for days on end.

SATURDAY 31 MAY

On Saturday morning when Millie flung open the front door wearing her all-in-one denim outfit, Esther burst out laughing. It took a huge amount of self-restraint for Millie not to slam the door in her smug face.

'Something amusing you?' Millie asked, holding the door open but not allowing anyone inside.

Esther gathered herself together.

'No. Sorry. I was thinking about something else.'

'What?'

'Um . . .'

Millie could see that Esther realized her mistake, which for her was unusual. They both knew Esther had a lot riding on keeping Millie happy.

'I was laughing, Millie, because I was happy. I'm happy you're wearing trousers. It's a real breakthrough. Dana must have worked wonders. We all said it would, didn't we?'

Adrienne was quick to soothe.

'You look wonderful, Millie. I've missed you. I've got some portable batwing-workers in my bag for a tryout if you're interested. Or maybe a bit of Frisbee in the garden?'

'The boots are nice with the new outfit,' said Florence, indicating the expanse of denim about Millie's body.

Harry put his head around the porch door. He took one look at Millie's dungarees and said, 'Where's your tool kit?'

'Do come in, everyone. Not Harry, obviously.'

Millie was furious. Harry had previously asked for her mother's number in case she wanted a bridge lesson and she said she'd think about it. She wouldn't give it to him now.

None of the women had actually seen Millie for three weeks, because she'd told them she was busy with her projects. There had been several texts, emails and a few cards popped through the door, but Millie was hardly ever in to notice them.

'You've lost so much weight, Millie!' Esther was amazed.

'I was always going to lose it, Esther. I'm not a flake.'

'No.'

'Unlike some people.'

The women looked at each other. Which one in their midst was the flake? Millie didn't know either, but she was riled. She didn't know why she was riled, which was especially riling. Maybe it was because her denim ensemble had failed, which was hurtful.

'Look, let's just get this done, shall we. Jesus!' Millie wished she hadn't bothered to share her triumph with her friends. It was all going wrong.

Adrienne surreptitiously went to the fridge. There was absolutely nothing inside. Not even the fridge deodorant. She felt along the shelves to make sure she hadn't missed anything.

'Fridge is pretty empty!' she said.

'I know it's empty. Been too busy, haven't I!'

When Millie stepped on the scales, they read nine stone thirteen pounds. Everyone stared at her.

'What?' said Millie. 'What is it? I'm normal now. This is great. Isn't it?' Millie had gone over to the cutlery drawer. She took the knives and forks out of it, gave them each a thorough wipe with a Brillo pad and put them back, streaked with pink liquid.

'You know what, can I just say something?' she began.

'Of course.' Esther looked at her watch and sat on the very edge of Mary's chair in the kitchen, so she could leave if things became unpleasant.

'I've worked my arse off for this campaign, guys. I mean, it's been hard. Really hard. I've denied myself, I've pushed myself, and I've been laughed at.' Millie looked up from polishing the sink to stare at Esther, who had the grace to look down at the floor. Millie was pleased to be scaring her. 'But now I'm on target, I've realized there's simply so much to do.' Millie was high with excitement.

'Like what?' Florence asked. Her friend was looking manic. The sink did not need scouring with wire wool. What was wrong with her?

'Well, there's a lot going on in the house now, as you can see, which made me think there's not enough time to do everything. In fact, I called you over because I wanted to help you guys stop wasting time on pointless activities and just get on with stuff that you can achieve like I have. For example, did you know that Aaron's gay, Florence? I can't believe you didn't see it. You could tell he wanted these DMs for himself. He was all over the leather. He likes *shoes*, Florence, not girls.'

Florence looked crushed.

'I think you should move on. Sorry to be the bearer of bad news, but life is too short, isn't it?'

Millie wondered if she'd upset Florence. Probably, if the wounded expression was genuine.

'Adrienne, you've got to get out more. I'm not your only client. Surely you had a life before you met me? And lose the silver trainers. They're too showy. Been meaning to tell you for ages.'

Adrienne hid her face in Vernon's fur and rocked herself.

'I won't clean the fridge, then,' could be heard through the fur.

Having got that off her chest, Millie told them she just couldn't help going at a slightly faster pace than perhaps they were able to go. She had her own agenda, and they had theirs. Life had suddenly become a rush of tasks and targets. And if people couldn't keep up, well, then so be it.

They didn't quite understand what they were being told, but Millie felt she had been clear, and grabbed her car keys. It was time to go. She needed to get on with her next project, which she assumed Esther would be pleased about. Esther roused herself and enquired what the project might be. She was in shock.

'I'm doing the photo shoot at the Bolt Whole now. Wall art, remember? I told you.'

'Oh yes.'

Millie knew Esther knew nothing about it but let it go.

'Which means I've got to go. Sorry, everyone. I've got to get the wallpaper before the shops close. Busy, busy!'

Millie ushered her friends out of her house. As they went one way, she went another. Harry was waiting on the porch to wave at Millie. He couldn't bear that he had upset his sweetheart.

'You look very endearing today, Millie.'

'Yeah, yeah.' She dismissed him with a wave of her hand.

Millie's plan was to set up an elaborate photo shoot at the Bolt Whole to showcase the designer wall and compare it with a display of five different designer wallpapers from five different shops. Millie had booked her visit with each shop – all she had to do was drive to the King's Road, choose five wallpaper samples at five different shops and get them back to the Bolt Whole to meet the photographer in one hour. This would be doable if the traffic was kind to her.

The only glitch in Millie's plan was that a red light seemed to have got stuck at a junction off the King's Road. She made an executive decision to drive through the faulty light and free up the traffic behind her. It was that or let people down on the other end.

So this is what happened. Millie put her foot down to cross the junction, only to collide with a taxi that was driving straight at her at the exact same time.

For a moment everything went very black, possibly because she had closed her eyes, followed by a very white shaft of light.

An angry taxi driver was shining a torch in her face and shouting. At first she couldn't quite understand – partly because he was Polish, but mostly because she was upside down. The shouting went on for some time until a kind cyclist decided to pull him off the window and call an ambulance.

Millie's stay in hospital offered up a mixed blessing. Both arms and hands were bandaged heavily due to the fountain of glass that had got caught in them, immobilizing her hands for eating chicken pieces, which was good, but also preventing further pill-popping.

Millie decided the doctor had a kind face, so she suggested a plan that might work for him. She would get her daughter, Mary, to ask the government to donate £1,000 to fund whatever wing they needing boosting if he would do something for her in return. The doctor asked what this might be. Millie wondered if a liposuction op could be fitted in while she was there in situ. Could he take off a clean six pounds? Could he do that?

The doctor couldn't. He went on to explain that since this was a Saturday, an operation (especially one that was unrelated to her injuries) would be unlikely to be considered necessary, and as the next day was Sunday, she would most likely be kept overnight until the Monday for observation. There was a slight risk of brain damage due to the impact of the taxi. The doctor seemed rather set on this course of events and made some secret notes on her clipboard.

Later the same evening the night nurse caught Millie out of bed and trying to open the pill jar with her teeth. She took them to show the doctor, who Millie decided had taken a personal dislike to her, and she never got them back. Florence collected her the next day after the pill confiscation. Millie had the use of her hands back but no pills.

MONDAY 2 JUNE

After two nights in hospital Millie was relieved to be out. Florence had come to pick her up, but Harry was sitting in the back of the car in the car park, which was an unpleasant surprise. He told Millie he'd put himself on standby in the event of her needing medical attention of any kind.

'I'll be fine, thank you, Harry. The damage has been done. Onwards and upwards.'

Harry leaned forward.

'And how are you mentally?'

'None of your beeswax,' said Millie. Her skirt felt loose. This was nice. She pinged the waistband and looked smug.

Florence regarded Millie carefully.

'Esther saw a receipt for the Divine Diet Clinic and put two and two together.'

Millie wasn't impressed with Esther's so-called deductive reasoning: the name and address had been on the receipt.

Harry tapped Millie's shoulder from the back seat. She brushed him away with an angry red hand.

'You'll be having withdrawal symptoms, Millie. Just want you to know you're not alone.'

'The point is, both of you, and you should know this, those pills have saved me.'

'Not entirely, Millie. You drove into a taxi and could have been killed.'

'I'm talking about before the taxi. They saved me then. Kahina told me I'd find an answer to my problem and I did.'

'She told you to take drugs?'

'She said I'd be shown the answer, in that lecture. Don't you remember? She said the answer would appear on a billboard.'

'What billboard?'

'Well, I had to Google it first. Then the answer appeared on a billboard. In the clinic.'

'They can kill you, Millie,' said Harry from the back. He looked worried, adding, 'Did you make a will? I'd like guardianship of Vernon, just so you know.'

Millie ignored him. She was annoyed with everyone, and suffering the pangs of withdrawal. She hadn't had a pill for forty-eight hours – ever since she'd been annoyingly rumbled by the nurse on the Saturday night.

'Blame Esther, then. It was her fault for taking us to the retreat, and Adrienne's fault for introducing me to Kahina.'

Millie was still mulling this over as she staggered out of the car.

'They're both to blame!'

Florence suggested it was best that it was all out in the open now, whoever made the introduction.

Harry insisted on helping Millie onto the sofa, but she pushed him away to rush towards the scales. She stood on them.

'Wow.'

'What are you?' asked Florence.

Millie was now a feather-light nine stone ten pounds. It was Monday 2 June.

'All I have to do is lose four pounds in a week for the final weigh-in jobbie on the 10th and I'll have done it!'

'You can do it.' Florence was pleased for Millie.

Harry beamed at her.

'You've made us so proud, hon!'

Millie winced at the word, but had bigger worries than Harry's cheese factor.

'There's a problem,' said Millie with a slow dawning that her old weakness was about to surface.

She shook her head and waved her arms up and down. The hands were now capable of self-feeding. She had also used her last spare cash on the diet pills, which were now most likely making some fat nurse in obstetrics very zippy indeed.

Her willpower was at risk again. She was starving, and

lack of sugar had made her crave something bad. She turned to Harry and smiled. He smiled back.

'You haven't got any crisps, have you?'

MONDAY 9 JUNE

It was the day before the final weigh-in. Esther called Millie to reassure her she'd patched things up with Very Medical, and together they would try and put their differences behind them with a party. There would be a photo shoot with the celebrity. The girls had finally, and rather unbelievably, secured Tessa Keltz. They would just have to say Princess Magdana was away at sea representing her country in a Commonwealth Games offshoot.

'What will you be wearing for the photo?' asked Esther.

'Skinny jeans and some kind of smock. Could be sleeveless,' said Millie proudly. She knew she was showing off.

This achievement was lost on Esther.

'Bring a dress for the ones with Tessa. They need it to cling.'

Millie and Tessa Keltz were to be photographed in the clinging evening dresses drinking a glass of water, as if they knew each other really well. The pills had to be featured in the foreground on a table, and they were each to be snapped looking at the pills in an affectionate but knowing way. They might have to do a few shots where they gave each other a wink. So there were a few options.

'Can't wait,' said Millie.

Esther then told Millie in confidence that she and Ernst had taken their relationship up a notch and Esther was seriously considering moving to Munich or at least exploring magazine opportunities over there for an Anglo *Die Hausfrau* demographic. Millie wondered when would be a good time to ask to be 'editor at large' – if that didn't make her sound too fat.

Millie bought herself an old-fashioned girdle, which was so tight she had to ask Florence to lace her up before they set off for the offices of Very Medical PR. As she was being laced in, Millie apologized for her extreme behaviour on the diet pills. She said she felt very volatile and depressed due to the withdrawal of the amphetamines. She told Florence she'd even sneaked two Kit Kats into her bed the night before. Then she had a nightmare about Harry, whereby he came into her bed and fed her a Crunchie while humming and pleasuring them both.

'Must be the stress of the weigh-in. Don't worry – you'll look great. Really slim. Last one!'

It was a relief to be talking like this. The pressure of having to share her second-best friend with her boss who worked for the other side had taken its toll. Soon all of this would be over and they could resume a simple life again. In the Bolt Whole with lots of drinks.

Florence also agreed that Millie had been right. Aaron was not going to be the One. She suggested they try speed-dating or climb Mount Kilimanjaro as a way to meet new people. Millie said speed-dating sounded more likely, as she needed to be accessible for Mary so she could make up for her bad behaviour. She wanted to be around to support her new job. Mary was about to host a science quiz on Sky Arts. It was exciting beyond belief and heralded a new era altogether. Eugene was out and Michael was in.

As Millie had suspected, Mary's new passion for her

tutor had been enthusiastically endorsed by Mary's agent, Emma, who equally fervently disapproved of Eugene. Apparently Mary's potential role as global adviser to the government and Eugene's association with alleged terrorist groups such as the VPL did not sit well together.

Millie weighed herself just before they set off. She didn't know if Florence had seen the dial, but she stepped off quickly. It read nine stone thirteen. She wasn't surprised. Just very, very disappointed.

She had failed herself, Mary, her friends and anyone else. Even Harry.

She panicked and slipped a hip flask into her jeans pocket. The pleasure of being able to have room to slip anything into her back pocket, let alone wear a pair of jeans, was almost entirely spoilt by the fact that she had failed to reach her target. But the withdrawal from the pills made everything very intense. She'd had to make repeated trips to the newsagent's since she'd got back from hospital. The owner had greeted Millie like a long-lost friend and was only too thrilled to get back to their previous system, whereby he would ask if she wanted to have a bag to hide the chocolate, crisps and flapjacks, and Millie would say that yes, she did on this occasion.

She knew it would be impossible to shed seven pounds in a single car journey, unless a limb was removed on the way, but Millie still held out for a miracle. Maybe she could die. Then she remembered she'd already tried that.

The Very Medical girls had prepared their offices for a party.

White sandwiches and crisps were scattered sparingly across the conference-room table, which had been covered with a paper doily. An old ghetto blaster was playing a 'Now' CD, and the Very Medical girls were dressed in almost matching chiffon dresses for the big denouement of the campaign.

Millie and Esther had sent out joint invitations to the weight-management team to thank them for their support, adding that they would get paid and photographed at the party. This, Esther explained to Millie, was to ensure they would turn up.

Adrienne, Joan and Jon were grouped round a paper plate of mini Scotch eggs when Millie and Florence arrived. Adrienne immediately rushed towards Millie and gave her a bear hug. When she released her, she whispered that she had recovered from most of the pain now that she had understood about the drugs. She didn't want Millie to be jealous, but she was going to be training Harry, so their paths would still cross. Then she followed Millie around like a puppy, which was annoying because Millie needed to get at the gin. She was shaking with nerves. Joan hadn't picked up on this, which was unusual, but it was probably because she was holding hands with Jon, who was talking a lot and who needed to be controlled socially.

Millie retired to the ladies' and downed half the gin. At least she looked thin. She had teamed the jeans with heels, which involved leaning on things at regular intervals if she needed to cover any distance. Running away would not be possible.

As she teetered out of the ladies', Esther was waiting, as was her habit, to guide her away from the mini Scotch eggs.

'Not good.'

'Thanks. I haven't even been weighed yet.' Millie was immediately defensive because she was guilty.

'The girls are in a terrible state. Tessa pulled out minutes ago and someone – I don't know who – has stolen the highly hi-tech scales.'

She looked at Esther.

'Was it you?' asked Millie.

'No.' Esther sniffed. 'Have you been drinking?'

'No.'

'Where's Ernst?'

Millie felt protective of Esther. She seemed to need calming down, but Millie wasn't really the right person to do that, given the circumstances.

Ernst was changing in the gents'. He'd just arrived from the Eurostar and needed to get into smart casual. He'd been in casual smart and needed to swap his cravat for a tie. Esther asked Millie if she should warn him about the news of the celebrity pulling out. She couldn't trust the Very Medical girls to do it.

'Let them do it. I would. They'll get blamed more,' said Millie.

Terri came up and blurted the news about the scales. Lucy had her arm around her. Terri looked as if she might cry. Esther and Millie tried to look suitably upset.

'Is there anything we can do?' Millie asked.

'They were behind the reception desk all day, but someone's just moved them.' Terri was beside herself.

Millie stepped in with a shrill 'I know!'

The sisters were so desperate they looked at her with hope.

'Listen! Why don't you just not weigh me? I'm nine six.

We all know that. I've done it. Look at me! You don't even need the scales.'

The girls looked disappointed. They thought Millie had a solution.

'We need to make it official,' said Terri. It was clear she didn't like Millie anymore.

'Well, I didn't nick them, if that's what you mean.'

'No, I didn't mean that,' said Terri.

'Good, because I'm fed up with being accused of wrongdoing. Do you get that? I'm sick of it!'

'And we're sick of your boasts and lies. How come your princess never materialized?'

Florence hurried over. She knew the signs, and she'd seen the hip flask.

Lucy put her hands on her hips and came up very close to Millie. She smelt the drink on her breath and nodded. Then she turned towards Esther and narrowed her eyes. This was not the timid plain-black-trouser PR girl of three months ago. Esther took a step backwards and looked around for Ernst, who was being pinned to a wall by Jon. He was talking about Joan's new website mock-up and it didn't look like he could stop. His iPad was preventing escape, and he was pointing a lot.

Lucy took a deep breath.

'Terri and I are both extremely fed up with being kept out of the picture all the time. We know you faked that email about the meeting, Esther, and that's not right. It's illegal practice, in fact, and we've taken advice on it.'

Lucy was very annoyed. Her voice was trembling because she wasn't used to confrontations in the workplace. In fact, this was her first one. But not only was she riled, she'd been on a one-day management course and had role-played being angry with a client, so she knew what to do.

The only way for Ernst to escape Jon was to usher Joan over to join the rest of the group. Jon followed closely. Adrienne was taking action shots of Millie on her iPhone to fill her 'memory box' of clients she had loved.

'Any news on the celebrity, ladies?' asked Ernst.

Terri and Lucy looked at each other but said nothing.

'Still no news, ladies?' added Esther sweetly as she looked at her watch with concern.

'I wonder if your incompetence will reflect on your final fee,' Millie said conversationally.

The girls looked furiously back at Millie and then at Esther. Their party was not going as planned. Florence and Esther helped Millie walk towards the water cooler.

'Best go gently, Millie. I think we can go in for the kill now, since Tessa cancelled, but do it my way.'

'Which is?' Millie teetered as she tried to pull off a paper cup for her gin.

'Blame the girls and get the cheque. Cheque first.'

'That's what I was going to do.'

'Yes, but you're not the right weight, are you?' Esther hissed through her teeth.

Millie glanced at Florence, who looked guilty. She'd obviously seen Millie weigh herself in her kitchen and tipped Esther off that the final weight was not quite what they had hoped for.

Suddenly, Ernst surprised them all with an announcement.

'I have booked a princess. One of your royals from the Duchy of Rutland. She has a crust.'

'Crust? Oh. Crest. Well, she may have a crest, but . . . is she a fat royal, Ernst? Or rather, *was* she a fat one before she wasn't?' Esther hardly dared hope. 'We'll need a "before" shot as well as an "after". Even a holiday one would do.'

'Very fat. Lulu knew her when she was fat. She has a photo from Leukerbad spa, where they took thermal waters at the same time, in a bathing suit. She was very fat. And sad. We can use this photo, and then of course she had much surgery, so now she is very thin and nice.'

'How perfect!' Esther looked at Ernst with pure love.

'I want to photograph the thin princess with Millie and the pills. She will meet us at the palace later today. She is in London and is happy to meet for this shoot.'

'The palace?' Millie thought she had misheard but realized she was drunk, so perhaps she hadn't. She would now be meeting the Queen.

'Easily done, Ernst. Adrienne's got all the data, haven't you, Adrienne?'

'Yes,' said Adrienne. She waved Millie's weight-loss book as evidence.

'What's happening?' asked Lucy, trying to keep up.

'Which palace?' Terri looked extremely put out.

'Crystal,' said Ernst. 'It will be full on with all the animal statues.'

'See?' said Millie, very drunk. 'Ernst wouldn't have got the idea for a princess if I hadn't met one first. You two are a waste of space if you ask me, and getting paid more than everyone else.'

Lucy had seen and heard enough. She'd been humiliated. She walked up to Millie and threw a glass of cava over her. Millie smiled back at her and kept smiling. The drips of cava fell into her mouth and she could taste something bitter-sweet. But she was now riled and angry. Debt, diet, love . . . she could sense the old, familiar surge of self-destruction well up and start to take over. She could feel it building and pushing its way out. She was going to mess up. Yes, she was ready – she was going to mess up on everything. It was meant; it was her nature; here it came.

'And do you know what, girls? I'm nine stone thirteen, OK? I'm not nine stone seven or nine stone six or nine stone five. I'm nine stone thirteen.'

The withdrawal from the amphetamines combined with the large injection of gin was powering Millie's innate desire to self-destruct. She felt as if she was inside a nightmare. She was about to watch herself blow everything she had worked for in one huge, massive gesture of stupidity. She had nearly got away with it. Esther had hidden the scales, she assumed, yet here she was needlessly showing her true hand.

Surprisingly to Millie, Lucy and Terri seemed prepared for this. Lucy pursed her lips and nodded to her sister. They both clacked over to their desk. Lucy picked up a pile of documents. She handed the pile to Terri, who removed the plastic cover with great ceremony. Lucy handed a copy to each guest. No one really wanted to take one in case it implicated them, but Lucy was determined.

She stood in the centre of the room and cleared her throat before speaking. 'Yes. We have issued a claim in the high court against Millie for breach of contract.'

'Yes,' said Terri, taking over. They had rehearsed this. 'You can rest assured, Ernst, the high court take this kind of breach very seriously. Millie will be forced to pay back all of her fee. With interest.'

'Yes.' Lucy took over from her sister again. 'The high court is very quick with these cases, and we have been advised by our solicitor to pursue "breach of trust perpetrated by Esther in association with her magazine", whereby a "ruination of reputation is inevitable".'

With more grim triumph they handed this second document to Ernst, but he waved it away and shook his head at them. He was happy with Esther. Very happy.

'I'm afraid your solicitor hasn't taken into account that German law protects me from your high court rulings, ladies.'

Terri was looking quite pale.

'But we've taken advice?' she asked, unable to stop herself from turning it into a slightly pathetic-sounding question.

'I'm sorry for your costs, in that case. Alas, I cannot pay Very Medical, for failure to deliver on agreed targets, and I will be invoicing you for my travel on the Eurostar. The final instalment will be issued direct to Frau Tucker. Please don't ever work for me again. Dismissed.'

The Very Medical girls looked mystified. They didn't get it. They retreated to the desk to plan their next move.

Millie attempted a makeshift sort of run, aiming herself at the drinks table. Then she caught sight of a familiar figure standing by the door. She stopped. And wobbled.

Mary looked concerned. Very concerned. Michael Morris was standing next to her, smiling in a nervous sort of way but holding a briefcase close to his chest for protection.

Millie assumed the smile on his face was to help defuse things. She hoped so. She didn't want to feel mocked at this heightened time by another potential son-in-law.

Joan and Jon had sought solace in the water cooler. Adrienne was hovering by Millie, while Esther stuck to Ernst.

Florence, as usual, took charge. She rushed over to Mary and pulled her forwards into the room. They'd obviously been in touch.

'Well done for making it, Mary. What time did you get in? Did the taxi pick you up? Your agent was so helpful. I didn't realize they did everything for you travel-wise.'

Millie was desperate to get to her daughter and take over from the gushing of her second-best friend. She got as far as a hatstand and grabbed on to it.

'Apologies, all. It seems I'm drunk.'

'You are,' said Mary. She walked towards it, having tactfully pulled away from the gushing Florence.

'And I'm not even nine stone six. I'm nine stone thirteen.'

'It doesn't matter, Mum.'

Millie broke down.

'I was doing it for you so you can come home to a house.'

'I don't need a house. I need you. I need you to be proud of me.'

'I am proud of you. I couldn't be more proud. Ever.'

Mary and Millie hugged each other properly, for the first time.

NINETEEN

~

THURSDAY 10 JULY

Millie's kitchen was very busy. Esther and Ernst were arranging bottles of green liquid on a tray covered in red gingham. Harry was painting a courgette with nail varnish. Adrienne was trying various moves on her Swiss ball.

'So we need the gunk, the veg, the blender, and we need Millie. Where are you?' Esther was calling out loudly and importantly from Millie's draining board.

Millie popped her head out from the airing cupboard.

'With or without pinny, Esther?'

Esther narrowed her eyes at Millie's waistline and considered. Esther was in her element. She loved photo shoots.

'Without, I think, don't you?'

'As long as I can pull it tight, Esther.'

Ernst was tying a gingham ribbon round a small plastic bottle. He stood back to admire and tweak the bow. This was a new side. It had always been clear that Ernst liked his trimmings, but who knew he liked them as much as this?

Millie looked with affection at this strange German man who had somehow ended up playing such a big role in all their lives. It was Kleinne Fett's money that had paid for Millie's Moulies. Her organic smoothies were to feature in Esther's new sister health and diet supplement, to be trailed as an insert in *Die Hausfrau* magazine. The surprising success of the herbal horse pills – endorsed by Millie and English royalty – had given Ernst's directors confidence to back a follow-up product. But this time he was entrusting the campaign to Esther. She had suddenly become softer and more approachable. The unnecessary cough had gone as well.

Esther fondled Ernst's hair, and Ernst fondled her dress fabric. They certainly made a tactile couple. At times it was almost too much to be in the same room with them, especially if Esther was in a wool-jersey mix, but Millie wasn't complaining. Esther had also stopped blocking her progress. Nathan's partner turned out to be an inspired graphic designer and had given the magazine a complete makeover – so much so Millie hardly recognized it.

Millie now felt that she and Esther made a good team. Esther had thrown the scales out of the window; Millie had doused them with cava.

'A German fourteen is our size ten, so you'll look practically minuscule to them, won't she, dear?'

Ernst nodded without looking up. The ribbon dressage of Millie's Moulies bottles needed his full attention again.

Harry was blowing on the courgette he'd just painted with a pastry brush. Millie could even say 'pastry' now without getting an anxiety attack. She tested herself.

'Is that pastry brush working out OK for you, Harry?'

'It is, Millie.' He looked surprised at Millie's sudden interest in his tools. 'Varnish just needs to dry, my love.'

Harry looked at her to see her reaction. Millie hadn't winced at being called his 'love'. She had found a new confidence. She knew she didn't have to show her inhibitions through anger in the same way. She had had her silver bowl chakra opened on a yoga weekend in Dorset and was now willing to overlook Harry's more irritating codependent behaviours. She would have explained this to Harry in more detail, but she didn't want to encourage him into a headstand – there was too much to do.

Al was trying to work out the most ambient light source for his 'pack shot', as Esther had told him it was to be called.

'Is that light going to work, Al?' asked Millie doubtfully. They were using Stan's camera and Al wasn't sure about the flash. A work light was being trailed from the ceiling.

'Should do,' said Al.

Millie thought Al looked almost rugged with a screwdriver behind his ear. She might ask him to wear that more often.

'And are you going to take the case off the camera, Al?' He didn't seem to know much about cameras, but Millie was trying to help him along.

'Yes, I am. Once I've sorted this.'

Millie was on a new mission to emphasize the positives, given the bank had allowed her to swap to a different kind of mortgage and prison was now off the cards. She felt asking pointed questions of those close to her might be better than expressing worried remarks. This may have been where she'd gone awry with Mary.

'And where do you want me, then?' Adrienne was flexing her upper arms. 'Shall I be found actually across the Swiss ball to signify that a toned stomach goes with the health drink, or just carrying it lightly?'

'Can you balance and drink the smoothie at the same time?' asked Esther.

Al said, 'Ready?'

'Stop!' shouted Harry, and rushed forward to powder Millie's nose. He checked Adrienne and nodded. 'You're good to go, hon.'

Millie had noticed Harry and Adrienne becoming quite familiar, which while sick-making on many fronts, in spite of her new resolve to be positive, at least kept Harry out of her hair, which was almost a double positive. Apparently their training sessions in the park had attracted quite a few pensioners keen to learn the splits.

In the end, they settled on a mise en scène of Adrienne flexing her six-pack, with Millie drinking her smoothie from a bottle. They all agreed this 'told the story with product'.

Ernst and Esther retired to the hall to say their very fond farewells.

'Keep my edelweiss safe.'

'I will.'

'See you in a week, *Liebling*.'

A loud snog followed.

Millie tried not to feel too grossed out by this overt display of affection. She knew she had to keep focused on what was to come. This was going to be a very important afternoon. Much, much more important than the smoothie photo shoot.

'Eugene!' she called upstairs. 'Car's due in ten.'

At that moment Florence arrived, holding a corsage in her hand. She reminded Millie of a flower girl, due to an extra-low lace camisole, very high boots and a frilly lace skirt. Millie didn't say this to her face, as this might not be quite the image she was projecting, but remarked that the carnation would set off Eugene's new outfit wonderfully well. Florence really had done Eugene proud. She made a show of pinning it on him with great care. The pinstripe suit, donated by yet another dead person's loved one at Pets Need Vets, projected the look of an antiques dealer, which was a vast improvement on the hessian robe that Eugene had wanted to wear. And given the trouser legs had to be halved for Eugene, the suit might be suitable to recycle as a page-boy outfit as well.

Joan and Jon arrived within the next few minutes and they all gathered in the kitchen for a glass of water, while Esther handed round the Bourbons to keep herself busy after Ernst's departure. Millie sneaked three of these into her handbag and forgave herself. It was going to be a nerve-racking occasion. As long as she didn't creep up from a size fourteen and a half in one afternoon, she would be fine. The flask of gin was added at the last minute just in case Mary forgot her words, or got stage fright, which Millie knew she wouldn't, but just in case.

Joan told Millie she had a good feeling about the afternoon at the studio. She had channelled her bird spirits, as had Jon. He was quieter today, which was a welcome result, and Millie mentally thanked whichever birds had shut him up. Millie was very nervous. She didn't think she could stomach Jon's relentless commentary at the same time as witness her daughter's first big TV debut, especially when Mary was to be teamed up with her ex-boyfriend, who was now her mother's temporary lodger.

They had already shot the pilot the week before, and Eugene had proved himself to be a very witty satirist. The programme was called *Fission Chips* and was aimed at a young but intelligent audience. Eugene's placement had been a bit of a risk, but the producer had wanted an 'outsider' figure to challenge establishment views of science. He also needed a young face to present the show. Everyone on the production team agreed that Mary was perfect, but it was just a case of finding the perfect foil.

Mary's agent caved in after pressure and put Eugene forward to audition for the role of Mary's witty saboteur. It had been Millie's idea. She knew Mary felt guilty about ditching Eugene for Michael, and as much as she could understand why Mary had chosen the quietly attractive Michael (over a short, impassioned tribesman), she also knew that Eugene was still special to all of them. Eugene had, after all, performed a rather important role in proceedings, one way or another.

Surprisingly enough, Mary allowed Millie to attend a meeting with her agent and the TV production company, which made her feel very special. She found herself passionately championing Eugene's cause for the need to save trees, animals and the planet, while Mary cleverly put her own case. She explained that her own research had differed from Eugene's in some ways, but these merely showed science to be complex. The producer jumped up at that and said, 'We love complex! Let's book them both – before someone else does!'

Eugene was ecstatic to hear he might now have a part to play in world politics. Even if the world viewing figures might be low, it was still on a bigger stage than before.

He was now officially Mary's regular guest and was to act as a political buffer to the more conventional scientists who made up the panel.

Eugene made a grand entrance into the doorway of the kitchen. Florence leaped forward to pin the corsage on his lapel and he murmured, 'Thank you, Momma.'

Millie observed more than a little preening from Florence in response to Eugene's juicy, smiley gratitude. Florence had just received her monthly patch top-up and there was definitely something cooking between them. Millie could smell the must. She didn't mind. Anything that could distance her from her 'impulse that has no name' had to be a plus. Mary would never know. Her daughter was the important one.

They all admired the antiques-dealer suit, which in Millie's opinion was slightly marred by a green padded waistcoat, but Florence insisted it would look good on TV. And from a distance, Eugene could pass as handsome, and especially handsome if he was sitting down.

They all piled into the free car provided by Angst TV Productions. Mary had texted Millie to say she would greet them all in the green room after the recording. Millie texted her back, 'I love you more than I can say.' Mary had texted back immediately, 'Me too.' At least she hadn't replied with an 'x'. This, to Millie, was very special and signalled a new era.

Al was wearing the cream jacket with the singe, but life could never be perfect. Millie knew this. At least he had sat next to her in the car. She wasn't sure if it was on purpose or not, but she was unusually pleased to have him so close.

Mary made a nervous entrance onto the studio floor, after a warm-up man had made a few jokes about Einstein and Darwin. He assured the audience that *Fission Chips* looked all set to be the next *Have I Got News for You* but without the jokes and with Mary instead. Millie and her weight-management team all cheered manically. Mary acknowledged them with a wave and looked more relaxed.

'My mother,' she said, and the audience laughed. Mary went on to explain that this was her first episode of hosting *Fission Chips* and that she hoped they would be kind. She looked very natural as she talked to the audience and Millie thought her heart would burst with fear and pride. The audience appeared to like her style and cheered and clapped, as they were told to do by the warm-up man with the bad jokes.

Mary took her seat behind a mock-up of a science laboratory on the set and the recording began. Two panellists either side of Mary were required to act out a scientific dilemma. Eugene was then invited to play a calypso reflecting the opposite view. He had to outwit the team with the funniest song. The audience loved Mary, but they also loved Eugene. Cleverly, the producer had already seated Eugene on a high stool, so no one ever saw the height discrepancy with the other contestants. He actually oozed exotic charisma and wit.

In the green room after the recording, Mary and Millie hugged again. Unlike the hug at the Very Medical party, which had been out of pity and need, this hug was about pride and respect and love on both sides. This was the closest they had ever been. Michael whispered to Millie that he really was very grateful for her asthma spray and asked if she wanted it back.

'I want you to have it, Michael.' She found herself giving him a little wink, which surprised them both. What had got into her?

Later on, after many congratulations to everyone, Millie decided to interrupt Florence, who was now smooching rather obviously with Eugene.

'Florence, thank you. Thank you for saving Vernon's life by asking Harry to feed him, and for lending me money and for being my first-best friend.'

Florence stopped stroking Eugene to smile at Millie with relief.

'You don't mind, then?' Florence looked back at Eugene, who grinned at them both with pleasure and just a little lust.

Millie took a step back. Just in case.

'No.'

Florence would never need to know that she had been promoted from second- to first-best friend. Or that Eugene had become downgraded to paying lodger and lover of her ex-second-best friend. Better leave it that way.

Millie even felt a new tolerance about Harry and Adrienne, who were handing over their business card to the producer's aged parents. It might come in handy to have friends in her new life.

Al took Millie aside and asked if he could suggest something. Millie braced herself. What now?

'Yes?'

'Erm, well, Millie, I was wondering whether you might like to come to the cinema with me?'

Millie smiled and popped another sausage with relief. She had got it all.

'And then maybe after that you might like to go for a drive.' Al was watching her face closely.

'In your van?'

'I've cleaned out the back.'

'Oh.' Millie looked disappointed.

'Well, I got rid of the magazines. They weren't mine in the first place.'

'I was wondering if we might road-test the mattress, Al?' Millie felt suddenly brazen.

Al looked at her, his eyes sparkling.

'Really?'

She had never been surer. The silver bowl was calling them both.

A CONVERSATION
WITH HELEN LEDERER

What inspired you to write this particular story?
Well, to avoid litigation, I might just say it happened to a 'friend'. She was offered money to promote a weight-loss capsule. Her life was in someone else's hands – several people's in fact – the trainer at the gym, the agent, the PR people and the client. No weight loss? No fee. And once you shake hands with the devil you can't go back. I thought it would make a funny self-contained tale. Millie either loses it, or she doesn't. But in this case there was more to lose than the weight.

Did you base Millie's character on anyone you know?
She is many women I know, and me. The inner layers of being bold, being angry, and being vulnerable, in turn drive the cycle of hope and disappointment – we all want the perfect body, sex life, and family backdrop, which is in fact unachievable. This doesn't stop us striving for it all . . .

What would you say the themes of the book are?
Desperation. Denial. Debt and chaos. Millie lives in chaos,

which means she spends more than she earns. Debt is inevitable, which makes her angry, but there's no one to blame except herself. She is scared of rejection, which is so unbearable it turns to anger, which she directs on those closest to her. Poor Florence.

Do you have a favourite moment in the book?
I like her sexual awakening – unseen, unsuitable, and unsaid, but unusually vivid. Words can paint rather affecting pictures, I discovered . . .

What do you hope readers will take away from your novel?
I want the reader to like Millie for all her weaknesses and to laugh at how she self-destructs, on occasion. I hope the reader will find the kernel of hope in there that very possibly leads to a cautious version of love? Basically I just hope the book might raise a laugh, every so often.

Do you have any favourite books or authors?
I love David Nicholls, Muriel Spark, Jane Austen, and C. P. Snow, among others.

Describe a typical day in your life.
Wake up. Feel anxious. Try not to feel anxious. Listen to a meditation if I can find my headphones. Put on trainers and gym gear. Wear them all day. I never get to the gym. Then comes hope: I meet people in a bar in the evening – people who might give me a job. I make sure we have a candle on the table. Drink too much. Forget that posh bars serve doubles . . .

Tell us something unusual about yourself.
Double-jointed thumb. Secret cheesecake recipe. Grade two guitar. Can make lavender bags if I'm in the right mood. I love laughing to the point of wheezing and needing my inhaler . . . My family used to call it showing off.

It's time to relax with your next good book

THEWINDOWSEAT.CO.UK

If you've enjoyed this book, but don't know what to read next, then we can help. The Window Seat is a site that's all about making it easier to discover your next good book. We feature recommendations, behind-the-scenes tales from the world of publishing, creative writing tips, competitions, and, if we're honest, quite a lot of lists based on our favourite reads.

You'll find stories and features by authors including Lucinda Riley, Karen Swan, Diane Chamberlain, Jane Green, Lucy Diamond and many more. We showcase brand-new talent as well as classic favourites, so you'll never be stuck for what to read again.

We'd love to know what you think of the site, our books, and what you'd like us to feature, so do let us know.

 @panmacmillan

 facebook.com/TheWindowSeat

WWW.THEWINDOWSEAT.CO.UK